JUDITH PELLA
AND
TRACIE PETERSON

A PROMISE FOR TOMORROW

BETHANY HOUSE PUBLISHERS
MINNEAPOLIS, MINNESOTA 55438

Books by Tracie Peterson

Entangled
Framed

RIBBONS OF STEEL*

Distant Dreams
A Hope Beyond
A Promise for Tomorrow

*with Judith Pella

9802

Books by Judith Pella

Beloved Stranger
Blind Faith

LONE STAR LEGACY

Frontier Lady *Stoner's Crossing*
Warrior's Song

RIBBONS OF STEEL†

Distant Dreams *A Hope Beyond*
A Promise for Tomorrow

THE RUSSIANS

*The Crown and the Crucible** *Heirs of the Motherland*
*A House Divided** *Dawning of Deliverance*
*Travail and Triumph** *White Nights, Red Morning*

THE STONEWYCKE TRILOGY*

The Heather Hills of Stonewycke *Flight from Stonewycke*
Lady of Stonewycke

THE STONEWYCKE LEGACY*

Stranger at Stonewycke *Shadows over Stonewycke*
Treasure of Stonewycke

THE HIGHLAND COLLECTION*

Jamie MacLeod: Highland Lass *Robbie Taggart: Highland Sailor*

THE JOURNALS OF CORRIE BELLE HOLLISTER

*My Father's World** *Daughter of Grace**

*with Michael Phillips †with Traicie Peterson

9802

A Promise for Tomorrow

Cover by Dan Thornberg,
Bethany House Publishers staff artist.

Published by Bethany House Publishers
A Ministry of Bethany Fellowship International
11300 Hampshire Avenue South
Minneapolis, Minnesota 55438

Printed in the United States of America by
Bethany Press International, Minneapolis, Minnesota 55438

Library of Congress Cataloging-in-Publication Data

Pella, Judith.
A promise for tomorrow / by Judith Pella and Tracie Peterson.
p. cm. — (Ribbons of steel ; 3)
ISBN 1-55661-864-6 (pbk.)
I. Peterson, Tracie. II. Title. III. Series: Pella, Judith. Ribbons of steel ; 3.
PS3566.E415P76 1998
813'.54—dc21
97-45442
CIP

To
Everett Daves,
Kansas Christian Newspaper

With thanks
for your friendship,
professional support,
and all the wonderful things
you've done.

—Tracie

JUDITH PELLA began her writing career in collaboration with Michael Phillips, a partnership that led to five major fiction series. She has also written the LONE STAR LEGACY series and *Blind Faith,* a contemporary romance story in the PORTRAITS series, with Bethany House Publishers. These extraordinary novels showcase her creativity and skill as a historian as well as a fiction writer. She has a bachelor's degree in social sciences and a nursing degree. With her storytelling abilities she provides readers with memorable novels in a variety of genres. She and her family make their home in northern California.

TRACIE PETERSON is a full-time writer who has authored over twenty-five books, both historical and contemporary fiction, including *Entangled* and *Framed,* contemporary love stories in the PORTRAITS series. She spent three years as a columnist for *The Kansas Christian* newspaper and is also a speaker/teacher for writer's conferences. She and her family make their home in Kansas.

Contents

PART FOUR
September 1851—January 1853

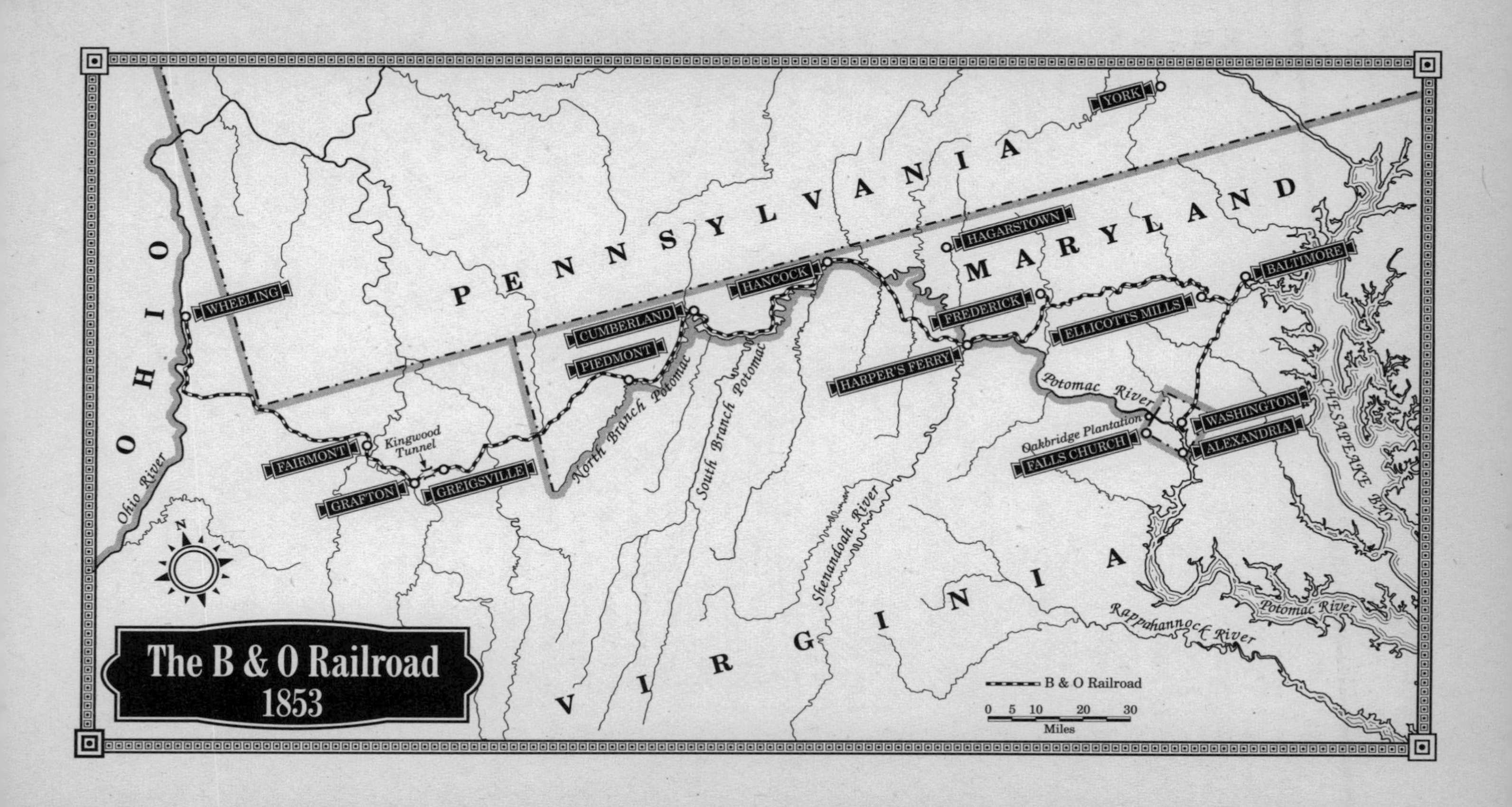
The B & O Railroad
1853
OHIO
PENNSYLVANIA
MARYLAND
VIRGINIA
YORK
HAGARSTOWN
BALTIMORE
WHEELING
CUMBERLAND
PIEDMONT
HANCOCK
FREDERICK
ELLICOTTS MILLS
HARPER'S FERRY
WASHINGTON
ALEXANDRIA
FALLS CHURCH
Oakbridge Plantation
FAIRMONT
GRAFTON
GREIGSVILLE
Kingwood Tunnel
Ohio River
North Branch Potomac
South Branch Potomac
Shenandoah River
Potomac River
Rappahannock River
CHESAPEAKE BAY
N
B & O Railroad
0 5 10 20 30
Miles

What Has Gone Before

Carolina Adams, a young woman of spirit and determination, enjoyed a pampered life in Oakbridge, her family's plantation, outside of Falls Church, Virginia.

Growing up as one of the middle siblings in a household of seven brothers and sisters, Carolina had always been eager to understand the world around her. Young ladies of the 1830s were not encouraged to educate themselves in the ways of masculine studies such as mathematics and science, but Carolina desired to cross those boundaries. She was especially enthralled with the railroad, which she fell in love with the first time she saw a train roar into Washington City. When her indulgent father, Joseph Adams, permitted her a tutor, James Baldwin, Carolina began to realize part of her dream. Carolina's older sister, Virginia, also hoped her dreams to be fulfilled by James Baldwin—her more conventional dreams of becoming a proper southern wife.

James had once worked for the Baltimore and Ohio Railroad, but while recovering from injuries following a rail accident, he was thrust into the job of tutoring Carolina Adams, and of courting her sister Virginia. What no one expected, least of all they, was that James and Carolina should fall in love with each other. James found healing in Carolina's friendship, and as she helped him come to terms with the past, James began to visualize his future with the railroad once more. In turn, Carolina found in James a man who was not threatened by her intelligence and regard for learning. She also found a soul mate with whom she desired to spend the rest of her life. Unfortunately, he had all but committed himself to Virginia, and Carolina was too insecure in her love to dare come between them, much less reveal her feelings toward James. Likewise, James refused to confront his growing affection for Carolina.

Torn by his conflicting feelings toward the two sisters, and pressured by family expectations, James allowed himself to be carried along by events, soon finding himself engaged to Virginia. But eventually realizing he could not marry a woman he didn't love, James broke off the engagement. However, in order to save Virginia from social embarrassment, he allowed her to publicly break the engagement herself. Then, unable to face Carolina and the social ostracism his ungentlemanly behavior would cause, James left Oakbridge and Washington for another position with the Baltimore and Ohio Railroad, a job that would take him far away to unsettled lands.

The loss of James, along with the death of her two younger sisters from yellow fever and her mother's mental breakdown, caused much sorrow and discontent in Carolina. This was not helped by the unwelcome advances of her father's commission merchant, Hampton Cabot, who had come to Oakbridge on business—and with his own personal agenda, which included snaring an Adams daughter. Further complicating Carolina's life was Virginia's resentment toward her because she believed Carolina was the cause of the broken engagement to James.

Carolina watched her family become torn apart as her remaining siblings went their way in marriages, careers, and activities, while Virginia's bitterness toward her grew. On the very morning that Carolina decided to accept Hampton's marriage proposal, Carolina learned that Virginia had eloped with Hampton. The growing tensions of the household finally forced Carolina to leave home on her own. She took a position as a nanny to Victoria, the infant daughter of Blake St. John, a wealthy widower who lived in Baltimore.

Blake was a cold, indifferent father and was constantly absent. After five years, Blake announced he was going to move west and requested Carolina to assume full responsibility for Victoria and the St. John house while he headed off to parts unknown. Carolina realized she had come to love Victoria as her own, but she felt that to accept such a proposition would have made her appear to be Blake's "kept woman." Not only that, but she feared that one day Blake would reappear with a new wife and take the child away from her.

This prompted Blake to make an even more startling proposal—a marriage of convenience to Carolina. She decided the sacrifice of a loveless marriage would be better than to lose Victoria to the orphanage to which Blake threatened to send her. All the while, however, Carolina's heart continued to long for James. She wondered how things might have been and of what she had lost as she took her meaningless marriage vows with Blake St. John.

When James finally reappeared in her life, he was crushed to find her married. She also confronted him with her suspicions that James' father, Leland Baldwin, was swindling her father and other railroad investors. They parted once again, not on the best of terms. Later, while doing business for his father, James became aware of Leland's illegal activities and realized that Carolina's concerns were well-founded.

When Blake was killed in a carriage accident, leaving Carolina a wealthy widow, she returned to Oakbridge and her father. Carolina ran into James on the same train, and they talked sincerely to each other. James finally confessed that he couldn't marry Virginia because he was in love with Carolina. Carolina, in turn, admitted her love for him. James, determined to let nothing else come between them, proposed marriage, and Carolina accepted. After they were married, their hearts turned back toward the dream that had first brought them together—the railroad. Their yesterdays were colorfully woven into a tapestry that represented their past, but a promise for tomorrow was yet to be created.

PART I

May–November 1843

For the structure that we raise,
Time is with materials filled;
Our todays and yesterdays
Are the blocks with which we build.

—Henry Wadsworth Longfellow

One

Bad Tidings

James Baldwin ran a hand through his dark hair and sighed. It was almost impossible to concentrate on the words of his father. Leland Baldwin had made a most unexpected visit to the St. John house in Baltimore, where James and Carolina chose to reside after their marriage six months earlier. James was anxious lest his father would still be on the premises when Carolina returned. That could prove disastrous. It wasn't that Carolina wouldn't at least feign hospitality and civility; it was that she held Leland in absolute contempt for his swindling of her father, Joseph Adams.

"It's not that I wanted things to be this way," Leland said, shifting uncomfortably in his seat. The rotund man rubbed his chest, a seemingly nervous habit of late, and waited for James to respond.

"I just wish you'd have come to me at the first," James finally said. "You have no idea how difficult it will be to make matters right again. There's not only this venture with Joseph and Carolina and the Potomac and Great Falls Railroad but also the land deals you've made in the West. What of those? The false deeds you've sold to unknowing people—people with dreams of settling in a new land and of owning their own property. Add to that the other paper railroads you've proposed to build. Railroads that only exist in the dreams and minds of hopeful men because you never planned to see them become reality. There are hundreds of investors, many of whom I'll probably never be able to locate, much less reimburse."

"I still see no reason to go to that much trouble. It's enough that I've ceased to participate in such affairs, is it not? Even though I've had nothing but disdain from your uncle Samuel. He thinks me an absolute addlepated ninny for worrying about such things. Then, too, I've nearly depleted all of my own resources."

"But, Father, you can't allow this to continue, and well you know it," James replied, then nervously rose from his seat and paced to the window that looked down on the front lawn.

"Looking for Carolina, are you?" Leland questioned. "I suppose she'd have a spell to know I'm here in her house."

James cringed inwardly at the words "her house." It had seemed a logical choice to stay on in the house of Carolina's deceased husband, Blake St. John. After all, Blake's daughter, Victoria, had grown up in this house, and her comfort was of great concern to James now that he was her stepfather. Carolina had suggested the temporary arrangement, reminding James that there was much to face and deal with as a new family, and that by staying on in the St. John house, they would at least avoid the complications of finding a new house, packing up the old, and making the actual move. James had agreed, seeing the sensibility in it from a standpoint of finances and time. But now, as had happened on many occasions, to hear his home referred to as "her house" left him with a strong desire to move and let the consequences be hanged.

"Carolina has a difficult time accepting what has happened," James admitted. He pulled back the edge of the damask drapery and studied the roadway some twenty yards away. "She feels perhaps an even deeper sense of betrayal than do I," he added and dropped his hold on the curtain. "You have to understand, Carolina is very close to her father. For you to have swindled her is one thing. But that you would endanger her father's good name—well, that is entirely different."

Leland's face reddened slightly. "She's too smart for her own good. You're going to have a constant battle with that one." He coughed and the gasping breath he drew sounded strained. "Your mother, God rest her soul, was the epitome of a proper, godly wife. My Edith could go into public and hold her head high knowing that she was a respectable, well-thought-of soul."

James felt weary under the strain of emotions. He sorely missed his mother, who had passed away nearly four weeks earlier. The memories of her love and kindness were all that James had to take with him through the days. He mourned her passing, but even more, he mourned the wasted time. And that was another reason he was desperate to put the past behind him and have his father's affairs resolved. He blamed himself for the despair his father must have felt to have given in to the heartless activity of swindling friends. He blamed himself for not realizing the pressures under which his father had been placed. First there had been the sale of his mother's family plantation. It had seemed reasonable at the time. After all, James' father wasn't a planter. Edith had inherited the place upon her father's death, primarily because there was no son to inherit it. She was the eldest of three girls, and therefore the plantation passed to her, with minor inheritances for her sisters. Already married with a child on the way, Edith had been proud when Leland had taken on her ancestral home in the hopes of becoming a farmer. But it wasn't to be. And without ever allowing her to realize the desperation that was slowly but surely befalling the place, Leland finally convinced Edith to let him sell the plantation and move to Washington, D.C. Now so many years later, Leland was once again having to sell off his possessions in order to account for his messes.

James felt sorry for his father. Sorry for the loss of control and respect that had befallen him. Sorry that he had never once felt confident enough to come to James with the truth of the matter. Oh, there had been that talk which had forced James to agree to seriously seek a wife, but even that had fallen far short of truth and honesty. Leland had spoken of a strain on the family coffers, but James hadn't realized the full degree of his father's circumstance. He had assumed that the real reason for his parents' pushing him into marriage was their concern for his own future and reputation. He knew his mother longed for grandchildren, and his father longed for a more elevated position in the social circles of Washington City. If James were to marry prominently, it would easily boost his family to even higher levels of acceptance.

Instead, James had ignored his father's demand to wed and had chosen his own path. A path he now found particular reason to regret. No, if James had only realized the desperation that had led his father down a path of poor choices, he might have helped. He might have been able to talk him out of his dirty dealings and actually find a way to alleviate the financial strain.

"Still, she wouldn't have been my choice for you, given her questionable reputation. After all, there was that awkward business with her sister's husband."

James startled back into the reality of the moment as he realized his father was speaking of Carolina. "You will not speak of my wife in that manner. She has never been anything but honorable, and I'll not allow anyone, even you, to speak ill of her."

"She started all of this, did she not? She's the one who made you suspicious and—"

"I'm glad she did," James said rather sternly. "You act as though this were some childhood lark. Some innocent prank. You could go to prison if she so much as opens her mouth to accuse you publicly. If the investors were to find out that you've swindled them out of hundreds of thousands of dollars, do you suppose they'd care very much that an overly educated young woman rang the alarm on such a fire? I think not." James watched as his father's face reddened even more. "What's more, if it weren't for the money left her by her dead husband, we'd never be so far along in quelling the concerns raised by other investors. So please don't sit there and insult her intelligence or character. The shame is not hers."

"I'm not proud of what I've done," Leland admitted softly. "I wish it could have been different. But I can't go back and undo the past."

"By paying back the investors and canceling out your contracts with them, you've made a good start. Mother's death seems a logical way to explain your inability to carry through on your word. Most people have been very understanding, even sympathetic. They realize that railroads take time, so the fact that you've been unable to proceed on your promises of new lines isn't all that startling. I only pray that the land swindles don't come back to haunt you. Those westward-bound folk who've bought up the land deeds you've offered will sooner or later find themselves the owners of nothing more than the paper they hold in their hands. When that happens, they will come looking for satisfaction."

"Very doubtful," Leland said, then rubbed his chest again. "It isn't easy, even in this day and age, to cross the mountains and go west. The trip takes weeks at best and oftentimes months. There won't be any real rush to spend additional time and money to come back east and hunt up a fictitious brokerage house, all in order to get their money back. No, they'll stay on, kick themselves for their stupidity in trusting a stranger, then pull themselves up by their bootstraps, and . . . and . . ." He gasped for air, and the look on his face left James little doubt that something was wrong.

"What is it, Father?" He moved quickly to Leland's side.

"Can't . . . seem . . . to . . . breathe," Leland said, groaning in pain and pulling desperately at his silk necktie.

"Here, let me," James said, pushing his father's fleshy fingers aside. He carefully loosened the tie and unbuttoned the stiffly starched collar that seemed to hold his father's thick neck captive. "Is that better?"

His father moaned and shook his head. "You'd best fetch the doctor, son."

James looked dumb struck for a moment. "Of course," he finally answered, realizing for the first time the severity of the situation. "Mrs. Graves!" he called for the housekeeper, rushing for the door. He threw it open and called again. "Mrs. Graves, send for the doctor at once!"

It was sometime later, as James sat in the downstairs drawing room with Carolina, that the doctor appeared in the doorway. His grave expression might have been enough to set the stage for the explanation to come, but James tried not to give in to his fear. He told himself that any physician of merit would take a serious approach to the condition of his patient.

"I'm sorry to have to tell you this, but your father has had a severe heart seizure," the gray-headed man said, taking a moment to remove his eyeglasses from the bridge of his nose. As he wiped the pince-nez carefully, he continued. "I wish I could afford you better news, but in truth I don't believe your father will live long."

"What can we do?" James asked, suddenly feeling like a helpless child.

The doctor shook his head. "He must be confined to his bed and allowed to do as little as possible for himself. I understand he is only here visiting, but I believe it would be far too traumatic for him to be removed from this place at present. Besides, it would be better that he remain in the home of loved ones and die in their bosom than to expire in the care of strangers."

James caught Carolina's stricken expression before she was able to lower her face to cover her reaction. He wanted to say something of comfort to her, but there would be time to smooth things over with her at a later time. Now there was much to be discussed with the doctor.

"Should we hire someone to care for him?" James asked the doctor. "Someone trained to deal with these kinds of things?"

"If that is your wish. I suppose a nurse of some sort would allow you a bit more freedom. Your father cannot be allowed out of bed, not that he would have the strength to do such a thing. His every need will have to be attended to by someone, so perhaps for the more delicate matters of personal necessities and such, I would suggest an additional care-giver."

"Can you recommend someone?" James asked, deeply concerned that he would somehow fail his father once again should he be unable to secure the very best of care for him.

"I'll send someone around," the doctor replied. "I wish I could say that I foresee a recovery, but the truth is your father is going to die."

James swallowed hard and nodded. "How soon?"

"Days. Maybe weeks or even months. We just don't know about these things. Part of it will depend on his will to live."

"Then he might find the strength to recover?"

"I don't foresee that," the doctor said, shaking his head. "However, if his care is of good quality, and the love of his family keeps him from despair, he might well linger for a short time. However, his discomfort will be great. His breathing will remain quite labored, and his body will slowly continue to weaken. I can't stop that fact. There is simply nothing in my earthly ability to keep your father alive. He's in God's hands now."

"Does he . . . well, that is . . . does he know the severity of his case?" James asked hesitantly.

The doctor put away his glasses and nodded. "He asked me to speak truthfully and I did. I told him that he had only a short time, and he seemed to accept it quite well."

"My mother died only four weeks ago," James admitted. "He's not been the same without her."

"So he said. You may send someone for me should his pain increase. I've left some laudanum with your housekeeper and have given her strict instructions for the dispensing of the medicine. Other than this, just make him as comfortable as possible."

James walked with the man to the door. "Thank you again for coming so quickly."

When the doctor had gone, James returned to the drawing room to find Carolina still stunned by the news that not only was her father-in-law in residence but he would remain and eventually die there.

"I'm so sorry about all of this," he began, moving across the room to take a seat beside her. Burying his face in his hands, James longed to say something that would dispel the anguish he felt inside. "This is all my fault," he said, his voice steeped in melancholia. "I drove him too hard. I knew he was unwell. You could tell just by looking at him."

"This isn't your fault, James," Carolina replied sympathetically. "Your father's health was not something you had the power to dictate."

He looked up and found her warm brown eyes considering him. How could he possibly hope she might comprehend his guilt? "You don't understand. All of this might have been avoided. He stopped by to talk to me about my uncle, and I brought up the affair of their illegal actions. I shouldn't have upset him that way. Not with Mother just a month in her grave."

Carolina placed her hand atop his, and for a moment James felt the warmth of her touch spread up his arm. She had always affected him this way. He closed his hand over hers and found solace in this moment of quiet comfort.

"I'm so sorry," whispered James as he looked through the open drawing room doors and to the staircase. "I'm so sorry."

"You mustn't blame yourself, James. For months you have blamed yourself for everything that led your father to make the choices he did. You can't take that burden on yourself. You didn't force him to cheat his friends. You didn't force him to swindle honest citizens out of their hard-earned money."

James shook his head. "But don't you see? He tried to tell me that things were not right. He tried to tell me that there was a crisis, but I refused to listen. I ran away like the coward I was."

"James, I've listened to you blame yourself until I'm weary of hearing it." Carolina pulled away from him with such abruptness that James could only stare openmouthed at her. She got to her feet, the pale lavender muslin gown swirling around her as she turned to face her husband. "How can you imagine that the deeds of your father—deeds begun long before you were old enough to account for your own actions, much less his—can possibly be your fault? This is a misplaced sense of honor. You aren't to blame for his poor management and decisions, and neither are you responsible for his heart attack. Please see the sense in what I'm saying."

James could see she had her temper up. He longed to calm her, to say the things she wanted to hear, but he couldn't. He knew otherwise. He knew that there must have been some way he could have prevented the actions of the past. And now not only did he have to deal with his father's illness, but he also had to consider the grief this event would impose upon his wife. "I could have done things differently," he said softly.

"Yes," Carolina admitted. "You could have married my sister Virginia. Is that what you wish you would have done?"

James looked stunned. "Of course not. You know better than that."

She softened. "Then tell me, what of the past would you recreate? What would you change that might not also change the fulfillment of our dreams? Would you give up the railroad? Would you take yourself back in time and become a banker at your father's side?"

James got up and began to pace the floor. "I don't know what I might have done. I suppose it doesn't matter now."

"Exactly!" exclaimed Carolina. She moved to his side. "Paul tells us in the Bible to forget that which is behind us. You can't change the past any more than I can."

James eyed her cautiously. "You can't put the past behind you. Why do you suppose it any easier for me?"

Carolina could not have looked more stunned had he slapped her. "If you are inferring that I refuse to let your father shirk responsibility for his own actions, then you are right. Everyone is called to account for his actions."

"Including me."

"You aren't making any sense," Carolina said, the anger in her voice becoming evident once again. "You didn't cause this to happen. I'm tired of you blaming yourself. It's almost as if you want it to be your fault. Is that it? Is this guilt a badge of merit that you somehow feel the need to possess?"

"How dare you!" James said, his own anger surfacing out of the tension. "My father lies dying upstairs, and you make insensitive accusations against my character."

Carolina drew a deep breath and folded her hands. "I'm sorry. You're right. I'm not being very sensitive. I'm angry and frustrated, but most of all, I simply do not know how to help you through this. Since the first day of our marriage, we've carried around all manner of trial and tribulation. This matter between ourselves and your father has weighed me down from the beginning, and it isn't easy to have the man in my house as a constant reminder of what's gone before."

James cringed at yet another reference to Carolina's possession of their home. He knew that she meant nothing by it, but nevertheless it wounded his pride, and because of this he struck out at her with words. "So there is to be no forgiveness in your heart for my father? Even though you would have me put an end to my past regrets, you cannot allow the past to be dismissed as easily when it comes to your own imagined grievances."

"Imagined? I daresay they are hardly imagined. Why, just the fact—"

"Stop!" James declared, his hands balling into fists at his sides. "I won't hear another listing of my father's sins."

"I would as soon forget them, as well, but the man lies dying in our house as a constant reminder of them."

"Well, I must say, this is the first time you've referred to the mighty St. John house as being *ours*." The words were no sooner out of his mouth than James wished he could take them back. This wasn't how he wanted it, and he knew full well it wasn't how Carolina wished it to be, either.

Carolina stopped cold. "What are you talking about?" Her expression was tightly pinched, as though she knew what he would say without James uttering a single word of explanation.

There was no avoiding the issue now, James thought, and gave her the only answer he could. "This place has never been a part of me. It is your house. Yours and Victoria's, and I am but an outsider."

"That's nonsense. You are my husband."

"And St. John was your husband before me."

"Not in any true sense," Carolina protested. "You know that very well."

James relaxed his hands and walked to the window to collect his thoughts. "I don't want to argue anymore. My father is dying, and whether you like it or not, he is going to die here under our care. He deserves better than your anger."

"Perhaps he is getting exactly what he deserves," Carolina said coldly.

James turned, barely able to contain the harsh words he might have hurled back in defense of a man who could not defend himself. He understood his wife's anger but not her cruelty. It wasn't like her, in any case, to be harsh and unfeeling. It was no doubt the shock and weight of yet another burden upon her shoulders. Still, he couldn't open his mouth without feeding off the tension in her eyes. Without another word, he walked from the room, pausing only long enough in the foyer to take up his top hat before exiting the house.

Carolina felt a deep, penetrating shame for the way she'd conducted herself with James. It was bad enough to harbor months of resentment toward her father-in-law, but even worse to suggest he deserved his affliction.

Falling on her knees, as she had so often done in this drawing room, Carolina began to sob uncontrollably. *Oh, God,* she prayed, *I feel so hopeless and tired. I thought marriage to James would be the awakening of all my dreams, and yet I find so many problems to contend with. I love him so much. But if I indeed love him, how can I hurt him in anger the way I did just now?*

"Carolina?" a voice called from behind her. It was Mrs. Graves, ever faithful to look out for her mistress.

"Why am I so cruel?" Carolina questioned, tears still streaming from her dark eyes. "Why can't I just keep my mouth shut and force my feelings into their proper place?"

Mrs. Graves smiled and came to sit on the sofa beside Carolina's kneeling form. "You aren't a cruel woman, Carolina. I've never known you to be that."

"Then you did not witness the horrible things I just said to my husband. Oh, but, Isadora," she said, calling the woman by her first name as she was wont to do in times of intimate friendship, "I was simply terrible. And all because I still feel such anger toward Leland Baldwin. I cannot bear the thought of caring for that man. And I can't help but wonder why God would force him upon me like this. I've tried to be fair about Leland and this horrible mess he created. I've used Blake's money to see the Potomac and Great Falls Railroad investments met. I've done what I could to help James repair the damages elsewhere, as well. What more can I possibly do?"

Mrs. Graves smiled in a motherly fashion that made Carolina only ache for the presence of her own mother. But Margaret Adams was confined to a mental hospital in Boston, and while there was hope for her recovery, she wasn't here to offer Carolina the wisdom she might once have offered. But Mrs. Graves was here, and more than once Carolina had sought this gentle woman as a substitute mother.

"I think you know what is to be done," Isadora Graves said softly.

"If you're going to suggest I forgive him," Carolina replied, "don't bother. I just don't think I can. I'm sure my father would agree and totally understand. Leland nearly ruined him. My father has often said that a man is nothing more or less than his name. His name should stand as a representation of the honor and integrity that lend themselves to the character of the man. Leland would have taken that away from my father."

"Leland Baldwin could no more take away your father's integrity than he could change the color of his eyes. Shame on you for believing that your father is no more than what another man deems him to be."

Carolina sniffed back tears and dabbed at her eyes with the edge of her lace cuff. "I suppose you are right. It's just that . . . oh, I wish I could feel differently about this. I know James needs me to forgive his father and to let the past be, but it is so hard."

"I know, deary," Mrs. Graves comforted. "But in time it will get better. You mustn't harbor anger against a dying man. Pray about it and search your heart. Think about what Jesus himself would do in the same position."

Carolina nodded. "Jesus would forgive him and welcome him back into the fold."

Mrs. Graves nodded. "We're to live by His example, are we not?"

Carolina stood up and smoothed the skirt of her gown. "It won't be easy."

"The Christian road seldom is," Mrs. Graves replied. "But 'tis the only way to know true peace and happiness."

"God knows this house could use a good dose of both," Carolina answered with a brief glance around. Her gaze fell to the stairs that would take her to the room where Leland lay. He would no doubt need some manner of attention after such a length of time alone, but try as she might, Carolina couldn't bring herself to confront him just yet.

"Would you sit with him for a time?" she asked Mrs. Graves.

"Certainly."

Carolina sighed in relief. "Thank you. I have a great deal to think about."

Two

Preparations

As Joseph Adams studied the latest correspondence from his wife's doctor in Boston, his heart was filled with hope. It seemed that Margaret was particularly fond of a matronly Christian nurse who had a miraculously calming effect on her patient. The doctor had, at last, given Joseph permission to make his first visit since Margaret's confining. Joseph wanted to run out the door and catch the next train north, but his more practical nature told him it was impossible. Nevertheless, he would make his preparations. The planting was done, the spring flooding that had caused problems in the lowlands of Oakbridge was now a thing of the past, and his son-in-law Hampton Cabot seemed more than capable of dealing with the management of the plantation. Even if he did manage things with a heavier hand than Joseph would like, Hampton's presence would enable Joseph to leave Oakbridge for several weeks.

Steeped heavily in thought of what arrangements he might make, Joseph folded the papers and put them back in their envelope. He gazed around him at the high-walled rows of books. The library was his favorite room at Oakbridge. It had also been his daughter Carolina's favorite room. How quiet the house seemed without her. Indeed, how silent the house had grown in the absence of many of his children. Mary and Penny had both died from yellow fever. York, his oldest and the true heir to Oakbridge, had shrugged his duties as a planter and had acquired instead a love of politics. He seemed content acting as a congressional aide to his father-in-law in Philadelphia. Together with his beautiful wife, Lucy Alexander Adams, they had two handsome children, Amy and Andrew, affectionately called Andy. And York had written that in the spring Lucy would bear yet another heir to the Adams line.

Joseph's only other son, Maine, was now preaching the gospel to Indian tribes in the far western reaches of the continent. Georgia, the youngest living member of the family, was happily married to a man twenty years her senior. She and the Major, as her husband, retired Major Douglas Barclay, was called, operated a horse farm south of Washington City, where they bred the finest livestock around. Carolina was happily married to James Baldwin and living in Baltimore with Victoria, her adopted daughter. And that only left Virginia, his eldest daughter.

Thoughts of Virginia brought a frown to his face. Virginia had eloped with Hampton Cabot on the eve of the morning when Carolina was to have answered his marriage proposal to her. There was bad blood between the sisters, and it grieved Joseph in a way that he could not shake. He longed for the days when his family might once again be united but knew it would never again be the same as when they were all small. Still, watching Virginia slip deeper and deeper into the grim hold of depression gave Joseph little time to worry about what would never be. Instead, he found himself desperate to ease the tensions of the future. Tensions that might yet be dispelled and eliminated.

There was so much he wanted for his family. So much that Joseph feared would never come about or be possible. He had hoped his sons might take an interest in the plantation, but neither one had been so inclined, and thus the responsibility had fallen to his son-in-law Hampton. Hampton had proven himself a worthy commission merchant for the family. Even when the banking crisis and depression of the late 1830s had destroyed many a family fortune, Hampton had used his foresight to protect the Adamses from suffering too much damage. It was for this reason alone that Joseph considered Hampton the logical choice to run Oakbridge, but there were residing conflicts that of late were making him think otherwise.

Hampton was often cruel to the slaves, something Joseph could not stomach. Joseph had long maintained that his slaves were not to be beaten, but Hampton often chose to ignore this standard. More than once, Joseph had been informed of whippings, and even brandings, that had been given at Hampton's insistence. And just as often as the stories reached Joseph's ear, he had admonished Hampton to cease such activities. Hampton had offered a pretense of acceptance in the early days of his training, but now after so much time had gone by, Hampton often ignored Joseph's warnings, knowing that Joseph needed him to assist with Oakbridge just as much as he needed the slaves. It was a constant source of worry. He hated to admit it, but he did need Hampton now with his attention so diverted by family problems, especially that of Margaret's condition. He needed to be free to go to her whenever called to do so.

So it was with a heavy heart that Joseph anticipated the arrival of his son-in-law to the library. It was also with mixed emotion that Joseph outlined preparations for Hampton to take over the running of Oakbridge while he journeyed to Boston. In and of itself, Hampton's behavior was not unusual or out of the realm of what others did. Even his domineering attitude toward his wife and children were perfectly acceptable in most other households. Few men would consider this to be a problem, while in truth, many would praise it as a virtue. It was considered that the man who could control his household was in keeping with biblical instruction; therefore, the social mores made it very difficult for Joseph to argue against Hampton's personal style, even if Joseph held it in contempt.

Still, the man had done well for him. Profits were up at Oakbridge, land was being reclaimed from rocky, unworked pastures and wooded fields, and prosperity was evident in every aspect of their life. Hampton Cabot knew his business well, and what he didn't know he learned with astonishing speed.

A knock at the door interrupted Joseph's thoughts. No doubt it would be Hampton responding to the message Joseph had sent nearly half an hour earlier.

"Sorry to be so long," Hampton said, coming in without waiting for Joseph's response. "I got caught up in overseeing the construction of the new slave quarters."

"Perfectly understandable," Joseph replied and motioned to the seat in front of his desk. "We have a great deal to discuss, so I'd suggest we get right to it."

"I told Virginia to see to it that we had some refreshments," Hampton said, pulling off his gloves and throwing them aside. He eased his large frame into the offered chair and blotted sweat from his forehead with a fine linen handkerchief. His blond hair was tousled and touched with dampness, but he seemed unconcerned with his appearance.

Joseph brought out a ledger, along with a list of noted instructions. "I brought you here because there are some things we need to go over. I have been granted permission by Margaret's doctor for a visit. I would like to leave for Boston within the next few days."

Hampton seemed to perk up at this suggestion. "Boston? That'll keep you away for some time."

"Exactly so," Joseph replied. "Which is why I wanted to meet with you. I shall turn Oakbridge over to your care during my absence. I have a list of instructions here that I would like to see executed to the letter."

He handed the list to Hampton and waited while his son-in-law gave it a quick perusal.

"I don't see any problem with this," Hampton said, glancing back up. "Is that it?"

"No, it isn't. Not exactly," Joseph said, already feeling uncomfortable with what he would say next. "Hampton, we've known each other a long, long time. I took you in when your parents died and saw to it that you received the start in life that you needed in order to succeed. You've served me well as a commission merchant, and you are now a part of the family."

Hampton threw him a lazy smile. "You hardly brought me here to sing my praises. What is it that you want to say, Joseph?" He slouched down and threw a leg over the arm of the chair.

Joseph shifted in his broad leather chair. "I want to leave with a clear conscience. I want your word that you will refrain from beating the slaves while I'm away." He saw Hampton's eyes narrow but continued before the man could reply. "This is my home, and I've opened it to you. I've allowed you a great deal of responsibility, but I will remove that responsibility if I believe it to be unwisely placed. Do you understand me?"

Hampton laughed in a short, strained manner. "I hardly think you would do that. After all, who would take my place? York is off in Pennsylvania playing at politics, and Maine is off saving the heathen world. Who else could you possibly get to do the job, if not me?"

"There are other overseers to be hired, Hampton. Don't forget that this is still *my* property."

"I suppose it is a fact that you could hire another overseer, but you'll never get the profits out of the land that I have. This is no small plantation, and therefore no small feat to keep it running smoothly. If I've taken a hard line with the slaves, it's because that's what was needed in order to get the work done. If you want to run a charity ward, then by all means do so, but it was my understanding that you wanted a profit on your investment. Your sons have no interest in this place, but I do. Who else would care as much as I do whether a profit is realized or not?"

Joseph nodded. "What you say is true, but the fact is, I've often thought of selling out and leaving the plantation to another owner. Last winter, when Bob Lee brought his family home to winter at Arlington, we spoke of his plans to educate and free his slaves."

"Outrageous!" Hampton declared, sitting up properly in the chair. "Education isn't allowed for them, and even if it were, they aren't capable of learning much. As for freeing them, wherever would they go?

Who would take them in and give them work? Then, too, who would work our fields?"

"If I sell Oakbridge, it won't much matter whether the fields are worked or not. I could just as well parcel it off to my children, in which case you'd still maintain a certain portion of the land. You could work that with or without your own labor force, or you could go back to commission merchant work."

"You aren't making sense, Joseph. I've advised you too long for you to ignore me now. Didn't I keep you out of hock when the depression hit? Hasn't my advice always been sound in regard to investments?"

"Yes, overall. But, Hampton, you already know very well the conflict and strife that is brewing in our nation over the issue of slavery. I can't simply ignore the direction the future seems to be taking. Bob Lee agrees. He plans to free the slaves at Arlington upon his father-in-law's death. They really belonged to him first, you know. Lee took on the place pledging to see to the old man's wishes, and, frankly, I am beginning to agree with his ideas."

"This is ridiculous, Joseph," Hampton declared, jumping to his feet. He slammed both hands down on the desk as if to accentuate his opinion. "Freeing darky slaves is not the answer for a productive future. Neither is selling a fine plantation such as Oakbridge. This is your ancestral home. Do you honestly believe your children will stand by and tolerate her destruction?"

"No one is speaking of her destruction," replied Joseph. "My heart isn't here anymore. Margaret is in Boston, and that's where I feel strongly drawn—I'm there physically a large portion of the time anyway. My children are grown and doing well for themselves, so I find myself considering all manner of possibilities."

"But to sell Oakbridge is ludicrous."

"Even if I sold it to you?"

"I could never afford this place on my own. Not yet, anyway," Hampton answered, calming only marginally. "But there's no reason for you not to let things go along as they have been. Go to Boston and take a house there. I'll manage Oakbridge and you'll see for yourself the comfort that will be had from the income."

"And what of the slaves?" Joseph asked, eyeing his son-in-law cautiously.

"The slaves are a very necessary part of the plantation, and well you know it. Would you free them, losing thousands of dollars in valuable assets, only to turn around and hire poor laborers? You'd be in ruins within months."

"I'm surprised you take this line, Hampton. You are a northerner by birth. Most of your life has been spent in New York, where for the most part slavery is considered an institution of grave reproach. How is it that you fight so fervently for slavery?"

"I may be a northerner by birth, but I'm not stupid. It is the ignorant man who looks upon the slaves and says, 'Free them.' There is no hope for this race of people outside the protection afforded them under the plantation system. Even you have said on many occasions that these people need to be cared and provided for."

"Yes, because we've allowed them no other position to be in," Joseph countered. "We give them no education, no training except that which suits our needs, and we degrade them by giving them no say in their lives. Believe me, I've long thought on this matter. I have been raised to hold slaves and to believe that the institution of slavery is in their best interests, given the circumstances surrounding their lives. I've stood my ground to defend my right to maintain slave labor, even spoken out about the good treatment I afforded my people, but honestly, Hampton, I see this entire slave issue as one that will someday destroy us. Already there are lecturers who do nothing but travel the country, stirring anti-slave sentiment. The country is restless, and I'm of a firm belief that this issue will not merely fade away."

"So a few imbeciles are stirring up conflict and strife. It has been that way down through history," Hampton said, his expression hard. "You are talking about Oakbridge and the life given you by your father. You took over the running of this plantation as an obligation to your family. I've heard the stories myself. You didn't want to run Oakbridge, never had planned to even stick around, but when your father and older brother were killed in a boating accident, you had no choice. Your heart and mind told you that the honorable thing to do was to take the reins of Oakbridge and run it as your father would have. Would you now throw that away? Would you destroy this plantation, and your father's dream, simply because you fear some future reprisal from a group of idiots?"

Hampton drew himself up and sneered down at Joseph as if he were considering someone of lesser social standing. "You aren't the man I thought you were, Joseph Adams, if you would deny your children and grandchildren their rightful heritage." With that he crossed the room, slamming the library door loudly behind him.

Joseph sat momentarily stunned by Hampton's outrage. There was some merit in what his son-in-law had said. Oakbridge was the ancestral home and it would be a pity to deny his family their right to it. On the other hand, Hampton could not begin to understand the future that Joseph saw in his nightmares. A future of devastating conflict as the slave issue threatened to unhinge every secret cabinet and closed room that southern gentility had quietly hidden from view.

Hampton felt the blood boiling in his veins. He couldn't contain his anger at Joseph's stupidity. To lose Oakbridge would be the ruin of all of Hampton's plans. Plans for power and social standing. Plans for financial empires that would stretch hungry fingers across the continent and even the ocean in order to plunder the vast wealth that awaited him.

Hampton stormed down the stairs in such a rage that he paid little attention to anyone or anything. *BOOM!* He struck his fist against the wall. "I won't let that old man cheat me out of my plans."

"Hampton?" Virginia, with their infant son in tow, stood just beyond the steps in the downstairs foyer.

Hampton met the questioning stare of his wife. How he despised her! She whined at him from dawn to dusk and even into the night when he would seek his pleasure with her. A very little pleasure, at that.

"What do you want? And where was the tray I told you to send up?"

Virginia edged back a single step, but the retreat gave Hampton a sense of power, and in the wake of his rage, it fueled the fire that burned within him.

"I'm sorry. I started to see to it, but Nate was fussing and I—"

"That's what we have slaves for, dear wife," Hampton said sarcastically. "Or had you forgotten? Perhaps you've already been drinking this morning, and your mind can no longer comprehend reality." He loved to torment her about her drinking. Perhaps because he knew it was her only refuge and driving her there put her away from him.

Virginia flushed and the baby began to cry. "I am not drinking. I'm trying to care for my child."

"Don't ever speak to me in that tone again," Hampton said, taking two long strides toward her with his arm poised to strike.

Virginia cowered against the wall and tried her best to shield the baby from his father's anger. "I'm sorry," she said, her voice a childish whimper.

Hearing a noise upstairs, Hampton cast a quick glance upward. No doubt Joseph would make an appearance at any moment, and the last thing Hampton wanted was to have his father-in-law browbeating him about his treatment of his wife. He returned his gaze to Virginia, lowering his hand as he did.

"Take that brat back to the nursery and go to our room. I'll deal with you shortly."

Virginia's face paled, and for a moment Hampton thought he saw tears glisten in her eyes. Good, he thought. She was afraid of him. It seemed her fear grew stronger with every confrontation. In no time at all he'd have her completely beat into submission and, maybe then, he would find her an acceptable wife.

Three

Confrontation

Carolina glanced down at the glass of water in her hands, and then toward the closed bedroom door. Behind that door her dying father-in-law lay awaiting her care. Somehow it seemed a cruel joke that she should find it necessary to nurse this man who had caused her such grief.

"Oh, Father, give me strength," she prayed aloud, grasping the door handle. The last thing in the world she wanted was to have to minister to this man. She thought of Jesus in the Garden, praying that the cup of responsibility might be removed from Him. That was precisely how she felt just now. She wanted very much to forgive Leland—even thought that perhaps she could do just that. But she needed time. She desperately needed time, and that was the one thing that had been taken away from her. Swallowing hard, she turned the handle and walked into the room.

He lay upon the bed, his complexion a pasty yellow with underlying tinges of gray. His chin rested in stillness upon his chest, with thick, fleshy jowls hanging loose at the sides of his face. His eyes were closed, and for a moment Carolina wondered if he had already passed from life. She panicked and rushed forward to put the glass of water on the nightstand, then nearly screamed when his eyes fluttered open.

"Carolina," he barely breathed the name and fixed his gaze on her.

She nodded. "I've brought your medicine and some water." She reached into the pocket of her apron and took out the bottle of laudanum.

"So good of you," he murmured. "You are good to care for me, in spite of what has happened."

Carolina heard the sincerity in his voice and was deeply convicted. Why did he have to be like this—so grateful and needy? His face contorted and a deep, chesty cough followed. Carolina waited for the spell to abate before lamely asking, "Are you in pain?"

"No, not much," he replied weakly.

His breathing was shallow and strained, and Carolina found herself breathing along with him as though to help ease the burden. "I'm sure the medicine helps with that," Carolina said quickly to keep from focusing on the rampaging thoughts in her head. The room smelled of death. She easily recognized the scent from the time she spent with her dying sisters. This man was dying. Right before her very eyes. And to make matters worse, she held him a grudge.

She poured the laudanum into a spoon and helped him take the medicine. Then ever so gently she offered him the water and eased the cup to his lips. With this action, Carolina's thoughts immediately turned to the Scripture in Mark. "And whoever shall give you a cup of water to drink in my name . . ." But she wasn't giving Leland a cup of water in Christ's name. She was giving out of duty and begrudged responsibility. Her hand began to tremble so that she nearly dropped the glass.

Seeing that she had allowed the water to dribble down Leland's chin, she quickly placed the glass on the stand and took up a towel. "I'm sorry," she said softly. Gently she dried his face, then met his gaze.

"You are so good to do this," he said, and his voice sounded both grateful and sad.

Carolina felt branded by the flames of his ingenuousness. "Do you need anything else?" she asked, barely controlling the nervousness in her voice.

"No, just leave me."

He closed his eyes as though dismissing her, and Carolina did not hesitate to take the opportunity to leave the room. She might have run had propriety allowed it. She couldn't fight the feeling within her. The feeling that she had come face-to-face with the opportunity to bear the love of Christ, and had failed.

Finding solace in the small library that had once doubled as Blake's office, Carolina sat down and fought the urge to cry. Convinced that it wouldn't help matters to give herself over to tears, Carolina tried to steer her thoughts toward a more positive outlook.

"Mama?" Victoria spoke from the doorway. "Are you all right?"

Carolina smiled and held open her arms for Victoria. Brown-black ringlets danced across her shoulders as Victoria skipped through the room and buried her face against her mother's neck. How very much Carolina loved this child. She could not love her more had she given birth to her. That she was Blake's daughter from his first marriage mattered little. That she was Carolina's daughter by choice and by heart made all the difference in the world. She held her tightly and found the calming effect most soothing.

"I'm just worried about things," admitted Carolina.

"Are you still mad at Grandfather Baldwin?" Victoria asked innocently.

Carolina tried to think of an answer to give her daughter. What could she say? To speak the truth of the matter was more than a six-year-old should be asked to bear. But to make light of the situation was also uncalled for.

"I'm not so very mad anymore," she admitted. "I'm mostly disappointed and hurt. Can you understand?"

Victoria pulled away and nodded most somberly. "He was naughty and did bad things."

"Yes," Carolina replied. "He did some things that hurt my feelings and made me sad."

"Like when I'm naughty?" Victoria asked.

Carolina didn't want to answer that. To compare her beloved child's mistakes to the willful actions of a full-grown adult was impossibly convoluted. "In some ways," Carolina finally answered. "But Grandfather knew that what he was doing was wrong and people would get hurt. When you do naughty things you often do not realize how the thing you are doing will affect people."

"But sometimes I know I'm being naughty," Victoria admitted. "And you still love me. You still forgive me."

Carolina nodded. "Yes, I do. I always will."

"Will you forgive Grandfather, too?"

The child's words shattered the icy wall Carolina held around her heart. To be confronted by one so young was possibly the most humbling experience Carolina had ever known. "I want to, Victoria. I know it is what Jesus wants me to do."

Victoria smiled. "Then just do it."

Carolina reached out to straighten the ribbon in her daughter's hair. "I wish it were that simple." The sound of the front door slamming shut brought Carolina up out of her chair. "Who could that be?" she questioned, moving toward the hallway door.

James stood in the foyer, eagerly shedding his top hat and outer coat. For days he'd barely spoken to her, in spite of her attempt to apologize. He was clearly preoccupied with many things, and while Carolina feared it was tearing apart their happy home, she knew she'd done nothing but add to his worries.

"James, you're home early. Is something wrong?"

He threw her an almost apologetic smile. "I am sorry for the noise. It's not your fault that the B&O would rather argue routes than actually move the railroad west."

Carolina leaned down to Victoria. "Go ask Mrs. Graves to have Cook bring us some refreshments."

"Cake too?" Victoria asked hopefully.

"Let Cook be the judge of what is best to serve," Carolina replied. Victoria nodded and scampered off in search of Mrs. Graves. "Why don't we go into the drawing room and you can tell me all about it? Have they given up on the idea of ending the line in Pittsburgh?"

"No, and that's a big part of the problem. They have three different routes, and all three are arguably the best in the eyes of those proposing the line," James replied and took a seat opposite his wife. "They are worse than Mother's social groups used to be in deciding where to hold the next charity event."

Carolina smiled in spite of the growl in her husband's voice. "Do you still favor the Wheeling route?"

Just then Victoria bounded into the room. James seemed to calm a bit at the appearance of the child. "Mrs. Graves said she would come right away," Victoria stated, then took herself to a favorite corner of the room where she liked to play with her doll Polly.

"Wheeling seems to be favored by a great many gentlemen. But the irritating fact is that the charters are in question, and permission has not yet been confirmed by the states."

"But I thought that was all taken care of," Carolina replied.

"So did we. Actually, the fault is just as often the B&O's as it is the states of Virginia, Maryland, or Pennsylvania. They offer us deals, and we refuse, based on one conflict or another. Or we simply allow time to run out, as was the case with the original charters."

"I am sorry, darling." Her voice was purposefully soft and soothing. She much preferred focusing on the railroad complications than on the problems that housed themselves under their roof.

"How is my father?" James asked, as if reading her mind and deliberately seeking to frustrate the fragile peace between them.

"About the same. He took a bit of broth for lunch but otherwise has preferred to sleep most of the time."

"Have you seen him?" questioned James.

Carolina's defenses were immediately put into place. "Of course I've seen him. I spent the entire morning checking in on him every few minutes. I gave him medicine not half an hour ago, and we spoke about his condition. He said the pain was not too bad."

"Oh."

James' voice left little doubt in Carolina's mind that he had presumed she'd spent her day avoiding Leland. Of course, the worst part was that she had. She had used one excuse after another to keep from having to sit for long at Leland's side. There was Victoria to concern herself with and, of course, the household, but all of that could have been managed in her absence had she but given the word.

Victoria's play became ever more animated, and as she began to sing loudly, James scowled. "Victoria, quiet down this minute."

Carolina frowned and tried to think of a way to move the focus away from the child. "The Reverend Wilcox came by earlier today and sat with your father for a time. I think Leland enjoyed his visit," she finally offered.

"I'm glad. I don't believe Father has ever truly understood salvation."

"No doubt that is true."

James looked at her sharply. "What is that supposed to mean?"

Carolina realized her mistake. "I simply meant that . . . well, it just seems that given all that has come to pass . . ." She fell silent.

"I'm sure I know exactly what you are implying," James remarked harshly. "Look, I'm in no mood to argue with you about my father."

Carolina opened her mouth to offer a quick retort, then closed it again. Thinking better of stirring up the same old conflict, she realized this was the first step to forgiving Leland and forgetting the past. "I'm sorry, James. I was wrong to speak out."

Before James could answer, however, a loud crash resounded in the room, followed by the unmistakable sound of breaking glass.

"What in the world?" James questioned angrily.

"I'm sorry," Victoria called out. "I broke Mama's vase."

"Victoria, I told you to settle down," James scolded. "If you had obeyed me in the first place this would never have happened."

Carolina started to speak, but James threw her a look that caused her to remain silent. Victoria's face held a stunned expression, mirroring Carolina's surprise. James had never so much as raised his voice to the girl in the past, and now it was clear he was taking the day's frustration out on her.

"I want this mess cleaned up, and furthermore, as punishment, you shall have no dessert with your dinner. Do you understand?"

Victoria began to cry and ran across the room to throw her arms around Carolina. "You're mean," she declared.

Carolina wrapped her arms around Victoria's quivering shoulders. "James, it was only a vase."

"It was broken because she didn't obey orders. I told her to quiet down. She knows the rules."

"I just think you're being too harsh on her. I don't think you're half as angry about the vase as you are that the B&O can't make up their mind which line to choose. You needn't take your frustration with the railroad out on this child."

"And you needn't intercede to take her side every time I try to discipline her," James said, clearly irritated at this latest example of betrayal. "I'm going to see my father. When I return, I expect to find this mess cleared away."

Carolina stared after him in shock. This was not the gentle man she'd married. But then neither was she the gentle wife he'd sought. What had happened to create in them such overwhelming discord? As she cradled the sobbing child against her, Carolina was torn between the need to vindicate Victoria and somehow to calm her husband. Both had erred in their actions, but she could neither change what had just happened nor truly smooth the rough waters that lay between her child and her husband.

"I hate him," Victoria declared. "He's mean, and he hates me."

Carolina shook her head and pulled the child with her to the chair. Sitting down, she drew Victoria into her arms and shook her head again. "He doesn't hate you, and I don't believe you truly hate him. He's hurting, Victoria. We all are. There is a great deal of pain in this house just now."

"Like when my other father lived here?" Victoria asked, hiccuping a sob.

"Yes," admitted Carolina. "Much the same. Your father is troubled by many things. He has been hurt and is trying to find his way through the pain."

"Like you, Mama?"

Carolina felt as though Victoria had exposed yet another chink in her armor. "Yes," she whispered almost too softly to be heard. "Like me."

Four

Judgments and Accusations

It was late when James came to their bedroom. Carolina had busied herself with mending James' shirts and socks, while hoping, even praying, that he would come upstairs and resolve the conflict that had kept them divided since his return home in the afternoon. When James finally did open the door to the room, his face looked haggard and his eyes lacked their usual luster.

"You needn't have waited up," he said, his voice almost apologetic.

"I thought perhaps I should," Carolina replied. She kept her own voice cool and objective. "I think we need to talk."

"Talk seems only to lead to arguments," James said, pulling loose the tie at his neck. "I have to leave early in the morning for Harper's Ferry, so I'd rather not fight with you at this hour."

"I have no intention of fighting," Carolina said, hurt that he perceived her to have a contrary nature.

James unbuttoned his striped navy-and-yellow waistcoat and casually tossed it aside. Carolina heard him heave a heavy sigh before speaking again. "Look, I'm sorry for the way I acted earlier. I know it was uncalled for, but it seems that there is nothing but heartache and tension in this house—in our lives. I'm not sure I ever expected things to be quite like this."

"Nor I," Carolina admitted. She smiled, thinking of her own youthful naivete. "I'm afraid growing up and getting married were games I presumed I'd be rather good at. Especially if I married a man who understood my passion for learning—" she paused, then added softly—"as you always have."

James didn't comment. Instead, he unbuttoned his shirt, pulling it out from the waistband of his pants. Then, as if having second thoughts, he plopped down dejectedly on the boot chest at the end of the bed. "Our marriage has been hard right from the start. Not because of you or me, but rather because of the complications that surround our union. My father . . . Victoria . . . this house . . . my job."

Carolina came around from the side of the bed to meet his gaze. "It seems most of those things are tied to me, so why not admit that I'm a major part of the problem? After all, I brought both Victoria and this house into the marriage with me. As for your father, there, too, the problem is mostly placed at my feet. Had I not exposed him for what he was doing, you would probably be content to overlook his affairs."

James looked hurt. "Why do you suppose something like that?"

"Because he is your father. My anger, as you so often have put it, comes from the fact that Leland's deeds could have ruined my father."

"But they didn't. You seem to forget that."

Carolina tensed. "I haven't forgotten anything."

"That's obvious," James said, reaching down to pull off his boot.

"I don't know what else you want from me," Carolina said coolly. "I've done whatever I thought I could to settle this situation."

"Everything but forgive the man. Maybe he doesn't deserve it, but you won't even offer it. And because of this, you grow more angry and bitter as the days pass. Frankly, I don't know how to help you." He pulled the remaining boot from his foot and stood to face Carolina. They were only inches apart, but it might as well have been miles.

"Help me?" Carolina shook her head, bewildered. "You've not seemed overly worried about helping me through this up till now." She let her anger surface to do battle for her and immediately regretted it. This wasn't how she had intended things to be.

"Every time I try, you throw it back in my face."

"You're no different. I've gone out of my way to try to ease your burden, and over and over you toss my help aside as though it was somehow belittling. The only thing you haven't tossed aside is Blake's money. You've been more than happy to use that to cover up Leland's deception."

James' expression turned stoic. "Is that what this is about? The money? Are you bitter because I agreed to let you use St. John's money to smooth things over with the investors?"

"I was merely trying to point out that if Blake hadn't left me the money—"

"But he did, and therefore anything else you might add is moot. You have the money, and you offered it up as a momentary solution to our problems. Even I know that you didn't do this out of kindness and concern for my father, but rather to protect your own father and see your dreams for the P&GF Railroad move forward. But I would add this, as you seem to have forgotten. While you were protecting your father, and inadvertently saving my father from shame, you were saving me, as well. The Adams and Baldwin names both stood to suffer, and in case you've forgotten, your name is now Baldwin."

"I haven't forgotten," she said, feeling his words pierce her soul.

"You offered up St. John's money because it was necessary to protect all of us."

"Yes, and all because of one man."

James' jaw clenched tight, and when he spoke, his words were barely audible. "He'll soon be dead. You'll have your revenge."

Carolina felt the color drain from her face. Is that truly what James thought she wanted? She walked away from him and sat down on the edge of the bed.

"There's nothing more we can do to change what has happened. But if we can't find a way to leave it behind us," James said, his voice void of emotion, "then I see nothing but destruction for our family."

Carolina began to tremble. She knew he was right. Why did this entire matter seem to take her up one hill, only to plunge her into a valley of despair on the other side? Just when she thought herself capable of letting go of her anger, something triggered inside her to make her hold on to it like a rope thrown to a drowning man. She glanced up to say something—anything that might show James how sorry she was—but he was gone. Their bedroom door stood open, and she had little doubt that James had gone to another room for the night.

Throwing off her robe, she crawled into bed and lay staring at the ceiling for a long time. James was right. Their entire life together stood at a critical crossroads. If she continued to hold a grudge against Leland, there would be nothing left between her and James. After all, James was Leland's son. How could she hate the father without something of that trickling down to the son?

"I don't care about the money," she whispered to the air. "So why did I bring it up? Why did I throw it in James' face when I knew it would only hurt him?"

She thought of all the years she'd longed for James' love and companionship, and now that she finally had it, she was isolating herself from him, building a wall of misunderstanding and bitterness that would stand between them like a fortress. Was that what she wanted?

"Certainly not," she murmured. "I love James. I don't want to lose him."

"Love forgets mistakes; nagging about them parts the best of friends," she could remember her mother telling her when she was a little girl.

Carolina smiled. She'd always thought her mother had made up that saying. It wasn't until years later that she found out it was a proverb from the Bible. But the wisdom in those words would have been just as true had they come from the local market. Dredging up the past had given her nothing but pain and misery. While she'd wielded Leland's sins like a sword of condemnation, James was the one who was taking the bite of each slashing move. She was killing her own beloved husband with the animosity she felt.

"Oh, Father," she prayed aloud, "this is so hard. How can I let go of what has already been done? How can I forgive Leland and, in turn, free myself from this misery?"

She prayed for a long time, hoping against all hope that James would return and she could plead for his forgiveness. But it wasn't to be, and when she awoke the next morning, she found that he had already left the house.

She ran to the window, hoping he might still be within sight, but there was no one even moving about on the street. James would travel to Harper's Ferry, still bearing the marks of her anger and the wounds of her selfish bitterness. Sinking against the window frame, Carolina began to weep.

Five

Turning Points

Carolina moved through the day with lethargic disinterest. James was gone, and left behind was the horrible memory of her caustic words. She had few choices in how to deal with the matter. She was hardly at liberty to get on the next train and follow him west. Leland needed her to remain in the house and offer him care, and Victoria's temperament still showed worrisome signs of agitation and conflict. No, she would have to wait until James returned in a week.

Taking up the *Godey's Lady's Book* magazine in hopes that she might find a decent dress design for Victoria's ever-growing frame, Carolina was surprised when a knock sounded at the front door. Knowing Mrs. Graves had already left for the market, Carolina answered the door herself. The older man on the opposite side of the door beamed a huge smile that spread from one muttonchop-whiskered cheek to the other.

"Papa!" she exclaimed, throwing herself with joyful exuberance into Joseph Adams' arms.

"I must say, this is quite a greeting," Joseph said with a laugh.

Carolina pulled away and drew her father inside the house. "I'm sorry. Here I stand outside making a spectacle of myself."

"You've never much cared in the past whether you made a spectacle of yourself," Joseph said, following her lead to the drawing room.

"That's before I had to become a respectable wife and mother," Carolina said with a smile. "Now, where are your things and how long will you be staying?"

"I can't stay long—only an hour or two," Joseph admitted. "I'm making my way to Boston. The doctor has agreed to allow me to visit your mother."

"Oh, that is good news," Carolina said, taking a seat. "Come sit and tell me everything."

Joseph did as she bid. "There's really not much more to tell. The doctor says that your mother is responding well to one of her nurses. The woman is rather motherly in her care, and she's a Christian, so she reads the Bible to your mother and prays for her. I found it a great comfort to imagine such attention being offered her."

"Yes, that is wonderful news. It would be an answer to all of our prayers if Mother would find a way to accept the past and live for the future." Carolina's words seemed to echo in her heart. Wasn't this the very advice she herself needed to heed?

"The trip to deliver your mother to Boston last year seemed to stretch out endlessly. But this time, I feel light as a feather, and the miles are simply eaten away as I dream of seeing her again."

"You love her very much, don't you?"

"I could love no other with more intensity of feeling. She is such a part of me that to leave her in Boston tore from my soul that very part which makes me wholly happy. I've missed her more than I could ever begin to put into words." Joseph's eyes misted and his look took on a faraway expression. "When I awaken in the night and find her gone, I startle to wonder where she is. Then when I realize she's in Boston, and I remember all that has come to pass . . . well . . . it's almost more than I can bear."

Carolina felt her own eyes grow moist. "I've never really thought about how hard this must be for you. I think from time to time about how much I wish I could just sit down and talk to her, but my family is here now, and so I fill my time with them. But you—" Her voice broke and she struggled to keep her emotions from running away with her. "You must ever face her absence."

Joseph fixed his gaze on her and smiled. "But all is well. God has been good to us, and I find great relief in having located a hospital with such a good reputation in its care of the mentally ill. I pray it will be but a short while until your mother completely recovers."

"Do the doctors believe it possible?" Carolina asked with obvious hope in her voice.

"They are more confident than they were a few months ago."

Carolina nodded and wiped her eyes. "I wish I could come with you to see her. How I miss my mother."

"Why don't you? You and Victoria could come. I'm certain it would do Margaret good, and if the doctor refused to let all of us see her, well, at least you would be nearer to her. Not only that, but you'd make marvelous company for me."

Carolina felt the anticipation of such a trip die within her as she remembered Leland. "I can't go." She knew the expression on her face would be enough to give her father reason to ask why, so before he could voice the words she continued. "James has gone west with the railroad, and his father is upstairs—" she hesitated, then added—"dying."

"Dying?" her father asked, his face showing proof of his surprise.

"Yes. The doctor said it is his heart. The attack was quite fierce, and I'm afraid he hasn't even the strength to be moved from the house."

Joseph reached out and touched Carolina's hands. She hadn't realized that she was twisting the folds of her skirt until he stilled her actions. "Tell me everything. Tell me about the attack and all that you have endured."

It didn't take long to explain the events that had created such misery in her heart. She told her father of the attack and of the problems that came with Leland's bedridden existence in her home. "It hasn't been easy," Carolina admitted. "James and I have argued many times over what his father has done. We argued last night, in fact, and James left for Harper's Ferry this morning before I could apologize or talk to him about my harsh words. Now I'm trapped here caring for a man who makes me most uncomfortable, and I have no idea how to make matters right again."

Joseph nodded. "I'd like to see Leland." The stern tone of his voice left Carolina wary.

"He isn't to be upset," she said, getting to her feet. "I'm sure you understand."

"I do," Joseph replied and stood. "I won't upset him, I promise. But I think it would do both of us good to see each other and share a few words. I would not want him to pass away without speaking my mind."

Carolina swallowed hard, wondering if her father would deliver a severe reprimand to the dying man. She'd never felt protective of Leland, but the idea of James coming home to learn that her father had severely attacked the dying man made her tremble. But when she met her father's eyes, she saw all the assurance she needed to put aside her fears.

"I'll show you the way," she said. How could she imagine such a thing of her father? Joseph's very nature was such that he would never hurt another living soul if he could at all prevent it. And although Leland had certainly performed an intolerable act of betrayal, her father wouldn't take it out on the dying man.

She directed her father to the room and paused outside the door. "Would you like me to go in and see if he's awake?"

"No," Joseph replied. "I'll wake him if necessary."

She nodded and watched her father enter the room. She knew she should draw the door closed, but something held her fast to the place where she stood. She observed as her father lightly touched Leland's hand, then watched as Leland opened his eyes and recognized his visitor.

"Joseph . . ." he said the name in a short gasp of breath.

"My good friend, it grieves me to find you like this," Joseph said, taking a seat on the straight-backed chair beside the bed.

"I had hoped to see you before I died."

"And here I am," Joseph replied in an almost lighthearted manner. "I had come to tell Carolina of my journey to see her mother in Boston. She told me you were here and gave me the details of your circumstance."

"It seems only fitting," Leland said, struggling to sit up just a little. Joseph reached out and helped the man up against the pillow. "I deserve nothing more than this."

"What manner of talk is this?"

Leland suffered through a fierce spell of coughing before offering Joseph an answer. "I'm sorry, Joseph. I'm sorry for the past and the wrongs I've done you."

Carolina felt her breath catch in her throat. What would her father say? Would he refuse the man's apology? She saw her father smile and pat his old friend's hand. The words that came from her father humbled and shamed her.

"We all make bad judgments, Leland. You did nothing more or less than each of us has done at different times. I only wish you would have come to me. If I'd only known that you were suffering from the depression and bank closure, I would have gladly given you whatever you needed."

Carolina watched Leland's face contort as tears slid down his cheeks. "I know you would have. But I was proud. I've . . . never—" He coughed again, gasping several times to draw a decent breath, and all the while Joseph held his hand tightly. Leland settled and resumed the conversation. "I've never managed things well, but I now know what I must do. Joseph, I know I don't deserve your forgiveness, but I'm asking for it nevertheless."

"Friend, you've always had it. You should have known that."

Carolina felt her emotions twist into a knot. She knew she was intruding on a very personal moment, but for the life of her, she couldn't move from her place outside the door.

"I fear I've done nothing to recommend myself to the good Lord," Leland said, making an attempt at lightening the mood.

"Few of us have," Joseph answered with a grin that took years from his face.

"But my deeds have taken me so far from the truth of the matter. I know I've strayed from the path, and I'm not sure that God would ever take me back, but that is my desire."

"It's God's desire, as well, my friend," Joseph assured him.

Carolina found herself deeply touched by her father's words of mercy. She longed to know the same peace and assurance as that which Leland sought.

"We don't always know what God's plan might be," Joseph explained, "but we can be confident that He knows what we need and how to bring it about in our lives."

"Just as He must have known how much I needed to receive your forgiveness," Leland replied weakly.

"Exactly," Joseph agreed. "God's thinking is not as ours. We see the moment—the detail of what is before us. But God sees it all. He sees the picture in total completeness. Yet He still allows us to choose our own path, and we can never stray so far that God would not take us back should we desire it."

"I've made plenty of bad choices," Leland said with a raspy attempt at a laugh.

"You've made good ones, too. Edith was one of those."

"Yes." Leland nodded. "Edith was, by far and away, the best choice I ever made. She would be sorely disappointed in me, however, if she'd ever known how low I had gone."

"Maybe disappointed, but she would never have stopped loving you, and neither has God. We must remember that He works everything out for His own purpose. Even our poor choices become the means to bring Him glory."

"I'm afraid the railroad was never my dream," Leland said after several moments of silence. "I knew your enthusiasm, as I did James'. I even knew Carolina's heart on the matter, but I could not bring myself to believe in the possibilities of such a venture. Then the bank closed, and in truth, it had already been in such peril for years that it was a wonder the deed didn't happen sooner." He paused, his breathing shallow. "I took your money and your faith, knowing that I would never see the project through. I figured I could make one excuse or another and soon it would all straighten itself out."

"Our own thinking often gets us in trouble that way," Joseph answered without condemnation. "But it is a thing of the past. We broke ground on the P&GF nearly a week ago. So you see, everything has worked itself out."

"I don't deserve this kindness, Joseph."

"Ah, Leland, we are friends. Friends overlook mistakes. Consider it no more an issue between us."

Carolina felt her chest tighten. A lump formed in her throat that forced her to move away from the door, lest she break into audible sobs. Her father had such a forgiving nature, and the wisdom that came from him gave her reason to hope for her own future. It was a turning point. One that had come most unexpectedly.

She had no sooner reached the bottom step than she heard her father bidding Leland good-bye. Struggling to regain composure of her shaken emotions, Carolina tried to greet Joseph with a smile.

Six

Strongholds

Joseph came down the steps with a questioning look. "Are you unwell, Carolina?"

Carolina shook her head, and even though she was tightly gripping the banister at the bottom of the stairway, she tried her best to appear unaffected by the scene she'd just witnessed. "No, I'm perfectly well, Papa," she offered, her voice sounding ridiculously childlike.

"Why is it, then, that I find your words and expression do not match?" He came to take hold of her arm, and as they walked back to the drawing room, he gently asked, "Why don't you tell me what's really wrong?"

Carolina felt her face flush. "It's just that . . . well, you see . . ." She fell silent and tried to imagine how she could explain. "I overheard you talking to Leland just now."

Joseph raised a curious brow. "And that has caused this despair?"

"In part," Carolina admitted. She took a seat by the fire and waited for her father to do the same. After he'd sat down beside her, Carolina forced herself to continue. "I'm afraid I don't understand how you can be so forgiving with him. After all, he's deceived our family and caused great pain. He promised one thing, then failed to deliver on that, only to turn around and do something completely different. And all while people were counting on him."

"That much is true," Joseph agreed. "But I suppose he had his reasons."

Carolina shook her head. "There is never a good reason to deceive. He lied to us. He knew how important the railroad project was to us, yet he took the money and went his own way."

"Desperation makes a man do things he might otherwise never consider. Leland is no different. He was never a good businessman. He tried his hand at farming and found that to his dislike. He attempted banking and made an even worse mess there. Leland is simply not cut out for those types of responsibilities."

"But that's no reason to lie and cheat your friends. You've been nothing but the best of friends to the Baldwin family, and still he stabs you in the back."

"Harboring hatred and malice toward the man will do little good. Bitterness only affords Satan a stronghold." He paused and studied her intently. "Are you harboring such bitterness toward Leland?"

Carolina looked away, ashamed to face her father. "I . . . it's just that . . ." She sighed and shook her head. "He nearly ruined you. He nearly caused the Adams name to be condemned."

"But it didn't happen that way, Carolina. You are holding something against the man that never happened."

"But it could have!" declared Carolina, turning to face her father. "His deception caused a great deal of harm."

"It delayed the P&GF's construction, but, Carolina, I believe all things happen in God's good timing. Perhaps this delay prevented an even bigger disaster. I certainly don't condone Leland's actions, but neither can I stand as the man's judge. And"—he reached out to gently cup her chin—"neither can you."

"But he probably wouldn't be even the slightest bit remorseful if he weren't dying. He and James argued the point of paying back the investors. He was certain that some excuse could have been made. I'm just not convinced that he's truly sincere in his repentance."

"Carolina Adams—" Joseph smiled and corrected himself. "Carolina Baldwin, do you really suppose yourself to have the right to judge Leland's actions?"

She put her hand up to cover his. "I don't suppose that, not really. But it is hard to accept that he can act as he did and suddenly be absolved of the entire matter."

"Yet you believed that should be the case for his son," Joseph reminded. "James was just as guilty of deceit, yet you pled his case on many an occasion."

"That was different."

"Was it? Was it really?" questioned her father. "James came into our home to tutor you and court your sister. He even allowed himself to become engaged to her. Yet all the while, by his own admission, he didn't love her—he loved you. He nearly carried that deceit to the altar, where he would have made pledges before God and man to love and care for your sister all of her life. He took my hospitality, yet lied to me on a daily basis. Should I then fail to forgive him, as you seem to imply I should fail to forgive his father?"

Carolina got to her feet and stood with arms outspread. "That is totally different. James did not seek to deceive. It merely happened. It was very nearly out of his control. Remember, Virginia is the one who proposed to him. He told me that much."

"He could have refused her, Carolina. You are making excuses for his lies, but you would refuse to offer a single exception for Leland's actions."

"I'm telling you, it's different, Papa."

"A lie is a lie, Carolina. Both men practiced poor judgment. Both men suffered and nearly lost the things most dear to them over such lies. Now that the truth is exposed and Leland is contrite, would you have me refuse to forgive him? Would you ask God to forever condemn his soul?"

Carolina shook her head. "Of course not."

"Then what do you want from him?"

"I don't know," she answered, her voice barely a whisper.

"You've already allowed yourself to take offense for me in this matter because it was my money, my trust, that Leland threatened. Certainly, your name was on the charter, but as my daughter and James' wife, little harm would have befallen you. So the wrong was done me, and you took up the cause as one of your own. Now I'm telling you that you needn't have done such a thing, and in fact, I cannot abide that you have done such a thing."

Tears rose in Carolina's eyes. "But I love you, and I hated to see you hurt."

"But I wasn't overly harmed. My feelings were hurt that, as my friend, Leland felt he could not come to me with his problems. But my reputation speaks for itself, and this small, insignificant event would not have destroyed years of trustworthy behavior. No, the shame would have fallen upon Leland, all the same." Joseph stood and opened his arms to embrace his daughter. "You must forgive him, child. There is nothing to be gained by harboring ill will toward a dying man. I must leave now, but I beseech you, talk to Leland. Talk to him and admit your anger. Tell him everything and then forgive him. The man is not long for this earth. Do not let him die with this standing between you. It will forever haunt you otherwise."

Carolina felt her father's arms tighten around her. She cherished his embrace and put her cheek against the coarse broadcloth coat. "I will talk to him, if it will please you."

Joseph pulled away and set Carolina from him. "Do not do this for me. Do it because it is right to do. Do it so that Satan will not be allowed a stronghold in your life."

Carolina nodded, tears blurring her vision. "All right, but it won't be easy."

Joseph smiled. "No, I don't imagine it will be. But you forgave James, and I'm sure you can find it in your heart to forgive your father-in-law."

"It's because of him that James and I are estranged."

Joseph's expression grew very thoughtful and he rubbed his chin. "Is it really? Seems to me that Leland probably had very little to do with it. After all, he wasn't even around most of the time, and now he's upstairs bedfast."

Carolina knew her father was right. The fights that had erupted between her and James were usually over something she said or did in regard to Leland. It wasn't God's fault, or even Leland's, that her marriage was now painfully strained. It was her own fault. Her actions and bitter pride had caused this. Hadn't James begged her to forget the past? Hadn't he tried more than once to smooth matters over and comfort Carolina in her fears for her father?

"You're causing me to see things that I'm not sure I want to see," she admitted, feeling rather sheepish about the entire matter.

Joseph laughed. "I can't tell you the number of times your mother has said the same exact thing to me. Or for that matter, the number of times she's caused me to see things that I didn't want to see, either."

"I suppose I have a great deal to sort through," Carolina said, her path suddenly quite clear. "Thank you, Papa. I know that I couldn't have begun to see these things had you not come here today."

"If not me, God would have sent another."

Carolina shook her head. "No, God knew that I would listen to you where I've failed to listen to others." Then she smiled and reached out to take hold of his hand. "I'm glad it was you."

Joseph squeezed her hand. "I'm glad it was, too. Now, come walk me to the door. I must be off."

"I wish you could stay."

"I know," Joseph replied, pulling her close as they walked to the door. "If time permits, I'll stop back on my way home and give you all the details of your mother's condition."

"Oh, please do, and do give Mother my love." She gave her father her happiest smile, then added, "Hopefully I'll have all of this behind me by the time you return."

Joseph hugged her tightly and kissed her cheek before taking up his top hat. "I know the kind of determination you have, Carolina. If you want to put this issue behind you, you will."

Carolina smiled. "Any more words of wisdom? Maybe something for James and me?"

Joseph turned at the door. "Don't go to bed angry. Resolve your differences even if you have to stay up all night long in order to do so. Otherwise, you might awaken to find that there is no opportunity to set matters straight."

"Just like what has happened to me today."

"Exactly," her father said with a nod. "Talk to James and bare your heart before him. Seek his love to help heal your wounds."

"I will," Carolina said, knowing that somehow she would do just that. "Good-bye, Papa, and thank you."

Carolina watched him go down the walkway and through the wrought-iron gates. The coachman, who had apparently been requested to await Joseph's return, assisted her father into the carriage. How she longed to go with him and leave the worries of reconciliation behind her. But she knew that would never work. Even as the carriage moved off down the street, Carolina knew that her place was here and her work awaited her in the upstairs guest room.

She was about to close the door when she spied Mrs. Graves making her way up the street. Victoria skipped alongside her, and Carolina smiled at the tender scene. Mrs. Graves seemed to babble nonstop to the child while Victoria would occasionally nod or laugh, continuing to match the older woman's brisk steps with her own energetic skipping.

The joy Carolina felt at seeing them reminded her that only through forgiveness and ridding themselves of strongholds of misunderstanding and fear had the three females knitted together to become a family. When James had appeared on the scene, it was again through the strengthening power of love that they had all opened their arms to accept him as a member of the family.

"God, please forgive me for my unkindness to Leland. Forgive me for not heeding the wisdom of my husband, and forgive me for allowing my tongue to put up barriers between us. Please bring James home to me safely so that I might make peace with him." Watching Mrs. Graves and Victoria turn before reaching the main entryway to the St. John house, Carolina realized they would come in through the back door, as was Mrs. Graves' habit.

Taking a deep breath, Carolina closed the front door and turned to lean against it. Spying the staircase, her eyes gazed upward. "Help me, Father, to face Leland," she whispered.

Seven

Choosing a Path

James found himself once again the traveling companion of Ben Latrobe. Riding in a private railcar, they made their way from Harper's Ferry to Cumberland. It was planned that James and Ben would meet up with several other members of the survey team and review some additional ideas on the three proposed routes to conclude the B&O. But James saw it as a good time to sort through his conflicting thoughts.

He had regretted leaving Carolina with their anger between them, but at the time James hadn't been able to bring himself to make yet another attempt at resolving their differences. He was tired. Weary of all that seemed to come between them. His father. The house. Victoria. He felt despair like that which he'd never known. Finally his dreams were being realized, and yet it wasn't enough to hold conflict at bay.

"I don't believe you've heard a word I said," Ben Latrobe said, pushing up his glasses.

"I'm sorry, Ben. Please continue."

Latrobe spread out a map on the small table between them. "The route that seems most sensible and obvious is to head straight out from Cumberland, follow down around the south branch of the Potomac and on west to New Martinsville by way of Fishing Creek, then through to Clarksburg and finally Parkersburg on the Ohio River."

"And the benefits of this route over the others?" James struggled to keep his mind focused.

"It puts us on a straight line with St. Louis, of course. It also lines up well with other proposed railroads to the west. Parkersburg is a very young town and quite small; however, this could be a bonus rather than an obstacle. We would have a free hand to develop our terminus the way we desired."

"And the negative side of choosing Parkersburg?"

"Namely the James River and Kanawha Canal Company of Richmond. They fear that should Parkersburg become the B&O's terminating location, Richmond trade will be given over to Baltimore. If the Virginia legislature listens to that caterwauling, then Parkersburg may become a moot idea."

"So what of the other two routes?" James asked, shifting uncomfortably and hating the heat of the day inside the car. Already Latrobe had given up on the June afternoon and tossed propriety aside, along with his outer coat. James, never one for convention, shrugged out of his coat, as well, and felt as though he was suddenly free of his bonds.

Ben wiped perspiration from his forehead and pointed to Pittsburgh. "Pennsylvania would like our western terminus to be Pittsburgh. The city is already comprised of nearly 70,000 citizens. The ports are well established with a monumental amount of commerce and trade moving through the city from the Ohio River on a daily basis. The city handles everything from cotton to pig iron and mass produces the latter in the form of everything from bridges to steamboats. There is daily packet service from Pittsburgh to Cincinnati and plenty of connections to canal trade for Erie and Cleveland."

James heard the words but cared little for their meaning. What would it gain him to be a part of deciding the Baltimore and Ohio's future when his own future was hopelessly muddled?

Latrobe didn't seem to notice James' dilemma, however, and continued on with his thoughts. "Of course, Pittsburgh is in Pennsylvania, and there is the matter of Virginia disallowing any portion of the B&O to pass over Virginia land, unless the western terminus is also in Virginia. That would create an additional routing problem in that we haven't even begun to survey routes that take themselves through Maryland and Pennsylvania without touching Virginia. And while I plan to do more surveys next August, my guess is that the added distance would create a monetary conflict that would take away the attraction of a Pittsburgh terminus.

"As for Wheeling, and I know this is your preference"—Latrobe marked the surveyed route with his finger—"it has a great deal of potential. It is a U.S. port of entry on the Ohio, and they are soon to become the home of the world's first wire suspension bridge across the same. Wheeling would solve the question of a Virginia-based terminus, and it already has the National Road, which brings in a great deal of freight and passengers."

Latrobe continued with the negative aspects of Wheeling. Something was mentioned of the location creating its own problem with three different proposed routes from Cumberland to Wheeling.

"I'm sorry, what did you say?" James asked, realizing his mind had wandered again.

Latrobe sat back and pulled off his glasses. As he gently rubbed the lenses he glanced across the table to James. "You've not been yourself since your arrival in Harper's Ferry. Want to tell me about it?"

James shrugged. "I don't suppose it would do any harm. Seems you are always helping me through my messes anyway."

Latrobe laughed. "And you have yet another mess?"

"The biggest yet." James leaned back against the leather-bound chair. "My wife and I have reached a point of disagreement."

"Is that all?" Latrobe replied. "Buy her a lovely trinket, apologize on bended knee, and complete the act by sweeping her into your arms. Minor conflicts have a way of not appearing quite so major an ordeal when a little humility is practiced."

"I'm afraid this is much more than a minor conflict. In fact, it is several very large conflicts all rolled together into one large, consuming problem."

"I see. Well, we have several hours ahead of us, so why don't you tell me all about it?"

"I wish I could. The fact is, I find it difficult to sort through it all in my own mind. First and foremost is the situation my father created." Latrobe eyed him curiously but said nothing, and James quickly continued. "My father, suffice it to say, practiced a bit of underhandedness, and my wife found out about it. The biggest problem in that was that it also affected her father, and she took that quite personally."

"I can understand why. Most women tend to be very defensive in regard to their family."

"Yes, well, that's putting it mildly. Carolina refuses to forgive my father, and the situation is further frustrated in that he recently suffered a heart attack—in our home—and is dying. I left for Harper's Ferry with Carolina being forced to remain behind to care for him."

"I'm sorry to learn about your father's attack. And you are right, that makes it more than an issue of trinkets and bended knee," Latrobe replied as he put his glasses back on. He squinted a couple of times as if to adjust the focus, then continued. "You say she refuses to forgive him, yet she must care for him while he dies?"

"Yes. The doctor was supposed to send someone over to help us, but the woman he had in mind was unavailable and no one else seemed suitable. My father's presence has added additional burdens to Carolina's already busy schedule, and given her feelings toward him, I know that weight to be doubled—if not tripled. Furthermore, I made matters worse by arguing with her about how much of this was my fault. I upset my father, and he probably wouldn't have had the attack in the first place had I left well enough alone."

"You cannot possibly know that, James. Besides, how can you take responsibility for your father's actions and health?"

"That's what Carolina said. I argued with her that if I'd only paid better attention to his needs, if I'd been a better son, then maybe he would never have found the need to cheat and deceive."

"His nature is what it is," Latrobe said in a nonchalant manner. "I doubt seriously that you would have swayed his nature by being more attentive. Without knowing all the details of the matter, I will add this." He paused and tilted his chin upward ever so slightly. "A man takes chances on the things he believes will make him happy. Be they right or wrong, he chooses for himself, and, in spite of the influence of those around him, he must still decide for himself what those choices will be. It's no different with the routes we're trying to decide on for the B&O. Each path a man takes must be carefully weighed and decided upon. Either he seeks to know the pitfalls of each way, or he ignores all warning signs and strikes out without any consideration of the consequences. Your father obviously did the latter."

"If that were the only problem I might not feel half so bad," James said in a dejected manner. "The truth is, besides this there is the growing frustration I feel from living in another man's house."

"Ah," Ben said with a smile. "Perhaps now we get to the crux of the matter."

"What do you mean?"

"Only that no man wants to believe he stands in the shadow of another. You've married the woman of your dreams, but in doing so you've taken on the responsibility of another man's child and home."

"Yes, and although I love Victoria dearly, she is becoming more and more of a problem. She resents my authority and often seeks Carolina out to keep from having to carry through with my wishes. Carolina most generally finds something objectionable to my instruction and thus, whether or not the matter is resolved, it always pits Carolina against me in dealing with the child."

Latrobe laughed at this, totally taking James by surprise. "That happens in homes where the children are born to both parents, James. Children, being children, will often see how far they can push their boundaries. They play one parent against the other, all in hoping to accomplish the most beneficial circumstance for themselves. My own children are masters at this. Victoria is simply doing nothing more or less than any of her contemporaries."

"So it isn't just me?"

"Absolutely not. There isn't a father alive who hasn't found himself up against the same thing. And while that doesn't solve the problem for you, at least you may take comfort in knowing that it isn't a unique dilemma."

"It may not be unique, but it's tearing Carolina and me apart. I can't get her to see that she needs to support me in this situation."

"Have you talked to her about it? Not in the heat of the moment when the problem is upon you, but rather in private, when nothing in particular is causing friction between you?"

"But that's the problem. There's been friction between us ever since we said, 'I do.' I don't know how to explain it, but as much as we love each other, and as much as we desired to be married, there hasn't seemed to be one moment of true peace between us since the wedding."

Again Latrobe smiled. "Welcome to matrimonial bliss, son."

James couldn't quite understand Latrobe's easygoing attitude. "Please don't tell me that this is all there ever is—that Carolina and I will be at each other's throats the rest of our lives."

"Of course I won't tell you that," Latrobe responded. "But I will say this. Marriage is work. It's hard work. Harder than anything else you'll ever do. Believe me, I know. And you want to know why?"

James nodded and Ben Latrobe leaned forward as if to impart a deep, mysterious secret. "Because marriage isn't about the wedding or the wedding trip afterward. It isn't about cozy nights spent in each other's arms or the way she makes you feel when she smiles. Oh, those things all have a part in it, but a very minor one. No, James, marriage is about sticking it out when it isn't so nice. Marriage is being there to pick up the pieces when your perfect world falls apart. It's seeing the mess you've made of things and being willing to work through it until you have created something better than you had before. It's listening to her fears, her troubles, and concerns. It's eating meals that don't taste as good as those your mother fixed, enduring her temperamental outbursts and tears, and not giving up when things get hard."

Latrobe paused for a moment and a frown lined his face where the smile had been only moments before. "True love is standing by your mate when his health fails, along with his business. It's holding on to what you have in each other and God when you watch your infant suffer and die. It's knowing that the world goes on and you can depend on each other even when everything else around you lies in ruins at your feet. Those things have happened to me, James."

Latrobe looked up then, and James could see the glint of tears in the older man's eyes.

"But through it all, my Ellen was steadfast. Not because she always agreed with me, and certainly not because I was always right in my choices. No, James, she stayed because of her commitment and her love. A love that she knew was completed in my love for her. I would imagine your Carolina feels the same. But you're both new to this. You've both had time on your own to decide how life should be, and now that you've come together you're bound to have disagreements in one area or another."

"It just seems I can't open my mouth without saying the wrong thing."

"Give it over to God, James. He has a way of working wonders. Don't be so hard on yourself, nor on Carolina. You two will need to make some definite choices where Victoria is concerned, but don't put yourselves on opposite teams. Remember, you are partners in life."

"I do remember that," James admitted, "but it's hard to know where to go from there."

"Like the railroad, eh? You have to pick one path over the other."

James nodded. "I suppose so. Only the positive and negative effects are more uncertain than the issues of where to lay tracks and what city to build to."

"Life is what it is—a journey. You start in one place and move to another, and along the way you experience the everyday complications of love, hate, trust, betrayal, hope, promise, and truth. You can take the journey alone or go with God as your full-time partner. It's one of those choices we each have to make."

James felt relief wash over him. He had chosen to take God along as his partner. Of that there was no doubt. That he had chosen to ignore His companionship was yet another issue. "I suppose as I've become more and more bent under the weight of my troubles, I've forgotten about God taking the journey at my side."

"He's happy to shoulder the burden, James. And He won't leave you to solve the problem for yourself."

The train rocked and bounced along the line while James silently prayed and put his mind at ease. He knew matters wouldn't solve themselves, but he felt confident that God could prepare the path for him to take. And by following that path and trusting God for the proper words, James felt a new hope that he could mend the rift between himself and Carolina.

Eight

Letting Go

For three days Carolina had the utmost of good intentions. Her plan was not only to talk to Leland but also to clear the conflict between them and deal with Victoria's obvious rebellion against James. But for three days she had suffered through her own bouts of troublesome health and watched Leland do likewise as he slipped in and out of consciousness. Leland's problem would eventually resolve itself in death, while Carolina knew her problem would resolve itself in new life. She was pregnant. And in the midst of the conflict and chaos that had become her life, she had very nearly missed all the telltale signs. Now, however, with the child growing rapidly within her, there was no mistaking the matter any longer.

She gently touched her rounding stomach. It seemed to have mounded up almost overnight. One day she was girlishly lean, the next she was carrying a child in an almost obvious manner. She knew it hadn't really come upon her exactly that way, but it seemed, with her worries over Victoria and James and her own crisis with Leland, that the excitement of bearing her first child had been swallowed up in grief.

Mrs. Graves had noticed immediately and was the only other person besides Cook who knew there was to be an addition to the family. Carolina had wanted to wait until the right time to tell James, but since the previous month, when she was quite certain about the life she carried, there had been no right time. Either James had been working or they had been arguing, and then Leland had suffered his attack. But now she was determined. When James returned home, she would tell him about the baby as well as the news that she had forgiven his father. At least she believed she had forgiven Leland. The final step was to go to the man and square the issue with him face-to-face. And that was what she was preparing to do.

Mrs. Graves had told her of Leland's rally; he was awake now and asking for James. Carolina saw it as the perfect opportunity to go to him and speak her mind. She surveyed herself in the mirror, grateful that her day dress was cut in such a fashion as to hide her changing figure. The powder blue print was complimentary to her complexion, and the full elbow-length sleeves eased the heat of the growing summer warmth. Soon, she thought, I will have to have new clothes made. She stood sideways and ran her hand down her figure, then turned to face the mirror head on.

She licked her lips and prayed for strength. It wouldn't be easy to humble herself before Leland, but after three days of prayer and fitful self-exploration, Carolina knew she was ready to let go of the past. This child represented the future. A future that she didn't want marred with ugly reminders of unpleasant times. The baby gave her strength to consider the future and how the arrival of their first natural-born child might forever change their lives.

Drawing in a deep breath, Carolina gave up her reflective consideration and went to Leland's room. She paused for a moment outside the door and once again murmured a prayer.

"Please, Father, let this go well. Let me do nothing to further upset Leland, but instead let my words give peace to us both."

She turned the handle and wasn't surprised to find Leland apparently anticipating her arrival. He was propped up ever so slightly and smiled weakly at the appearance of his daughter-in-law.

"I had hoped to talk to James, but you are a welcome sight nevertheless," he said, his voice barely audible.

"I'm sorry to say, James has not yet returned from his trip west. He should come home soon, however." She moved to the chair by the bed and took a seat. "I had rather hoped that we might talk before his return."

Leland's expression registered surprise. "I would like that."

Carolina smiled. "I would, too." She glanced away and tried to think of how she might bring up the subject that weighed on her when Leland all but took the words from her mouth.

"I would also like it if you could find it in your heart to forgive me." He managed weakly to hold up his hand to wave off any protest Carolina might offer. "Please hear me out." She nodded and he continued. "I was wrong to do the things I did. I know that your silence and money are the only reasons I'm not yet in prison. For that mercy, I am grateful." His body was wracked with a hideous spell of coughing, which brought a premature end to his words.

Carolina leaned forward to offer assistance should Leland need to sit up any farther, but again he waved her off and soon the cough spent itself, and he drew a deep but ragged breath to continue. "Carolina, I'm deeply ashamed of what I did. I know that may not mean much, but it is the truth. Your father helped me to see that the only hope I have now is in making my soul right with God and mankind. Yours is the only forgiveness I have failed to obtain."

Carolina's eyes blurred with tears. "You haven't failed, Leland. I do forgive you. I didn't want to at first," she admitted, "but God would not let me be. I knew it was wrong to hold anything against you, but I was so hurt at the betrayal."

"I do not blame you for hating me."

"But I didn't really hate you—I only wanted to." She paused and smiled. "Does that sound out of place? A Christian woman seeking to hate someone? But I thought hate would make the matter less painful. If anger and bitterness took the place of the hurt I felt, then I supposed somehow it would be easier to deal with. But it wasn't, and I am sorry."

Leland smiled and moved his hand to touch her arm. "I completely understand your motives. I would like you to understand mine, as well. You see, Edith was the light of my life. I wanted so much to be the man she needed. Her father had been a strong man. A powerful man, capable of leading others and making things happen. I was a simple clerk, and not very good at that, but I fell in love with Edith from the first moment I laid eyes on her. Probably much like James did with you." He paused for several moments, his breathing rapid and very shallow.

"I wanted very much to make Edith see the potential in me, and when she did, I felt as though my life had become complete. It no longer mattered that I was but a simple clerk. It didn't matter that I couldn't offer her great wealth. She loved me, and it was in this that I found my self-worth. When her father died and she inherited her childhood home, I tried my best to fill her father's shoes. Plantation life had never appealed to me. I didn't have the land in my blood and could just as soon take it or leave it. But it was precious to Edith, and so for her sake I gave it my best effort. It was your father who eventually convinced me to sell the place."

"My father?" Carolina asked, surprised at this news.

"He had become such a good friend. I had known him long before Edith agreed to marry me. He advised me often in the plantation business, showing me such things as what horses to purchase, when I had finally saved enough to obtain my own carriage and team. He could see that the plantation was rapidly declining under my care—or rather lack of it. He helped me see the sense in letting go of my desire to fill the position of the former master. When I approached Edith and told her how miserable I was, she understood and did not object to my selling the place. We sold it, then took the proceeds with us to purchase a house in Washington City and to start up my bank."

At this he glanced away, and Carolina thought his expression had taken on a look of painful remorse. "You don't have to go on," she offered gently.

"Oh, but I do. For you, I want to go on. I want to tell it all so that you might better understand. You see, I knew I had cheated James out of his birthright. The plantation should one day have gone to him, but because I was unable to maintain it, I felt somehow I would have to make it up to him. I put everything I had into the bank, and when that, too, began to fall apart, what with the problems that haunted all of us in the banking business, I knew I would either have to find some way to bail myself out or suffer the ridicule of those I loved most. I sent James off to college, arguing with him about his interests, demanding that he take on mine. I didn't have the proper funds to put him through school, but I knew that to pull him out would be to announce to the entire world that I had failed again."

"Is that when you began to create counterfeit bank notes?" Carolina asked.

Leland nodded. "My brother Samuel—you know, the one who came to visit last week?" Carolina nodded and he continued. "Samuel had always rubbed elbows with men of lower class and more corrupt natures. I knew he would know what to do, and soon the matter was resolved and times looked better. I didn't think of it as hurting anyone in particular. After all, what were a few drafts here and there, drawn against huge banks with solid reserves? I never worried about the corruption of my own soul.

"Then I saw things get worse, and I pushed James to marry for money and social power. I knew it was wrong, but arranging marriages for children was perfectly acceptable, as you know."

"Yes, I know it very well," Carolina said with a smile. "Mother used to have a rule about the eldest daughter marrying first. Arranging a marriage for Virginia became a most consuming business."

Leland nodded. "James never loved her. He came to tutor you in arithmetic and science, and instead lost his heart. I don't blame him. You were always my favorite, as well."

Carolina felt her face grow hot. "I didn't know that," she offered lamely.

"It's another reason that having your forgiveness is important to me. I admire you, Carolina. For as much as I fought against your participation in masculine ambitions such as the railroad, I have to admit I felt intimidated by your knowledge of such things."

"Most men have been. I think only James and my father remained unaffected."

"Oh, I won't speak for your father, although I know his pride in you is strong. But James I know full well, and I know he has been anything but unaffected by your intelligence. He loves it. He respects and welcomes it, and it has changed his outlook on life. Never forget that."

"I'm afraid I've hurt him very much in all of this," Carolina admitted. "I didn't mean to let things get carried away. I didn't mean to hold this grudge and create such hurtful feelings between us. Leland . . ." she spoke his name drawing a deep breath, "I hope you will forgive me. I know I was wrong."

Leland's expression was pained. "You did nothing wrong."

"Yes, I did. I held this thing against you, and I knew that I should forgive you, even as God has forgiven me for my bad judgments, but instead I became stubborn and unyielding. I don't deserve your forgiveness, but I do seek it."

Leland reached out and took hold of her. Carolina felt how cold and lifeless his hand was, and she barely contained a shudder when she realized how close death was to consuming him.

"I can't imagine," he began, his voice growing ever weaker, "that you should need such a thing, but, yes, with all that is within my power, I forgive whatever wrong you believe you have done me."

Carolina let her tears fall freely. "Thank you . . . Father Baldwin." It was the first time she had addressed him in such a fashion, but it seemed right and good, and left her feeling warm and happy.

"You make the perfect daughter-in-law, Carolina. I'm so proud of James and his choice. I wish I could have had his convictions and strength of character. Maybe then I would have stood my ground and this talk would be unnecessary."

"We have to let go of what might have been," Carolina said, knowing it to be the truth.

"I only wish," Leland said softly, "that I might have lived to see my grandchildren. You and James make such good parents to Victoria. I would have liked to have seen you with a baby in your arms. A Baldwin baby."

Carolina flushed and squeezed Leland's hand very gently. "I'm going to have a baby in November."

Leland's face lit up for the first time, and for a moment Carolina thought it might be just the thing to give him the will to live.

"James said nothing to me."

Carolina smiled. "He doesn't know yet."

"He does now," James called out.

Carolina turned to find him standing in the doorway. She had no way of knowing how long he'd been there, but his eyes were full of tears, and now, in spite of his obvious exhaustion, he was beaming a smile that stretched from one side of his face to the other.

"James!" she exclaimed and hurried to his arms. "I've missed you so—" She could say no more, for his lips had come down to cover her own in a much-longed-for kiss.

She relished the feeling of his arms around her, and when his kiss deepened, Carolina melted against him happily. This was as it should be, and Carolina wanted to forget that anything else existed except for this man and this moment.

Leland's raspy cough broke the spell, however. Both Carolina and James pulled away to come to his aid. He laughed as he settled his body and reached out a hand to his son. "I'm so glad you have come. There are some things I want to say before it's too late."

"I know. I overheard a great many of them," James replied.

"I don't want to die without your knowing how very proud I am of you," Leland answered.

"Thank you, Father. It means the world to me that I have not shamed you."

Leland shook his head. "You never could. However, I have shamed you, and I know that full well. Forgive me, and my life will be complete."

"I do forgive you, just as I pray you have forgiven me for not seeing your need."

"It wasn't a son's place," Leland said, dropping his hold on James. "I'm weary now and I think I would like to sleep." He glanced up at Carolina and smiled. "Take good care of her, son. She's a rare and lovely woman, and I could not have chosen better for you."

"I will," James said and put his arm around Carolina. He looked at her with such tenderness that Carolina forgot about the pain of the past few months.

They left Leland to sleep and went to the privacy of their bedroom. No sooner had James closed the door than he let out a yell of enthusiastic approval. "We're having a baby!"

Carolina laughed as he picked her up and spun her around. "I wanted to wait for a more perfect time to tell you."

"The timing could not have been better. I was so touched to eavesdrop on your conversation with Father. It truly humbled and blessed me, darling." He put her down but held her tightly in his arms. "I love you so much, Carolina."

"And I love you, James." She pushed away just enough to see his face. "I've been so wrong, and I'm very sorry for the trouble I've caused and the pain I've needlessly inflicted on you. I felt so torn up inside. I knew what God wanted me to do, but it was so hard to let go of my anger and pride."

He put his finger to her lips. "It's done now. Peace has been made. I know married life has been anything but easy for us, but from this point forward you have my assurance that I will do anything in my power to make it better."

Carolina nodded. "And I will do anything in my power, as well." She took hold of his hand and placed it on her rounded abdomen. "We will look forward to our future."

James' eyes glowed in wonder as he added, "And the promise of what is to come."

Later that night, Leland Baldwin passed away. He had made his peace with man and his Maker and longed for nothing more than to see an end to his pain and suffering. When Mrs. Graves found him in the morning, she told Carolina that it seemed almost as if the man were smiling. Carolina liked to believe it was so and took great comfort in the fact that she had heeded God's prodding and sought Leland out the day before. She shuddered to think what might have happened had she left things as they were.

Leland's body was taken by train back to Washington City, where on a cloudy afternoon he was buried beside his beloved wife. James and Carolina stood side by side, surprised by the rather impressive turnout to Leland's funeral. Carolina was glad they had preserved his name and reputation. She would have hated to know that her malice would have sent the man to his grave without anyone to mourn his passing.

The service concluded, and Carolina gripped her husband's hand. "Are you all right?"

James drew her close and put his arm around her. "I'm fine. I shall miss them both," he whispered with one final glance back to his parents' gravestone.

"As will I," Carolina agreed. And she felt happy to know that deep down inside, she really meant it.

Nine

Adoption

Carolina looked over the latest reports regarding the Potomac and Great Falls Railroad. The aching in her back made it easy to give up on the columns of figures, and the activity of the child she carried within her made it equally easy to put her thoughts elsewhere. Rubbing the small of her back, Carolina shifted first one way and then another, trying futilely to relieve the pressure.

The baby was due in a matter of weeks. The crispness of the late-October mornings had relieved the heat and humidity, but much of Carolina's misery would only find relief when she delivered the baby.

A baby! It still amazed her to think that she carried a new life within her body. Her hand gently passed over her bulky stomach, and she laughed when the baby kicked playfully at her hand.

"Soon, little one," she said affectionately. "Soon."

Carolina straightened in her chair and was just about to return her attention to the ledgers when the sound of breaking glass and Victoria's adamant declaration of "I didn't mean to" filled the air. This was followed by James' stern voice demanding to know what was going on and why Victoria had been so careless.

Carolina immediately got to her feet and moved in awkward strides to the library door. This was the third argument she'd heard between James and Victoria in less than an hour. It seemed that no matter how hard she prayed, there was no peace between the two. This caused Carolina no end of grief. She had brought an innocent child into a marriage where a virtual stranger had become her father. Now nearly a year to the day that she and James had married, matters between Victoria and James were worse than ever. The once shy but gentle-spirited six-year-old had turned into a rather unbearable tyrant.

James and Carolina had spoken on many an occasion as to how

they might deal with Victoria's actions and attitude, but nothing seemed to work. Victoria alienated herself from everyone, including Carolina. Whenever Carolina tried to speak to her daughter, it was almost as if Victoria was afraid to get too close to her. She would suspiciously eye Carolina's growing midsection, then very nearly cower when her mother would reach out to embrace her. Carolina wondered and had even discussed the possibility that Victoria was simply jealous of the baby, or maybe even worried about what the arrival of a baby might mean to her position in the household. But no matter how Carolina tried to approach the subject, Victoria grew more and more distant.

"I didn't do it on purpose!" Victoria screamed.

This rallied Carolina's thoughts back to the present, and quietly she opened the library door and made her way to the front parlor. It wouldn't be easy to deal with yet another episode. Especially feeling as she did. Her back hurt, the pressure of the baby was ever upon her, and quite frankly she was exhausted from dealing with the constant battles between Victoria and James.

"You are going to clean up this mess, young lady," James said sternly as Carolina came into the room.

Carolina found the standoff to be ridiculously mismatched, and she would have laughed at the sight of Victoria, chest puffed out, standing on tiptoe to meet her father's reprimand, had the situation not been so serious. But then her gaze fell to the object Victoria had broken. The delicately crafted porcelain figure of a woman playing a harp lay in pieces on the floor.

The figurine had been a long-ago gift from her mother, and seeing it broken affected Carolina in a way she had not anticipated. Tears began to stream down her face, and an involuntary sob escaped her.

This had a great sobering effect on both James and Victoria. James hurried to her side just as Carolina put her hands to her face. She hadn't meant to break down like this. After all, it was only a material object. But the more she tried to reason with herself, the more she cried.

"Come sit down," James whispered, taking hold of her very gently.

He led her to the nearest chair and helped her sit. She wanted to thank him—wanted to laugh off her reaction—but her emotions were so overwhelmed by the circumstances that Carolina could do nothing but cry.

"That figurine meant a great deal to your mother," James told Victoria.

"No, no," Carolina tried to speak. "It's all right, James. She didn't mean to do it."

Victoria gave James a look of smug satisfaction. Her mother would take her side, the expression suggested, and Carolina suddenly felt very guilty.

Victoria nearly danced her way over to Carolina. "I told him I didn't mean to break it," she said, patting Carolina's arm.

Carolina caught her husband's expression and knew that she had deeply wounded him. She had to find a way to make it clear that she stood with James on the matter. If they were less than united, Victoria would simply go on playing them against each other.

"Go get the broom," James ordered Victoria.

"You can't boss me around," Victoria suddenly declared. She took hold of her mother's arm as if to prove to James that she was speaking for both of them. "You aren't my real father, and you can't tell me what to do."

Carolina stiffened at the words. When had Victoria become so hostile and ugly in her actions? As Carolina caught the look on James' face, she knew he was close to losing his temper in full. This made Carolina only cry all the more.

"Go get the broom," James ordered again. His teeth clenched together as if to keep him from saying anything else.

Victoria tightened her grip on Carolina and stared back defiantly. "I don't have to. I want to stay with Mama."

James reached out and took hold of Victoria, but the child wrapped her arms around Carolina and pleaded for help. "Mama, don't let him take me away."

Carolina could hardly think clearly. She wanted very much to assure Victoria that James' love for her was just as real as her own. She wanted to insist that Victoria stop this nonsense and do what she was instructed to do. And she wanted most of all for the hostility in her family to be dismissed and forgotten. But that wasn't going to happen, and Carolina knew that this pivotal moment required her to make a choice. Either she could make her stand once and for all with James, or she could usurp his authority and belittle him in Victoria's eyes and side with her child.

Suddenly it seemed very clear to Carolina that Victoria had forced this issue on more than one occasion. And while in the past Carolina had managed to assuage the anger of both parties, this time was clearly different. This time definite battle lines had been drawn.

"Mama, I want to stay with you," Victoria pleaded.

Wiping her tears and struggling to regain at least partial control of her emotions, Carolina looked once again to James and then to her daughter. "Do as your father says. I'm ashamed that you would disrespect him as you have just now."

Victoria could not have looked more surprised had Carolina slapped her. "But, Mama!"

Carolina disentangled herself from the child and got to her feet as James pulled Victoria away. "Go get the broom," he told the child for the third time.

Begrudgingly, and with a look that registered Victoria's feelings of having been betrayed, she finally left the room. James came to Carolina just as she started to move for the door.

"Thank you for supporting me in this. I know it wasn't easy, and I can tell by the look on your face that it caused you great pain."

Carolina felt exhaustion wash over her. "The fact that you two cannot seem to get along causes me great pain. I feel as though to love either of you means I have to forsake the other, and it just doesn't need to be that way."

"Of course not. Listen to me, Carolina. You're weary from carrying our child and your heart is heavy-laden with the concerns of this household. Give me a chance to work through my problems with Victoria. We'll make things right; you'll see."

Carolina tried to smile. "I know you'll do your best."

"I will," he said, kissing her forehead. His hand came to rest on her abdomen. "Soon," he whispered. "Soon our child will be here and things will be much better."

"I pray it is so," she replied, noting that Victoria had returned and was watching them with a sad expression. "I'm going to go rest," she told James, nodding in Victoria's direction. "I'll leave this matter to you two."

James had given Victoria ample time to clean up the broken figurine and retreat to her room before he attempted to go after her and speak his mind. He felt new strength in the fact that Carolina had stood beside him in dealing with Victoria. He thought of Ben Latrobe's words and how children were given to playing games with their parents. He could see how Victoria had worked at them both, and now he longed to reach out and find a way to meet the child on her own level. Somehow he had to show her that he loved her as much as Carolina did.

"Victoria?" He came into the nursery to find the child staring in silence out her bedroom window. "Victoria," he spoke her name again, this time a little more sternly.

She turned, acknowledging him with a glance, then returned her attention to the world outside her window.

"We need to talk," James said, taking a seat at the miniature table Victoria used for her studies and playtime.

She turned, eyed him suspiciously, then finally spoke. "You are going to send me away, aren't you?" Her voice was quite refined for a six-year-old.

"What?" James was so stunned he couldn't believe his ears. "Send you away? Where in the world did you get that idea?"

She shrugged. "Are you?"

"Never!" declared James adamantly. "Is that what has you worried? Do you feel the need to test my love for you?"

Victoria's lower lip quivered, and James thought for sure she might start crying at any moment. He patted the chair beside him. "Come sit here and tell me why you feel this way."

Victoria pushed back her dark hair and got up from her window seat. She took the chair James offered her and folded her hands in a fashion that James knew best as her church pew pose.

"Victoria, I know you think I'm too hard on you, but the truth is, it's because I love you and care about the person you become that I discipline you." He looked at her, softening his expression in order to make her less afraid. "Sometimes mothers and fathers have to be stern with their children. It's important to set rules and have limitations; otherwise, everybody would simply do whatever they felt like doing."

"I like to do what I feel like doing," Victoria admitted in childlike honesty.

"So do I," James said with a smile. "But it isn't always prudent."

"What's that?"

"Sensible. Doing whatever we want, when we want, isn't always the sensible or the right thing to do. Sometimes we have to do things in order to be helpful to others, or we might have to obey certain rules in order to be safe—like when I'm working with the railroad. Understand?" Victoria nodded, but James could tell she was still not completely convinced.

"Victoria, you must understand something," he began, reaching out to take hold of her hand. "I am your father now. Just like God is our heavenly Father, and—"

"God is Jesus' Father," Victoria interrupted quite seriously.

"Yes, He is. But we become His adopted children when we accept Jesus as our Savior. He accepts us as His own and He loves us more than we can ever know. It's like that with you and me. You are my adopted daughter, and I accept you as my own and I love you more than you can ever know."

"But you have a new baby in Mama's tummy. Now you don't need me." Her voice wavered as she fought to control her emotions.

"Is that what you think?" James asked, giving her hand a gentle squeeze. "Do you truly believe that, Victoria?"

"I'm naughty, and you don't want me to upset Mama or the baby."

"Sometimes your behavior has been naughty, and I don't want to see Mama upset. But that doesn't mean I would ever send you away. We are a family, Victoria. We stay together because we love each other. We don't just give up on each other when times get hard. I would never send you away just because we have problems."

"You won't?"

Her face looked up at him so hopeful in expression that James couldn't help drawing her into his arms. "Victoria, you are my little girl now. And when the new baby comes he or she will need you to be the big sister. I'm counting on you to be helpful, but I'm also counting on you to be my little girl and to take walks with me and to talk to me and to do all the fun things we do together now."

"Won't the new baby need you?"

"Of course, but I'll need you, too, and I hope you'll need me, as well."

Victoria remained silent for several moments, then she reached up a hand to touch James' cheek. The action touched James in a way he had not expected. He hugged her close and cherished the moment. This was their moment alone. Just theirs. There was no Carolina or Mrs. Graves. No Grandfather Adams or anyone else. It was just Victoria and James. Daughter and father. He wanted that moment to live forever in his memory. He wanted to take it with him when times were hard and he had to be far away from home.

It was only after thinking on these things that James suddenly realized that Victoria was crying. "What's wrong?" he asked, lifting her chin so that he might better see her face.

"You said God 'dopts us 'cause He loves us," she replied, hiccuping a sob.

"That's right. We become His children with full rights to all of His blessings."

"But you didn't 'dopt me. Mama said you would, but you didn't. My name is still St. John, but your last name is Baldwin."

Between her tears and little-girl voice, the name came out sounding like Botwin, but James didn't mind. He knew what was troubling her heart now. Was it possible that this insecurity had been the culprit to stir up all of the conflict between him and Victoria? Before he could comment, however, Victoria continued.

"Mama's a Baldwin and even the new baby will be a Baldwin. I know, 'cause Mama was picking out names and she always stopped with Baldwin."

James smiled and let go of her chin in order to wipe her tears with his handkerchief. "Is that why you've been so angry at me? Did you think I didn't love you enough to give you my name?"

Victoria's huge dark eyes beheld him with hope. "I'm not mad at you. I just don't want you to send me away."

James shook his head. "I will never send you away, Victoria. And if it meets with your approval, I would like very much to adopt you and call you Victoria Baldwin. Would that be all right with you?"

Victoria nodded enthusiastically. "Can we do it now? Before the baby comes? May I be a Baldwin first?"

James laughed. "You most certainly may. I will go right away and see my lawyer about it. We will change your name as quick as this," he said and snapped his fingers.

Victoria smiled and tried to imitate the snap but found it impossible to coordinate her pudgy fingers. She was content, however, to let the matter go and instead wrapped her arms around James' neck in a tight, possessive hug. "I love you, Papa," she whispered in his ear.

It was James' turn to grow misty-eyed. "I love you, Victoria," he replied, then added with great pride, "Baldwin."

Ten

New Birth

Carolina's labor started with the dawning of November the sixth, and by afternoon she was tired of the wait and tired of the pain. Through the window in her bedroom, Carolina could see the snow lightly falling. It had come early and would probably amount to nothing more than a dusting, but the hypnotic pattern of falling snow was the only thing to draw her attention away from the suffering.

"Does it always take this long?" she asked as Mrs. Graves wiped a cool towel across her perspiring forehead.

"Sometimes much longer," she admitted to her young charge. "I figure this little one ought to be born sometime this evening."

"This evening?" Carolina nearly screamed the question as another pain tore through her abdomen. She pulled against the leather birthing straps that Mrs. Graves had secured at the headboard of her bed. It helped only marginally to have something to pull against as her child pushed for freedom.

"There, there. It's all a part of birthing. You'll forget all about the pain once you're holding the baby in your arms."

"I seriously doubt that," Carolina said, falling back against her pillows as the pain subsided.

Mrs. Graves chuckled and rinsed the towel in a basin of cool water. "There's not a woman alive but what says the same thing during her laboring time. But I promise you, it's true. Now, you just rest easy while I go and check on the master and Victoria."

Carolina nodded and closed her eyes. All she wanted to do was rest, but there was no rest to be had. There was no comfortable position in which to lie, and even if there were, the pains were close enough together that anything more than five or ten minutes of rest would be impossible.

She tried to think about the baby and of what Mrs. Graves had told her all along about delivering a child. She had heeded the woman's advice in every way possible and knew that the time would pass more easily if she remembered the end goal. Her baby. James' baby.

She smiled at this thought and sighed. Life had been so much easier these past few days. James and Victoria were bonding in a way that she had once only dreamed was possible. Victoria's entire mood seemed lightened by the process of adoption, which James had moved through rapidly. He had found Carolina's attorney, Thomas Swann, to be of tremendous assistance, and Carolina felt grateful that Swann had understood their need. And so it was in a process of one friend calling upon another and then another that Victoria's adoption was all but signed and sealed. Already she called herself by the Baldwin name, and no one said anything to discourage her from doing so.

"May I come in?" James called from the door.

"Please," Carolina answered, seeing his worried expression turn to one of sheepish uncertainty.

"Are you sure?" He came to her bedside in hesitant steps. "If you'd rather I not be here—"

"*I'd* rather not be here," Carolina announced with a smile. She reached out her hand and took hold of her husband's long, lean fingers. "But, of course, we know it is most necessary for me to remain."

James seemed to relax at this and took up the bedside chair. "So my son is giving you fits, I hear."

"What makes you so certain it's a boy?" asked Carolina with a stubborn upward tilt of her chin.

James grinned. "Because that's what I want him to be. Besides, we already have a lovely daughter."

"True enough, but what if this is another lovely daughter?" she asked and grimaced, feeling the beginnings of another contraction.

"I would love another daughter, just as I would love a son. Never fear," he assured her.

Carolina was determined to keep from making an issue of her pain, but as the strength of the contraction gripped her, she cried out and lunged forward against the leather straps, dropping her hold on her husband's hand. "Oh, James," she said, moaning in misery, "please pray for me. Pray for us."

The color had drained from his face. "Let me get Mrs. Graves."

"Not . . . necessary." She gasped for breath, fighting the pain.

"But the baby!"

"Isn't coming yet." Carolina nearly growled the words. She found herself extremely irritated that James wouldn't just pray as she had asked him to do.

James was frozen in place, however, and Carolina knew she had probably scared ten years from his life. As the contraction let up, Carolina struggled to draw a deep breath. She felt completely exhausted and let her aching body ease back against the bed, without concern for her appearance.

"James," she whispered and reached up to encourage his touch. He stared at her hesitantly for a moment. It seemed he was afraid to touch her, lest he cause her even more pain. "James, don't look at me like that."

"I'm sorry," he said, leaning forward ever so slightly. "Like what?"

"Like I'm about to pass from this earth. I'm only giving birth, and while I know many women suffer complications and such—"

"Don't even speak it!" James exclaimed, taking hold of her hand with such sudden alacrity that Carolina was left momentarily speechless. "Please don't say a thing like that," he said, fear obviously edging his voice.

"James, don't be afraid for me. This is all very natural. Mrs. Graves says I'm doing fine, and I'm certain that when the time comes for the doctor, he will say the same thing. It's painful, yes. But not so that my life is in jeopardy." It was as if in dealing with her husband's fear, Carolina could finally let go of her own fears. She had certainly worried that she might die giving birth. Women she knew from childhood had passed away during childbirth. Why should she be any different? But seeing her husband's uncertainty caused Carolina to put aside the worries that had haunted her throughout the day. She would give birth to this child, and she would live to raise the baby, as well.

"Before the pains come again, could we just pray together?" she finally asked James. "Would you pray for us?"

James nodded and moved to sit beside her on the bed. Gently he put his arm around her shoulder, and as he did Carolina leaned against him and lingered in the memories of other times spent in his arms. There would be other times. This child would be born to them, and life would be good. She had found new strength, and from somewhere deep inside her, Carolina knew it would be the strength she needed to get through.

"Father," James prayed, "please protect my wife and child. Ease their pain and suffering, yet bring a speedy and healthy ending to this labor. Let us all focus on what is to come, to the joy that we will share in this new child. Let us cast aside our fears and the oppression of the moment as we trust you."

Carolina could feel her stomach tightening but forced herself to remain still in James' arms. She bit at her lower lip and tightly gripped the bedcovers as the pain became almost unbearable. Then the pain changed. It was almost indescribable at first, then the urgency to bear down against the pain overtook her with surprise. With a gasp, her head snapped up and Carolina looked at her husband in stunned wonder.

"Get Mrs. Graves," she commanded, knowing from what she had been told that her labor was making the transition into a new stage. "Hurry!"

James jumped up from the bed, stumbling over the chair as he went. "Mrs. Graves!" he called out frantically. "Mrs. Graves!"

Carolina would have laughed at the scene had she not been so intent on the new feelings controlling her body. The contraction passed as the others did, and with it the urgency to push subsided. Mrs. Graves had told her that when these feelings came upon her, it wouldn't be long until her child would be born. She paused, glancing around, feeling the safety and assurance of familiar things. Her child would soon be here and in her arms, and the wonder of it all brought tears to her eyes.

Brenton Phineas Baldwin was born in the early hours of the evening. He screamed with a hearty vitality that left no one wondering about his health and well-being. The doctor had pronounced him one of the finest specimens of new life that he had ever had the privilege to deliver, and Mrs. Graves had assured Carolina and James that Brenton's handsome features ran a close second to Victoria's newborn beauty. The latter was said especially in light of the fact that Victoria hovered between James and Carolina, studying her new brother with a look that alternated between extreme pride and cautious exploration.

"He is perfect," Carolina declared, running a hand over the baby's dark brown matting of hair. "I think he looks like you, James."

"What? All ruddy and wrinkled?" James asked with a laugh.

Carolina and Mrs. Graves laughed as well but Victoria seemed not to hear the joke. "I think he looks funny," Victoria said, reaching up to touch his cheek. Just then baby Brenton yawned and gurgled. "Oh no!" Victoria exclaimed. "God forgot to give him teeth!"

The adults burst into laughter, much to Victoria's surprise. "Well, look," Victoria told them, not understanding. "His mouth is empty." At this Brenton began to fuss.

"I'd wager his stomach is, too," Mrs. Graves suggested, then patted

Victoria on the head. "Never fear, deary. Your little brother doesn't need teeth just yet. The good Lord knows exactly what each of us needs and doesn't need. Right now Brenton only needs to be loved and cared for. When he needs teeth, God will send them along. And when he needs sisterly advice, you'll be there to help him out."

Victoria exchanged a look with her father and mother as if to assure herself that Mrs. Graves spoke the truth. Carolina smiled at her daughter and used her free arm to pull her close. As she did, Brenton seemed to settle down. "Look, Victoria, I think he already likes you."

"I like him, too," Victoria admitted, "but I still think he needs teeth."

Mrs. Graves slipped out of the room, and when she did James took up the place she'd vacated and stood beside Carolina and Brenton. "I'd say we make a dandy family," he declared.

"I second that motion, Mr. Baldwin," Carolina agreed. "We have a fine daughter and a fine son. What more could anyone ask for?" She looked up to find James' loving gaze fixed upon her.

"And we're all Baldwins," Victoria announced, as though someone might have forgotten. "Even me."

"Especially you," James added, and Victoria nodded quite soberly.

"We are truly blessed," Carolina said, giving Victoria a squeeze.

James eased down onto the bed to sit beside his wife and son. "We are blessed, and we need to always remember that. We have each other and that is very important. We are a family and we must always stand beside each other through good times and bad."

"For better or worse, eh?" Carolina asked with a grin.

"For richer or poorer," James countered.

"Even without teeth," Victoria declared.

James chuckled and reached behind Carolina to tousle the child's hair. "Even without teeth, for there may one day come a time when I shall lose all of mine and be just as wrinkled up as Brenton. I will especially count on your love then."

Victoria took hold of his hand. "I will love you then, Papa. I promise."

Carolina leaned against James, her face nuzzled against his. "I will love you then, too. Maybe even more than I do now, although that is difficult to imagine," she whispered softly, placing a tender kiss upon his cheek.

James turned and caught her lips with his own. "I'm counting on that, Mrs. Baldwin," he murmured as he pulled away. "I'm counting on that."

PART II

February 1849–February 1850

Life consists in motion . . . the United States presents certainly the most animated picture of universal bustle and activity of any country in the world. Such a thing as rest or quiescence does not even enter the mind of an American.

—Francis Grund

Eleven

Nightmares

The heavy, dank mist threatened to swallow Carolina whole. She tried to move, to run, but her legs were held fast as if in shackles.

"Help me, please!" she cried out over and over, but no one heard her and no one came to her aid.

Then, just as the darkness closed in around her, Carolina heard one of her children cry out. It was enough to give her the strength to pull free from the cryptic stranglehold. She pushed her way through the swirling fog, fighting for some handhold, something familiar that might pull her up from harm's way.

The crying intensified and Carolina felt her heart begin to pound. This was no ordinary cry. This was the cry of a child in jeopardy. Gaining speed, Carolina pushed blindly ahead until the sound was nearly upon her. A door materialized before her eyes, and just as she reached for the handle, a huge hand clamped down on her arm and dragged her backward.

The scream that tore from her throat was enough to awaken Carolina from her nightmare. Drenched in sweat and panting heavily, she reached out to James for comfort. But James wasn't there. It seemed he was never there.

Aching from the emptiness inside, Carolina ran her hand over James' pillow before pulling it close. Holding it tight, she tried to steady her ragged breathing. Five years of listening to the Baltimore and Ohio argue about the routes that did nothing to move the railroad west, but did everything to steal her husband away, were beginning to take their toll on Carolina.

It wasn't only that James was frequently absent from their home, but even when he was in residence, he was preoccupied with the routing issues and incessant arguing of his peers. It wasn't enough when the route had finally been established to complete the B&O in Wheeling, but in choosing that location, a hundred other problems arose. And while Carolina found the entire matter quite fascinating, she seldom had a chance to join in the discussions because she was nearly always busy with the running of her household and the children.

Thinking of the children, Carolina threw off the heavy winter covers and slipped from her bed. The nightmare still haunted her. She had felt suffocated and weighed down, and there was no one to help her. Were her dreams merely playing out her realities?

She went first to Victoria's room and found the twelve-year-old sleeping soundly. Moonlight flooded the room through the open curtains and fell across the bed, illuminating Victoria in an ethereal way. She'd only just had her birthday, and Carolina smiled to see her clutching the doll James had sent from Pittsburgh. Victoria's special relationship with James warmed Carolina's heart in a way that eased her worries. The years had bonded them together, and for all that James had adored having a son to carry on his name, he had reserved a special place in his heart for Victoria.

Carolina smoothed back a brown-black ringlet and let the silky curl slip through her fingers. She's growing up so quickly, Carolina thought. It seemed only yesterday that Victoria had been a baby in her arms. Now she was nearly grown, and in a few short years she would be at a proper age to wed and bear children of her own. It made Carolina feel suddenly old, even though she'd not quite reached her twenty-ninth birthday.

She left Victoria to go in search of her son. The nursery was quiet and only the rhythmic sound of breathing could be heard to break the silence. Brenton, just turned five last November, lay in a gangly manner all sprawled across the bed. He had managed to lose his covers in the night, and Carolina quickly located them at the foot of the bed and gently eased them back in place.

Brenton sighed, rolled to the opposite side, and settled once again. Carolina found that he'd managed to re-expose his left leg to the chill of the night, but she gave up trying to keep him under wraps. Instead, she watched him for a moment. He was the spitting image of his father with dark brown hair and brows. For a child, he was most serious and devoted, and he loved to mimic his father. It made her laugh to watch Brenton assume James' stance or posture. He would follow James around the house, always studying him, watching and waiting as if to learn some great secret about his father. And almost always he seemed far too serious for a little boy. It was hard on Brenton to be without his father so much of the time, but there was nothing Carolina could do to change matters. They couldn't very well trek west after him.

The faint sound of sucking came to Carolina's ear, drawing her away from her son and to the far side of the nursery. Here, not quite three-year-old Jordana, the youngest of the Baldwin clan, sucked her thumb, unaware of her mother's presence. Where Brenton was serious and reserved, Jordana was humorous and rambunctious. She reminded Carolina of a little clown, constantly performing for an audience and always looking for a laugh. Jordana kept Carolina and Mrs. Graves too busy to worry about much of anything else. It was not at all unusual to find Jordana shinning up a tree or dangling from the wrought-iron fence that encircled their house. Carolina adored the precocious child, and often it was Jordana alone who managed to keep Carolina's spirits up when things turned gloomy.

All was well. The children were sleeping soundly, and there was no reason to feel the despair and anxiety that Carolina felt within her soul. But the feeling haunted her nevertheless. Hugging her arms to her now-chilled body, Carolina longed for other arms to hold her. If only James were here to comfort her and reassure her that nothing was amiss. But he was gone. And Carolina wasn't even certain where he was. Two weeks ago he had been in Pittsburgh discussing iron for rails, but the brief letter that accompanied Victoria's gift stated he would soon be leaving on a boat that would take him to Wheeling.

Frustrated by her churning emotions, Carolina left the nursery and went back to her bedroom. For a time she sat by the window and stared out into the starry sky. The clock chimed the quarter hour, but Carolina hadn't bothered to see what quarter it might be announcing.

"I don't want to feel this way," she said aloud, and yet for all she tried to reason it away, Carolina couldn't even put a name to her emotions.

Fear seemed to rank close to the top, but then again, it wasn't exactly fear. Anxiety was definitely a companion, but it was more than that; it was something akin to dread.

"But I have nothing to dread," she murmured.

Cold seeping in from the window caused Carolina to get up and pull the draperies closed. Climbing into what now seemed a mammoth bed, Carolina drew the heavy quilts around her and settled back on her pillow. Even here, where she felt closest to James, Carolina could not shake her misery.

"Oh, Father," she prayed, "what's wrong with me? Why can I not simply dismiss this and be done with it?" She stared up into the darkness of her room. With the drapes drawn tight, the room held nothing but shadowy images and unbearable silence.

Determined to feel better, Carolina tried to focus her attention on thoughts more pleasing. She'd just received a letter from her father, and the news about her mother was more than she'd ever hoped to hear. Margaret had made tremendous steps toward recovery. She could now sit and discuss the past with Joseph, and while she often grew teary eyed, she was no longer given to spells of violence.

Carolina rejoiced in this news. Her mother was actually asking questions about the family and made efforts to send messages via Joseph to each of her children. To Carolina she sent a word of thanks for the lengthy letters that she received from her every month. Margaret delighted in the news of her grandchildren and promised that one day they would all be together and get to know one another properly. Carolina had asked her father what had stirred this miraculous recovery in her mother. For even though it had been nearly seven years since Margaret had gone to the hospital in Boston, Carolina had read a great many accounts of people who never recovered from mental illness.

Perhaps that was the curse of intelligence. In her desire to better understand her mother's situation, Carolina had read everything available to her. Anything at all that dealt with sicknesses of the mind came to Carolina as the possibility of holding answers for her mother. There were, of course, those articles that offered such ridiculous suggestions as depriving patients of sleep, food, or water, or inducing pain in delicate parts of the body in order that the brain pain might be lessened as the body focused on pain elsewhere. Carolina had prayed that the Boston doctors would forsake those methods of treatment for methods less frightening.

In the case of Margaret, Carolina knew that there had been a great deal of sound practice on the part of the doctors and nurses. One nurse in particular, a godly woman of infinite patience, had befriended Margaret and taken her on as a personal project. Carolina credited this woman with much of her mother's recovery. The rest was clearly credited to God, for Carolina knew that without His mercy, her mother would surely have never survived her ordeal.

The tensions brought on by her nightmare were now lessened somewhat, but still the oppressive feelings lingered, and Carolina was hard pressed to know what else she might do to cast them off.

"The children are well. Mother is recovering. Father is happily back home at Oakbridge," she recited. "James is making a way for the B&O and, God, you know better than I how much he enjoys his work. There's no reason for me to feel this way. None at all."

She shifted in the bed and rolled to her side. Once again she caressed James' pillow and wondered where he was sleeping on this cold February night.

"If you were here," she whispered, "you'd tell me I was being silly. Then you'd hold me close, and I would see the folly in giving myself over to such things as bad dreams." She paused and shook her head. "But you aren't here, and I miss you, and I resent that you're gone, and I resent even more that I'm not with you, sharing in the building of our dreams."

There, she thought. She'd said the one thing she'd promised herself she wouldn't ever think on. She was envious of James' dealings with the railroad, and she longed to be at his side, immersing herself in the growth and transformations of the line. But she had three children, and travel to the wilderness was no easy matter. Even with the train established to Cumberland, it was no small feat to travel with children in tow.

But she loved her children. She adored them. And while it was true that she had never expected to have them quite so soon, Carolina knew that she'd never have traded a single one of them, even if it would have meant being able to work on the railroad for herself. She sighed. It wasn't that she didn't find it rewarding to be a wife and mother. Nothing gave her more comfort than to hold her children, and nothing pleased her more than to be in James' arms. But she'd wanted so much more. She'd planned an entire future around her education and her love of trains. She had married Blake St. John in order to adopt Victoria and provide the child with a real mother, but even then she had seen herself moving forward with her plans. Blake had gifted her with a large portfolio of railroad stock, and when he died prematurely, Carolina found herself with a vast fortune in stocks and cash. Of course, the depression had devalued most of her stock, but even so, there had been more than enough money for her to purchase up stock at half the original price from desperate men seeking to dump their unwise investments. The investments themselves had not been unwise, but the future had seemed so uncertain at the end of the last decade. Now prices were rising nicely, and Carolina held major portions of stock in several small New York lines, as well as a good portion of stock with the Baltimore and Ohio. And there was still the Potomac and Great Falls Railroad on which they had finally broken ground and begun to build.

Carolina felt a twinge of guilt as she contemplated the matter. She was a woman, and as such, she was unwelcome in board meetings and anywhere else where opinion was offered for the future of the railroad. Only her father and James seemed to consider her ideas as having merit. But even they found their hands tied when it came to others. Why, Carolina wasn't even allowed to come and vote her stock on the B&O. She had tried once, but it raised such a ruckus that Thomas Swann, her ever-faithful attorney, suggested she allow him to represent her. Carolina had no choice but to agree.

Then the previous fall, Thomas had taken on the position of president of the Baltimore and Ohio Railroad. Carolina had been pleasantly surprised, but James had shrugged it off, saying that everyone had known for some time that Swann was being groomed to replace Louis McLane in the position. Carolina remembered the feeling of betrayal that she had somehow been left out of this news. James had never mentioned it to her, and even though she'd been very busy with the children, she knew he could have made an effort to keep her informed.

With Thomas at the helm, Carolina thought this would be the perfect opportunity to assert herself as a stockholder, but even James thought it unnecessarily foolish for her to stir up the other members. He laughingly told her that she'd find the meetings as boring as Sunday tea with the Baltimore Ladies Mission Society, but Carolina wasn't convinced. Most women very well might have been bored, but not her. She knew she would have thrilled to the talk of proposed lines and routes. She would have been fascinated with the suggestions for repairs and purchases of new equipment. But what hurt most of all was that she knew James recognized the truth of the matter, as well. He knew her better than anyone, save her father, and he knew that such a meeting would be just the thing to keep Carolina on the edge of her seat.

And now he was gone, as always. Away with the railroad—working at a future that should have been her own. She pounded the mattress with her fists and tried not to feel the frustration that poured over her once again. This was doing nothing to ease her mind from the strangling hold of her nightmare.

"James loves me, and I love him," she said aloud, as if to convince some unseen entity. "I love the children, and I know that what I am doing is right." She paused and sighed. "But oh, God," she again broke into prayer, "I want so much to be a part of it all. I want to know the sights and sounds of the rails being laid. I want to hear the clanging of the picks and shovels. I want to smell the smoke from the engines and feel the rumble of the locomotives beneath my feet."

The tension mounted in her soul, and Carolina knew that whatever peace she'd found with images of her mother was now eaten up with unfulfilled dreams. She had so much to be grateful for, and at least with James working for the railroad, she shared in the process and completion in her own way. It should be enough, she thought. It should be enough to have all that I have, to be loved and to love. It should be enough.

But it wasn't.

Struggling with emotions that threatened to overwhelm her, Carolina closed her eyes and tried to think of James. If only James would come home and stay for a time, Carolina was certain her haunting nightmares would ease and the feelings of loneliness and anxiety would be put aside.

"Please, Father, please bring James home to me. Let Ben Latrobe or Thomas or whoever else is using him no longer need him. At least for a short while so that we might have him with us again." She murmured the words even as sleep overcame her. There was nothing more she could do. Nothing that would bring James home any sooner. Nothing else would fill the void.

Twelve

Landslide

"It'll be good to be home," James told Ben Latrobe.

The eastbound train from Cumberland was making slow but steady progress, and even though cold seeped in from every possible angle, James found it completely tolerable. He had much on his mind, not the least of which was his family, and the cold seemed a small price to pay.

Ben Latrobe, ever bent over his paperwork and maps, nodded. "Agreed. There's a great deal of work awaiting us there. I've reread our missives from Swann and find that the business of moving this railroad westward is going to take every bit of money and man power we can muster."

"At least Swann is aggressive in the area of raising cash."

"Yes," Ben commented and looked up from the stack of papers. "He's also more easily attainable than McLane. I was truly beginning to fear for the line."

James nodded. It had become well known that Louis McLane had taken to removing himself from the details and physical aspects of the Baltimore and Ohio. It was even said that he would receive no one in his office who had not first set an appointment well in advance. "I suppose like anything else, McLane ran his course. I like Swann. So, too, does my wife. He was her attorney for a long time before giving his duties over to the Baltimore and Ohio."

"Yes, and I'll wager he'll not stop with our little attempt to reach the Ohio. Swann seems a man destined for big things."

"He can certainly talk circles around anyone in his way. I've never heard a man speak more eloquently," James added and rubbed his eyes.

Latrobe nodded. "I'm telling you, he'll go far. Why, you should have heard him when we spoke of the routes out of Cumberland. He thought it ridiculous we'd taken so long to move. Yet when presented with the problem of whether to build an expensive tunnel through Knobly Mountain at the Patterson Creek cutoff, battle with the Chesapeake and Ohio Canal Company for right-of-way through their marked territory, or just go around the town in a broad U-turn, Swann was thoughtfully humbled. He considered the consequences of each and suggested that the most important thing was to move forward. He said, 'We may delay it for a season but the result is inevitable.' Then he told me at this point to just get around the city as best we could and get the line headed west. Thomas Swann wants this railroad built as badly as we do, and he will use his savvy, eloquence, and intellect to see it done."

James smiled, knowing Latrobe was right. "Swann told my Carolina that the true worth of the railroad wouldn't be realized until we reached the Ohio River. He was rather put back on his heels that McLane had sat on the Maryland bonds for all of this time. In fact, he was rather livid about it. He told us that the bonds represented the company's greatest resource, and they should be used, not held back in reserve. After all, the railroad is in better condition than ever before. People are finally seeing the potential, and to use the bonds would be physical proof to the company that we have faith in the completion and prosperity of the B&O."

"True enough," Latrobe said with a chuckle. "And it's not only the prosperity of the B&O. Seems lines are springing up everywhere, and all of them are beginning to realize profits. Speaking of lines springing up, what's this I hear about your Potomac and Great Falls reaching completion?"

"Well, not actual completion. It still comes short of Great Falls proper, but the line is in place, and even though the cars are horse drawn for now, we have the potential to put a locomotive engine on the line within the next few years."

"Designing one yourself?" Latrobe asked casually.

"I haven't worked in design for some time. You know full well you keep me far too busy for that kind of work." The rhythm of the locomotive changed, causing James to glance out the window. "We're slowing," he commented, then got up to better survey the situation.

"Problems?" Latrobe questioned, more out of courtesy than any real interest. Already he was tracing a map with his finger.

"From the looks of it, we're approaching Doe Gully Tunnel."

"That would put us some sixty miles from Harper's Ferry. I suppose the engineer is taking it slow in case of slides. You know, I heard there were some rather large rocks thrown across the entry last week. Probably nothing more than that."

But as the train slowed even more and finally stopped, even Ben Latrobe took a greater interest. By this time, however, James was already at the door to the car and making his exit.

"What has happened?" James called out to a man standing not far from the engine.

"Landslide," the man announced.

"How bad?" Latrobe questioned, catching up with James.

"Bad." The man turned and eyed both James and Ben with caution. "You ought to stay in your seats. Leastwise till we figure out what's to be done with the passengers."

"I'm Ben Latrobe, Chief Engineer for the Baltimore and Ohio," Ben said by way of introduction. "This is my assistant, James Baldwin. I'd like to know who's in charge here and what's being done."

The man snapped to attention. "Certainly, sir. Didn't mean no offense, sir."

"None taken. I appreciate your concern for the safety of your passengers."

"Mr. Bollman, Master of the Road for this division, he's the one what's in charge."

"Bollman, eh? Good man. He's been moving in and out of B&O crowds since he was fourteen. He'll have a good handle on this."

James followed as the man led them to Wendell Bollman. Up ahead he could already see the gravity of the situation. A huge piece of slate looking to be at least two hundred feet long and some twenty feet thick had broken away from the ridge just prior to the western portal of the tunnel.

"Bollman, Ben Latrobe." Ben extended his hand and paused to glance over his shoulder at James. "This is James Baldwin. What's going on here?"

"Pretty much exactly what you see. I've been put in charge of cleaning this mess up. There are some two hundred workers scheduled to be put on this. Some are already in place as you can see; others are coming in with provisions from Cumberland."

"Looks serious. Anyone killed when it came down?" Latrobe asked, looking at the slate, where a dozen or more men were already working at it with picks and sledges.

"Not that we know of."

"Well, thank God for that," Latrobe murmured.

James heard their conversation continue as he moved away to get a better look. He walked to the place where the slate clearly blocked the tunnel. Alongside the massive ridge piece were hundreds of smaller, more easily moved rocks. Leaning down, he picked up a chunk of stone and turned it over and over in his hands as he considered the situation. Moving across the work field, he passed the men slinging sledges and picks and moved to the opening of the tunnel. There was little doubt that this would close down the line for some time to come.

James tried to imagine the repercussions of such an accident. Already investors were angered at the delay in reaching the Ohio, and with good reason. After all, they'd been at this project for over twenty years and still had not reached their objective. It was always one accident or another, or a flood or depression that slowed the works and gave a reasonable answer to the delay, but even James wearied of the excuses. Broken slate sealing off the track seemed to simply add itself to the list without much fanfare or importance. Delays were delays, and one accident seemed pretty much like another. It meant money and time, and those were the only two words investors seemed to understand these days. It would take more than Swann's optimistic use of bonds to keep investors focused this time.

He glanced up at the huge barrier and shook his head. It was a seemingly impossible task. They would literally have to move a mountain, and that would require a great deal of effort. Men overhead walked the distance of the huge slate slab and discussed the best theory for breaking it up. He could hear their conversation in bits and pieces. Black powder was mentioned, along with the need for more workers to break and shovel. James was just about to turn back when one of the men above him yelled out. "Rocks!"

Men scrambled back toward the train, but James merely stared upward, dumbfounded as a runaway piece of slate crashed toward him from the ridge above. It was moving too quickly for him to react soon enough. As he tried to dive out of the way, he heard shouts and even saw the frantic waving of arms.

The first pieces slammed into James, knocking him from his feet and carrying him a short distance in the wake of its momentum. He thought of Carolina and how he wouldn't be able to make it home that night after all. Then he felt what must have been a boulder crash down upon his head, and everything blurred. He knew he was losing consciousness. Knew that the day was suddenly fading to night.

He reached up to protect himself from the rock, but it was to no avail. His arm burned with fiery pain, as did his head. Piece after piece rained down upon him, smothering him under the dust and weight of the slate.

"Carolina," he whispered her name, reaching out for an imagined hand, and then he fell silent and gave in to the swirling blackness.

Ben Latrobe sat beside the unconscious body of his friend. They'd been brought over the tunnel in order to connect with the Cumberland supply train, and now they were making their way to Harper's Ferry and the medical facilities there. A doctor accompanied them. He was an older man who had been found among the passengers of the stopped eastbound locomotive, and when word of James' accident had spread through the crowd, this man emerged to offer his assistance.

"Well, doctor," Ben asked, "will he live?"

"Hard to say at this point. He's suffered a pretty good blow to the head. I've managed to stop the bleeding, but there's no telling what might happen with an injury like that. He might wake up and be fine, then again he might never wake up. He's got a broken arm, maybe some ribs, as well. Can't really tell for sure."

Latrobe nodded and tried to imagine breaking the news to James' wife. He liked Carolina Baldwin. She was feisty and straightforward, but every inch a lady. She had acted as hostess to more than one gathering of Latrobe's survey team, and not only welcomed them graciously but actually took interest in their work. Now as he sat in a stunned stupor, he couldn't imagine being the one to break the news of James' accident, much less, if it came to that, his death.

Latrobe stripped off his wire-rimmed spectacles and rubbed his eyes. They were filled with dust from his frantic efforts to extricate his friend from the rubble. His hands were even more filthy, and it seemed a useless effort to wipe one with the other. Taking out his handkerchief, he attempted to clear his eyes.

"We're going mighty fast," the doctor said, eyeing the passing countryside.

"It doesn't seem half fast enough," Latrobe muttered. Even though James was as stable as they could make him, it seemed to take forever to move down the track toward Harper's Ferry.

Closing his eyes, Latrobe leaned back in his seat and prayed for James' condition to improve. There was no sense in giving up just yet, he reminded himself. Things always had a way of looking worse than they were. Hadn't there been other times when situations seemed bleak and hopeless, and hadn't those times worked together in proper order?

"It's a real wonder no one else was hurt in that disaster," the doctor said, and Latrobe found reason to open his eyes and nod.

"Yes, it is," Ben replied, knowing that fact would offer little comfort to Carolina Baldwin or her children.

Thirteen

Thomas Swann

It was said of Thomas Swann that while he enjoyed his fine wines and Havana cigars, he could just as easily be found at ease sharing a mug of ale with the common man. It was a gift, some said, that Swann could appeal to the aristocratic, genteel assemblage, while equally conducting himself with the dock workers and ragtags from poorer neighborhoods. Swann neither set himself above nor below those in his company but had a way of making all mankind feel as though they were his equal.

A big man, Swann was as opposite his predecessor, Louis McLane, as two men could be. McLane held an aristocratic air that often alienated him from others. He was driven in the early years, but as time passed, it became increasingly apparent that McLane's interest and efforts were waning.

Swann, a stockholder and an active supporter of the railroad, was one of the first men considered in the search for a suitable successor to the retiring McLane. He was motivated, dynamic, and astute. If anyone could get the B&O to the Ohio River, it would be him. Swann would be successful. Thus, when McLane resigned in September of the previous year, Swann was the natural replacement.

But now as Thomas Swann's carriage approached the wrought-iron gate of the Baldwin home, he felt anything but successful. Words failed him as he considered how he might break the news of James Baldwin's accident to his wife.

Watching in silence as the driver expertly maneuvered the horses through the open gateway, Swann drew a deep breath and set his jaw. He had been in the acquaintance of Carolina Baldwin for many years, and for just as long had handled her business affairs with her complete and consummate trust. She would not find it in the leastwise odd that he should approach her house on this day. He was a frequent visitor there, usually speaking to them on some matter pertaining to the railroad, but just as often stopping by on less formal occasions to share their company. And while he had given over her legal affairs to his former partner, Swann found that she still solicited his advice from time to time on matters of a more personal nature.

It was through these gatherings that he had come to know James, as well. He had heard of James through Ben Latrobe's reports and the word-of-mouth praise that often passed among men bent on one particular goal. He found James Baldwin a good match for the spirited young woman and could easily see their union as something ordained by God. He had always known that she hadn't married St. John for love, nor had she wed him for the money he possessed. No, Carolina had instead lost her heart to St. John's daughter, Victoria, and that was what bound her to the marriage. That St. John had died in a carriage accident so soon after their union seemed an uneventful moment in Carolina's life. He had loved neither his daughter nor his wife, and had in truth spent very little time in the house, even when Carolina had been working as his nanny. But as awkward and unfitting as St. John and Carolina had been for each other, Swann easily recognized the opposite was true of her and James Baldwin. They appeared together as the best of all possible fits. Both were intelligent and driven, but where James tended to be more reserved and quiet, Carolina was all fire and turbulence. They worked well together. But now Swann would have to tell Carolina that her husband had been in an accident.

Only that morning he'd received the telegraphed message that James had been injured the previous day. The details of his condition were unknown at that time, but his injuries apparently were extensive. Ben Latrobe had sent the message, and he promised to keep Swann apprised of the situation. For now, Swann felt he had little to offer Carolina except the dreaded news of James' present condition.

Disembarking his coach, he shivered against the bitter February winds and pulled his collar up to shield himself from the worst of it. The walkway seemed longer than usual, and with each step, Swann's eloquence failed him. What would he say? How could he possibly offer her any real comfort when he knew so very little? He reached for the brass knocker on the ornate oak door and let it fall against the wood once, then twice more. Mrs. Graves, showing her age and a bit of extra weight, greeted the man with a beaming smile.

"Well, now, Mr. Swann, and to what do we owe this pleasure?" She noticed the carriage driver and waved. "Have your man come around back for something warm to drink."

Swann motioned the man to the back of the house, then doffed his top hat and gave the woman the slightest bow. "Mrs. Graves, I see you are faring well through this bitter winter."

"I'm not so certain about that," the housekeeper said, stepping back from the door to allow Swann entry. "This cold has left me chilled to the bone."

He nodded and put his hat upon the receiving table. "Is Mrs. Baldwin at home?" he questioned as he unfastened the buttons of his heavy wool coat.

"She is indeed. She'll be quite happy to see you, in fact." Mrs. Graves leaned closer and spoke in a conspiratorial manner. "She's missing Mr. Baldwin something fierce. Maybe in his absence you will offer second best."

"I'm afraid not today," he said, letting the housekeeper take his coat and gloves. "I've come with ill tidings."

Mrs. Graves paled. "About the master?"

"Yes." Swann hesitated to say anything more, wanting to break the news to Carolina in as gentle a way as possible. If she saw her housekeeper in a fit of tears, there wouldn't be any chance to make this easy on her. "Please, just call Mrs. Baldwin, and we'll discuss this together."

Mrs. Graves nodded and showed Swann to the front parlor. "Wait here, please."

He did as instructed, taking a seat in the sturdy-looking wing-backed chair he found by the fireplace. His thick shock of dark hair had fallen down onto his forehead, and it was while attempting to right this problem that Carolina entered the room with a stricken look on her face. Obviously Mrs. Graves had already lent an air to the nature of his visit.

"What is it? What has happened to James?"

"I'm afraid there was an accident," Swann began. "Please come sit with me, and I will share what I know. For now, James is safely in the care of doctors and doing well." He elaborated on the latter part, praying that it was true.

A look of relief seemed to wash over Carolina as she hurried to take up her position opposite Swann. "What kind of accident? Was it another derailment?"

Swann knew about James' near-death experience when Phineas Davis had lost his life. "No, it wasn't a derailment. It involved a landslide near Doe Gully Tunnel."

"Doe Gully? That's west of Harper's and Martinsburg, isn't it?"

"That's right. It seems a shelf of slate broke loose and fell across the tracks, blocking the west portal of the tunnel. I don't really have the details, but somehow James was injured."

"I see," Carolina said, twisting her hands.

Swann studied the young woman for a moment. Even though they'd known each other for nearly seven years, he thought she had changed very little. Her skin was still a milky white and youthful, despite the fine lines about her eyes and mouth, which seemed only to add depth and interest to her lovely appearance. Her eyes were warm and dark, and though they held grave concern in their expression just now, Swann thought them to be most beautiful. They had certainly never held such sorrow in them when Blake St. John had passed away. As St. John's attorney and manager, Swann had also had to bring the news of that tragedy to Carolina, and while shocking, the news had certainly not given her reason to grieve overmuch.

He reached out a hand and patted her arm. In his thirty-nine years of life and fifteen years of marriage, he had never been good at dealing with women's sorrow. Oh, his own Elizabeth had said he was quite compassionate and perfect in easing her miseries, but Swann never felt confident in such things. Give him a meeting room with caterwauling investors and argumentative board members any day.

"He's been taken to Harper's Ferry," he began again. "Although I'm uncertain as to why they didn't just take him back to Cumberland. Maybe they felt it would be wiser to get him home to Baltimore for more extensive medical help." He regretted the words as soon as they came out of his mouth, and he quickly sought to soften them. "Then again, maybe he was well enough to travel and refused to go back. That would be just like James. Always pushing forward."

Carolina nodded and dropped her gaze to her lap. "I suppose it would be like him."

"I'll send a telegraphed message to Ben Latrobe. He's there with him. I'll find out how soon James will be heading back to Baltimore. I'd imagine he'll be here before you know it."

"No!" Carolina exclaimed, her head snapping up. "I want to go to him. I can't just sit here in Baltimore waiting to learn of his fate. I want to go on the very next train. I need to be at his side."

"It's too late to go today. I can arrange for it tomorrow morning."

Carolina nodded and turned to Mrs. Graves, whom she had requested to remain to hear Swann's news. "Will you pack my things?"

"Certainly. And I will also tend to the children while you are away." The housekeeper hurried off without a further word, apparently to see to the task immediately.

Carolina was more thankful than ever for her loyal housekeeper, who was so much more than a hired servant. When Carolina had decided not to place her children in the care of a nanny, Mrs. Graves had said, *"And why should you, when you have a substitute granny right here to help out whenever you need?"*

Carolina turned to Swann with pained intensity. "If you know something more, something that you aren't telling me—"

Swann shook his head. "I promise you, I have told you everything. I only know what little the telegram explained."

Carolina sighed. "Wondrous things, telegraphs. Linking people together faster than even locomotives," she murmured absently. Her mind, however, was hardly on the great invention, nor on her good fortune that the B&O had seen the potential of such communication and had allowed for the use of their right-of-ways to put up telegraph poles. But without that telegraph she might not have known of James' condition for days. "I only hope it was fast enough," she mused her fear aloud.

"Carolina," Swann said softly, casting aside all formality, "he will be fine. You'll see. I'm sure his injuries will be treatable, and before we know it James will be back on his feet. After all, he's gone through a derailment and lived to tell about it."

Carolina smiled weakly. "I'm sure you're right. It's just that—"

"What, my dear?"

"I suppose I feel guilty. I was praying that God would send him back to me for a good long time. I wanted him here in Baltimore, Thomas. I didn't want to have to go even another day without him." She began to weep softly into her hands. "I'm so selfish," she whispered.

"Not at all. I would say it is quite a statement of love that you should find his companionship so welcome, even after all these years. Many a couple would happily be parted and rid themselves of the constant turmoil of their miserable existence."

"I could not bear to lose him," Carolina said, lifting tear-filled eyes. "I could not live without him."

"Nonsensical talk, Carolina," Swann replied. "You aren't going to have to live without him. I've never known you to give in to speculation like this. Where is your faith?"

The sound of children squealing and arguing came from upstairs and grew louder as the noise of numerous feet pounded down the steps. Carolina instantly dried her eyes with the edge of her sleeve, and Swann watched as her entire countenance changed. She would be strong for her children. This was evident in the way she positioned herself straighter in the chair. She cast him one quick, wordless glance, but it spoke volumes and Swann gave her a brief smile. It was understood that the children would be kept from fear and concern.

"Give back!" Jordana screamed at Brenton as they entered the parlor.

"Mama," Brenton called, pushing away from his sister. In his hands he clutched a cloth-headed stick horse. "Tell her no!"

Carolina surveyed her children, then spoke. "Cease this yelling at once and tell me calmly what is going on."

"She took my horse," Brenton said indignantly.

"Mine too!" Jordana said, reaching out for the wooden stick pony.

"He's mine, not yours!" Brenton protested.

Carolina got up and took matters into her own hands. "Jordana, you know that this pony belongs to Brenton. Now, I'm sure we can find something just as much fun for you to play with."

"Want pony," Jordana said, kicking her feet as her mother lifted her into her arms.

Swann watched as Carolina allowed herself a brief moment of weakness as she nestled her face against Jordana's dark hair. He alone saw the anguished look that passed over her face. It pierced his heart, and he longed to find some way to take the pain from her.

Just then Mrs. Graves appeared at the door and hurried into the room to take Jordana and Brenton in hand. "I'm sorry, Mrs. Baldwin," she said, speaking formally. "I was bringing down your trunk, and they slipped out of the nursery."

"It's all right. No harm has been done, except that poor Brenton fears his pony will find its way to a new stable."

"Miss Jordana, you come with me, and we'll see if Cook has something good to eat. Maybe you can help make biscuits for dinner."

"Want cookies," Jordana said, clapping her hands together. "Cookies. Cookies." At this, Brenton lost interest in the hobby horse and trailed after Mrs. Graves, insisting that he, too, would find much pleasure in a sugary treat.

"I should be going," Swann commented, seeing this moment as the perfect time to excuse himself from Carolina's company. "I will arrange for your passage in the morning. I will meet you at the station, and if I can get away, I will accompany you myself to Harper's Ferry."

"Thank you, Thomas," Carolina said, squaring her shoulders and drawing a deep breath. "I am so grateful for your assistance. Thank you for coming yourself to tell me of James."

He took her hand and kissed it lightly. "I would never have dreamed of doing otherwise."

Fourteen

Shared Interests

The passage to Harper's Ferry was uneventful. Carolina spent most of the time in contemplative silence. Thomas Swann, respecting her need, kept his interest to the most current issue of the *Niles Register*. Carolina greatly appreciated his kindness in accompanying her to see James. She knew his schedule was quite hectic these days, and it deeply touched her to know that he cared enough about her family to offer this gesture.

When the locomotive finally arrived at the depot, Carolina scarcely even noticed the surroundings. She allowed Swann to lead her from the passenger car, but when he mentioned that James was in a hospital, she nearly broke down at the station. Carolina held the common notion that hospitals were where people went to die. It was unbearable that James should be in such a place.

Carolina was silent during the carriage ride to the hospital. Her mind raced with thoughts of what she would find upon her arrival. Would James already be dead? Or would he be alive but suffering painful injuries? She tried not to let her imagination get the best of her, but it was so hard.

"I'm certain we'll find everything in top order," Swann told her as he assisted her across the hospital threshold.

"I pray it is so," Carolina whispered.

She was impressed by the whitewashed walls and newly mopped wood floors. The air seemed stale, but the building was warm, which was a great comfort after the frigid cold of the train. Although March was nearly upon them, the winter weather seemed to hang on with a fury all its own, and even now the skies were gray and heavy-laden with snow.

An older woman in a starched white apron and coarse gray wool dress appeared and began to question the approaching couple. Carolina found herself instantly impatient and spoke before Swann could manage to announce their need.

"I'm Mrs. James Baldwin. I believe my husband is a patient here."

The woman nodded and pointed. "His bed is in the last ward on the right."

"Thank you." Carolina didn't even wait to exchange a glance with Swann. All she could think of was seeing James again. She thought of the way his eyes lit up when he smiled, and the way he always set her nerves to right when his hand touched hers. Oh, James, she thought, picking up speed with unladylike strides, please be all right. Please be safe.

"Here we are," Swann said, reaching out to push open the door.

Carolina hurried into the room and came to a halt at the sight of a redheaded woman kissing James' forehead. She felt the blood drain from her face, even grew light-headed at the sight. Who was this woman and why was she being so familiar with James?

"I see you are faring very well," Swann said, attempting to introduce their presence.

Carolina stood in complete silence as the woman straightened up and met her stare. She barely heard James' words as he spoke. "Carolina! Mr. Swann! What a wonderful surprise."

This caused Carolina to turn her attention back to James. His head was swathed in bandages, and his face was scratched and bruised. Her chest felt tight as she met his gaze and saw the joy in his eyes. Surely if anything were amiss, there would be some form of embarrassment or anxiety rather than happiness in his expression.

But still she remained fixed in her place beside Swann. In truth, she wasn't sure what to do. The woman at James' side was very attractive, although she wore a moderate amount of makeup, and Carolina was certain her hair was anything but natural in color.

Thomas Swann cleared his throat uncomfortably. "I gave Carolina the news of your accident. She insisted on coming immediately to be at your side."

"I'm grateful that you brought her to me, Mr. Swann. We've been apart nearly a month, and I can't tell you what a vision she is to behold."

Carolina again turned to look at her husband. He spoke as though unaware of her discomfort. But surely he would have to know the startling effect of seeing another woman kiss her bedridden husband. Swann seemed to completely understand the situation and sought to put his friend at ease.

"If you two would like some time alone, I would be happy to escort your other visitor home."

Carolina offered Swann a look of gratitude. Somehow she had to fight the feelings that were building inside her. Feelings of confusion, jealousy, and most disturbing—insecurity.

"That would be fine," James said. "But first we must share introductions. This is Annabelle Bryce, world-renowned actress and good friend."

Annabelle laughed. "I don't know that the world-renowned actress is all that important, but I do value the friendship we share." She moved forward to greet Carolina. "You must be James' wife. I've heard so much about you that I would know you anywhere."

"I'm afraid I've heard nothing about you," Carolina replied, knowing her words poorly hid her dismay. Nevertheless, Annabelle's smile remained fixed and sincere.

"I am Thomas Swann, Miss Bryce," he introduced himself. "I am the president of the Baltimore and Ohio Railroad." He gave her a slight bow, then moved forward to put himself between the two women. "Might I accompany you to your hotel or . . . ah . . . home?"

"I'm staying with my sister." She put her gloved hand upon his arm. "Thank you."

"Carolina, I will see to Miss Bryce and return later to accompany you to the hotel," Swann said as he turned to go.

Carolina said nothing until the door had been drawn closed behind the exiting couple. She wanted to run to James and throw herself into his arms, but images of Annabelle Bryce caused her to remain standing. She lifted her head and caught James' strange expression. It was as if he studied her for some reason. She quickly glanced away, noticing the rest of the ward for the first time. There were a half dozen beds in the room, but James' was the only one occupied.

"Are you going to talk to me, or are you afraid I'm a ghost?"

She glanced back to find him giving her a lopsided grin. Taking a deep breath, she clutched her handbag tightly. "I was so afraid." It was all she could manage to say. For the first time she saw further indication of his injuries as she eyed his right arm in a sling.

"I was too." He extended his left arm and beckoned her to come to him.

"And when I heard you were in a hospital, I didn't know what to think."

"The boardinghouse where I usually stay was full, and this seemed more convenient than the hotel. But you can ease your fears, my dear. I am a bit battered, but I will survive."

Carolina moved forward, desiring nothing other than to be in his arms, but she halted as if Annabelle herself stood between them. "She's very beautiful, James. Why did you never speak of her?"

James surprised her by sitting up quickly. He grimaced with the pain the movement caused but refused to let it stop him as he reached out to take hold of her hand. "Because it seemed unimportant. Now, come here and kiss me like a proper wife."

Carolina gasped as he pulled her down beside him. "James, this isn't how a proper wife acts," she protested.

"No, I don't suppose it is," he whispered, slipping his hand behind her head. "But you mustn't fight me. I'm very injured, you know. Any struggle and I might strain something and lengthen my recuperation period."

Carolina looked at him in surprise, but his grin reassured her, and if not that, then his kiss did the job in short order. He kissed her long and passionately, as though his hunger for her canceled out the pain of his injuries. Carolina forgot about Annabelle and the fears of whether James lay near death's door. It took very little encouragement for her to return the kiss, and without realizing it, she sank onto the bed and melted against him.

"I've missed you more than words will ever express," he whispered as he eased away slightly. "Your face was all I could see, even as the darkness claimed me. When I thought I might die, my real regret was being parted from you and the children without being able to tell you one more time how much I love you."

"I feared I'd never see you alive," she managed to say, choking back a sob.

"Now, now. You aren't allowed to cry," he said in a teasing tone. "You may only cry when a person is truly in jeopardy. I'm merely dented a bit, but hardly all that broken."

Carolina straightened up and immediately noticed that she'd transferred smudges of dust and coal smoke onto James' white nightshirt. "I must be a sight," she said, trying to wipe away the dirt.

"You are," he answered, his blue eyes dark with appreciation. "A most welcome sight."

"I . . . ah . . ." she stammered to think of just the right words. Reaching up a hand to her stylish velvet bonnet, Carolina could feel strands of her carefully pinned coiffure coming down. "I didn't have time to freshen up," she said, trying to resecure the hair.

"I don't care," James said, reaching up to pull her hand back down. "I think you look wonderful."

Carolina could only envision the exacting fashion of Miss Bryce.

The actress, whether given to dying her hair or not, could boast that not a single strand had been out of place. Even the woman's afternoon walking dress had been freshly pressed and in perfect order. Then, too, the image of Annabelle giving James a loving kiss on the forehead positively eroded her last pretenses at being strong. Without warning she began to weep, and soon her sobs were quite uncontrollable.

James eased her back to him and let her have her cry. She felt the tension of the last twenty-four hours overtake her. He might have died in that landslide instead of only sustaining injuries. She might be viewing his dead, mutilated body instead of feeling the warmth of his arms around her. Suddenly all the security of husband and home faded from her and the haunting reminders of their frail existence overwhelmed her reason.

"You mustn't take on so," James finally said, his left hand lovingly stroking her back. "Everything will be all right. You'll see. I'll be fit as a fiddle before you can even say jack-a-dandy."

Carolina shook her head. She couldn't explain her insecurities to him. She couldn't tell him that Annabelle Bryce had been her undoing. That even when faced with James' accident and the possibility of his death, she had remained strong. Why should it be that this stranger's attentions toward her husband should be the one thing to undo her resolve?

"Carolina, listen to me," James said, shifting with some difficulty so as to allow her to get nearer. "It was just an accident. Did they even tell you the details?"

Carolina shook her head and eased away from her husband in order to see his face. "I only know it was a landslide at Doe Gully." She drew a ragged breath and attempted to dry her tears with her dusty handkerchief.

James took the cloth from her and reached up to wipe her face. "It was indeed a landslide. The big slide had taken place prior to our arrival. I was inspecting the site when another piece broke loose and tumbled down upon me. I have a concussion and nasty gash on my head, as well as a broken right arm. My ribs are sore, as is most of my body, but otherwise I am well."

"Are you truly?" she asked in a barely audible voice.

James smiled and gently dabbed her cheeks. "I promise you, I am well on my way to recovery. In fact, Ben tells me that I shall be allowed a job at home in Baltimore, so see there, this thing has its good points, too."

At this, Carolina remembered her selfish prayer to bring James home to her for a good long time. The thought that somehow her prayer might have caused James' accident sent her into yet another fit of tears. "I'm . . . sorry," she said, trying hard to control her sobs. "I know . . . I shouldn't cry."

"I'm sure your worries have been many, but"—he lifted her chin in order to force her to face him—"Annabelle isn't one of them."

Carolina couldn't even attempt to hide her expression of surprise. How could he know what she was feeling? How did he understand that Annabelle's poise and confidence were her undoing?

"I thought that might be a matter of grief to you," he said, shaking his head slowly. "Do you not yet know how much I love you? How you hang the moon and stars for me? Annabelle is a dear, dear friend. She was there for me in a time when you were totally unavailable, but she is only a friend. You needn't fear that I prefer her company over yours. Even our conversation lent itself to you."

"Me?" Carolina questioned, taking the handkerchief from James in order to wipe away the new tears.

James laughed. "Does that surprise you? You come in to find a woman kissing your husband, and you find it hard to believe we had just discussed you?"

For the first time since her arrival, Carolina offered her husband a weak smile. "It did seem rather odd to have spent the entire trip worrying about whether you lived or died, only to find you in the clutches of another woman."

James touched her cheek lightly, and where his fingers traced her face, Carolina felt a tingle of warmth spread. "My home is with you. I've always come home to you."

"It's just that railroading is so unpredictable—so dangerous. I love the railroad, but I love you more."

A grin broke James' serious expression. "I was never quite sure about that."

"Oh, don't tease me now," Carolina said, shaking her head. "I don't understand sometimes what it is I feel. You make me cast aside normal thought, and my emotions are never so churned up as when you have stirred them with your words or actions." She reached a hand up to lightly touch his bandage. "To think that I might have lost you—it's unbearable."

"And unnecessary. You didn't lose me, and in time I will be back to perfect order. You'll see."

Carolina frowned. "Until the next time." Her insecurities crowded in around her, placing a wall of fear between her and her heart's desire. She knew perfectly well that her feelings defied her more logical nature, but this was life and death, and the life that hung in the balance belonged to the man she loved.

"You are borrowing trouble," James whispered, eyeing her very seriously. "None of us knows the future. The end will come to each of us, even as it has come to those who've gone before us. We can't stop living just because of the things that might happen tomorrow."

"I know you're right. My head hears your words and comprehends them just as it did the algebraic expressions you taught me as my tutor. But my heart—" she paused and drew her hand over her breast—"my heart isn't as easily convinced."

James took hold of her hand and placed it on his own chest. "My heart is convinced of only one thing. My love for you. The rest seems unimportant."

"The rest is completely wrapped up in that one thing. If something should happen to you—"

He put a finger to her lips and hushed her. "Our faith for tomorrow is in God. Our faith in each other is bound there, too, for as we seek Him, we draw closer to each other. Our trust is strengthened and our love purified and refined. We must believe that He is in control of even the slightest detail of our existence." He let his fingers trail down her jaw to her neck.

"I do believe," Carolina said, shivering from the emotions stirred by his touch. "I must believe."

He kissed her again, this time less urgently. "Believing often requires practice, just like algebra," he said with a smile. "We'll work at it together and you'll see. It will all work together."

Fifteen

The Confession

Carolina stayed beside her husband until the doctor and nurse arrived to shoo her out. She stepped into the hallway, fully intending to find Thomas Swann awaiting her arrival, but instead she found Annabelle Bryce.

"Mr. Swann and I had a lovely talk, and I begged him to allow me to wait here for you," Annabelle explained. "When Mr. Latrobe arrived in desperate need of discussing railroad business, Mr. Swann was finally convinced."

Carolina swallowed hard and took a deep, steadying breath. "I see," she managed to say without sounding like a complete fool. "How very kind of you."

"I thought it might be nice if we could talk. I've long heard of you from James, and I would find it delightful to share supper with you. Would you do me the honor?"

Carolina felt a wash of insecurity rush over her. The woman looked so well kept and lovely. Her stylish black wool mantelet was ornately embroidered with fiery red birds and silver branches. Trimmed at the neck and hem with mink, it was the epitome of popularity that season. Under this, Miss Bryce's damask gown of red, black, and green plaid jutted out in the highly desired bell-shaped fashion, giving her a very smart appearance. An involuntary frown crossed Carolina's brow. Alongside Annabelle Bryce, she felt quite dowdy in her gray traveling suit and black winter coat, all smudged and wrinkled from her journey.

"Please, Mrs. Baldwin," Annabelle said, coming forward, "I would like very much for us to be friends."

"I am quite hungry," Carolina admitted, then met the other woman's gaze. She would have much preferred going to her hotel room to freshen up, but there was an urgency in Annabelle's voice that she couldn't ignore. "I would be happy to share supper with you. The doctor said I might return to see James later today, so if there is somewhere we might go that is close to the hospital—"

"But of course. There is a cafe just across the way."

Carolina nodded and followed Annabelle into the street. The cold weather had hardened the muddy thoroughfare, but still Carolina gently raised the edge of her skirt to avoid any additional dirt and wear to her hem. The traveling gown was several years old, and seeing Annabelle only made Carolina more aware of how much she'd allowed herself to become out of pace where fashion was concerned. She had become the perfect example of the nonsocial housewife and mother. She seldom ever gave herself over to entertaining, and with James gone so much of the time, she avoided the parties and socials of other families. It was difficult to attend events alone, and oftentimes it was simply considered in bad taste. So Carolina had slipped out of the social circles with exception to her charity work and Sunday church services, which often only served to further her loneliness.

Sighing as she contemplated the woman before her, Carolina chided herself. It's not like I ever cared one whit for being stylish. Books always took precedence over ball gowns. But there was something about Annabelle that made Carolina acutely aware that perhaps she'd become overly reserved and remiss in her social responsibilities.

"Here we are," Annabelle announced, pushing open the door. "It isn't much, but the food is good and they know me here, so no one will be upset at serving two unescorted ladies."

"I'm sure it will be fine," Carolina commented. Immediately her mind took off in another direction. She wondered how long Annabelle had sat outside James' room, all in order to invite her to supper. *Why would Annabelle Bryce spend her day awaiting me? What is she about?* Carolina pondered as they took a seat at a far-removed table.

"We can have a little privacy here," Annabelle said with a smile.

Carolina took her chair and nodded. Just then a woman looking to be in her mid-fifties appeared. She wore a serviceable gown of brown cotton and a pinafore-styled apron of bleached muslin. Her hair was graying and pulled back in a tight, secure bun, making her countenance seem almost angry. But where the fashion made her seem stern, the wrinkles around her eyes suggested a less severe nature, and when she smiled in welcome, all thought of formality faded.

"It's mighty cold out there today. What can I get you ladies?" she asked in a motherly fashion. "Something to warm you up, no doubt."

"Do you have a special today, Naomi?" Annabelle asked in a manner that suggested complete familiarity.

"Why, we sure do, Miss Annabelle. Thickest beef stew you'll ever set your lips to. Apple pie and fresh-baked biscuits, as well."

"That sounds perfect for me. How about you?" Annabelle questioned, looking at Carolina for confirmation.

Carolina nodded. "Yes. It sounds just fine. I'd also be grateful for a cup of tea, if you have it."

The woman beamed her a smile. "Why, we sure do. I'll have it all out here directly."

She bustled off to see to their order, leaving Carolina painfully aware of Annabelle's fixed stare. She felt a desperate need to freshen up but was determined not to give in to her emotions. James had already assured her that Annabelle was nothing more than a friend, but Carolina remembered that at one time she and James had only been friends, as well.

"May I call you Carolina?" Annabelle suddenly asked. Carolina was so surprised by this that she could only nod in mute agreement. "And you, of course, must call me Annabelle. Everyone does."

"All right," Carolina managed to say.

The women engaged in several minutes of small talk—the weather, the traveling conditions, the amenities of Harper's Ferry, with which Annabelle was quite familiar. Then the waitress returned with their meals, and it was only after she had gone to attend to a new arrival of customers that Annabelle once again took up the conversation.

"I met James a long time ago, in case you wondered." She paused to study Carolina's reaction, and Carolina found herself trying all the more to retain a straight, stoic expression. She had no desire for this woman to pry into her wounded pride and damaged self-confidence.

"James attempted to help me from the train. We were stopped because of snowdrifts, and it was necessary for a carriage to bring us on to Harper's. We both ended up plopped down in a snowbank, but it was the start of a great friendship. I soon learned that James admired spirited women who possessed the ability to think for themselves. He told me I reminded him of someone. I didn't yet know that you were the one I reminded him of. He was running away at the time—or so it seemed—and it turned out to be pretty much the truth. He was going west with the railroad and seeking to forget something very painful."

Carolina nodded, knowing full well it was most likely when he had broken his engagement to Virginia.

Annabelle continued between samples of her steaming stew. "I later learned he had left your sister because he'd come to recognize his love for you. I don't have a single memory of James when he was not pining for you. Over the years, we've shared many conversations and kept each other company during painful times. But always, always, it was you he thought of. I knew you must be a very special woman, and even then I knew someday I would have to meet you for myself."

Carolina didn't know what to say, so she busied herself with the food. It was difficult to listen to what Annabelle had to say because it only served to stir up the jealousy Carolina already felt burning down deep inside. She tried to counterbalance those emotions with James' earlier words, but sitting across from Annabelle made it difficult to focus on those things.

As if seeing that Carolina was far from convinced, Annabelle continued, this time dropping any pretense of polite chitchat. "There was a time when James was quite devastated by his loss. He found you married to another, felt you were forever lost to him, and sought me out to share his misery."

Carolina felt the intensity of Annabelle's watchful eyes. She hadn't a clue as to what Annabelle wanted from her. Why should she bring me here to tell me all of this? Has she no mercy or consideration for my feelings? If James esteemed this woman for her kindness, then where was such a quality now?

"I could have had him for myself," Annabelle stated bluntly.

This caused Carolina to drop her spoon. "I beg your pardon?" she questioned in a whisper.

"I believe you heard me," Annabelle replied. "James was well into his cups one night, and his anguish over being too late to take you for his wife was more than he could endure. He found you promised to that commission merchant who later married your sister."

"You seem to know a great deal about my family," Carolina said in a rather hostile tone. She thought to straighten Annabelle out on the fact that she had never been promised to Hampton Cabot, but she let it go.

Annabelle smiled, not in the leastwise insulted. "James was very thorough in his confessions. As I recall, you had seen each other at some social event in Washington."

"Yes," Carolina replied, remembering the moment in full clarity. "I was accompanied by Mr. Cabot, who did, indeed, marry my sister Virginia."

"James was told by your friends that you two were to be wed. He returned to Baltimore a broken man. I found him wandering the streets drunk, or at least well on his way to being so. I took him home, fed him, and let him pour out his miseries. It was then that he suggested we be married."

Carolina felt her chest constrict. Her stomach suddenly churned, making her wish most fervently that she had never taken a single bite of the delicious stew. "Why are you telling me this?" she asked, but down deep inside she really wondered why James had never mentioned it.

Annabelle put down her spoon and her expression softened to one of complete sympathy. "Because I saw the look in your eyes when you found me kissing your husband. Because I see it still and know that it can lead to no good. If left untended, it will only cause grief between you and James."

"So you tell me that you could have had my husband? How does that resolve anything?"

"It should stand as proof to you of James' devotion. It wasn't me that he was proposing to. As I mentioned, he'd had more than a little to drink. He spoke of always needing me and what an important part of his life I'd become. He even said he could not imagine living a single day without me in his life." She paused and Carolina could see tears glistening in her eyes. "He was talking about you, not me. I could have agreed to his suggestion of marriage—trapped him into an awkward obligation—but it was you he wanted. It is you he loves."

Carolina said nothing, but she knew in that moment that things had changed. She knew Annabelle to be honorable, at least in part. And while the woman remained a stranger in most ways, Carolina easily read the sincerity and honesty in her words. What purpose could be otherwise served than that which Annabelle suggested?

They ate in silence for several moments, and it wasn't until the woman returned to bring two huge pieces of apple pie that Carolina spoke. "None for me, please. I'm afraid I've made a glutton of myself with your stew and biscuits."

Annabelle nodded. "The same is true of me. Please just put this on my account, Naomi. I'll take care of it later."

"No, that isn't necessary," Carolina protested, reaching for her handbag.

"Please, let me do this one thing for you."

Carolina thought to refuse, then realized it was her turn to be gracious. She nodded. "Very well, but you must allow me to return the favor sometime."

"I'd like that very much. I can't think of anything I'd enjoy more than to share time with you and James before you return to Baltimore. But for now, let me accompany you to your hotel. I'm sure you would like to see to your things, and then you can feel free to go back to the hospital and be with James."

They left the cafe and walked in silence until they came to the hotel where Thomas Swann had arranged for rooms. Carolina continued to wonder at the woman beside her. A great many women in Annabelle's position might have used their past relationships to bring harm and misery upon others, but this woman was clearly different. There was something about Annabelle that seemed almost noble and admirable. She carried herself regally, and although upon closer inspection, Carolina found her face to be a bit poxy and scarred, she was lovely in a way that seemed to come from the inside out.

She still wondered who Annabelle Bryce really was. She was an actress, of that James had made clear during their introductions. So maybe this was all staged for Carolina's benefit. Maybe Annabelle was merely playing a part.

"I could have had him for myself," she had told Carolina simply. *"I could have agreed to his suggestion of marriage, but it was you he wanted. It is you he loves."* Carolina followed Annabelle into the lobby of the hotel, all the while replaying Annabelle's words in her head. It had become increasingly obvious that while Annabelle had spoken of James' feelings for her, she'd not confessed her own feelings for James.

Stopping abruptly, Carolina eyed Annabelle cautiously. "You told me that James didn't love you, but you never said whether or not you loved James."

Annabelle seemed taken aback for a moment before replying. "No, I didn't, did I." It was more a statement than a question.

Carolina immediately put up her guard. Her body tensed with the expression of unmasked admiration in Annabelle's eyes. Admiration that was certainly intended for James. Turning to leave, Carolina was surprised when Annabelle's gloved fingers closed over her arm. The actress patted her gently and smiled.

"You do not need to worry about my feelings in this, Carolina. I am a Christian woman, and I honor the commitment of marriage. I would never present myself as a complication to your marriage or to the love you two so obviously share." She paused for a moment, seeming to need to control her own emotions. "I may well be envious, but I am not an adulterous woman. You need fear nothing from me."

Annabelle's words stayed with Carolina throughout the rest of the evening. When she retired for the night, she lay in her hotel bed, contemplating the reason she had been privy to such personal feelings and thoughts. Annabelle clearly admired, maybe even loved, James, and while at first Carolina found this most alarming, now it gave her cause to dwell on yet another aspect. After six years of marriage and three children, Carolina realized that she'd allowed herself to become complacent about her marriage. She had never lost sight of the blessings she found in the security of home and hearth, husband and children, but she had lost sight of the dream.

Their dream. The dream to push forward into the future together. To share their lives in such a mission and always stand as ready partners to aid the other. Carolina lay staring at the ceiling, suddenly remembering the night of her coming-of-age party. She had stirred a gathering of male guests into a hardy brawl, and James had rescued her and taken her to the safety of the gardens. There under the moonlight and stars, James had awakened in her a desire that she'd never known. She longed for his touch and his kiss, but it was more than that. She longed to share his life—to bear his children—to help him accomplish his ambitions and goals. She admired him for his intelligence and quick wit, and she loved him for his fierce loyalty and honorable nature.

I had forgotten my first love, she thought, remembering the feeling of giddy joy that bubbled up inside her when realizing James' love had been returned all along. Somewhere along the way she had removed herself from that joy. In the fuss and bother of everyday life, she had grown weary and harsh in their separations and trials.

"Marriage is indeed no easy task," she said aloud. She thought of her immaturity and pride and determined there and then to cast aside her childish nature. "I am nearly a score and nine. Surely it is time to put aside self-serving ideals and focus on the benefits of what we have together."

She thought of James sleeping alone in the hospital bed and longed for him to be beside her. "Father," she prayed, "I ask for James' recovery. I ask that it be speedy and void of pain. I long so much to hold him. To have him beside me, to share our thoughts and dreams again. Help us find a way to avoid being separated for so long, and if that cannot be granted, then help me find a way to survive in spite of it."

Sixteen

The Road Ahead

James and Carolina found Baltimore unchanged upon their return after a week in Harper's Ferry. Thomas Swann met them at the station and offered them the use of his carriage for their journey to their house. James still suffered from attacks of pain to his arm and head but otherwise felt a glorious wonder at being alive to see his family again.

"I'm grateful for all you've done," he told Swann. "Allowing me to work here in Baltimore while I heal is more than I could expect."

"A man needs an income, and we have much use for a man like you," Swann said good-naturedly. Then, gazing in another direction, added, "Say, do you recognize that man?"

The man in question was tall and lean and seemed almost awkward as he moved across the platform. "No, I can't say that I do," Carolina replied, trying to get a better look at the stranger.

"That's Abraham Lincoln," Swann said. "No doubt he's returning to Illinois after a rather dull single term as a United States congressman."

"How do you know him?" James asked, watching as the man disappeared from sight.

"I first met him in Washington last year. I was impressed with his ideas on a variety of subjects. We shared legal views and discussed the Baltimore and Ohio."

"What did Mr. Lincoln think of our endeavor?" Carolina asked, her interest piqued.

Thomas Swann smiled down at her. "Well, the man is investing in a ticket that costs nearly nine dollars to take him from Baltimore to Cumberland via our railroad. He'd no doubt prefer our rails all the way to the Ohio rather than give himself over to the stage. We estimated his trip will take him some twelve days, once you consider the stage and steamer packet that he will take to St. Louis."

"Still, it is a wonder," Carolina said and allowed Swann to assist her into his carriage. "Imagine going nearly six hundred miles across mountains, valleys, and plains, and all in twelve days. It seems a moderately short amount of time, considering that many of our ancestors spent weeks, sometimes months, just getting over the barrier of the mountains."

"And it will only get faster," said James as he settled himself in the carriage. "I look forward to our progress. Has the route to Wheeling been agreed upon, then?"

"No, not entirely. There are routes surveyed for Wheeling, Grave, and Fish Creeks. Any of which would bring us to the destination of the Ohio River and, eventually, the city of Wheeling."

"What do you mean 'eventually'?" asked Carolina.

"Well, that is a source of much controversy at this point. To proceed with the line via Fish Creek is the route farthest from the city of Wheeling. They fear if we adhere to this choice, we might never complete the line to Wheeling and thereby deprive the city of its full potential. The citizens of Wheeling believe, and maybe fairly so, that if we take the Fish Creek route, we will come upon the Ohio some eleven or more miles south of their city. Of course, we would complete the line up the Ohio to Wheeling, but they fear that this would only create the birth of yet another rival town on the Ohio, should we fall short of coming to the river via their great town.

"Of course, Latrobe favors Fish Creek rather than Grave because the latter calls for four tunnels and twenty-three crossings of the stream itself. The Fish Creek route calls only for moderate bridging and one tunnel. Fish looks to be our cheapest route to build; however, Wheeling Creek would take us directly into the city. It's a great dilemma and one which will not be easily resolved." He paused and gazed out the carriage window. "Ah, here we are."

"Won't you come inside and warm up?" James invited.

"Thank you, but no, I believe this reunion should be one of family. I know your children will be half wild to see you, and, no doubt, Mrs. Baldwin would prefer not to entertain."

"Nonsense, Thomas," Carolina said, dropping all formality. "You know you are always welcome."

"But this time I will pass. I have a very important meeting in the morning, and I must be prepared."

The driver halted the carriage, then quickly jumped down from his seat to help first James and then Carolina from the carriage. He left them long enough to deliver their luggage around back, then returned to take his seat topside again.

"Take care, Thomas," James said, "and thank you again for bringing Carolina to me."

"It was my pleasure. I will see you in my office next week, agreed?"

"Agreed."

They watched Swann's carriage pull away and might have lingered there in the chill of twilight, but already Mrs. Graves had opened the front door, and the children were clamoring around the aging housekeeper in order to see their parents.

"Papa!" Victoria called out, determined to be the first to greet him. "I missed you so much!" She skirted past Mrs. Graves to run to her father. "What happened to your arm?" she questioned, coming up short.

"I'm afraid it's broken," James replied. He extended his left arm and smiled. "But this one works perfectly well, and I only need one to hold you close." Victoria easily moved into her father's embrace.

"Papa! Mama!" Brenton and Jordana chanted from the doorway.

Carolina went to embrace them both, then urged them all inside. "Come, come. We can have our reunion by the fireside."

"I've got some tea already hot," Mrs. Graves offered. "Coffee too."

"Sounds marvelous," James replied, Victoria clinging to his left side, Brenton hurrying to wrap an arm around his father's waist. "I don't suppose Cook has made any of her lovely jam tarts?"

"I don't suppose she would dare not, knowing that you were returning today," Mrs. Graves said with a laugh.

It was hours later, when the children had been sent to bed and James and Carolina had retired to their room, that Carolina grew reticent. James wondered at the change. She had been quite animated and spirited with the children, but as the evening waned, James had watched her become more and more reserved.

"Want to tell me what's bothering you?" he asked softly as he watched her take out her hairpins and let down her hair.

Carolina picked up her brush and shrugged. "I suppose I'm just tired." She brushed through the thick chestnut hair and appeared for all purposes to be quite absorbed in her task.

James slipped out of his coat, then turned to Carolina. "I'm afraid I'll need your help to rid myself of this waistcoat and shirt."

Carolina put down the brush and came to him, her long dark hair rippling in waves down her back. James couldn't help himself. He pulled her close and buried his left hand in the mass. "Nothing feels quite as good as this," he murmured. "Unless, of course, it's this." He lightly kissed her neck. "Or this," he said, trailing up her jaw to her lips. He heard her sigh and knew that she was quite content to share his passion. This moment alone was all that he could think of during the time they'd spent in Harper's Ferry. Upon his release from the hospital he'd even suggested they take a few days together at the hotel, but Carolina had been most insistent to return to Baltimore.

"This isn't getting that waistcoat off any faster," Carolina said, pulling away.

"Maybe not, but it's certainly more fun." He allowed her to undo the buttons and waited while she slipped the article from him.

Next, she silently went to work on the buttons of his shirt, and when these were all unfastened, she helped him free his arm from the sling.

"Come sit and talk with me," James said, leading her to the bed.

She raised a quizzical brow, as if to question whether his intentions were truly bent on conversation, but never offered protest, in any case. James drew her close and smiled. "I am so happy to be back with you. It almost makes the accident worth it."

"Don't say that!" Carolina exclaimed.

"Well, God knows that I'd not choose this path," James admitted, "but He also knows how much I've missed being with my family. There's a great deal of work to be done on the line, and the future of my business is not here in Baltimore. I suppose it makes for a good respite to have this time here and now with you and the children." He felt her stiffen and eyed her quite seriously. "Is that what is bothering you?"

"I don't like to think of you going away. I worry about you."

"I see," he answered, still trying to study her expression. She had bowed her head slightly, making it difficult for him to survey her completely, but he could tell she was deeply troubled. He let the silence linger between them for several moments, knowing from experience that it would get the better of Carolina. She hated to wait in silence. It was almost a threat to her.

"Annabelle was very nice," she finally said.

"Yes. Annabelle is very agreeable company."

Carolina's head snapped up and her eyes widened as she met James' gaze. "She's obviously quite devoted to you."

"And that bothers you, doesn't it?"

Carolina lifted her chin in her trademark look of defiance. "It would bother any wife to know that a beautiful actress finds her husband to be, as you say, agreeable company."

James instantly recognized her jealousy and chuckled. He'd never seen this side of her and it was rather flattering. "You are jealous," he stated matter-of-factly.

"I am not!" she exclaimed and sought to move away from him. "I'm simply . . . well . . . I'm . . ."

"What? You're what?" pressed James playfully. "If not jealous of a woman who means nothing more to me than what the bounds of friendship offer, then what is it that has set you in this mood?"

Carolina's eyes welled with tears. She tried to bury her face in her hands, but James would have no part of it. "Tell me," he gently commanded, then added, "please."

"I'm lonely," Carolina said, trying to smile through her tears. "I know that sounds foolish. I have Mrs. Graves and Cook, and of course the children, but it is you I long for."

"I'm right here," he said, somewhat confused by this sudden confession.

"But for how long? Three, maybe four weeks. Long enough for the arm to mend. Then you'll be off again for the West and I won't see you for weeks or even months. I can't bear it. I don't want to stay in Baltimore if it means that you'll be somewhere else."

James saw the seriousness of her expression and felt the genuine need in her soul. "Would you have me give up the railroad? Give up the dream?"

"No," she replied, shaking her head most vigorously. "But I used to be a part of that dream. It used to belong to both of us. Remember?"

"Certainly. But I still don't understand. If you don't want me to give up the railroad, what is it you're trying to say?"

Carolina wiped her eyes. "I want to come with you. I want us all to come with you. Thomas told me he has some tunnel project for you out west of Cumberland. He said it would take a good long time to complete and you would act as liaison between the contractor and the railroad."

"That's true. Construction is to begin on the tunnel sometime this fall. But, darling, I don't understand how you can possibly suggest coming with me."

"Is there no town?"

"Well, there is a town of sorts. It's hardly more than a widening in the road. You certainly can't desire to give up your comforts here in the city. What of the children and your family at Oakbridge? As it stands now, they are only a day away by rail. If you follow me into the wilderness, there won't be the comfort of hopping on the next train."

"You're building a railroad tunnel, aren't you? Surely that means the railroad will accompany the tunnel," Carolina argued.

"Yes, but not for a good long while. Swann is setting up a series of small contracts that will be let in sections. The Kingwood Tunnel is only one section. There are many unfinished sections between that point and Cumberland."

"I don't care. If it means we'll be together, I will endure whatever it takes."

"But is that fair to the children? They have their friends here, and they are used to a fine home and plentiful food. I have no way of knowing what kind of supplies we might find in Greigsville."

"Greigsville?"

"Yes, that's what they're calling that particular location. It's hardly more than a few clapboard buildings and tent structures at this point."

Carolina seemed to consider this for a moment, then got to her feet and paced a line in front of where James remained sitting on the bed. He watched her, her face contorting into several expressions before she finally stopped before him.

"I suppose it's hard to explain to a man how a woman feels inside. I know we are very different, James, but the truth of the matter is, when you are gone I feel as though a part of me is gone, as well. I seem barely functional as half of a whole that can only be fulfilled when you are at my side. I despise the social circles here in town, and I'm even coming to dread church."

"I don't understand," James said, searching her face for answers.

"I despair of going places without you. It isn't that I can't perform my duties while you are away, but I find it all rather meaningless and dull. Church makes me lonely as I see other husbands and wives sitting side by side with their families. I know God is there for me, and that I am never truly alone, but, James," she said, falling to her knees in front of him, "I long for you to be there. I desire it as I desire no other thing in this life. Not the comforts of the city, nor the wealth of goods it affords me." She put her head on one knee and her hand on the other.

James stroked her hair with his good hand, while he ached to hold her close with both arms. "I'm sorry," he offered softly. "I had no idea you felt this way."

"How could you?" Just a hint of her old bitterness returned to her voice. "You're seldom home longer than to say hello and good-bye. Even when you are here, there is often one thing or another that takes you away for hours on end. At least those distractions will be minimal in this Greigsville town you speak of."

"Perhaps, but it's just as likely that an entirely new set of problems will emerge."

"Yes, but we would be together. You would come home to our bed every night. I would see you most every day, and I would be able to properly care for you and you for me."

"But Greigsville is so isolated. I have no way of knowing if there are other women there with whom you might become friends."

Carolina lifted her head and reached up to touch James' face. "None of that would matter, so long as I had you."

James found the intensity of emotion in her eyes to be almost too much to bear. He pulled her up to sit beside him on the bed, and for several moments simply studied the woman he had married. She was still young and beautiful, and his passion and desire for her had never waned. He, too, knew the frustration of their long separations. He could remember all too well the many nights of tossing and turning, wishing fervently for her companionship. He wanted more than a life of visiting his own home and family. He wanted more of a relationship with his wife than to simply give her another child and move off to the wilds of some unsurveyed countryside. Seeing her here, like this, he remembered the reasons he had first found her so appealing. He loved her sense of humor and her intelligent mind. He loved the way she hungered for knowledge and the fact that she looked to him for much of her teaching. He had also appreciated her sense of adventure and had once envisioned them sharing such adventures. He suddenly had a more complete picture of what his absences had meant to Carolina—more than just missing him, but also missing being part of the life they should be experiencing together.

"It would require a great sacrifice on your part," he said, knowing that the decision had already been made. "Are you certain?"

"Oh yes."

"I can't promise you that it will be easy."

"I don't care," she replied eagerly.

James saw the excitement in her eyes, and it touched his heart in a way he could not explain. She was willing to give up all that she had in order to follow him. She could not have the entire dream for herself, but she was willing that he have it, and that through him she might share it in some small way.

"Thomas wants me there by September. Will that give you enough time to square away matters here in Baltimore?"

She smiled, and it was a smile that lit up her eyes in a way he'd not seen in some time. "Tell me what is to be done."

"You will have to figure out what will be needed and what can be left behind. I'll go on ahead of you. Not only to set up arrangements with the railroad contractors but also so that I can see what lodging is available, and maybe we can better plan from that."

"You truly mean it?" Carolina questioned in joyful enthusiasm.

James grinned. "I truly mean it. I think it's a capital idea." He reclined on the bed, pulling her with him. "I think it might well be the best idea I've had in a long time."

Carolina raised herself up on her elbow. "What do you mean *your* idea?" she teased. "I'll have you know, James Baldwin—" she began, but he gave her no chance to finish.

"Tell me later," he murmured as he passionately pulled her back against him. "Much, much later."

Seventeen

The Long Night

Margaret Adams sat under an outdoor canopy on the meticulously tended lawns of the South Boston Mental Asylum. The May morning was bright and beautiful, with the sound of birds in the trees and the wafting scent of flowering vegetation filling the air.

"Your husband has written you another letter," a rather portly woman said, laying an envelope on the table in front of Margaret.

Margaret smiled and touched the letter almost reverently. "He's good to do that," she commented.

"Soon he'll come," the woman said with a smile.

"Oh, Esther, I shall look forward to that day."

Esther Jacobs smiled. For as long as she had acted as nurse to Margaret Adams, she had never known a time when her charge hadn't looked forward to her husband's visits. Even when she was newly arrived at the hospital and quite spent with grief over the deaths of her children, Margaret would pine for the man in a way that made Esther question the sense in keeping them separated.

"Why don't you come take a walk with me now, dear? Soon it will be time for the noon meal, and then you'll find yourself too busy to enjoy the day."

Margaret nodded, getting to her feet. She slipped the letter into her pocket and awaited instructions from her nurse. Esther came around to resecure the shawl that had fallen to the lawn. "You may need this." Margaret pulled the edges closed in front and looked down the path as if to consider their route. "I believe if we walk down this way, you will positively delight in the apple blossoms," Esther said, leading her patient.

Margaret was never given to much conversation, but Esther knew how greatly she enjoyed hearing from home. "I'd imagine that letter is burning a hole in your pocket, eh?"

"It is difficult not to tear into it," Margaret admitted.

"Well, we will find a lovely bench near the trees, and you may take time to read it through."

Esther directed her to just such a place, both panting and slightly out of breath as they took a seat on the wrought-iron bench. Margaret, accustomed to Esther's companionship, pulled the letter from her pocket and began to scan each line. "Oh my," she suddenly gasped and Esther took note.

"Something wrong?"

Margaret shook her head, then lifted her gaze to meet Esther's face. "He says the doctors are considering the possibility of my returning home." Esther beamed a brilliant smile as Margaret added, "Did you know of this?"

Esther nodded and the look that passed between the two women was one of complete joy. They'd both worked long and hard for this day. They'd both endured moments of testing when such an announcement seemed impossible.

"It might yet take months to convince the deciding panel, but I feel confident it will happen," Esther replied. "You've made great progress."

Margaret's eyes moistened and Esther patted her hand. With their gazes fixed, a peace seemed to pass between them. It was as if in that moment the past had suddenly fallen away. Esther likened it to a rebirth, and while she'd not seen many patients recover to claim such a prize, she overflowed with happiness that Margaret Adams should be one of those who did just that.

"Oh, Esther, what if—" Margaret fell silent.

Esther knew the turmoil within the woman. She had come to the asylum barely more than a raving lunatic. Her two youngest children had died from yellow fever, and this on top of babies who had passed on many years earlier. Her husband, a good and gentle man, had wept uncontrollably at seeing his wife physically carried away as she shouted and screamed accusations at him. Esther had thought it might well rob the man of his will to go on, but she realized quickly how wrong she had been in her assessment. Joseph Adams was a strong, compassionate man. He had proven himself to be a loving husband, in spite of his wife's inner turmoil and rage, and as Margaret had improved and found her way back through the insanity that gripped her, Joseph, too, was transformed.

"Remember what the Good Book says," Esther told her. " 'Therefore if any man be in Christ, he is a new creature: old things are passed away; behold, all things are become new.' "

Margaret looked her square in the eyes as if searching their depths to find assurance that her words were true. Esther smiled and immediately the tension in Margaret's face eased.

"The old is passed away," Esther said softly, taking Margaret's hand in her own. "God has brought you through the fires of testing, and you are a new creation by His hand."

Margaret gripped her hand tightly and nodded. "I know the truth in this," she whispered.

For a moment neither woman spoke or moved. The minutes lent themselves to reaffirming Margaret's faith. Esther knew how she had labored to understand how God could be a loving, trustworthy Father, even while, for some reason unfathomable to her, allowing her children to pass from this life. Margaret had likened it to a never-ending night of darkness, and Esther had easily recognized the truth in her comparison. Margaret labored to accept that the foundations on which she had built her entire life were indeed fixed and solid. That God was still God, and that He still loved her with an everlasting love. Once she had come to terms with this, Esther knew it would only be a matter of time before her mind and heart would knit back into proper order. And so that day had come, and Esther could only rejoice with her patient. The long night would soon be over.

Joseph Adams lingered over his ledgers for only a moment longer before snapping them shut. He had once again summoned Hampton to the library, and true to form, the man was taking his time. Still, Joseph couldn't concentrate on facts and figures, not with so much else weighing on his mind. The night had seemed endless as he had tossed and turned. Many things in his life were amiss, and the one bright spot in his otherwise dismal world was that it was time once again to journey to Boston for a visit. He could only pray that soon the doctors would find Margaret completely healed and allow her to return home. He longed for that day as he did no other. He missed her companionship and conversations. He mourned that she had missed out on so many of the changes in her family over the last few years, yet even this seemed unimportant compared to her recovery and return.

But there were other problems that overshadowed Margaret's absence. The issue of slavery was gradually becoming a nightmare of massive proportions, and as ridiculous as it seemed, the issue was tearing the country apart. York, his elder son, had written letters from Philadelphia that spoke to the heart of the matter. After serving one term in

Congress, York had failed to win a second term in the elections of 1848. He knew now the first win had been purely on his father-in-law's coattails. When York's proslavery views became more widely known, his constituency turned on him. Northerners found it impossible to understand the institution of keeping huge numbers of slaves in order to run large plantations. The northeast coastal population was far more industrial than agricultural, and it was difficult for residents of those areas to understand the amount of work that went into farming. York was understandably bitter about this and the fact that it had damaged his political career. Quite frustrated, he had told of protests and lectures that spoke to the cruelty of owning human lives, and until Hampton's heavy-handedness at Oakbridge, Joseph had thought it a circumstance that didn't involve him.

It was easy to forget about those plantation owners who acted with disregard for their slaves, when few in his immediate circle acted in such a way. Robert E. Lee would certainly never allow for cruelty at Arlington House. Neither would a half dozen other good men with whom he had shared friendships over the years. Still, he knew full well that such horrors were the reality of the institution. He'd known of circumstances where Negro families were split up—sold to different owners, all because of profit margins and marketability. But he'd never played a part in that, so he wasn't guilty. Or was he? Wasn't he just as guilty because he'd turned away, refusing to acknowledge what was happening? When he heard rumors circulating around Oakbridge and saw the marks of Hampton's cruelty, wasn't he just as guilty in looking away as he would have been had he wielded the whip himself?

With a heaviness he could not shake, Joseph wondered what recourse he had. He'd spoken many times to Hampton about his actions, and while things went along smoothly for a while, he had a sneaking suspicion that Hampton had merely threatened the slaves into silence and submission. But Joseph was gone so much, spending weeks on end in Boston, that it was difficult to keep a tight rein on his son-in-law. It was too easy to allow the situation to be superseded by his need to have someone run things while he was away.

A knock sounded at the door, and Hampton Cabot entered the room without further warning. He wore fawn-colored riding pants and a white shirt that was open at the collar.

"There's trouble stirring up again," Hampton said, seemingly unconcerned that it was Joseph who had summoned him to the library, instead of the other way around. "Two of the Willminghams' slaves have escaped, and I've a notion they may come here to seek refuge."

"What gives you that impression?"

"I overheard a couple of the house girls talking in their bedchambers. Essie and Lydia to be exact."

"What were you doing on the third floor?" Joseph asked, fearful that he already knew the answer. It was rumored that his son-in-law had remained anything but faithful to his wife. Without clear proof Joseph could only wonder about the parentage of two very light-colored infants born to two other slave girls who worked in the weaving and sewing houses. Joseph had never accused Hampton to his face, but the implication lay between them like black powder awaiting a spark.

Even now Hampton's expression dared Joseph to accuse him of wrongdoing. Instead, Joseph waved him to take a chair, feeling much the coward for not standing up to his son-in-law. In truth, he wasn't completely convinced that Hampton was to blame. Joseph's now-deceased overseer, Walt Durgeson, had a rather ruthless grandson who'd lived with Walt at Oakbridge. And while the young man had since moved on, the timing could have just as easily put him in the position of fathering the slaves' babies as Hampton.

"I told them both," Hampton continued without bothering to account for his presence on the third floor, where several of the house slaves were quartered, "that I'd beat them to within an inch of their lives if those slaves showed up and they didn't tell me about it right off."

"Hampton, you well know I don't approve of beating confessions out of people. I doubt Willmingham's slaves will come here. They'd be wiser to stick to the river," Joseph muttered.

"Nevertheless, I intend to see to it that we don't inadvertently harbor them."

Joseph nodded, wanting to say so much more. Instead, he reached for a piece of paper. "I will be leaving soon for Boston. Here is a list of things you will need to attend to while I'm gone."

Hampton perused the list and nodded. "It appears completely manageable."

"Yes, well—" Joseph paused to consider his next words, "it will be if you remember moderation and refrain from allowing your temper to take over resolutions."

"I only lose my temper when incompetence costs me money."

Joseph didn't correct Hampton's reference to the money belonging to him. He knew that his son-in-law considered it only a matter of time until Oakbridge belonged to him in full. And while Joseph hadn't made up his mind that such a thing was going to happen, he knew that all indications pointed in that direction.

"Nevertheless, Hampton, I don't want interference where I have made changes. If you think something can be handled in a more efficient manner, then speak to me on it before I leave. However, I will brook no nonsense concerning the education of the slaves. I don't want to hear that you have disallowed Virginia to continue working with the slave children to teach them to read and write."

"It's a waste of time," Hampton protested, "but it's of no difference to me."

"Good. I'm still proposing to free them, and as the children come of age, they will need skills and education in order to make it in the world outside what they've always known."

"You'll be losing good assets."

"I can always offer to hire them back on," Joseph replied.

"It will eat up all of your profits," Hampton protested.

"Not if I lessen the responsibilities. I am still of a mind to parcel off the bulk of Oakbridge and leave myself with just the house and a small plot of land to work. Then I won't need slaves."

"I'm telling you, Joseph, that would be sheer madness. You can't hope to remain profitable doing business that way."

"Profits aren't everything, son." Joseph used the familiar term hoping to defuse Hampton's ire. He feared Hampton would only turn around and take it out on someone else if Joseph didn't find a way to smooth matters over. "Besides, we've other things to discuss. If the runaways turn up here, simply return them to their masters. Let them decide the punishment."

Hampton said nothing, but Joseph could see the disdain in his eyes. He hurried to move their conversation forward. "I have arranged for another private railcar to be built. I want to have one here at Oakbridge and another situated at the line's terminus on the Potomac. That way, anyone desiring to travel on the P&GF from Washington to Oakbridge, or in the opposite direction, will find it no more difficult than taking their place on board the car."

"I'm certain the cost of that must be outrageous," Hampton replied in a barely civil tone.

"Yes, well, I can afford it." Joseph eased back in his chair and smiled. "It won't be long now until I'll be able to bring Margaret home. I'm certain she will be anxious to be among family once again. She'll no doubt find Nate and the twins quite charming." Joseph referred to Hampton and Virginia's brood. Not quite five years earlier, Virginia had stunned the family by producing twin daughters. Levinia and Thora—Lightning and Thunder, as Virginia had explained the meanings of the names—had been born in June of 1844. Although terribly small, and frightfully early by the doctor's calculations, the twins had thrived to grow into two beautiful little girls. Joseph thought them precocious and a bit spoiled at times, but they had a way of charming their grandfather that usually made him overlook their behavior. The girls were as different as night and day in their personalities, but their appearance was identical.

"So when is the big day to be?" Hampton questioned, his voice clearly under strained control.

"I'm not sure. I would like to believe it would come by Christmas, but there's simply no way of telling. I could just remove her from the hospital on my own, but I'd like for them to give her every benefit. Up until recently, Margaret has said very little about returning to Oakbridge. It's another reason I've considered parceling Oakbridge off, or selling it outright. Margaret may not feel up to returning to this place and the difficult memories it holds for her. If that is the case, we may well take a home elsewhere."

"That certainly is no reason to sell," Hampton reasoned. "I could stay on and keep the place working in good order, while you go wherever you desire. I'm telling you, Joseph, selling now would be a mistake. Look at what's going on around you. They've struck gold in California, and manifest destiny rings true in the hearts of Americans. There are people leaving in droves to consider the opportunities in the West, and they will need food, clothing, and livestock, all of which you can produce here on this plantation."

"Someone else could just as easily provide those services. The new owner could simply pick up where I've left off. Believe me, Hampton, I wouldn't consider the matter lightly. It will come or not, only after intense discussions with York and the others. That's another reason I'll be gone for a longer period this time. I intend to spend time in Baltimore with Carolina and James, and then move on to Philadelphia to visit York and Lucy. I'll probably discuss this matter with each of them before going on to see Margaret in Boston."

Hampton's jaw clenched tight. Joseph could see a notable tick in his cheek and realized there would be no reasoning with the man at this point. "Well, there is much for me to see to before my departure. If you'll excuse me," Joseph said, getting to his feet. At the door he paused and added, "Hampton, stay off the third floor. If you need something from the attic or elsewhere, send someone else." His meaning was clearly understood if judged by the blaze of fury he saw rise up in his son-in-law's eyes.

Hampton sat seething, unable to move in his anger. How dare Joseph risk his security and future! It was bad enough that he had to play second fiddle to everything he did, but Hampton would be hanged before he'd allow Joseph to sell Oakbridge. As for his dalliance with the female slaves, well, Joseph had little say over it. The girls were terrified of him, and he knew they'd never risk admitting to his nocturnal visits. The only other person to have knowledge of his actions was Virginia, and he'd beat her senseless if she dared open her mouth.

It was at this inopportune moment that Virginia made the mistake of appearing to solicit Hampton's aid. She looked haggard and worn, and Hampton found her less and less appealing, but now with her face pinched in worry and her hair streaked with bits of gray, he found her positively repulsive.

"What do you want?"

His growling voice set her back a step. "I . . . well . . . I thought perhaps you should have a look at Nate."

"Have a look at him? What in the world are you talking about, woman?"

"Well, he slipped out of the nursery, and Miriam didn't find him until he managed to get outside and up into one of the trees. He fell before she could get him down, and I'm worried that maybe he's broken his arm."

"How in the world did this happen to my son?" Hampton demanded, springing to his feet in one fluid motion. Virginia cowered against the wall of books as he moved toward her for answers. "Well?"

"The girls were . . . ah . . . having an argument," Virginia began.

Her hesitancy and intimidation fueled Hampton's already infuriated temper. He moved to within inches of her. "You aren't making any sense. Where's Nate?"

"He's downstairs with Lydia. Miriam is trying to make some sort of order out of the nursery. It was just an accident, Hampton. The girls were fighting—tearing the place apart. Miriam went to quiet them, and Nate slipped out of the room."

"I'll have her hide for this. No darky slave is going to endanger my son's life."

"But, Hampton—"

Virginia started to protest but quieted when Hampton threw her a warning look. "And just where were you when all of this was happening? Hitting the bottle?" Virginia's expression left him to believe there might be truth to his accusation. Hampton eagerly picked up on her guilt and drove home his merciless point. "What kind of mother are you to let your child risk death while you console yourself with sherry?"

"It was an accident. I fell out of a tree when I was six. No one was drinking sherry when I slipped out of the nursery," Virginia said, finally seeming to stand up to him.

Hampton narrowed his eyes. "Where is that stupid woman?"

"Who?"

"Who do you suppose? Miriam. I want that slave brought to the whipping post, and I want her there now! Do you understand me? Find her, then send one of the stable boys for the doctor. I'm no physician to be judging the boy's arm, but if it's broken, I'll do more than beat that Negress. You hear me?"

Virginia nodded, eyes widened in fear. Hampton felt elation at the expression of horror on her face. "If Nathaniel's arm is broken, I'll break both of her arms as payment."

"Hampton, no!" Virginia exclaimed as he strode from the room. She hurried after him, her voice frantic. "Father will never allow it. Miriam was born and raised here—she's like family."

"She's a slave, nothing more—certainly not family," he sneered, then added, "unless your father sowed wild oats that we don't know about."

Virginia's mouth dropped open in stunned recognition of Hampton's implication. Hampton laughed loud and hard. "Oh please, Virginia, don't play the ingenue with me. Go find that idiot and have her brought to the post."

Eighteen

Revelations

Joseph sat across from his second daughter and admired the strength of character he found in her. Carolina, at twenty-nine, was a mature and lovely woman. She greatly resembled her mother, but there was also a hint of the strong Adams jaw and deep-set eyes. He still thought from time to time that Carolina should have been born a son. She was given to an interest in everything from the railroad to the construction of the new pier at Locust Point on Baltimore's harbor to world finance. On the other hand, she was graceful and feminine, fashionable and lovely, all while maintaining a household and children. It was this perhaps more than her dark eyes and hair that reminded Joseph of Margaret.

"You are staring at me as if I've smeared axle grease across my face," Carolina suddenly commented. "Is something wrong? Is your breakfast cold?"

"No," Joseph laughed. "Everything is fine. I was just thinking of how much you favor your mother."

Carolina smiled. "It won't be long, Papa. Soon you'll be able to bring Mother home and all will be as it was before."

He shook his head. "No, never that. And perhaps it is better that it not be that way. I'm praying it will be better. It's a new start for us."

Carolina nodded, then took a sip of her tea. She seemed thoughtful to Joseph, almost as if she had something of importance to speak to him about but was weighing the situation before doing so.

"How's James doing? Is that arm giving him any trouble?"

Carolina nodded. "The trouble comes in the form of not being able to use it. James is far too active to suffer a broken bone."

Joseph couldn't help but chuckle. "No doubt his activities are what brought him to this end in the first place."

"True enough, but he can barely abide his ordeal. But enough of us. I've told you everything about the children and James; why don't you tell me the news of home?"

Joseph felt the joy slip from his expression. "I wish I could report that all is in order there, but frankly, Carolina, it serves as another reason for my visit here."

Carolina put down her fork. "What's wrong, Papa? I can see in your face that something is not as it should be."

Joseph nodded. "You know what's happening in this country regarding the slavery issue?"

"Of course," she replied. "It would be difficult not to know."

"Well, York writes of the growing tensions in the North. Seems northern folk have trouble understanding the need to continue with slaves. They believe all slaves should be freed and rehired as paid laborers. I can't deny that I've considered such ideas as holding great merit. Not that I don't also note the loss of profit and comfort in knowing that my staff is permanent under one institution but perhaps unreliable under the other."

"Still," Carolina said, "what's the difference between hiring free men who live elsewhere and provide for their own needs for shelter, food, and clothing, and the slave for whom you are entirely responsible? Surely the money issue is very slight."

"Indeed, that, too, is a consideration. My problem, I suppose, is not with what is happening across the states, but rather with that which is under my own control."

"Hampton?"

Joseph nodded. "Something has happened; in fact, it nearly kept me from making this trip." He fell silent remembering the hideous details of Miriam's beating. He wouldn't tell Carolina of the horror of finding the young woman so severely beaten by Hampton that she could barely stand. Nor would he tell Carolina of Hampton's taking the lash in his own hand to administer her punishment until her back was reduced to strips of bleeding flesh. Such a thing was too horrible to hold in his own memory, much less burden another with.

Carolina seemed to sense his anguish. She reached across the breakfast table to touch her father's arm. "Tell me."

"Hampton had Miriam beaten. Well, that is to say, he beat her himself."

"Miriam? But why?" Carolina pulled away in angered frustration. "Miriam has been with the family since her birth. She's never caused a single bit of trouble. Why would he beat her?"

"Miriam is in charge of the nursery, and while the twins were spatting, Nate managed to sneak out. He ended up outside long enough to climb a tree and fall out before anyone could help him down."

"Is he all right?"

"Just bruised and scared, although we worried about whether his arm had sustained a break. The doctor looked it over, however, and found only a sprain. Hampton felt the responsibility to be totally Miriam's and punished the woman unmercifully."

"How unmercifully?" Carolina asked in fearful tone.

"Quite." Joseph saw the pained expression flash across his daughter's face. "She'll live, but she'll be scarred."

"How did this happen? Why was it allowed to happen?" Tears sprang to her eyes. "How could anyone be so cruel and heartless?"

"I'm as much to blame as anyone, although the matter was quite simply kept from me until the deed was already done. Hampton took matters into his own hands, as is often the case, and when he learned of Nate's accident, he took it out on Miriam. I confronted him afterward, and he admitted to losing his temper—even showed a bit of remorse. He swore he'd never do such a thing again. But that temper of his can't be trusted."

"Why don't you just take control away from him? Hire another overseer and leave Hampton to go back to being a commission merchant."

"I've considered that, but I once mentioned such a thing to Virginia and she seemed quite devastated at the thought of leaving. She is not a happy woman, and I believe she receives some solace from being at Oakbridge."

"Why is she so unhappy?"

"I believe she is not happy in her marriage. Hampton can be somewhat overbearing toward her and the children."

"Only overbearing? He would not harm them, would he?"

"No, of course not. Even Hampton must have limitations. I only hope that after this incident with Miriam he will mend his ways."

"But what if he doesn't? Oh, Papa, Miriam deserves so much better."

"Yes, I know that. I fear this might not be the end of it."

"What if you were to give her to me?" asked Carolina. "I love her dearly and she could come stay with us. She could help me with the children and move with us when we go west. After all, Mrs. Graves can't go along. As much as she'd like to, she doesn't wish to be so far from her own family, not to mention that moving to the wilds of Virginia would be most difficult for a woman of her age. Miriam would be the perfect answer, however. She wouldn't mind going west and—"

"Hold on there, child. What are you talking about? Are you planning a move?"

Carolina flushed slightly. "I'm sorry, Papa. I planned to tell you this morning, only your news came first and took my mind from it." She beamed him a smile, then added, "James is being posted to Greigsville, Virginia, to act as liaison between the B&O and the contractors responsible for the new tunnel being built nearby. It's one of the many sections being contracted out in hopes of finally connecting the railroad to the Ohio River. We've discussed the matter, and the children and I are going to move with him."

"Is that wise? That's very rough country, as I have heard. Hardly anything there—certainly nothing in the way of a big city and the comforts it might afford."

"But none of that matters," Carolina replied and looked away as if trying to decide how to explain. "When the landslide threatened James' life, I realized I couldn't be separated from him like that again. He was often gone for weeks, even months at a time, and the loneliness—" She paused and smiled again at her father, only this smile was more sympathetic than anything. "I know you understand the loneliness of having your mate far away. I don't know how you've endured these last few years."

Joseph felt warmed by his daughter's sudden understanding of his loss. How had he endured? It was only by busying himself elsewhere and concentrating on God's promises that he could find the will to go on. Then, too, was the fervent hope that Margaret would get better. "Separations between soul mates can never be easily handled."

"No indeed," Carolina agreed. "Which is why it doesn't matter whether there is a single store or church or school. Nothing matters as much as us being a real family. By living in Greigsville, James will come home to me every night, or at least most every night, and the children won't have to wait weeks on end for their father to spend time with them."

"You won't find it easy," Joseph told her.

"No, I don't imagine I will. But I am realistic about it. I'm not fooling myself into believing that just because we are together, there will never be any hard times. I know that hard times come to everyone, but I think overall the change will be good for us."

"What did James say about this decision of yours?"

Carolina grinned at her father. "What makes you so sure this was my decision?"

"I know you. You set your mind to a thing, then God have mercy on anyone who gets in your way. It wouldn't matter if James had been dead set against it—you would have found a way to convince him otherwise."

"You know me very well. Maybe too well."

"Can a father ever know his child too well? I hardly think so." He returned her smile. "I'm glad for your ability to set your mind to a thing. Just never forget to consult God before mapping out a plan."

"Is that what you are doing now regarding Hampton and Oakbridge?" she asked quite seriously.

He nodded. "Yes, I am. I've been in constant prayer over this entire matter. Hampton—slavery—Margaret—Oakbridge. I've never wanted to be a plantation owner. You know that as well as you know anything else about me." Carolina nodded and he continued. "But I always saw my duty to my family, and to those who'd gone before me to create such a dream and ambition, as a sacred trust. A trust that I should never take lightly or discard because of disinterest or difficulty. But now I'm not so sure. Now the dreams and ambitions of generations past seem very unimportant in the wake of the future. Slavery is dividing this country, and with good reason. More and more, I'm convinced that it's a way of life that will not exist much longer.

"The plantation itself has never meant anything more to me than a burden and a way to keep my promises. It kept me from living my life in my way, but it also provided blessings for my family, in spite of my disappointments."

"Perhaps the time has come to rid yourself of the burden," Carolina remarked quietly. "I suppose that's how I see my move to Greigsville. Not only do I get to have my husband with me more, but I also get to be closer to the dream of working in some capacity with the railroad. Oh, I know I'll not be out there on the line, but I'll be near enough to observe, and James will be there to tell me what's happening and how the line is coming along. Ben Latrobe will still, no doubt, come to visit and to work with James, and so we will continue to hear news regarding the rest of the line. Perhaps, just as I'm setting aside a lifetime of familiarity and comfort, you should set aside Oakbridge and the responsibilities of ownership."

"But to whom would I sell the estate?"

"Why not approach York? He is, after all, the rightful heir. He has been unhappy and restless in Philadelphia since losing the election. His work administering his father-in-law's business affairs is hardly challenging for him. Perhaps if you told him you longed to be free from the burden, he would leave Philadelphia and take his place at Oakbridge."

"But the last thing I want is to cast onto my children the same burden which was put upon me," Joseph answered quite sternly. "I know what it is to feel the desperation. To have no choice in the matter. To see the road clearly set for you rather than being allowed to choose for yourself. I can't do that to my own child."

"But rather than sell to strangers, York should at least have the opportunity to refuse or accept it," protested Carolina.

"Granted. I can see the fairness in that much."

"He doesn't have to accept responsibility of Oakbridge, and you can make it quite clear that you don't care either way. But rather than go down the line offering it first to one child and then the next, I would leave off with York. If York doesn't want to assume the duties, then sell it outright to someone else. Don't open yourself up for arguments and complications, and don't leave it to the point of Hampton Cabot taking control."

Joseph nodded. "I've considered the problem of that very thing. Maine will certainly have no interest, and I know that Georgia is quite content with her horse farm. She has no need for a plantation the size of Oakbridge. You have made it clear that Oakbridge is unnecessary to your happiness, and after York, that only leaves Hampton and Virginia."

"Exactly. We all know that Hampton would love nothing more than to usurp your authority. He's wanted control of Oakbridge ever since first coming to the house to announce the impending banking disaster of 1837. He saw a way to get what he wanted through marriage to one of your daughters. It didn't much matter which daughter, so long as he became a valid part of the family. Now we can see where that has led."

"True enough," Joseph said.

"Just don't make any rash decisions," Carolina pleaded. "Talk to York, even if you don't ask him to take over at Oakbridge. Talk to him and ask him what he would do in your position. Perhaps he will volunteer his services. I wouldn't be surprised if he's actually had enough of politics and northern ways, and he's ready to come home."

"Even so, there is still the matter of Virginia and the children," Joseph replied.

Carolina nodded. "But Virginia made her choice. You can't be responsible for that. After all, she didn't seek your counsel before running off to elope with the man."

"Sadly enough," Joseph commented and took a long drink of coffee. "I probably would have eagerly given consent had she approached me on the matter. After all, I was ready to push you into his care."

"Well, we simply did not know his true character. Perhaps we still don't. I would say there is probably a great deal about Hampton Cabot we don't understand. I realize that Virginia's happiness, and that of the children, is uppermost in your mind. Why not speak with Virginia about it? Maybe she would willingly stay behind with the children."

"And break apart her marriage? Should I play a part in such a circumstance?" Joseph threw his napkin down and shook his head. "And herein lies my dichotomy. If I stay and allow Hampton a hand at overseeing Oakbridge, he might well continue to use brute force in order to get what he wants. If I hand Oakbridge over to York, then Hampton and Virginia will need to find another home—and Hampton another job. I can't think of anything that would irritate the man more. And if I sell or even divide the land, I still require that Hampton take the initiative to care for his family somewhere other than Oakbridge."

"Poor Papa," Carolina said, coming to stand beside him. She hugged him close, and Joseph knew her sympathy was genuine.

"I know that God will guide us through this, but it has become such a difficult matter. However, I do like your idea of sending Miriam to your care. I will happily give her to you, if that is her wish, and you may do as you like from there. Keep her, free her—it will be entirely up to you."

"First we will care for her. She'll have a long recovery, no doubt."

Joseph pushed his chair back and got to his feet. "Please don't worry overmuch about this, daughter. I know things seem quite bleak, but God will provide the answer."

Carolina smiled. "I know He will, but I also know what it is to wait and wait for an answer and feel that it might never come." Carolina drew her father along to the front parlor. "I still believe some sort of bargain might be struck with York. Perhaps he and Lucy would even sell a parcel of land to Hampton in order to do right by him."

"Could be. Could be. But enough of such matters. I wanted to share with you the success I'm having with the P&GF Railroad."

"Oh, do tell."

They took a seat together on the sofa before Joseph continued. "I've contracted for another private car to be made. That way I can leave one at Oakbridge and one at the Potomac terminus. Then whenever you get a chance to venture back from that wilderness you will soon call home, there will be a car ready and waiting for your use."

"Oh, Papa, that sounds wonderful."

"Hampton didn't think so. Thought it a terrible waste of time and money."

"No doubt. But Hampton doesn't share our dream." Carolina's eyes were alight with love for her father and excitement at this news.

"When do you think we might acquire a real steam engine?"

"I would like it to be soon, but we both know that the line is hardly profitable as it is. The real money needs to be invested in completing our line to Falls Church. The horse-drawn cars are good enough for now. At least it should prove a great deal more profitable to transport crops to the Potomac come harvest."

"I'm certain that will be true. You know, Papa, there is the money Blake left me. I still have a great deal of it and—"

"No. You save that for your daughter and for the future of your family. You may well need it more than the P&GF needs a steam engine or a completed line." He saw her frown of disappointment. "Now, now. Don't take on so. Things will work out in proper timing. You'll see."

"I know you're right, but I'm impatient."

"Once you're nestled in the Virginia wilderness, you'll have few concerns about the P&GF. You would do well to have your husband go ahead of you and design a list of everything you'll need. That, in and of itself, will require a good investment of money."

"He already plans to do just that," Carolina admitted.

"Good. The future may seem a bit sluggish in its arrival, but it will come together in God's timing. Your mother's return home, your move, Oakbridge—all will be resolved and cared for."

Carolina leaned over and kissed her father. "We simply need to have faith."

He smiled. "Yes. Faith is the key."

Nineteen

Shaping the Future

In September of 1849, after two weeks of mishaps and conflicts en route, the Baldwin family finally managed to navigate the distance between Baltimore and Greigsville. They had traveled by train to Cumberland and found this stopping place the real point of origin for their adventurous journey west. Without the luxury of a train, the family was forced to travel either by stage or wagon, and since they had brought possessions enough to start their new housekeeping, wagons seemed the best choice. At least for James to accompany their supplies. James, however, didn't feel that a freight wagon was exactly appropriate for his young wife and children.

"We will be better off together than separated," Carolina had insisted. "I assure you that none of us will perish simply for want of better traveling conditions."

So it was that after their arrival in Cumberland, and Carolina's arguing to have her own way, James went in search of a freighter service.

Staying at the same hotel in which she and James had stayed on their wedding trip, Carolina found herself more than a little aware of her surroundings. Cumberland, for all its growth in the past seven years, was still painfully small compared to Baltimore. With some six thousand residents, the town could boast new hotels, mills, shops, and a growing coal industry that caused folks in Baltimore to sit up and take notice. But because Cumberland had set its sights on the Chesapeake and Ohio Canal providing them transport and connection to the rest of the world, the city fathers had paid very little attention to the potential of the railroad. But that was now starting to change.

Still, Carolina began to wonder exactly what she had imposed upon her family. Cumberland would be nearly one hundred miles away from their new home, and Fairmont, Virginia, the next largest town, would be some forty miles away. And even though both towns were small compared to Baltimore, Carolina knew they would be her only link to immediate comfort. What if something happened and they needed help that could not be had in Greigsville? Carolina tried not to worry herself overmuch. Time alone would tell of their circumstances. She had to maintain faith and trust that God would watch over them. She had to trust that this was the right thing to do. When James returned with the good news that a local freighter would transport not only their goods but the family, as well, Carolina put aside her worries and tried to concentrate on the work at hand.

The trip had played itself out in coordinated comfort, at least for the most part. The children, with exception to Victoria, thought it novel to sleep outdoors in a tent. Carolina had tried not to feel panicked as they went farther and farther away from civilization and the comforts she had always known. She worked instead to focus on the fact that they were starting a new adventure together. She and James wouldn't have to be separated, and the B&O Railroad would spring to life practically outside her front door. At least that was what she told herself on the trip to Greigsville.

But now as they stood before the clapboard house that was to become their home, an overwhelming sense of disappointment descended. She began seriously to question her own judgment in having made this decision. It had seemed the perfect solution to their situation, but when faced with the reality of the adjustments she would have to make, Carolina wondered if she was truly up to the challenge.

As the freighters went to work unloading the wagons, Carolina moved closer to the building to consider her home.

"Well, I told you it wasn't much," James said in an apologetic tone. "I did what I could, however, and as you can see for yourself, this is the best Greigsville has to offer."

Carolina nodded, trying not to show her dismay. The house wasn't even painted. It had merely been slapped together in what appeared to be someone's attempt at house building. The two-story structure seemed foreboding, if not downright frightening, but Carolina knew James had done his very best. And there was always the possibility of building something else. After all, money wasn't a problem. Surely they could contract some workers to assist them. Of course, supplies would be an issue. Until a rail line was in place, it would be difficult to transport finished lumber and other building materials. Maybe someone could set up a lumber mill. Carolina pondered that as she struggled to keep from focusing on the abomination in front of them.

"We can fix it up," Miriam offered. "Wert never a house built but what a little care din't fix it jes right."

Carolina nodded. "I'm sure that's true."

The children were clamoring to be let down from the wagon, and already Brenton was over the side and running up the dirt walkway. Jordana was attempting to follow her brother's example when James caught her by the back of her pinafore and held her momentarily suspended in midair.

"And just where do you think you're going?" he asked.

"Wanna play," Jordana told him in no uncertain terms.

"You have to mind your step here," James told her and hoisted her into his arms. "Remember what Papa told you about snakes?"

"Don't play with snakes," Jordana said in a serious tone edged with anticipation.

James smiled. "That's right. Somehow I think they'd come out on the losing end if you made such an attempt." He put her down on the ground, then turned to help Victoria from the wagon. "And now for you, my dear."

"We can't stay here, Papa!" Victoria protested.

Carolina turned at the sound of her daughter's voice. She could tell after a lifetime of problem solving and heartaches that Victoria was desperately close to tears. Of the children, Victoria had been least supportive of the move west. Carolina prayed that God would comfort her eldest daughter, because if Victoria started to cry, there was just no telling whether or not Carolina could restrain her own tears.

"Now, now, Victoria," James told her as he gently lifted her from the wagon. "We'll just have to set things right and then it will be a splendid home."

Carolina caught his expression over Victoria's head. It was a pleading look, begging for her to confirm what he'd just told their child. "Your father is right, Victoria. We'll have to work hard together, but no doubt we can make it look just fine."

"I didn't want to come here anyway. There's nothing but trees and mountains, and I think this is a horrible place. I want to go back to Baltimore and live with Mrs. Graves." She stomped her foot to make certain everyone knew exactly how unhappy she was.

"Victoria, I can't change what has happened," James offered. "Your mother and I discussed this with you more than once. This will allow us to remain together. If I had to live here without you, I'd seldom have a chance to see you."

"But there isn't even a real store," Victoria said, tears welling in her eyes. "I'll bet there are no other young people, and I'll die of boredom."

"I don't believe boredom will be an immediate problem," Carolina said with a weak smile. "There's going to be far too much work, and I'm going to need your help. Here it is already September, and we have to make ready for winter. Not only do we have to find a way to make this home fit before the first snows, but we have to make certain that we have enough supplies laid in just in case the supply freighters have trouble making it through."

"We'll probably die out here, and nobody will even know it," Victoria complained and folded her arms against her chest.

Brenton had already made his way into the house and was returning with his report. "There's a hole in the wall and a raccoon tried to get in, but I chased him out."

"There probably be all manner of critters inside," Miriam said, laughing. "I best see what I can do."

"I'll help you," Brenton offered.

Miriam cast Carolina a sly smile, and Carolina was amazed at how good-humored the woman could be. After her long ordeal of recovering from Hampton's beating, Carolina could only stand in amazement at Miriam's attitude. She was cheerful and loving, just as she always had been. Carolina had asked her one day about it, and Miriam had assured her that she didn't hold Hampton a grudge but rather prayed daily for the man. She told Carolina that praying for a person's enemies accomplished a whole heap more than spending your time trying to get revenge. Besides, what could a mere slave do to avenge herself?

"Well, the work won't do itself," Carolina announced, determined to put forth her best effort. "James, what should we do first?"

"I'd suggest we get a good meal going. These men are going to be ready for something hot and nourishing after we unload all of this," he answered, waving a hand over to the two wagons.

Just then two redheaded men came lumbering up alongside the first wagon. They'd come from the direction of the small tent city that housed the Irish laborers. These men had been contracted to work on the Kingwood Tunnel, and James had already warned Carolina of their rowdy ways.

"Mornin' to ya," the elder and taller of the two said and tipped his hat in Carolina's direction.

She nodded, noting that his large hooked nose appeared to have suffered more than one break in its time. His wild red hair was a coppery color, and together with his emerald green eyes, Carolina had little doubt the man was Irish.

"Good day to you, gentlemen," James answered for his family.

"I'm Red O'Connor and this mite is me brother, Kiernan."

The "mite," as Red had referred to Kiernan, stood a good head taller than Carolina but did indeed seem rather dwarfed by his larger, beefy brother. Kiernan's hair was not quite so red. Carolina thought it a more pleasant shade of auburn, and it wasn't as unmanageable and unruly as Red's hair. It lay straighter and more orderly beneath a billed seaman's cap, which Kiernan properly doffed in greeting the Baldwin family.

"I'm James Baldwin," Carolina heard her husband introduce himself. "This is my wife, Carolina. This is our daughter Victoria." He glanced around to find the others. "I've a son and another daughter about the grounds somewhere, but no doubt they are too busy to concern themselves with our neighbors."

Red laughed, and Carolina could see that he was missing several teeth. It rather confirmed her first thoughts that this was a brawling man. She turned to say something to Victoria and found the girl staring in wide-eyed wonder at the younger Kiernan.

"We're very pleased to make your acquaintance," Carolina said, continuing to watch her daughter. She glanced across to find Kiernan smiling at Victoria, and suddenly she felt the urge to hide her child away. Frowning, she slipped an arm around Victoria's shoulders and hoped the protectiveness of her action was evident.

"Would ya be a part of the railroad men a-comin' to see this tunnel through?" Red asked, ignoring Carolina's frown.

"Yes," James replied. "I work for the Baltimore and Ohio. I will be the railroad's eyes and ears on the Kingwood Tunnel project."

"Will ya, now," Red more commented than questioned. "We're workin' on that very same tunnel."

Carolina was fascinated by his heavy brogue. It was almost lyrical. "Do you live in the tent city?" she asked, almost hoping it would open a lengthy reply just in order to hear the man talk.

"That we do."

"Well, this is to be our new home," James said, moving his gaze back to the clapboard house. "It needs some work, but I'm sure we'll make the best of it."

"We might be able to lend you a hand," Kiernan said without awaiting his brother's approval. "Leastwise, I might."

"Ever the do-gooder," Red said with a smile. "But he's right. We might be able to lend ya a hand o' welcome."

"I'm uncertain at this point what we need to do first," James replied. "I'm afraid constructing houses isn't on my list of experiences."

"Shouldn't be hard to fix this place up. Looks to be somebody pounded together a few nails and boards in short order without much consideration to the finished product." He glanced up at the house, then beyond to the sky. "First things first. I'd suggest we get your gear stashed inside," Red said, pointing to the wagons. "It'll come a rain in a little while."

James looked heavenward. "Do you think so?"

"Ofttimes that's the case. These afternoons have been fairly wet ones."

"I trust your opinion," James replied, then turned to Carolina. "I'll help unload these wagons. You wait inside and direct the men as to where to put things."

Carolina nodded and released Victoria. "You go round up your little sister and keep her out of harm's way."

Victoria nodded and walked away, glancing not once, but twice, over her shoulder at Kiernan O'Connor. Carolina looked up to find Kiernan's green eyes fairly twinkling from the added attention. Judging by his face, he looked no more than fifteen or sixteen, but his physique was more that of a man than a boy, and Carolina wouldn't have him dallying with her young daughter.

"We'll give ya a hand," Red said, then punched Kiernan to draw his attention. "Come on, ya useless thing."

Carolina found it impossible to do anything but adhere to James' directions. She went up the path, hesitant to survey her new home. What if the inside was worse than the outside? She stepped across the threshold and grimaced. There was no flooring in place. Someone had literally put up the building and left off at the floor. The dirt had been packed down hard and someone had thoughtfully put a tent tarp down in the first room, but it was evident that this would only serve as a temporary solution.

She lifted her chin ever so slightly and determined within herself to be strong. This meant the world to James, and to her. She had, after all, been the one to suggest the move. To back out now was unthinkable. Just then Miriam appeared, and it was as if she could read her mistress's mind.

"There, there, Miz Carolina," she said, coming to pat Carolina's arm. "We's gwanna have a good home here."

"I pray you are right, Miriam," Carolina replied. She looked around and shuddered. "What did you find upstairs?"

"Jes four rooms," Miriam answered. "Downstairs, there be another two with a lil' cranny in back that can suit jes fine to be my room."

"Well, I suppose that's a good start. I presume one of those rooms is a kitchen?"

"It will be," Miriam said with a grin. "Gots no stove jes yet, but I'm a-reckonin' that when that gets here, it'll make a fine kitchen."

"Oh dear," Carolina said, feeling despair wash over her. "Can you cook over an open hearth, Miriam?"

"I ain't never done it, but I suppose it can't be too hard."

Carolina shook her head, realizing anew what a pampered life she had lived. "Can you put something together for lunch? The men are going to unload the wagons, and then they'll probably be ready for some sort of meal."

"I's gwanna have it all ready. Jes you trust Miriam to see to it."

Carolina smiled as the woman took herself off to find the necessary supplies. She looked around and sighed. Six rooms total, and only two for living space on the ground floor, she thought. Still, the front room was plenty big and they could always build on a room or two in the future. She tried to bolster her courage.

"Where do you want this?" one of the freighters asked as he entered the room with a large trunk on his shoulder.

"Upstairs," she murmured. "I'm not sure which room, so you'd better let me lead the way." Carolina hurried to precede the man. She glanced in each of the four small rooms and picked the one on the front side of the house that appeared to be slightly larger than the others.

"This one," she motioned to the man. The trunk was full of serviceable clothing that belonged to her and James. This room would serve as their bedroom, while the room across the hall would be perfect for Jordana and Brenton. Perhaps she'd find Victoria and give her a choice of the other two rooms.

She didn't have far to search. Victoria was leading the way up the stairs with a most insistent Jordana tailing behind. "She wanted to see the house," Victoria said with a shrug.

"It's just as well," Carolina replied. "I've chosen these two rooms for your father and me, and Brenton and Jordana. I thought you might like to take a look at the other two and decide which one suits you."

Victoria nodded and went to peer inside each of the rooms. Carolina could see by the frown on her face that she wasn't overly impressed with either one. "I suppose this one," Victoria finally said, picking the room on the front side of the house. "At least I can see what's going on from here."

Carolina ignored Jordana's animated exploration and went to hug Victoria. "It will be all right," she told her daughter. "You'll see. Together we can make this a wonderful home."

"But there's not even paint on the walls," Victoria said, shaking her head. "And the floor downstairs is dirt."

"I know," Carolina replied. "And there's no stove in the kitchen, and only two rooms downstairs. And I haven't even a single clue as to what we'll find in the way of a necessary, but we could always dig out the chamber pots."

"I hate this place," Victoria said, her voice filled with disgust.

"I know. It's not the best of places, but your papa did what he could. We mustn't let him see us unhappy; otherwise, he'll feel as though he's failed us."

Victoria nodded. "I won't complain," she assured her mother, and Carolina smiled.

"You're a good girl, Victoria."

"Me good girl. Me good girl," Jordana chanted, dancing circles around her mother and sister.

Carolina laughed. "Yes, indeed. Now, I need to go direct the men. You two stay out of trouble and out of the way."

She took herself back downstairs, her heart a little lighter. I need to heed my own medicine, she thought. I need to focus on the fact that we have a roof over our heads instead of a tent, and that we have the means to improve our lot. Those thoughts did much to improve her attitude.

The men made short order of the work, and it wasn't fifteen minutes after the last of the load had been brought into the house that the rain came just as Red had predicted. Carolina was grateful to have her things protected but couldn't help despairing at Miriam's trials in fixing a meal with rain leaking into the chimney. She offered what help she could—which wasn't much—as the men stood around discussing how to temporarily fix the leak.

James had directed the dining table to be positioned near the center of the kitchen, and it was here that Miriam happily plopped down the steaming caldron of stew when it was finished cooking.

Miriam shook her head. "Don' hardly seem right that our trials should come one atop the other." She glanced at another leak in the roof, then frowned. "We gwanna have ta get sumptin' to cover up this floor, else we be walkin' in mud."

Carolina managed a laugh. "I don't imagine it's going to much matter for the time. However, I plan to speak to James straightaway and see about getting a plank floor put down. Is the stew ready?"

"Ready as it's gwanna get. Them taters could be a mite hard, but most ever' thing else was canned first."

"I'm sure we'll all be grateful for it. I'll let the men know." She left Miriam to fuss around looking for bowls and silverware, and approached the men. "Miriam has managed to put together some stew," she announced. "She tells me the potatoes may well be a bit underdone, but I assured her that given the circumstance we will all be happy for what we receive."

"Folks in Ireland would be mighty happy for a potato, cooked or raw," Red said with a hint of sadness in his tone.

"Did you go through the potato famine?" Carolina asked the big man.

"Aye, that we did. Folks there are still goin' through it. Crops ain't been worth eatin' for years."

"Potatoes turned black almost as soon as you dig 'em up," Kiernan said. "It seemed a cruel joke. At first you'd dig a hill and think you had a fine-lookin' crop. Next thing you know, they were black and moldering."

"How awful," Carolina commented.

"Tain't the half of it," Red said. "Folks half starved, half crazy from want of food. People hurtin' each other over crumbs. Parents a-watchin' children die. Everybody seekin' out even the tiniest morsel of food."

"They were even eatin' the grass," said Kiernan.

"The grass?" Victoria questioned. "How could people eat grass?"

"When your stomach is empty and there's little chance of anything else comin' along, grass seems mighty reasonable," Kiernan said soberly.

"But I thought the worst was past," Carolina remarked.

"The famine just gave the landlords reason to come in an' strip away the land from the workin' folk. Sheep now graze where crops once grew, and farmland is scarce in some regions. Many a family was just left out of work and home and given over to die."

"How terrible!" exclaimed Victoria.

Carolina saw the way his words affected Victoria and thought to change the subject. "We will be extra grateful for our fare, indeed, given the stories you've shared with us this day."

"Absolutely," James replied and nodded. "We have been blessed to make our way through the wilderness, and now we have been blessed to make new friends. We share a future," he told them. "A future that will require each of us to work together just as we worked together this day. May we always remember that many hands together make the load lighter, and that even small blessings are still blessings that shouldn't be overlooked."

Red grinned. "You're quite the speechmaker, now, aren't ya?"

James laughed. "From time to time I'm inspired. But right now I'm mostly hungry."

"Aye," Red replied. "I could go for some of that stew meself."

Carolina watched them exchange glances. She was torn in many ways regarding their new friends. Red seemed oppressive and demanding, while Kiernan was quiet and restrained. She wondered what the future might hold in store for the group, especially given her daughter's intent interest in the young Irishman. Only time will tell, she thought and followed the group to the kitchen.

Twenty

The Connaughtmen

Sitting outside the opening of their tent, Kiernan O'Connor watched his older brother with guarded interest as Red slipped out and lumbered down the path to a gathering some five or six tents down the way. For days he'd watched the man come and go at all hours of the night. Always there seemed to be some secret meeting somewhere, and always it involved the work force on the Kingwood Tunnel.

They'd hardly been in America for more than two days when Red had hooked them up with canal work on the Chesapeake and Ohio. Red had assured his brother that while canal work was mostly digging and mucking out, it was better than the alternative of having no money at all. Kiernan wasn't that sure he was right, but having been only fourteen at the time, he respected his older brother's direction and put his heart and soul into his work.

Railroad work seemed to come along as a natural alternative to canal work, and once again Kiernan followed his older brother's lead. Then the trouble started. First one skirmish and then another. Someone would say something against the Connaughtmen, from the Connaught region of Ireland, of which Red and Kiernan were proudly a part. The next thing Kiernan knew, that person ended up either badly beaten or just plain dead. Of course, that required a balanced response from the other side, which more often than not consisted of the Irish Corkians from County Cork.

Kiernan had grown up with county brawls and rivalries all of his life, but it seemed that these things were escalated when the Irishmen came to America. Desperation made the Irish turn against each other, and if you weren't aligned with your own people, from your own county or region, you were often made to suffer unbearable punishment. Kiernan thought it a pity that Irishmen should fight against one another when so many Americans were happy to fight them all and even instigate fights among the immigrants. It seemed the Irish were considered the lowest form of scum to ever wade ashore, and with exception to positions of hard labor that few others wanted, the Irish were seldom welcomed in American society. But their willingness to do the dirty work of the upper class was challenged by other immigrants like the Germans and Swedes and even free blacks.

It was clearly understood that if the men fought and killed or ran off one side or the other, then that many fewer men would draw pay for the week.

Kiernan tried not to think of Red being one of those among his own people who were sowing seeds of strife. It was well known that Red had a temper, but Kiernan liked to give him the benefit of the doubt. He wanted his brother to settle down, maybe even take a wife. Anything would be better than seeing him in the center of bitter hatred and turmoil.

Pushing those thoughts aside, Kiernan tried instead to focus on the month-old newspaper in his hands, wishing for the millionth time that he could read. He made out letters and symbols, thinking he just might have a grasp of what the various advertisements were about, but there was no real way of knowing. Red didn't read; in fact, he thought it foolishness to desire such a thing. Reading wouldn't turn a shovel or pick its way through rock, and therefore it couldn't possibly be important to them.

But Kiernan felt otherwise. He longed to know what the words and letters on the page meant and often imagined himself passing the evening reading one book or another. Not that he felt like doing much else after twelve- and fifteen-hour days at the tunnel site. He didn't mind hard work. He'd never known anything else. His home back in Ireland had lent him nothing but work from the time he was able to walk and talk.

Tossing the paper aside, Kiernan stared into the fading light of the evening skies. The clouds hung heavy and blanketed the valley with growing swirls of fog. It suited his brooding. And as he sometimes did when in such a mood, he wondered why things had gone as they had. The famine in Ireland had come upon them without much warning. Oh, to be sure, there had been bad crops in the past. His granddaddy had told him of times when the potatoes had failed, leaving them to wonder how they'd ever see the winter through. But this had been different. The crops had failed and then continued to fail, until year after year had passed by and no hope was left to any of the folk remaining.

Kiernan had watched his mother suffer as she saw her children go hungry night after night. She had prayed and cried and wailed to God. When their da had died, leaving her a widow, Kiernan had felt sure there would be a funeral wake to rival all others, but instead, his mother had given up on life and died, as well. That left Red in charge of the family, and his answer to all of their troubles was America.

But there were five younger siblings to worry over and the three youngest were girls. Kiernan felt it was wrong to leave them behind, but Red had little difficulty putting them off on their two married sisters, both of whom had scarcely been wed a year. They took their responsibility seriously and accepted Red's edict with few objections. Even their husbands had respected Red's wishes and his promise that he would send for each one as the money came through. But now after two years, Kiernan feared the time would never come when he'd see his brothers and sisters again. Always when the money was saved up, Red would throw it into some harebrained scheme. Mostly he'd drink it away, and for that, Kiernan truly resented him. Kiernan had often thought of deserting his brother in order to return to Ireland, but he knew it was an impossible dream. He had neither the money to go to them nor to bring them here to America. Red thought Kiernan crazy for wanting to return to Ireland when America had so much to offer.

But Red couldn't go back to Ireland. Not after what had happened. Even thinking of that cold dark night caused the hair on Kiernan's neck to bristle. It was before Red had truly made up his mind to go to America. Red had hoped to convince their landlord to give them just one more year of tenancy. But the man was hardhearted and couldn't care less that Kiernan and Red were now responsible for five children. He demanded Red empty the small hut and burn it to the ground on his way out the door. Other plans had been made for the property.

Red had once been a reasonable man, if not exactly peaceable. But he had started to change even before the problem with the landlord. It had begun with the death of his new wife and infant son in the beginning of the famine. The bitterness and rage began to seethe within him. And it wasn't helped by the death of their parents and so many friends.

Thus it was no real surprise when Red flew into an instant rage at the landlord, who was Red's elder by at least two-score years and no match for the brawny younger man. Red had pummeled the man, all the while demanding he reconsider his position. As his blood spilled out, the landlord firmly held his ground, promising he'd see Red sent to prison for his actions. But within moments the landlord's threats were silenced forever. Red had killed him, and as surely as the sun would rise in the morning, the law would hunt him down and see justice served.

Kiernan shuddered and looked up once again to the hillside and then the stars. America was a good land, a rich and bountiful land, and while he was glad to be a part of it, Kiernan longed for the arguments and fighting to be put behind them. Red said it was important to keep lesser men in their places, but Kiernan thought it was more because of his brother's hunger for control. Red led the Connaughtmen with a severity that sometimes frightened his younger brother. He spoke in hushed tones among tight circles of men about the need to unite in their causes. Connaughtmen should stand with their kind and see to it that no one broke the circle. Their enemy was any man who wasn't a Connaughtman, and there were plenty of those. Ulstermen from the northern reaches of Ireland, Corkmen from the south, even Longfords from the same Irish midlands as the Connaughts—all were to be considered enemies, right along with the Americans themselves.

Kiernan thought of the Baldwin family. He liked their open friendliness and the kindness they'd extended him and his brother after they'd helped to unpack their wagons. He especially liked the young daughter Victoria. She looked at him as though he might be someone important, and that made him feel like someone important. He knew she was only a child—her mother made that more than clear—but still he found himself drawn to her dark doe eyes and brown-black hair. She was unlike anyone he'd ever known, and in spite of the fact that she was young, Kiernan knew that time would remedy that problem. What might not be so easily remedied was the differences in their cultures and backgrounds. Kiernan was a poor Irishman with little hope for his future and a fierce loyalty to a family left behind in Ireland. Victoria Baldwin was obviously well on her way to becoming an elegant young woman. She was the very type of girl he would have been forbidden to associate with in Ireland.

And despite their kindness, Kiernan had no doubt James and Carolina Baldwin would hold the same prejudice against him where their precious daughter was concerned. He was nothing but a poor railroad Mick, and there was little hope for a decent future in that. Sighing again, Kiernan hadn't heard Red sneak up on him. It wasn't until his brother gave him a playful fist to the arm that Kiernan realized he'd passed a great deal of time in daydreaming.

"And what are ya doin' out here lookin' all calf-eyed?" Red asked him, stomping mud from his boots. "I suppose ya might be a-pinin' for that little lassie down the way. A bit young, don't ya think?" he asked and pulled out a pipe and pouch of tobacco.

"She'll grow," Kiernan answered carelessly.

"Ah, and so it was the lassie," Red said with a devilish laugh. "Ya might as well try to catch a fairy in the woods. Or had ya forgotten where ya'd be a-comin' from?"

"I know full well where I'm comin' from," Kiernan replied in complete irritation. "Seems yar all-fired stirrin' of conflicts and troubles won't let me forget."

Red took a stool beside his brother and began packing tobacco into the bowl of his pipe. "And well ya shouldn't be forgettin'. This might well be America, but we're just Micks to break the rock and do their dirty work. No gentleman is goin' to let the likes of ya touch his daughter, and of that ya can be sure."

Kiernan eyed him suspiciously and sought to change the subject. "So what troubles have ya been stirrin' tonight?"

Red chuckled. "Troubles a-plenty for the supervisors and railroad men. It won't be long now until we strike and put them all in their places."

"Why a strike?" asked Kiernan. "Why is it always a strike? We scarce get settled into a job than ya have the men to arms over money."

"It's just smart business, me brother. They can afford it, and we can use it. It's just that simple."

"I still think it would be smarter to work hard and earn a decent name for ourselves."

"Nobody cares if a Mick works his fingers to the bone. They'd still flip him half the wages they pay anyone else and kick him when he bent over to pick it up."

"So ya plan to strike? When?"

"Now, mebbe we'll be a-strikin' and mebbe we won't. There's other business at hand."

Kiernan watched him lean over to light his pipe from the lantern. He appeared so casual and nonchalant, yet his words spoke of real trouble and hardships to come. Kiernan couldn't refrain from asking, "What other business?"

Red straightened, sucked hard on the pipe, and blew out a puff of blue smoke. "Well, ya might say there needs to be a bit o' housecleaning."

Kiernan tensed. "Ya mean get rid of the Corkmen and Fardowns, don't ya?"

"Well, now yar startin' to think like a true Connaughtman."

"I didn't say I approved."

"Well, ya should," Red said, glaring at Kiernan as though he'd dared to speak out against a sacred trust. "They come in here and put up their shacks and rival us for jobs. They know better, yet they still come."

"But I suppose ya will be seein' to their ignorance and helpin' them along their way," Kiernan stated in disgust. "Why can't we just settle down and put our minds to earnin' enough money to bring our kin to America?"

"In time, lad. In time. First we make America a decent place for them to come to."

"And we do that by killin' our own kind?"

"Corkmen and Fardowns are hardly our kind."

"They be Irish, just the same as us," Kiernan protested.

"But they ain't men of Connaught." Red seemed to find Kiernan's disgust amusing. "Never fear, lil' brother o' mine. I'll not be expectin' ya to soil yar hands. Leave the work to the menfolk."

"I'm a man, only ya treat me like a child."

"Then stop speakin' like one." Red took another couple of draws on the pipe before tapping out the bowl against the leg of his stool. He stood, ground the burning embers of the tobacco into the dirt, and yawned. "Mornin' will come mighty early. I'm thinkin' it'd be best to leave this conversation for another time."

Kiernan nodded and allowed Red his routine of securing the tent flaps while Kiernan climbed onto his cot. There was a definite chill to the air that made him grateful for the thick wool blankets Red had insisted they buy before coming to Greigsville. Red promised they'd soon have a shanty of their own, and the idea of walls and a stove in the place of a cook fire and tent gave Kiernan pleasant fuel for his dreams.

But on this night another fuel was supplied. As soon as he closed his eyes, Kiernan envisioned Victoria Baldwin. She was young, he reminded himself. But just as easily he reminded himself that his own mother had scarcely been ten and four when she'd married his da. Victoria had told him she was nearly thirteen, and while he knew womenfolk in America did things different from Ireland, he'd seen plenty of them married young with babes of their own.

He smiled to himself, just as Red turned down the lantern. She was young, but she would grow, and while she did, Kiernan would make sure he stayed in her company.

Twenty-One

A Bit o' the Blarney

The first heavy November snows buried Greigsville in white before Carolina felt the Baldwin house had become an acceptable place to live. Through the assistance of their Irish friends they had managed not only to patch the holes and resecure the frame of the house, but also to add two coats of whitewash to the outside and paper the walls of the inside. Miriam had taken Carolina's beautiful Persian rug and added strips of canvas from the tenting material, all in order to make it large enough to meet the corners of the front room. The remaining piece of tarp was large enough to cover over the kitchen floor, and once the stove arrived and cabinets were built, the room didn't look half so bad.

Even Victoria had taken on a new attitude about their dingy little house. She arranged and rearranged her dolls and books until she found just the right balance. James, feeling bad because they'd been unable to bring her writing desk, hired Kiernan to build his daughter a simple table and chair. Kiernan had surprised them by turning out a much more complicated piece of furniture in the form of a small table with drawers down one side instead of regular spindle legs. Victoria had fussed over the piece as though she'd been given some of the Crown jewels. She immediately set to work to make a little pillow cushion for the seat, announcing that it would be just the thing to make the set complete.

After discovering Kiernan's ability to craft furniture, James quickly put in an order for other pieces. They'd been so limited in what they could ship before winter that he thought it would be most appropriate to have Kiernan put together some of the bits and pieces that would turn their house into a home. Two clothing chests were added to those they'd brought with them, as well as a bookshelf and a very simple whatnot cabinet or "étagère," as Victoria insisted they call it. Little by little the house took on a very personal feel, and with it, everyone's attitude and dismal outlook changed.

"In the spring," James promised, "we'll get a whole wagon train of things brought out."

"We ought to help set up a store," Carolina said thoughtfully. "This town is sure to grow, what with the tunnel and railroad. Perhaps we could invest in building a dry goods store—even have Kiernan produce furniture for the store."

"He's going to have his hands full with the railroad. As it is, he put together those pieces for us on his Sundays off."

"I know," Carolina replied, "but it might be something he'd like a chance at. Maybe it would allow him the extra money he and Red need for bringing their family to America."

"It's possible." James seemed to consider her suggestion for several moments. "A store wouldn't be such a bad idea. The investment could only be profitable given the fact that the alternative is to travel to Fairmont or Cumberland. Yes, I see your point."

Carolina smiled and went to where James sat by the fireplace. "In spite of the hardships, I'm glad to be here with you."

He looked up at her and extended his hand. Then without warning, he caught her hand and pulled her down on his lap. Carolina giggled like a schoolgirl and wrapped her arms around his neck.

"I'm glad you're here, too. I would be very lonely without you and the kids."

As if on cue, Brenton came padding down the stairs. "Papa! Come see! The sky is orange."

James shook his head and sighed, while Carolina slipped off her husband's lap and went to her child. "What do you mean, the sky is orange?"

"I looked out the window. Come see."

Carolina let him lead her to the front window, but the frost prevented her from seeing much except a hint of muted light. "There does appear to be something going on," she told James.

He got up and went to the front door. "I'll see to it. You stay here." Just then an explosion sounded from a distance. The ground shook around them, leaving Carolina and James to stare at each other in dumbfounded silence while Brenton danced around chanting, "Fourth of July! Firecrackers!"

"Hardly," James said, his expression instantly given over to grim concern. "It's the Irish." His voice was resigned to the fact. "I'd heard rumors that there was to be a purging of the workers."

Carolina was instantly at his side. "What do you mean, a purging?"

"Apparently it isn't enough that they're all Irish. Red explained to me that they are separated in a rather clannish order. Regional people associate only with others from their region. Kiernan told me the problem has actually become worse here in America. Probably because they are vying for the same jobs." Fires rose up to illuminate the night skies. "I'd better go down there and see if I can do anything to help the sheriff."

"No!" Carolina exclaimed. "Don't do that. It isn't your fight."

James turned to her and put his hands on her shoulders. "Keeping the peace here is everyone's fight. If we don't find a way to quell this, we will only have to face it over and over again. You stay here with the children."

By this time, Miriam had been awakened by the blast. She came into the front room, her shawl wrapped tightly around her shoulders to ward off the chill. "Miz Carolina?" James took that moment to go for his coat and hat.

"The Irish are fighting, or so it would seem," Carolina answered by way of explanation. "James is just now going to see what can be done."

"I want to go, too!" Brenton declared.

"No, suh, young master," Miriam said sternly. "You is goin' to bed."

Carolina nodded. "You go along with Miriam and be a good boy."

Miriam took him upstairs, much to Carolina's relief. She didn't wish for her children to see the fear in her eyes.

"I'll be back soon. Sit tight," James told her and kissed her lightly on the forehead before rushing out into the night.

Carolina stood at the open door for several minutes. She could hear the raised voices of the men in the distance. Angry voices. Murderous voices. She shuddered. "Oh, God, keep James safe," she whispered the prayer, feeling very inadequate.

Miriam returned, and upon her suggestion, they began to roll bandages out of a couple of old sheets in order to help with the wounded. Carolina found herself passing the time after the bandages were done by sitting in silence beside the hearth. If only someone would tell them what was happening. If only morning would come and put an end to the frightening shadows that danced out across the firelit skies.

"What has happened?" a sleepy-eyed Victoria asked. She descended the stairs with a blanket wrapped securely around her white flannel nightgown.

"The Irish are having some sort of fight," Carolina explained to her daughter. "Your father has gone to check it out."

Victoria's eyes widened and it seemed she came instantly awake. "Papa's gone into the fighting?" She hurried to the window, but finding it impossible to see into the night, she threw open the front door.

Carolina came to take hold of her, fearful that Victoria would try to join her father. "We should hear something soon," she told her. "Come back inside and keep warm."

Victoria did as she was told, but she wasn't at all happy about it. With her dark hair streaming down her back, she suddenly looked much younger and very vulnerable.

"Just pray for him," Carolina whispered. "God is watching over him as surely as He's watching over us."

"It's hard to just sit here and do nothing but wait," Victoria whined.

"Then you can help us roll more bandages." Carolina handed her a wad of material. "There will no doubt be plenty of wounds to mend after this ruckus."

Victoria paled and Carolina wondered if her daughter was not only fretting for her father but also for the young Irishman who seemed to have so completely captivated her interest. Kiernan O'Connor had done nothing inappropriate in his behavior, but his interest in Victoria was nevertheless obvious. Carolina tried not to take offense at Kiernan's attention. She tried to remember what it was to be young and how fanciful youth could be in regard to love. Still, she didn't like to see Victoria turn her attention to infatuation at such an immature age. There was a great deal the girl had yet to learn, and Carolina feared she would throw it all away.

It wasn't until that moment that, with some surprise, Carolina realized she'd already planned out Victoria's future. Here she was already envisioning Victoria in a university or college but had given very little thought as to whether or not Victoria wanted such a thing.

Carolina had just opened her mouth to question her daughter on that very subject when the door burst open and James entered, disheveled and smoke smudged.

"Papa!" Victoria cried out. Dropping the bandage roll, she hurried into his arms. "Are you all right?"

"I am fine." He gave her a brief hug, then turned to his wife. "Carolina, the sheriff is putting together a posse of townsfolk. We're going after the ringleaders in order to capture them and put them in the jail up north in Kingwood." He went to the fireplace mantel and took down his musket. "The sheriff has also asked for women to help tend the wounded."

"Are there many?" Carolina asked, her heart pounding hard at the sight of James with gun in hand.

"Quite a few. The Connaughtmen burned the shanties and tents of the Corkians and Fardowns. Seems nearly three hundred Connaughtmen chased off their rivals from the tunnel work earlier this evening, and the matter continued to build until a full-fledged war broke out." He looked at her anxiously, then turned.

"Wait!" Carolina called, dropping her own bandages and crossing the room to her husband. "How long will you be?"

"There's no telling."

"Victoria, quickly! Go get your father the extra blankets. Miriam, pack him some food." Both hurried to do Carolina's bidding. "You can't go without provisions," she told James. The snows were fierce and the mountains nearly impossible to navigate. And what if the men were hiding out in places of ambush? "Please be careful," she said, her gaze locking with his.

James pulled her close. "I'm sure we'll be fine. There are quite a few of us going in search of those men."

"Do you suppose Red is one of them?" Carolina dared the question only because Victoria hadn't yet returned.

"I'm afraid so. At least, that's what it sounds like."

"Do you suppose Kiernan is also involved?" Just then they heard Victoria's feet on the stairs.

"I honestly don't know," James told her.

Miriam and Victoria returned. James kissed Carolina soundly, then released her and took up the blankets and cloth-wrapped provisions. "Pray for us," he called over his shoulder as he disappeared into the night.

"I already have been," she whispered from the open doorway. "I'll never stop."

Victoria hugged her tightly and laid her head against Carolina. "Will Papa be all right, Mama?"

Carolina realized that once again she had to be the strong one. "I'm sure he'll be fine," she told her daughter. "We must keep him in our prayers."

"We bes' get the bandages down to those hurt folk," Miriam suggested.

"Yes," Carolina agreed. "Victoria, gather up the ones we've already made. You can watch the children and work on making more while Miriam and I go tend the wounded."

Victoria nodded and went about her task, while Carolina hurried upstairs to put on warmer clothes. Within minutes she was standing at the door as James had only moments earlier. "I'll check in when I can," she said. "Be sure to keep a close eye on Jordana. There's no telling who might still be out there looking to stir up trouble. Keep the bar across the door, and keep the door locked."

"I will, Mama," Victoria promised.

An hour later, Victoria, weary from making bandages and lack of sleep, heard a scratching noise on the backside of the house. She felt her heart leap to her throat. Quietly she put the bandage down and got to her feet. Maybe it was just the wind. She paused, straining to hear. The noise came again, this time causing Victoria to jump. Someone or something was nosing around the back of the house.

Bears and mountain lions were plentiful, but it was the dead of winter, and her father had told her that both were most likely hibernating. Could it be one of the Irish her mother had warned her about?

She heard the noise again; this time it sounded more like a knock. She went to the archway between the front room and kitchen—afraid to look through the window but afraid not to look, too. Finally she gathered her courage and, taking a deep breath, forced herself to step through the arch.

Her hand flew to her mouth just in time to stifle a scream. A face peered back at her through the frosted glass of the kitchen window. She started to dash from the room, but the sound of her name being called instantly froze her in place. She turned again and listened.

"Victoria!" the muffled cry came.

It was Kiernan. Of that she was now certain. Against her mother's instructions she hurried to lift the bar and unlock the door. "Kiernan!" she gasped as his battered face peered back at her in the dim light.

"Can ya help me?"

"Of course, come in." She shivered, then realized she'd dropped her blanket wrap somewhere along the way.

"No, they'd be a-findin' me here. Do ya know of a place to hide me?" He was limping as he stepped toward her and swayed so far to the right that he had to catch himself against the cabinet.

Victoria tried to think of the best course of action. She could put him upstairs in the spare room. It was seldom that anyone went in there. But seeing the footprints in the snow, she knew that others might track him here. Then a thought came to her. "There's a cave just a short way from our yard. Papa had it cleared out and boarded it off. We store food there."

"That would work," Kiernan agreed.

"Let me get a lantern and some blankets," Victoria said, turning to go.

"Turn the light completely down," he advised. "We can't have anyone seein' us."

Victoria nodded. She gathered up the blanket she'd earlier warmed herself in, then went quickly to pull another from the trunk in her room. Frantically she searched the house for anything she might use to help Kiernan. She took up a few of the bandages she'd rolled, then grabbed a pail with half-frozen water. The last thing she did was wrap her cloak around her and take up the lantern. Remembering Kiernan's warning, she turned the wick down until only a hint of fire burned on the wick.

"Can you take these?" she asked, handing him the blankets.

"I can manage," he responded in a whisper.

"Good," she said, motioning him to follow. "It's just over here."

Twenty-Two

Kiernan

Victoria scarcely heard the exchange of conversation between her mother and father. Nearly a week had passed since the riot and still Red O'Connor and many of his men were at large. From what she had managed to glean from the adult talk, her father's friend Ben Latrobe had arranged to hire armed guards to patrol the work site, and that was stirring up unfriendly feelings among the workers and their supervisors.

Daily she had performed her chores, grateful they included helping Miriam in the kitchen. Whenever Miriam needed something from the cave, Victoria happily volunteered to fetch it, giving her the perfect opportunity to see to Kiernan, who was still hiding there, nursing a badly sprained ankle and unable to move. Those were her happiest moments, for it was here that she enjoyed the friendly banter that passed between them. Kiernan didn't treat her like a child. He asked after her, actually seeming anxious to know more about her life in Greigsville and in Baltimore. In turn, she listened to his stories of Ireland and longed deep within her soul to one day see the country for herself.

"Latrobe convinced the contractors that twenty-five men armed with muskets and bayonets would be enough to put things right," James was telling Carolina. "The contractors are willing to give the men another chance, but of course Red will have to account for what he's done when he's found."

"What of the others?" Carolina asked, casting a quick glance at Victoria.

Victoria was certain that her mother truly meant to ask after Kiernan but refrained from speaking his name so as not to upset her. In order to give them no indication that she had the slightest idea of his whereabouts, Victoria joined in. "Yes, what about his brother?"

James shrugged. "That I do not know. I suppose he might have gone off with Red."

"Surely not!" Victoria exclaimed. Her only thought was that Kiernan might face the same blame as Red. She found her parents staring at her in open surprise at her outburst. "I can't believe Kiernan would want to see men hurt like you described," she quickly offered as explanation for her disruption.

"I don't like to believe he would, either," James finally said, reaching out to pat Victoria's small hand. "I wouldn't worry overmuch. I'm sure they know how to take care of themselves, whether together or apart."

Victoria nodded and hurried to finish her breakfast.

"Miriam, I think it would be nice to have some of that venison Kiernan brought us. Why don't we have stew for supper this evening?"

Miriam nodded and Victoria seized the moment. "I'll go get it for you after breakfast."

"That would be very nice of you," Carolina said, beaming her daughter a smile. "When you finish with that, we'll get right to your studies. I'm afraid if you don't concentrate, Brenton is going to pass you by in arithmetic."

"I don't like it very much," Victoria admitted.

"But you'll need it if you're to go on to college," Carolina said matter-of-factly.

Victoria could hardly count her mother's many references to sending her off to college. It was very important to her mother, and up until recently Victoria assumed she could grant her this wish and not rebel or protest, in spite of her dislike for bookwork and learning. Now with her mind constantly thinking of Kiernan and Ireland, Victoria didn't like to imagine going off to some northern university where progressive minds allowed men and women to learn together. Not unless Kiernan could go, too, and that wasn't very likely given the fact that he couldn't read.

But he was learning, she thought and smiled to herself. As soon as he'd begun to knit back to health, Victoria had offered to loan him a book with which to pass the time. It was then that he had confessed his inability to read.

A loud knock sounded on the front door. Victoria's father and mother exchanged looks.

"Who could that be?" James wondered out loud, getting to his feet.

Victoria peered through the open archway as her father opened the door to reveal one of the young townswomen who'd befriended her mother.

"Hello, won't you come in?" James asked.

"Thank you kindly, but there isn't time," the woman said anxiously, then glanced through the doorway. "I need your missus. Mrs. Smith is havin' her baby and it's a-comin' hard."

Victoria saw her mother's eyes widen at this announcement. Carolina got to her feet and Victoria followed, leaving Jordana and Brenton to play with their food. "I'm sorry, but I've hardly any experience in such matters," Carolina said, coming to stand beside her husband.

"You've a sight more experience than me, what with me being newly married and the youngest in my family. Weren't no brothers and sisters to help birth, and leastwise you have three of your own," the young woman protested.

"I see," Carolina said, nodding. "Well, then, I will come, and I will bring Miriam with me."

"Your slave?" the girl asked in wide-eyed wonder.

"Miriam is a free woman," Carolina told her. "I gave her papers and now she works for us willingly. But Miriam knows birthings, and I'm sure she can offer up more help than I." She turned to Victoria. "You keep your brother and sister out of trouble while I'm gone."

"I will," Victoria assured her. With her father, mother, and Miriam gone, Victoria knew she would have a perfect opportunity to visit with Kiernan. Her only problem would be keeping Brenton and Jordana busy.

After the house emptied, Victoria decided on a plan. In order to keep a constant watch over Jordana, she would have to take the child outdoors with her. Brenton wouldn't be a problem. He loved to cipher, and she knew that she could simply leave him with a slate of addition problems and he would be content. Still, if she took Jordana with her, her sister might well later mention Kiernan's whereabouts. She just couldn't risk that.

"Brenton, I need your help," she told her brother. "I'm going to have you practice your reading, but I want you to read that nice storybook Mama has for Jordana."

At this Jordana began to clap her hands. She loved to be read to, and Victoria realized if only Brenton would cooperate she could count on at least ten or more minutes to visit with Kiernan. She wiped Jordana's face off and helped her down from the table while trying to arrange everything in her mind.

"I need to go outside to the cave and get the venison for our stew. Then I'll probably need to bring in some wood," she told Brenton, careful to notice that the woodpile beside the stove was running low. "I'm going to be a few minutes because I don't know exactly where Miriam and Mama put the venison." It was a lie, but she knew it would buy time with her brother.

"I'll read to her real good," Brenton promised, helping himself down from the table.

"You'll have to make sure she stays right with you and doesn't go near the fire or get outside," Victoria admonished, clearing the last of the breakfast dishes away. She had never thought to enjoy menial tasks, not after her privileged upbringing, but her mother had told her that it would do her good to learn. And now she was happy to have learned because she was beginning to realize she would be very content marrying and having children.

Kiernan had observed her homemaking talents when he had visited the family and had been impressed. He had also been pleased by her ability to cleanse his wounds and tend to his needs. When she had stitched his shirt back together and darned the holes in his socks, Kiernan had offered her high words of praise. It was because of his reaction that Victoria thought perhaps sewing and cooking might well become her only ambitions in life. Her mother might enjoy book learning, but she felt happier working with her hands.

Arranging Brenton and Jordana in the front room, Victoria knew she'd have to hurry. She decided to leave the dishes until after seeing Kiernan. She put water on to heat and paused only to gather up a bit of leftover breakfast to take with her. Kiernan was a big eater, and her most frustrating problem this last week had been to supply him with food. Twice she'd gone to see him only to find that he'd helped himself to some of the canned foods they'd stored in the cave. It had been no easy task to hide the empty jars from her mother until she could clean them and replace them along with the other empty containers.

"I'll be right back," she promised Brenton and Jordana. "Be good and maybe Mama will let me bake cookies."

She slipped out the back door and hurried down the path, past the outhouse and to the wooded area that butted up against the rocky wall of the mountain terrain. The cave was scarcely twenty yards from the back door, but still Victoria worried about leaving her siblings alone.

She reached the cave, lifted the bar that held the board gating in place, and swung the door open. "Kiernan?" she called out.

"Top o' the morning to ya," he replied and eased out of the shadows.

"I've brought you something to eat."

"Ah, a lil' traveling food," he said, sweeping a hand through his disheveled red hair.

"What do you mean, traveling food?" Victoria asked, fearing that she knew only too well what he meant.

"I need to be gettin' back to my people. I need to find Red and see if he's alive or dead." He took the cloth-wrapped breakfast from her and went to sit on a nearby rock. He munched on the biscuits and bacon while Victoria paced a path in front of him.

"What will they do to you when you go back?"

He shrugged. "Don't rightly think I'll announce my arrival." He grinned. "Then again, don't rightly think anyone'll care."

"But what if they do? My father says that the sheriff intends to find out whether Red started this thing or not. He says that they'll put Red and anyone else responsible in jail until they learn the truth of the matter."

"What they say and what they do is ofttimes different. They're shorthanded for workers now. I don't think they'll be carin' about the skirmish half so much as keepin' time with their contract."

"But they might," Victoria protested. "They just might throw you in jail because you're his brother."

Kiernan laughed. "Couldn't be any worse than the ship I came over on. Coffin ships, they call 'em, and with good reason. Either ya end up in one or ya feel like ya've just spent yar last moments buried alive."

"Tell me about it," Victoria said, hoping to stall for time. There had to be some way she could keep Kiernan from risking his life by rejoining the workers at the tunnel.

"Not much to tell. At least not for yar delicate ears. It was dark and cold and smelly, and death was all around us." His face contorted at the painful memory. "We ate porridge once a day, and after a week of it, most would just as soon go hungry. I wouldn't be surprised if that's why I have such an appetite now." He grinned apologetically. "Now, ya don't need to be hearin' this. What of yar folks? Have they been a-wonderin' about yar trips to the cave?"

Victoria shook her head. "I've tried to plan it out for when they weren't around. I didn't want to get you in trouble."

Her heart ached to tell him how she really felt. Looking at him now, she could almost speak the words. His laughing green eyes and auburn hair were only a part of his attraction. She loved his rugged face with the prominent nose that suggested a Roman ancestor or two; she even adored the broad set of his eyes and the fullness of his mouth. She fancied herself to be in love with him, and it hurt that she couldn't simply speak the words and let him know how she felt. But what if he didn't return her love? She would simply die if he rejected her. Best to just leave things be for now.

"Well, ya won't have to be a plannin' anymore," he said, getting to his feet. "I'm leavin'. Do ya suppose the way is clear for me?"

She nodded, not knowing what else to do. "Papa has gone to the tunnel, and Mama and Miriam are delivering a baby."

"Good." He grabbed up his blankets and folded them over for her. "I can't thank ya enough for what ya did."

"I wish I could have done more. I should have hidden you in the house instead of this cold cave."

"Ah, but ya be forgettin'," he said, touching her chin gently with his fingers, "I was livin' in a tent before this. The cave is a mite bit warmer, truth be told."

She felt her knees begin to shake at his touch. He was so close to her, and the warmth of his fingers on her face was enough to make her feel faint. "I'm . . . ah . . . I'm glad . . ." She couldn't find the words to speak. It was as if his eyes could look through hers clear down into her heart.

"Yar a good girl, Victoria. I won't forget yar kindness." He kissed her gently on the cheek, then went to the opening of the cave. He was limping a bit, but he could put weight on his leg without grimacing in pain. He paused and quickly glanced back at her. "I'll be comin' to see yar family later. Now, don't ya forget me."

With that he was gone and Victoria was left behind. She reached up to touch the place where his lips had kissed her. His Irish brogue rang in her ears. *"Now, don't ya forget me,"* he had told her, as if such a thing were possible.

Victoria hurried to the opening, hoping for one more glimpse of him, but he was gone. Only the tracks in the snow suggested that he'd truly been there. "Oh, Kiernan," she sighed and wished fervently that she might age by at least four years in the next few minutes.

Gathering her wits about her, Victoria barely remembered to retrieve the venison before exiting the cave. She moved as if in a dream. He was so handsome, and she loved the way he talked and the way he cared about his family back in Ireland.

The house was quiet except for the monotone reading of Brenton. She sighed. All was well. Her escapades hadn't caused any problems for her brother or sister, and relief washed over her as she realized suddenly just how much might have happened in her absence. She would have to be more responsible in the future.

The future. It seemed so unreachable. So distant. How she longed for it, and the maturity it might offer her. "Please wait for me, Kiernan," she whispered and lovingly touched her hand again to her cheek. "Please don't forget me."

PART III

February—December 1850

Not enjoyment, and not sorrow,
Is our destined end or way;
But to act, that each tomorrow
Finds us farther than today . . .

A Psalm of Life
—Henry Wadsworth Longfellow

Twenty-Three

Margaret's Homecoming

It was to festivities celebrating the birthday of George Washington that Margaret and Joseph Adams returned to Washington City. Margaret found herself duly impressed with all that had transpired in her absence. Washington had always been a city in one form of transition or another, but the evidence of this was never so clear as when Margaret stepped from the train. New buildings stood as proud sentinels to the nation's capital, while all around these rang the bustle of activities, with vendors seeking to ply their wares and disgruntled congressmen arguing as only congressmen could.

"My, but it has changed," Margaret commented as they boarded a hired carriage.

"You'll find the world greatly changed, my dear," Joseph told her as he took hold of her gloved hand.

Margaret smiled. Her subdued nature greatly contrasted the celebratory spirit that was evident in the streets around her. Washington's birthday was rivaled only by the Fourth of July in celebration and anticipation. "It seems so chilly for them to be out and about like this," she commented, noting a group of children playing a circle game of tag.

"I remember many were the times in our youth we endured the cold for the sake of a good party in honor of the general."

"But, of course, you are right," Margaret replied, still taking in the sights and sounds of the town from which she'd been so long absent. "I have missed it in some ways. In others, I'm just as glad to have left it behind." She stared thoughtfully around, wondering how it would be to see Oakbridge again. "I do long for home."

Joseph squeezed her hand. "We will be there before you know it. Remember I told you about our little railroad?" She nodded and he continued. "I have a private car which will stand by ready to take us to Oakbridge. The trip will pass quickly and smoothly, taking just less than an hour. It's really quite a wonder. We don't have a real locomotive engine, but the horses have a much easier time pulling along the rail than they would over open roads."

"I think I prefer the horses," Margaret said, smiling at her husband. "It will give us a pleasant time to sit alone and enjoy each other's company."

"I'm grateful for that time, and for the times to come," Joseph admitted. "I thought I'd lost you, but now I find that you are returned to me." His eyes misted with tears, and Margaret knew in her heart what the years of separation had cost him. They'd cost her no less.

"I can scarcely remember those early years in the asylum, and yet the one thing lingers—I never stopped wishing for you to come and make everything right."

"I wish I could have," Joseph said, his tone revealing his sorrow.

Margaret shook her head. "It's for the best, I suppose. I learned so much from my time away. In truth, as we've discussed before, I was a totally different woman then. I was self-absorbed and concerned with much that had no real bearing on our lives." She gazed down at her hands, knowing the futility of wishing that she could take back the hurtful things she'd said and done in the past. "I feel renewed. God has brought me through a dark shadowland and into the light. I am resolved to be a good wife and mother."

"But you always were," Joseph countered. "We raised children, not perfect beings. They needed direction and faithful guidance, and you always offered that. We have beautiful, accomplished children, and you are as much to credit as anyone."

"I long to see them all," Margaret said softly. "I wish Carolina had remained in Baltimore until we passed through. Still, I understand her need to be with her husband. I'm glad she is happy with James. Perhaps one day soon she will come and bring her family to see us."

"I'm certain she will. I know how she longs to be with you again."

"She told me when she visited a few years ago. I believe it was before the birth of her youngest."

Joseph smiled. "I remember. She'd just learned that she was expecting Jordana and she wanted to come and share the news with you."

"She was so grown up I scarcely knew her. So mature and graceful."

"So much like her mother."

Margaret shook her head. "No, she's always been more her father's daughter. Adventure runs in her blood."

"Along with the wanderlust, eh?" Joseph said with a laugh.

But instead of laughing, Margaret frowned. "I should never have kept you from your desires to travel. Wanderlust does not have to be a bad thing."

"It was exactly as it should have been. We aren't going to spend our new future together regretting a past that can't possibly be changed."

"Oh, look!" Margaret exclaimed. "We're crossing the Potomac. How cold and gray it looks."

"Well, it is February."

"February. Time ceased to have meaning to me while I was sick. It seemed days lasted for years," Margaret said wistfully.

"For me, as well," he whispered and pulled her into his arms. "I was never complete without you."

Margaret turned in his arms and gazed into the loving blue eyes that held her captive. "It will be a good life, Joseph," she promised him. "No matter our course, it will be a good life—together."

"Grandmother's home!" a chorus of children called out.

Entering the foyer of her home, Margaret peered out from her cloak to find a half dozen children dancing circles around her. She didn't recognize the faces. They were her grandchildren and yet she was meeting them for the first time.

"Let your grandmother take off her cloak and warm up near the fire," Joseph suggested to the brood. He reached up and helped to take the wrap.

"Mother," Virginia said in a hushed tone.

Margaret glanced up to find her eldest daughter standing at the foot of the stairs. She looked to be at least ten years older than her actual thirty-three years. Gray streaked her hair and her body was desperately thin. No more the belle of the county, Virginia had become a haggard old woman before her time.

"Virginia," Margaret whispered her name as if trying it for the first time. She held open her arms and received her daughter's hesitant embrace. "How I've missed you."

It seemed those simple words broke through the tension of their reunion. Virginia tightened her hold and sobbed. "Oh, Mama, I've missed you, too. You don't know how many times I wished desperately to have you here."

"Well, I am here now," Margaret said, trying to cheer her daughter.

Virginia pulled away. "You need to meet my children."

Margaret smiled. "I would like that very much."

Virginia motioned to the now silent gathering of children. "Nathaniel. Girls. Come and meet your Grandmother Adams."

Nathaniel Cabot, at seven and a half, was blond like his father but took the Adams nose and chin from Virginia. "You must be my grandson Nathaniel," Margaret said, sizing him up. "My, but you are tall and handsome."

Nate beamed a smile at her, proving the recent loss of several baby teeth.

"And these are the twins," Virginia told her. "Levinia and Thora."

"That means lightning and thunder," one of the girls said.

"I see," Margaret replied, trying her best to sound very impressed. "And which one are you?"

"I'm Thora," the child replied and curtsied.

Her sister, a near perfect mirror image of the first, curtsied and in a more hesitant voice declared, "I am Levinia."

"I am pleased to make your acquaintance, my dears," Margaret said, smiling up to Virginia. "Twins are very rare. I don't know of a single case in our families."

Virginia shrugged as if the newness of such a thing had long since worn off. "I suppose it must be from Hampton's side."

Margaret eyed her daughter curiously. Perhaps another time would lend itself to a more intimate discussion with Virginia.

"Mother!" Georgia, the youngest of the Adams daughters, declared from the grand staircase.

Margaret looked up to find her daughter in a navy blue riding habit. Joseph had already told her that this was Georgia's most common mode of dress these days. The love she had developed for anything equestrian caused her to stand ever ready to perform. My, but she has grown into a beauty, Margaret thought. Her hair, though brown like the others, had a slight auburn cast to it and had been piled and secured beneath a sturdy wool riding hat.

Virginia stepped aside as Georgia rushed to greet Margaret. "Oh, Mother, I had despaired of ever seeing this day. How good you look!" Georgia declared, then stepped back to survey her mother quite critically. "Well, you have lost weight, but no doubt Naomi's cooking will put a bit of flesh back on you."

Margaret laughed. "You sound every bit the part of a doting parent. Have our roles somehow reversed themselves?"

Joseph chuckled at the exchange. "Our Georgia prides herself in her doting. These three little gentlemen," he said, motioning to the little boys who had not yet been introduced to her, "are her sons. And there's yet another son, little David, in the nursery."

"Yes, as well as a baby daughter. You will positively love her."

"You needn't convince me of that."

"Will you love baby Deborah more than you love us?" Thora asked rather haughtily.

Margaret thought the child rather insecure to ask such a question and immediately sought to allay her fears. "Not at all. I have been blessed in my life with nine children, although four of those are no longer here with us. I loved each one of my children the best for entirely different reasons, and I would expect it to be no different with my grandchildren." This seemed to appease Thora for the moment, and Margaret turned to the three quiet little boys.

Georgia went to stand behind them. "This is Phillip and he is six." The child gave a much-practiced bow. His light brown hair fell across his forehead as he leaned forward, and when he arose, he jerked it back in place with a movement that suggested it went along with the bow. "This is Michael, who is five, and Stephen is four. David is a most rambunctious two, and that is why he is in the nursery instead of hanging from the fixtures down here. And finally there's Deborah, who is just six months."

Georgia's boys mimicked their brother's bow, although Margaret noted the absence of the head snap to secure their hair. "You are all very handsome brothers," she told them and opened her arms. "Come and give me a hug."

The boys looked obediently to their mother, then finding her approving nod, stepped forward and allowed their grandmother's embrace. It amused Margaret that moments before Georgia's appearance on the stairs, her boys had acted just as rowdy as Virginia's children. Georgia seemed to hold great control over them when standing in the same room.

"Where are your husbands?" Margaret asked her daughters as the boys stepped back to stand beside their mother.

"Hampton is discussing horseflesh with the Major," Georgia replied.

"He'd like to buy a new team for the brougham," Virginia added.

"Well, I shall look forward to seeing them both," Margaret replied, trying hard to stifle a yawn.

Joseph noted the action, however, and instantly came to put an arm around his wife. "Your mother has been traveling all day. I suggest we allow her a rest, and then we can celebrate further over dinner."

"That would be wonderful," Margaret replied, feeling a sense of contentment wash over her. "I've scarcely had such busy days these past years."

"Papa said you were crazy," Thora Cabot declared.

"Thora!" Virginia exclaimed, reaching out to take her daughter in hand.

"It's all right, Virginia," Margaret said, coming to where they stood. "Thora, for a time, I was very crazy. At least it felt that way inside, and do you know why?"

The little girl, refusing to be intimidated by either her mother or her grandmother, shook her head. "How come?"

The room fell instantly silent, and Margaret actually felt relieved that Thora had dared to bring up the unspeakable. "Because my babies had died from a bad sickness. I was so sad to lose them that my mind grew very sick. I had to stay in the hospital for a long, long time, but God helped me to get well."

"So you're not crazy no more?" Thora asked, evidencing her five-year-old curiosity.

Margaret smiled, then chuckled at the stunned expressions on her daughters' and husband's faces. "No, I'm not crazy anymore. But I am very happy to be here with you all. I feel God has truly blessed me with His love."

Again, Thora appeared satisfied and Margaret felt as though she'd just passed some sort of inspection. It was as if the child, although only five years old, had somehow designed a test of sorts to see exactly what kind of person she was dealing with. Margaret wondered if the girl had repeated what her father had said as a means of stirring additional strife, but it was hard to believe that a little child would be capable of such a thing. Still, she seemed quite smug in offering up her father's words.

"Come, my dear," Joseph said, taking hold of her arm. "Let's retire you for a rest, and then you can listen to all the gossip and news of the county."

Margaret promised her return, then allowed Joseph to lead her upstairs. He seemed most apologetic once they were behind the closed doors of their bedroom.

"I am sorry for what Thora said. It seems the child is given over to moments of intrusion."

"I'm not at all sorry," Margaret declared, unfastening the buttons of her wool traveling jacket. "If not for Thora, the tension might have gone on for days. Someone was bound to broach the subject sooner or later. Better a child in her innocent way than an adult in a more covert manner."

"I suppose I should have warned you about the twins," Joseph said, shaking his head. "They are a bit of a handful at times. Virginia tries to keep them under control, and Hampton hired a governess, a Miss Mayfield. She's older and very respectable and brooks little nonsense from the children. But the twins can be very conniving, if I do say so. Thora, obviously, is the more outspoken of the two, but Levinia can be sneaky, as well."

"Don't fret over it. I'm certain that it is only a phase." Margaret rid herself of her jacket and began unfastening the lace collar and ribbon at her neck. "I find everything the same, and yet so different," she said with a quick glance around the room. "This room is just as I left it, yet not so the family."

"There is much changed," Joseph agreed. "And perhaps it is only the start."

"Pray tell, Mr. Adams, what have you concocted now?" She sounded so much like her old self that they both laughed out loud.

"I haven't really concocted anything just yet," he admitted. "But it has been uppermost in my thoughts to change a great many things. I suppose I've put it off in hopes of discussing these changes with you."

"Such as?" she asked, going to the dresser where she knew without doubt she'd find her nightgowns. They were there just as she had thought. How good it would feel to sleep in her own bed once again.

"Well," Joseph began, his voice clearly filled with hesitancy, "there is so much to consider these days. The slavery issue has escalated to a point where it consumes nearly every point of interest in the government. States are considered for admission to the union based almost solely on whether they will be slave or free. Doctrine and policy are set with this issue overshadowing every point, and you can scarcely go anywhere, even to church, without being assured of a rousing conversation on our peculiar little institution. I've thought hard of being done with such matters and moving on."

Margaret stepped behind her dressing screen and slipped into her gown of white lawn. A feeling of familiarity washed over her. There was such contentment in simple things. "And how would you move on?" she said as she stepped out.

"It isn't important." He paused and smiled. "My, but you are beautiful. You've scarcely changed at all."

"Oh, but I have," she replied. "I've learned that so many things needn't be the issue that we make them. You have spoken to me before of freeing our slaves. Is that still a thought in your mind?"

"That, as well as other things." He sat down on the boot box at the end of their bed. "Suddenly slavery and public issues seem less important. I have to admit, my dear, bringing you home to Oakbridge has filled me with great apprehension."

"Because of the past?"

He nodded. "I didn't want you to suffer. I didn't want to force you to stare all the memories in the eye again. I thought perhaps of dividing the property among our children, or of selling it outright. That would free us up to go wherever you would like. We could live anywhere."

"Ah, I see the wanderlust is still with you, Mr. Adams." Her voice was teasing and gentle. She came to where he sat, and for the first time in a long, long while, realized how very much she still desired this man.

Joseph looked up rather sheepishly. "I truly thought of your welfare."

Margaret laughed. "I do believe you, husband dear. I am deeply touched that you care so much for me. But honestly, you must be at peace about this. I have long thought of this day and knew that it would come. I hoped and prayed that it would come. Being here isn't any harder than being somewhere else. There are those empty places that were once filled by our children, but there are still others who fill the void. I will mourn Mary and Penny and the baby sons we lost so long ago for as long as I live." Her voice was emotional, and Margaret knew that with little trouble she would soon cry. Drawing a deep breath, she chose instead to touch Joseph's cheek with her hand.

"Don't be afraid for me," she told him softly. "Do what pleases you. For once in your life consider what you want first, and know that it will be my pleasure, as well."

"I am so blessed to have you," Joseph whispered.

"And I you," Margaret agreed. She dropped her hold and went to the side of the bed. Turning down the covers, she smiled. "You look tired, Mr. Adams. Perhaps a midday respite would serve you well."

Joseph got to his feet and shook his head. "No, no, my dear. You are the one who—" He fell silent as he caught what Margaret hoped was her most appealing and hopeful expression. As the meaning of her words sunk in, Margaret thought he looked twenty years younger.

Joseph cast a quick glance at the door and then again to the woman from whom he'd been so long parted. "I believe I am in need of a rest," he replied with a roguish grin replacing his surprise. "Good to have you home to look after me, Mrs. Adams."

Margaret laughed and slipped under the covers with a yawn. "It's very good to be home, Mr. Adams."

Twenty-Four

Conflict and Strife

Hampton Cabot poured himself a good portion of whiskey and sat back to consider his plight. His mother-in-law's arrival back home had been heralded with enough fanfare to rival that of any character of nobility. The dinner they'd enjoyed, now two evenings past, in celebration of her return, had left them all sated and satisfied physically, but Hampton became instantly aware of an undercurrent that he could not quite put his finger on. It unnerved him to be so completely in the dark on matters that clearly affected his future.

Tossing back the whiskey, he poured another glass and studied the amber liquid as though it might mystically reveal the answers he so desperately sought.

"I thought I might find you here," Virginia said, coming into the drawing room generally reserved for the male members of the family and their guests.

"So, wife. Come to get yourself a drink?" he asked sarcastically. "I thought you generally drank alone or I might have invited you to join me." He took a long swallow, then shook his head. "No, on second thought I would not have done that. Your company leaves a great deal to be desired."

"It doesn't seem to keep you from my bed," Virginia replied harshly, the anger in her voice apparent.

"As is my right," Hampton countered smugly. "And don't you forget it."

"I have little opportunity to do so, especially now."

"What nonsense are you speaking of? Your mother's arrival home hardly has anything to do with my conjugal rights."

"I'm not talking about Mother's return," Virginia said hatefully.

"I'm talking about being pregnant. Once again, you've given me another child."

"Is that what all this is about?" Hampton asked and laughed. "I say, good for me!" He held his glass aloft and smiled. "To yet another Cabot heir!" He swallowed the remaining whiskey and slammed the glass down on the table. Then knowing what would hurt her the most he added, "If you can manage to keep from miscarrying this one." Although she'd given him three healthy children, Hampton could count nearly half a dozen other times she'd lost his children before they came to term.

"I despise you," Virginia said between clenched teeth.

"Yes, I know you do, and it matters very little to me. You see, I have what I want, and I do what I please. I care very little for what you think or feel about that, so long as you stay out of my way when I want you gone, and come when I call."

"I don't want this child," Virginia adamantly declared. "I don't want any more of your children. You are hateful and mean, and far too heavy-handed with the children."

"I simply discipline them when they need it," Hampton replied, surprised that he wasn't more irritated by Virginia's bold outbursts. In fact, he almost found the matter amusing, even entertaining. She was so serious, standing there with her hands on her hips, fire blazing in her eyes. It made him want to goad her on—just to see what she might say next.

"Of course," he said, picking his words carefully, "I could just ignore them as you do and find my solace in a sherry bottle."

"Stop it! Life with you has been sheer misery. Were it not for my family I would have long ago found a way to rid myself of this marriage. However, since divorce is not an option, I suppose I have little recourse but to endure your abuse."

"How very right you are," Hampton said, narrowing his eyes in anger. "I am your master, just as I am master over the slaves your weak-spined father owns. You will do as I say, and you will be grateful for the attention and protection I afford you in return." He got to his feet and moved toward her with deliberate slowness. "You do understand, don't you, my dear?"

Virginia stared him down, refusing to cower. It surprised him but made for a more intense sport. But just as he would have pushed the matter, the sound of voices came from just outside the drawing room door. It sounded like Joseph speaking to Thora and Levinia. With a shrug, Hampton moved away from Virginia and went to see what the disturbance was.

Throwing open the door, he saw Joseph watching the twins scamper off in the direction of the kitchen. "What's going on?" Hampton questioned.

"I found those two with their ears pressed against the door," Joseph replied quite seriously. "Seems a bad habit they've picked up."

Hampton smiled. "No doubt they were just excited about their mother's news."

"News?" Joseph questioned.

"Yes. It seems we're to be blessed with another child. Virginia is expecting."

Joseph smiled. "Congratulations, my dear." He went to Virginia and embraced her.

Virginia hugged her father but scowled mercilessly over his shoulder at Hampton. He threw her a devil-may-care look that he was certain she would interpret as his final word on the matter. He was delighted that she was pregnant. Children represented vitality in a man. The fact that Virginia had miscarried at least five other children was a point of frustration but certainly not a poor reflection on him. That his wife had trouble carrying his children to term was clearly a point of inability on her part, not his.

"If you don't mind, Virginia," Joseph told her and affectionately slipped an arm around her waist, "I'd like a few private words with your husband."

Virginia nodded and complaisantly exited the room. Hampton didn't take issue with her for failing to seek his approval; instead, he poured himself yet another glass of whiskey and offered to do the same for Joseph.

"No, thank you," Joseph replied and took a seat. "I have a great deal to say and I don't wish to be distracted."

"Very well." Uneasiness gripped him as he anticipated what his father-in-law might wish to address.

"Now that I am not required to make my trips between Boston and Oakbridge," Joseph began, "I want to relieve you of many of the duties you've performed on my behalf. For the time being, I don't plan to move ahead to sell Oakbridge, nor even to divide it among my children. I do, however, plan to take a personal stock in the circumstance and situation of my property and decide what is to be done from that point forward."

"I see," Hampton replied dryly. "And what is it you would have me do? Sit idly by?"

Joseph seemed to consider him for a moment before answering. "I'd expect you to abide by my wishes. Something you've deemed unnecessary for some time. There's more than enough work to keep the both of us busy, if you've a mind to continue learning the plantation business, but I will take charge." Joseph paused for a moment and drew a deep breath. "You've long defied me in matters related to my slaves. Time and time again, I've asked you not to take a heavy hand with them, and yet you go behind my back and do as you please. You've badgered and belittled my people until they've been frightened half out of their wits. That is completely uncalled for."

Hampton tried to protest, but Joseph held up his hand. "Hear me out." The command was firm and demanding.

"As you well know, I cannot abide your cruel treatment of the slaves."

"Are you suggesting I take my family and go?" Hampton questioned, knowing that Joseph had long feared he might do that very thing. But to his surprise, Joseph merely shrugged.

"If you think that's the only way to handle this matter, then of course I have no choice but to let you go. However, if you are of a mind to curb your temper and refrain from using physical violence to see things resolved your way, then I welcome the assistance you can lend me."

Hampton said nothing. He couldn't very well speak without revealing his inner rage and thus destroy any pretense of following through with Joseph's suggestion.

"At times, I've almost believed you capable of finding pleasure in the cruelty you inflict," Joseph continued. "I don't want to believe that of you, but I find it quite reasonable given your indifference to the matter. But that aside, I thought you should know that I plan to move ahead with my desire to free the slaves at Oakbridge. Whether I sell this place or pass it on, it is my intention to free my slaves beforehand. If they choose to hire back on at laborers' wages, that will be entirely up to them."

"You'll regret that day," Hampton managed to mutter.

"You might believe so, but I do not. I feel confident and good about setting them free. However, I'll not throw them to the wolves. They've been with me far too long and they are dependent upon me for their well-being. It would be my Christian duty to send them into the world with the basic essentials necessary to keep them alive and safe."

"Oakbridge will fail without them." Hampton forced himself to be calm. "You know it will."

"Perhaps," Joseph said with a thoughtful nod. "But I seriously doubt it. Georgia hired free Irish laborers and has a staff of over thirty to pay, yet her horse farm thrives and does more business than she can keep up with."

"That's horses, not farming. Crops require an entirely different manner of attention, as you well know. Then, too, you have your own stable of animals and livestock in the fields, as well as the house staff and various other positions required to make this place profitable."

Hampton finally felt capable of pressing forward and gave Joseph no chance to reply. "I've made this plantation more profitable than you could have ever dreamt. I saved you from ruin time and time again. I show you ways to cut costs and to reap benefits you hadn't even bothered to consider. I made Oakbridge the plantation that it is today."

Joseph stared at him sadly and shook his head. "Perhaps, but at what price? In all my years of ownership prior to your arrival on this plantation, I never suffered a single runaway. Do you realize that, Hampton? Not a single man or woman felt the need to escape their lot here and make a run for it elsewhere. People were happy and productive. Yet since you have been allowed authority, there have been over twenty runaway attempts, many beatings with one death related to these, in addition to several deaths from sickness, improper care, and just plain exhaustion."

"It's cheaper to work a slave, even to the point of death, than to hire free men," Hampton said snidely. "And you know that very well. Slaves are an asset you can't afford to live without. Not if you intend to keep Oakbridge running."

"Then perhaps," Joseph said quite seriously, "I won't keep her running."

"Madness!" Hampton declared and got to his feet. "Sheer madness."

"Perhaps to your way of thinking, but to mine it seems quite reasonable to consider. You see, I never wanted this life to begin with. And as my dear wife has pointed out, perhaps now is the time to seek the life I want."

"You can hardly trust what she has to say. She's just spent the better portion of a decade in an insane asylum."

"I won't have you talk about Mrs. Adams that way. We all know very well what happened to grieve her and rob her of her senses. But as even you can see, Hampton, she is perfectly healed and quite capable of handling the matters of her house." Joseph got to his feet and walked to the door. "I had hoped," he said, turning back to face Hampton, "that we could see eye to eye on this matter. I hate to have further conflict and strife develop over a disagreement as to how *my* plantation should be run. If you find you cannot bring yourself to agree with me, then I will understand if you choose to leave. But I will add this one simple thought. If Virginia should find it necessary to remain here at Oakbridge with her children, I will not force her to go with you from this place."

"She's my wife and she'll do whatever I tell her to do," Hampton growled the words. "The laws of this land will not allow for your interference."

"She might well be your wife, but she was my daughter first, and I will protect her in the best way I can. I have powerful friends, Hampton. Including my heavenly Father, who is a most powerful ally in times of trouble. I am praying to resolve this matter in an amicable way for all of us. I hold you no malice and wish you no harm. I believe only that you are misguided in your beliefs, but you are not beyond reason. I will continue to pray about this, and I hope you will do the same."

With that he exited, leaving Hampton to consider his father-in-law's words and to seethe in anger. Hampton might have thrown something at the door had he not known that it would only further Joseph's resolve that he was right in treating Hampton like a wayward child.

"A slave is a slave," Hampton muttered. "And a wife is a wife." He paced the room for several moments before shaking his fist at the closed door. "You'll not take either one from me, old man. You'll see. I'll have it my way, with or without your approval. With or without you."

Without him.

Hampton smiled to himself. Now, there was a thought. If Joseph Adams ceased to live, Oakbridge would be dependent upon Hampton for guidance. York wouldn't want it, as he still had political ambitions, and Maine was off preaching in California. If something happened to Joseph, Hampton would be the natural one to take over Oakbridge's concerns.

"Perhaps I've been going about this the wrong way," Hampton murmured.

Twenty-Five

Secrets

Margaret took advantage of the surprisingly mild March day to venture outside for a brief stroll. She knew exactly where she wanted to go and without hesitation made her way to the small family cemetery. It pleased her to find that the graves of her four children had been meticulously cared for. Miniature picket borders framed each grave, and tiny new buds of crocuses were peeking their heads through the ground.

"My babies," she whispered thoughtfully. "You were all so young. Too young." Now, even many years after their deaths, Margaret felt the pain as if it had been yesterday. "I'm so sorry, my little ones." Tears rose to her eyes. "I wish I could have kept you here with me. What a joy you each were."

Concluding her visit, Margaret walked around the grounds a bit and slowly made her way back to the house. Staring up at the fluted marble pillars of her Greek revival home, Margaret felt a contentment that overtook her earlier feelings of sorrow. This home of hers represented a lifetime of dreaming and working and loving. It seemed so right that she should return to this place, and suddenly she was very glad that Joseph hadn't sold it off or divided it among the children. She wasn't ready yet to say good-bye to Oakbridge.

She glanced around, noting the orchards with their tiny buds of green, seeing beyond to fields not yet planted with new crops. The earth was just awakening from a sleep, and that was exactly how Margaret felt. The sense of renewal and refreshment gave her energy to face whatever life presented.

"Thank you, Father," she prayed aloud, her gaze falling back to the mansion itself. "Thank you for giving me a faithful husband and for blessing our lives with children."

Movement caught her eye from one of the upstairs windows. With little more than a quick glance, Margaret felt certain she'd seen Virginia behind the filmy curtain panel. "Oh, Lord," she whispered, "she's so troubled. How can I help her?"

The wind blew gently, chilling Margaret ever so slightly. Perhaps she would return to the house and speak with Virginia about what had happened to make her so unhappy. Suddenly that seemed a very reasonable idea, and Margaret took off in search of her eldest daughter.

Moments later, Margaret located Virginia in the upstairs music room. She was seated on a lounging sofa, letter in one hand and glass in the other. Margaret might have wondered at the contents of that glass, but Joseph had already mentioned Virginia's attraction to sherry.

"May I join you?" she asked softly.

Virginia looked up, not bothering to hide her drink, and shrugged. "If you like."

Margaret decided to ignore the obvious and instead drew up a chair beside the lounge and focused a tender smile upon her child. "I've longed to have some time alone with you. It seems there is much we should discuss."

Virginia tried to maintain a look of indifference, but Margaret read the pain in her eyes as she answered, "I suppose you've come to lecture me."

"Not at all. You have been Oakbridge's mistress for these past years, and now it would be wise for us to speak of the changes and needs—" Margaret paused, then added—"if I'm to be of any use to you at all."

"Any use to me?" Virginia questioned. "I'm hardly any use to anyone."

"I seriously doubt that," Margaret said, smiling. "We both know this plantation does not manage itself."

"Well, it doesn't get managed by me, either," Virginia said. Then without giving it much thought, she downed the contents of her glass. "Hampton runs things quite well without my help."

"I very much doubt that." Seeing they were getting nowhere, Margaret nodded her head toward the letter. "Who is that from?"

"Carolina. It's for the family," Virginia said, as if she felt the need to explain why she was reading the missive.

"And what has she to say?"

Virginia shrugged again. "Her perfect life is a little less perfect because she's chosen to move to the Allegheny wilderness. But no doubt she'll have everyone civilized and set in proper order before summer."

Margaret chuckled. "Yes, I suppose she might at that. Why don't you tell me about it, or read it to me if you like."

"Well," Virginia began, glancing back down to the letter, "the tunnel that James is working on is well under way. They are having trouble with some of the laborers. Irish laborers." She looked up at Margaret as if to emphasize this latter bit of news. "They had a spell of fighting and such, but it seems to be under control for the time." She looked back down at the paper. "Carolina says the house they live in is quite primitive compared to what they had in Baltimore or here at Oakbridge. They arrived to find it with dirt floors, but James has since arranged for wood planking, and when the freight routes aren't quite so muddy, they intend to have a proper floor put in."

"How are the children?" Margaret asked, trying to picture the scene in Greigsville.

"They are all well. Victoria is now thirteen, and Carolina says she has her eye on some young man there. Carolina thinks she is much too young to consider such things but admits that with few women in the area and Victoria being such a beauty, the attention was bound to be there, even if her interest were not stirred."

"Probably very true," Margaret said, smiling to herself. She could well imagine Carolina's concerns.

"Brenton and Jordana are well. Carolina says it is a full-time job just trying to school the three of them, but plans are already under way to build a school. Victoria has little interest in studious work, while Brenton—" she paused to read a passage from the paper—" 'Brenton is ever his father's son. He strives to learn all manner of subjects and even asked to be taken to the tunnel site so he could learn about black-powder blasting.' "

Margaret grew teary eyed at the thought of the grandchildren she'd not yet had the privilege to know. Virginia stopped abruptly, an expression of grave concern on her face.

Margaret waved her handkerchief. "I'm fine, honestly I am. I'm just a bit sad for the time I've lost. So many children have come into this family while I continued to mourn the passing of my two." She wiped at her eyes and smiled. "I've a great deal to make up for."

"Maybe I should pour you a drink," Virginia offered.

"No, that's not necessary," Margaret replied, realizing that this was how Virginia dealt with her problems. "I suppose I am just now coming to see how much time I wasted on things of little importance. When I was young, I worried about what society thought of me, and of whether or not I was involving myself in just the right causes, for the proper amount of time and effort."

Virginia looked at her as though her words made little or no sense, so Margaret continued. "When Mary and Penny died it was simply too much for me to deal with. I withdrew into my own world in order to protect myself from the pain. Much as you drink your sherry to ease your own pain."

Virginia flushed but didn't deny her mother's words. Instead, she dropped her gaze to the letter on her lap, as if looking at her mother would require her to deal with the truth of the matter.

"Virginia," Margaret whispered her name and reached out to touch her daughter's hand, "I cannot express to you how sorry I am for the time we've lost. I feel if only I had been stronger, I might never have fallen apart and been forced to desert my still-living children."

"How can you say that?" said Virginia. "You were the best mother we could have had. It wasn't your fault things happened as they did. You were—are—a good Christian woman. You worshiped regularly at church, helped the poor, arranged charities for the orphans. Why, you even prayed with us nightly when we were small children. God should have protected you better."

"God can be blamed no more than I should blame myself. Things happen as they will. But even if I shouldn't take the blame, I do feel regret—I just can't help it. I had completely missed the importance of living on more than pretense and deeds."

"I don't understand."

Margaret thought for a moment. "I suppose it is difficult to put into words. I wanted everyone to think well of me, and so I did the things I thought would bring me praise and admiration. I worked hard to make my 'goodness,' if that's what we should call it, apparent. I wanted people to see me as the perfect wife and mother—the perfect hostess and social matron. These things became more important than simple faith in God."

"But you no longer think they are?" Virginia asked, surprised.

"No, Virginia dear, I don't." Margaret smiled.

But Virginia was bewildered. "I still don't understand. You don't think it matters at all what people think?"

"Yes, I suppose to some extent it does, but that cannot be the basis for a firm foundation of faith. I lost sight of what was important. I may have even lost sight of God. And there were times that I did as I pleased, knowing full well I was being willful. There were even times I opposed your father, although I knew him to be right. I thought I knew what was right, but when troubled times came, my foundation crumbled. Much like yours has."

Virginia grimaced and stiffened. "I'm doing the best I can."

"Yes, you probably are," Margaret agreed. "But I do worry about what the sherry might do to you."

"I only use it to calm me."

"But it doesn't calm you. Not really. I can't see where it has benefited you at all. You are worn out and exhausted. You look to have aged at least ten years beyond your time, and although I've been home for just over three weeks, I have yet to see you smile."

"I don't have anything to smile about. I have a horrible marriage, three bratty children, and another child on the way. I live here as a virtual prisoner of my husband's will, and frankly I don't understand why God has done this thing to me."

Margaret eyed her intently. "Why God has done this? How do you suppose this is something God has done? Did you or did you not choose to elope with Hampton Cabot without your father's consent?"

Virginia tried to mask her pain. "Go ahead and blame me. Everyone else does."

"I'm not trying to blame you for anything, but neither do I want you to blame God for something that you clearly took out of His hands."

"You can't take anything out of God's hands," Virginia retorted haughtily. "He is God, after all."

"Yes, but He has also given us the free will to either choose or reject Him and His ways. Just as your father and I tried to raise you to hold a certain set of standards as truth, we also realize that you will pick and choose what you will. All we could do was set that standard before you. You had the free will to decide whether or not those standards were acceptable to you."

"Marrying Hampton seemed the right thing at the time," Virginia offered weakly.

"Did it really?"

Virginia lowered her eyes. "I don't want to talk about this anymore."

"All right. If that's what you truly want." Margaret got up to go, then changed her mind and sat down beside Virginia on the lounge. "I only want you to know how very much I love you. The mistakes of the past are unimportant when it comes to how much I care about you and your happiness."

At this, Virginia looked up. Her eyes overflowed with tears. "You needn't be kind to me. I don't deserve it."

Margaret opened her arms to pull Virginia into her embrace. Her daughter stiffened and tried to pull away, but Margaret held her fast. "I love you, Virginia." At this, Virginia broke down and sobbed.

"I don't want to live like this anymore. I just don't want to live."

"It's all right, sweetheart," Margaret soothed. "I had much the same feelings once."

"I can't do this anymore," Virginia said, pulling away. "You don't know what it's like—what I'm going through."

"I may not know all of the details, but I recognize the pain." Margaret reached up and touched Virginia tenderly. "You may not believe this, but I swear to you that it is true. Your peace will come when you take your focus off of all that is wrong and painful to you and put it back on God. He longs to ease your miseries, Virginia. You can count on His love to be real and true and faithful, even when mankind fails you."

"I'd like to believe that," Virginia said, trying to wipe her tears. "But I've listened to religious discussions all of my life. It didn't keep you from having troubles."

"I didn't say it would. The Bible tells us that in this world we will have trouble," Margaret replied. "But it also adds that we can be of good cheer because God has already overcome for us."

"But troubles will still come, is that it?"

"Most likely."

Virginia shook her head. "Sounds like something people use to comfort themselves when the bad times come. 'Oh, God is with you—take heart.' But still you suffer and still the heartaches come. Mother, I wish I could have your faith, but I've seen too much. I know too much now to go back to that naïve little girl I used to be."

Margaret's heart ached for her child. If only she could find a way to help her see the truth. "I will pray for you, my darling. And perhaps you can pray, too."

"I can't," Virginia said, getting to her feet. "I can't even begin to find the words."

Margaret nodded. "When I was at the asylum, I was much the same way. I had a wonderful nurse who used to pray for me. She said it was like the story of the paralyzed man who didn't have a way to get to Jesus, so his friends did it for him, lowering him through the roof. Do you remember that story?" Virginia nodded. "I will do that for you now. I will take you to Jesus in prayer."

She got up to stand beside Virginia, then leaned over and kissed her lightly on the forehead. "It will get better."

Virginia's face contorted and the look seemed to say she wanted to believe her mother, but doubt and past experience left her hesitant.

"You'll see," Margaret assured her. "With God, all things are possible."

Twenty-Six

The Strike

Carolina was the first to hear the pounding that signaled someone at the back door of the house. Groggily, she shook her husband and heard him moan in recognition of her touch.

"James, someone is knocking at the kitchen door."

"Huh?"

She shook his shoulder again. "James, listen. Someone is raising quite a ruckus downstairs. Miriam is probably half out of her wits."

"All right," James replied, sleepily sitting up.

Carolina had already slipped from the warmth of her bed to don her robe. "Hurry, James. It must be very important if they're waking us up before sunrise."

By this time, James was starting to come fully awake. "It had better be important," he muttered. "I feel like my head barely touched the pillow."

They hurried downstairs and met Miriam coming upstairs to find them.

"Don't know who'd be a-callin' at this hour," Miriam told James as he took the lighted lamp from her hands.

"Who is it?" James questioned before opening the door.

"Kiernan. Please hurry and let me in."

James opened the door. "Do you know what time it is?"

"I'd not have come if it weren't important." Kiernan took his cap off and twisted it nervously in his hands. "I had to warn ya."

"Warn me of what?"

"There's gonna be trouble at the tunnel today. Ya'd do best to stay here and let matters resolve themselves without interferin'."

"What sort of trouble are we talking about?" James questioned.

Carolina felt her heart in her throat. Trouble had already reared its head on more than one occasion, but for the past month things had been peaceful, almost serene. After the November riots a few of the ringleaders had been caught and arrested. But others, including Red, had eluded arrest and, after a time, had returned to work. For the sake of the work, the bosses had been willing to let things slide. Moreover, they feared if they fired Red, all the other Connaughtmen, who made up the majority of the work force, would quit in protest, leaving construction seriously delayed.

Had they all been lulled into a false sense of security? The contractors had even declared that there was no longer a need for the armed guards hired to watch over the Kingwood Tunnel after the last November riots and had let them go. But now for Kiernan to feel the need to risk his own safety in order to warn James, Carolina knew the trouble must be serious, and it left her feeling weak in the knees. Without the armed patrolmen, they would be at the mercy of the Irish.

"Red said the men are gonna strike, but because a great many of the Corkians will be against the Connaughts in this matter, he'll have to convince them."

"In other words, he plans to beat them into submission, is that it?" James fairly growled the words.

"Ya know me brother well."

"Well, it makes no sense to me that you people have to fight each other. At any rate, I'll not stand idly by and watch work on the tunnel come to a standstill. We've got a railroad to build, and I'll be hanged if I let Red O'Connor dictate the course of our plans."

"He won't like your interferin'," Kiernan said quite seriously.

Carolina knew that he spoke the truth. She'd heard only too many horror stories about people who crossed Red O'Connor. Mostly she'd been made aware of the conflicts through other wives. Some had experienced his wrath firsthand when Red had beaten their husbands and threatened to burn down their shanties.

"Go on back, Kiernan," James said. "I don't want you getting yourself in trouble. No doubt Red would forget that you're a Connaughtman, and his brother at that, if he found out you were warning me."

"'Tis true enough," Kiernan admitted, "but in a way, I'm just tryin' to protect Red, as well. He'll never see it for himself. Mebbe when he's hangin' from a noose he might understand, but I doubt it."

James nodded. "Look, just go back and protect yourself. I'll come down to the site, business as usual, and when I see what's going on, I'll deal with it from there. No one need ever know that you brought me the information."

"Thank ya," Kiernan said, barely raising the bill of his cap.

James closed the door and had turned back around when Carolina came out from the shadows. "Are you truly going down there?" she asked, though she already knew the answer. "You heard what he said. Better yet, you know very well the things he *didn't* say."

"Strikes and riots seldom lend themselves to reasonable thought," James rejoined. "The railroad is my responsibility. I am the eyes and ears of my employer. Those contractors for the tunnel are hardly going to be in a position to protest this strike. After all, the money won't come from them; it will come from the B&O Railroad. And because this is the case, I have to do my part. I have to try to negotiate this conflict to an amicable solution. But I promise you I'll be careful." James reached out to take her into his arms.

"I'll still worry."

"I'd be surprised if you didn't. But perhaps it will ease your mind to know I have no intention of going alone."

"What do you mean?"

"Remember the men hired last winter to stand guard along the tunnel site?"

She nodded. "The same ones the contractors let go because they didn't feel the cost justified their employment?"

"The very same. Most of those men are still in town. I'm going to round them up and put them back on the payroll. I think the contractor is going to have to accept the fact that we're dealing with a real powder keg here and that in order to keep from allowing someone to light the fuse, we're going to need to keep guards full time. The B&O should probably help pay for it, and in that way, guarantee each man a secure position."

"Do you really suppose they'll go with you this morning?"

"Most of these men are in need of money. I don't anticipate being turned down. I suppose that for money they will do most anything I ask," James replied with a grin.

He drew her once again into his arms, and this time he kissed her long and tenderly. Carolina felt the familiar feeling of pleasure wash over her. How she loved this man! She clung to him tightly before letting him go. *Oh, God,* she prayed, *don't let any harm come to him.*

James rode west from Greigsville and headed to the tunnel site. The early morning mist covered him with a damp chill. The muffled clopping of the horses filled the uncanny silence, and James found the racing of his heart to be an almost audible sound. The men who rode with him hardly seemed concerned. They carried their muskets and bayonets as though they were all a part of a bizarre hunting party rather than a police force going to put down a potential riot.

Three additional men remained in Greigsville to recruit and locate other guards to be hired on for work at the tunnel, while a fourth man rode out in order to get word to Ben Latrobe. He prayed it would be enough to quell any possibility of an actual riot, but in his heart he held serious doubts as to his abilities to negotiate this battle. Kiernan had made it clear that Red was in pursuit of higher wages and better conditions. Neither was something James had the power to grant. He could, of course, listen to the demands and be sympathetic to their needs, but otherwise he was powerless.

As they neared the tunnel site, loud voices carried across the morning air, and from time to time gunshots could be heard. James prayed these were for the purpose of drawing attention and not for killing. He urged his horse forward and rode into the camp just as Red mounted a large rock and shook his fists at the cowering contractors.

"We're not animals to be pushed around and forced to live in crates and tents. A man can't give a good day's work without the comforts of a decent place to live and sleep. The wages ya pay can scarce put food on the table, much less buy the things a man needs elsewise." A hearty roar of agreement rose up from a group of men crowded around Red. He turned, seeing James enter the camp, and scowled a greeting.

"Red, can we talk?" James called.

"No," the man shouted back. "I have too much yet to do. I've not got the men to understandin' the need for our strike. Corkmen are a hard lot to reason with."

The men of Cork were gathered a good distance away, near the mouth of the tunnel. They were clearly outnumbered by the Connaughtmen, and fear clearly etched itself in their expressions. Some of the men had obviously already experienced the physical side of Red's reasoning. They remembered too well the tragedy of the previous November. They no doubt also realized that Red had managed somehow to distance himself from accountability for those actions.

Sounds of discord rose from inside the tunnel, and Red smiled down at James' openmouthed expression. "I told ya they're a hardheaded lot."

"Red, you can't go around beating these people into submission simply to suit your desire to strike. I won't have it," James said.

"Oh, ya won't, now? And who do ya suppose will stop me?" the burly Irishman challenged, his green eyes alight with amusement.

James dismounted and drew his weapon. "I suppose I will," he answered.

Red's lips broke into a smirking grin. "Did ya hear him, boys? He thinks he can put down a Connaughtman."

The group around James turned glaring expressions in his direction, but the sound of the other patrolmen taking their places beside him bolstered his courage. "I don't want to fight any man," James said. "I don't think it's necessary. In fact, I think it's an act of cowardice to bully unarmed men."

Red's smile faded and an open expression of hostility replaced it. "Would ya be calling me a coward?"

"Only if you continue to harass these honest men," James replied. "But you are a bully, Red. There's no denying that."

"We got 'em all," a man shouted from the opening of the tunnel. He pushed several battered men forward, throwing them off balance and into the dirt. The man waved his musket at Red and added, "I think these Corkians have reconsidered joining us." The Corkmen stared up in mute silence, blood streaming down the sides of their faces, their eyes even now turning black.

James stoically faced Red. "Hard to fight facts when they stare you in the face."

"So what?" Red retorted. "I'm the stronger man. Connaughtmen are always the stronger." A cheer rose up from the men at Red's side.

"Strength isn't everything," James said, trying hard not to appear in the leastwise shaken or unnerved. "Wisdom often takes a man further than might."

"Flowery words!" Red shouted. "But pretty talk does not a tunnel make. Ya think ya know our plight so well, but ya haven't lived as we've lived. Ya have a fine house, and family, and plenty to put on the table for them to eat. Our families are in Ireland, starvin' because there isn't food enough to make a meal. Our houses are tents and shanties that do naught to keep out the cold."

James nodded. "I agree. Things do need to change. But look around you, man. There is lumber for the taking and resources that have scarcely been tapped. But just as one group or the other manages to put together some kind of shelter, you come along and stir up a war and destroy everything in your path."

This brought affirmation from the Corkians, who by this time had pressed forward to stand closer to James as he continued. "So instead of acting like a jackeen, why not give yourself over to some reasoning? Tell me where you've made things better with your badgering and rioting. You and your fellows burned down half of shantytown last November. I fail to see how your actions propose an improvement in housing."

"It's true!" yelled one of the Corkmen.

"Yeah, well, ya deserved worse," one of the Connaughtmen hollered back.

This brought about a volley of insults from each side until Red called them all to silence. "What's happened has happened, Baldwin. It don't change nothin'."

"Perhaps not," said James. "Then again, perhaps it changes everything. Maybe the biggest mistake we've made at the Baltimore and Ohio is that we've hired unreasonable men. Men who can't abide by the rules. Men who don't really need the work."

"Are ya threatin' me job?"

James considered his question for a moment. To fire Red would be to turn a snake loose in the grass. There was no telling when he might rear up and strike. Still, to allow Red to run the show was unacceptable.

"Is that what it will take to make you get down from your perch and talk sense?" James challenged.

"I don't cotton to folks threatin' me," Red retorted.

"Nor do I," James replied evenly. "I'm willing to try to make some kind of arrangement toward the needs of these people. What I'm not going to stand for, however, is your threats. These men have come here to work." James nodded toward the Corkmen. "They have families and needs same as you and the rest of your men. If you kill even one of them, you'll go to prison, and I'll see to it that you never work for the B&O again. There will be another hundred men standing in line happy to take the job you've just vacated. Think about that for moment, Mr. O'Connor."

"He's right, Red," Kiernan called from the crowd of men. "Nobody cares whether it's one Mick or another. A Mick is a Mick, and there'll be plenty to replace us when we're gone."

Red looked down to where Kiernan emerged from the crowd. "If I want yar opinion, I'll be askin' for it."

"Then tell me what kind of box ya want to be buried in," Kiernan replied in a nonchalant manner.

"Ah, go on with ya, boy," Red answered, refusing to be moved. "We've got a right to better ourselves."

"Of course you do," answered James. "Just as I have a right to protect what is mine, and that which I represent. If you insist on making this a bloodbath, then yours can be the first blood shed."

Red eyed him suspiciously for a moment. "Ya'd not have the guts to pull the trigger yorself."

"Oh, wouldn't I?" James had nearly forgotten the gun in his hand. He now aimed it at Red and took his sight. If it saved the lives of all the other men, he'd put a bullet in Red's leg and incapacitate him for a while.

"Enough!" Kiernan declared, jumping up on the rock, putting himself between James and his brother. "Let's go speak of this together. Mr. Baldwin needn't shoot anyone today."

"Get out of here," Red growled, trying to push Kiernan aside.

Kiernan held his ground and James lowered his gun. The boy had a fierce loyalty for his brother, even though he had stolen away in the night to tell James of the strike. James admired the courage Kiernan showed, both in his actions then as well as now.

"I'll not go," Kiernan replied. "Ya'll have to kill me first and drag me cold, dead body from this place. I'll not see ya shot through just because yar too pigheaded to listen to what the man has to say." Then he turned to face James. "And if ya even try to harm him, I'll hunt ya down meself."

James nodded. Kiernan's anguished look evidenced his torn loyalties. "I don't want to shoot your brother, Mr. O'Connor. I simply want the work at the tunnel to go on and for us to negotiate an amicable settlement in this matter."

Kiernan nodded and turned back to Red. "Ya heard the man. Can't ya give that much? See if ya can get what ya want without shedding any more blood."

"A peaceable strike, is that it?" Red questioned.

James nodded. "That would be acceptable to me." Just then ten additional mounted patrolmen appeared on the edge of the camp. "And just to see that it stays that way, I've reinstated the guards we had last winter."

"We can't afford to pay for those men," one of the contractors declared, coming from his hiding place. "You can't force us to hire them on."

"Mr. Bradley," James said to the contractor, "unless you want to lose this contract altogether, I'd suggest you accept the facts for what they are. These men are necessary to keep the peace at this time. Mr. O'Connor and his representatives will sit down to discuss matters with you and with me, and hopefully we will iron out an agreement that will meet the needs of all parties. Until then, the B&O will be responsible for the payment made to the guards. Their continued presence will be a matter of negotiation between you and the railroad."

"Well, I suppose that's all right, so long as I'm not having to pay it out of my pocket."

James rolled his eyes. The man clearly cared only for the money. He turned as Red jumped down from the boulder. "So are we agreed to talk?"

"We can talk, but it don't mean we'll agree," Red said, his eyes still ablaze from the excitement of the moment. "And while we talk, we don't work."

"Agreed," James replied.

"So be it," Red said, lacking any real enthusiasm in his voice.

But James wouldn't and couldn't let him off that easy. Without even glancing at the men around him, James spit into his hand and extended it. "Shake on it?"

Red grimaced, looked at his brother momentarily, then nodded. Spitting into his own hand, he reached out to take James'. "Ya drive a hard bargain."

James grinned in spite of the fact that Red was threatening to squeeze his hand right off his arm.

Relief washed over Carolina as she spied James approaching the house. "You look tired," she said, putting the sewing aside when he entered the house. "I've kept supper warm. Are you hungry?" she asked, leaning up to kiss him.

"Starved."

When he was seated before his warmed meal, she asked, "So how did it go?"

"Red agreed to talk," James said. He told her a few more details, then, noting the unusual silence in the house, asked, "Where are the children and Miriam?"

"I sent them down the way to help Mrs. Kaberline."

"Help her do what?"

"Jordana and Brenton are keeping the Kaberline children occupied while Victoria and Miriam help clean and ready the building next door for the new store. Remember the freighters that are promised to arrive by the middle of March?"

"Oh yes. I suppose I'd forgotten."

"Well, I haven't. I hope they bring plenty of everything. I penned a letter to Mrs. Graves and instructed her to crate up enough to fill half a train. There's so much I miss, and I admit I am anxious for it to be here with us."

Carolina brought James a steaming cup of coffee. He wearily smiled his appreciation, then took a long, slow drink, and sighed. "I wish I could pour this all over my body. The dampness makes me ache."

"I'll fix you a hot bath after supper, but now you must tell me more about today," Carolina said, her curiosity getting the best of her.

James told her all about the talk with Red, adding with frustration, "Frankly, I think the Irish just like a good brawl."

"James, what a prejudicial thing to say! Of course not all Irish want to fight. I'm sure the women and children find it abominable. Probably most of the men do, as well. Kiernan certainly doesn't seem to be given over to fighting."

"No, and that young man is truly an enigma."

"How so?"

"He put himself between Red and me."

"Why did he need to do that?" Carolina's eyebrow raised. She wasn't liking at all the feeling she was beginning to get. She'd already let her imagination run wild throughout the day, and now she feared James was going to tell her that her fears had actually materialized into actions.

"Red refused to listen to reason. I thought I was going to have to shoot him to get his attention." Carolina tried to conceal her surprise but knew she'd done a poor job when James continued. "You needn't fret. I probably couldn't have even brought myself to do it. But I didn't have to find out because Kiernan jumped between us and managed single-handedly to calm things down. He's quite a young man."

"He and Victoria seem far too chummy for my comfort," Carolina replied without thinking.

"There are certainly worse men in this world to consider for a future son-in-law."

"But he's Irish," Carolina replied, as if that perfectly explained her misgivings.

James raised his own brow and grinned. "Now who's sounding prejudicial?"

"I only meant that there's a world of difference between them, and I know Kiernan plans to go back to Ireland for his family."

"Right now we have more pressing matters to resolve. The next couple of days are going to be extremely tense. I think it would be wise for you and the children to stay close to home. Vendettas are never easily resolved."

Carolina nodded. She could only hope and pray that Red's vendettas would not bring harm to James. Red wouldn't like the fact that James and Kiernan had humiliated him in front of his men. And because of that, he might well decide to pay James back.

Twenty-Seven

Compromise

Red O'Connor sat opposite James at the negotiation table, with Ben Latrobe at the head. For nearly two weeks the strike had continued, and matters were only made worse when the Cumberland freighters arrived bringing in free Negroes as additional laborers. Most of the Irish resented the Negroes, in spite of the fact that their plights were similar. The Irish shared many of the same negative reactions from whites that the Negroes endured. But instead of drawing the two groups closer, it served to pit them against each other just as it did among regional groups of Irish—especially when it came to available jobs. Immigrant Irishman or free Negro, it was all the same to many who would employ them. They were the lowest form of human life, and some even questioned whether they were human.

"We won't be a-workin' with them," Red declared during the negotiations, referring to the Negroes. "If you bring them in, I promise there will be blood spilled."

James suggested that Ben Latrobe send the men elsewhere on the line. He hated to think that they would have to isolate each group out to separate sections of railroad, but it was appearing more and more as if this would be the most amicable solution.

Ben Latrobe didn't appear quite so convinced. "Mr. O'Connor, we all have people we find difficult to get along with." His meaning wasn't lost on Red, and he continued before the man could react. "But if I simply sent away every man who irritated me, I'd not have workers, nor would I have friends. We've agreed to increase the pay of common laborers to eighty-seven and a half cents a day, while increasing those with actual mining experience and duties to a full dollar a day. Work will be done in eight-hour shifts underground, and eleven-hour shifts for those working above ground. Work stops at sundown on Saturday and starts again at sunrise on Monday. Building materials are available for new houses, and I will even look into your suggestion of building a hotel to house workers until the completion of the railroad.

"What I can't agree to is to sift out the non-Connaught workers and ship them off to other locations. If the men leave of their own free will, and I do mean at their will and not at the point of gun, then so be it. But I will not be dictated to in regard to filling those positions. A good worker is a good worker, and all are welcomed to hire on so long as they do a fair day's work. So you see, should you decide to covertly rid yourself of these people, I will not oblige you by bringing in Connaughtmen to take their places."

"We'll not work with *Negroes,*" Red said, straining at the final word. He'd already exhausted a vast repertoire of derogatory names before Ben threatened to put an end to negotiations if he didn't refrain from such language.

"I think," James told Latrobe, "this is one area we might reconsider. I agree that every worker should be treated as any other worker, regardless of the color of his skin, but given the conflict already running amuck concerning the Negroes and the issue of slavery, I don't think we need to add to the problem."

Ben grew thoughtful for a moment, then nodded. "I suppose I see the wisdom in reconsidering. But for now, I want the work to continue. Not only to continue, but to exceed our earlier expectations. You've cost us a good bit of time and effort here, Mr. O'Connor, and while you may feel quite content with what you've accomplished, I cannot look at the tunnel and say the same. It is my fervent hope that our good faith in this compromise might be rewarded with your supreme efforts to see that tunnel completed."

Red got to his feet. "Yar tunnel will get built, I promise ya that on me life."

"Well, as added assurance that the peace remains on a permanent basis, I'm going to keep the guards on the payroll. The contractor has agreed to share the cost with the railroad, and I believe it will be in the best interests of all concerned."

Red said nothing, but his gaze locked momentarily with James' as he nodded. With that he exited, and James let out the breath he'd been holding. It was over. The strike was finished, the negotiations were complete, and all parties were satisfied. He felt as though a tremendous weight had been taken from his shoulders.

"At least no one was killed," he said, thinking aloud.

Latrobe smiled. "Did you expect there to be?"

"With O'Connor and his incessant Connaughtmen rights and rituals, who was to know? I wearied so much of the conflict between the two parties that I wanted to dismiss them all and start over."

"Well, I think the real solution comes not in segregation of the regional groups, but in evening the sides."

"What!" James realized he'd nearly shouted the word, and he forced himself to calm down. "Sorry, Ben, but I don't follow your logic on that at all."

"It's really quite simple. If we bring in enough men from the other factions, then all sides will be equal, and you won't have one group bullying or holding court over the other. They will be equals and therefore find it necessary to deal with each other fairly."

James shook his head. "That isn't how these men work. If there were five hundred Corkians and only one Connaughtman, he'd still stand and fight. That's just how they are. And it isn't just the Connaughtmen. It's every single group. Each faction believes they are the most important, that their ways are the right ways. They very nearly have no fear of the other's wits or numbers, and they certainly will not stop at an all-out war just because you even the sides. It won't work."

Ben leaned back in his chair and considered James for a moment. "Perhaps you are right, but what if you aren't? What if this is the perfect solution? I've already discussed this matter with Thomas Swann and others on the board, and they feel it makes good sense."

"But neither they nor you work one-on-one with these men. You put me here to be your eyes and ears. Now that I'm trying to be honest with you about the holes in your solution, you refuse to listen." He knew his tone was taking on an air of frustration, but in fact James could very nearly see the bloodbath that might occur should Latrobe carry through with his plans.

"I'm still listening, James," Latrobe assured him. "But ofttimes we are too close to a problem to see the solution. I think perhaps you have been somewhat given over to their way of thinking. Perhaps you've been unnerved by their threats and their pitiful attempts at action."

"Pitiful attempts?" James asked indignantly. "Ben, you weren't here last November. Families were thrown out into the streets and their houses were burned to the ground. The Connaughtmen forced Corkmen to leave the town, driving them out into one of the worst snowstorms of the year. I don't know but what men died from that attack, and just because it didn't happen in a big city like Baltimore doesn't qualify it as a pitiful attempt."

"I didn't mean to suggest that the violence was acceptable behavior. I do realize what happened and how it affected this town and work production. Why do you think I've insisted on the patrolmen becoming a permanent fixture at the site?" He paused and offered James an apologetic smile. "Come now, let us not be at odds. I think you might well be surprised at the success of my solutions if you just give them a chance."

James held back the retort he might have made if the man had been anyone but Ben Latrobe. He genuinely respected Latrobe's thinking—most of the time. But this time he was dead wrong. If he brought in men to equal out the numbers from each faction of Irish, it would serve only to kindle the flames of another uprising.

Seeking to give them time to consider the matter without anger, James chose to change the subject. "So tell me about the new Camel engines."

Latrobe described Ross Winans' popular new design that was notable for its extremely powerful engines. "I want Camels here at the tunnel site to help in transporting supplies up the steep grade."

"I've read some on the design," James said, "but I still can't imagine putting the engineer on top of the boiler." He'd seen a drawing of this, and the entire engine looked anything but normal because of this feature.

"It's true that Winans put the cab on top of the boiler. It allows for an increased size in the firebox, while removing the weight from the same. The weight is centered over the drive wheels, about three tons figured for each."

"How much were they able to increase the firebox?"

Latrobe thought for a moment. "With the firebox behind the frame, it allowed Winans to make it the same width as the outside width of the frame. The firebox itself slopes downward from the boiler to the tender, where a fireman stands ready to shovel in coal."

"Staying with the coal burners, eh?"

Latrobe smiled. "Since that's what the Camels mostly haul, it makes little sense to go to wood."

"Ah," James commented. "We've had Grasshoppers, Crabs, and now Camels. The roundhouse is becoming a regular zoo."

Latrobe chuckled.

"So now you have your powerful little mountain coal hauler," James remarked. "I suppose they know what they're doing, but from what little I've seen, I'm just not sure it will ever catch on."

"Doesn't really matter much whether it does or not. The B&O is more than happy to keep the shops busy developing them. But that aside, let's talk about our tunnel."

James nodded and leaned forward as Latrobe stretched out the design prints they'd worked from all winter. "As you can see, in spite of the weather and the labor problems, we've made decent headway." James pointed to the map. "We've had mostly slate and sandstone to excavate, and while that's a blessing in regard to removal, after exposure to the air and elements, the slate tends to crumble. The entire tunnel will have to be arched and lined."

"All 4,100 feet of it?" Latrobe eyed the map thoughtfully.

"I believe so. I know it will be costly, but in the long run it will be far more costly to ignore this problem," James replied. "We've sunk three shafts at points that you can see here. Moving from the east portal we have the first shaft going down one hundred eighty feet, the second here"—he pointed to a spot about a third of the way from the first shaft—"at a depth of one hundred seventy-five feet. And the last at one hundred sixty-seven feet. Each shaft is basically fifteen by twenty feet and lined with heavy timbers to discourage cave-ins. I'd be happy to escort you up to take a look."

"I'd like that."

James nodded and continued. "As I wrote you, the horse gins are working well for lifting out the rock. Those winches were mounted horizontally on a sturdy timber framework, and from them we ran two pulleys up and down the shaft. As the horses walk in a circle, the full container lifts up excess dirt and rock and the empty one is lowered into the shaft."

"I'm glad to hear they are efficient."

"They are for now. I do see the time coming, however, when steam gins would work better. But it can certainly wait for the time being. You'll be happy to know the western portal has been started, as well as the eastern. We've run into some hard rock there, so progress has been slowed. It may even be postponed in order to focus on the more easily achieved sections."

"Probably wise," Latrobe replied. "Let's definitely inspect the shafts, but after lunch. I for one am growing hungry, and your wife promised me a meal fit for a king."

James grinned. "She does a good job. Miriam and the women in town have taught her a great deal. I never thought to see her in a kitchen, but she gets in there and works right alongside Miriam, and what's more, she has told me at times she actually enjoys herself."

Latrobe laughed. "I'm sure she'd rather be going over tunnel formulas instead of cake recipes. Say, why don't you take a copy of these home and show her exactly what's going on here? No doubt she'd be delighted with the chance to see what's happening."

"I will do that," James said, then grew rather sheepish. "In fact, I've already promised to bring her to the tunnel site when the weather is stable. I might even let her go down into the shaft."

"The Irish won't like that. They'll see a woman on the grounds as bad luck."

"How about if she doesn't look like a woman?" James added, shrugging. More than once that winter, Carolina had pulled on an old pair of James' wool trousers to add warmth to her own wool pantalets. It was seeing her do this that gave James the idea to disguise her and bring her to the tunnel in order to get a firsthand look at their progress. He knew it was hard for her to be removed from the workings of the railroad, and the family had demanded so much of her time and attention that she rarely had a moment for anything else. But James remembered her eagerly poring over his own engine designs when he'd been her tutor at Oakbridge. He could still see the delight in her expression as she pondered the ideas set forth by the Baltimore and Ohio Railroad.

"I think she'd make a jim-dandy young boy, don't you?" James asked, unable to keep from smiling.

Latrobe chuckled. "I'd like to see that myself."

"Stick around," James replied.

"I'm afraid I can't. I've made a promise to the board and to the men. I'm going to constantly move up and down this line until it's completed. It's good for morale and it helps me to have a firsthand knowledge of exactly where we stand. Swann thinks it a perfect solution to knowing for sure whether or not we can boast completion by 1853."

"And what do you think so far?"

"I think we can do it," Latrobe replied. "Maybe even by late 1852. The most difficult tasks will be the bridges and tunnels, but we will do it this time. Swann will get us there come drought or high water."

"It's hard to imagine after all these years," James said, thinking of how impressive it would be to find the line completed. "It seems we've struggled so long to reach the Ohio."

"Well, it isn't over yet. Not by a long shot. There are many problems to deal with, and no doubt there will be conflicts and trials aplenty before we actually find ourselves on that muddy bank of water. If we can keep down the labor disputes and squabbling among the townsfolk and legislators, we will certainly progress more rapidly."

"I believe the compromise reached here was a good start," James said. He tried not to frown at the thought that Red might just turn around in another six months and strike again. Worse yet, he fully expected the man to continue retaliation against those who were not Connaughtmen.

"Compromise is the key to every productive partnership," Latrobe remarked, gathering his things.

Twenty-Eight

The Hands of Time

To Carolina, spring and summer of 1850 passed not in dates on calendars or the ticking of the clock, but in new skills mastered and wisdom attained. Life in Greigsville, Virginia, was certainly not what she had imagined it while dreaming away in her plush Baltimore home. Somehow, while she knew it certainly would not resolve all the problems of life, Carolina had convinced herself that living together as a family and being near the action of the railroad would be enough to keep her content. But that wasn't the case.

There was a growing restlessness inside her that caused her to turn inward, desperately searching for some missing element. How could she not be happy? She had her lovely family, all safe and healthy. She and Miriam had managed to create a comfortable home, and with the arrival of additional Baltimore supplies, the house was taking on a strikingly pleasant air. James had even arranged to add two rooms to the first floor, as well as a porch that wrapped around the front and side of the house, giving them a place to pass the evenings together.

Greigsville itself had also grown and developed over the past year. In fact, it had rather experienced an explosion of people and services. They could now boast two schools, two churches, and several stores, one of which she and James owned, with the Kaberlines hired to manage it. There was also in the town a post office and resident doctor. Much of the St. John money was invested in the town and Carolina couldn't think of a better use for it.

The Irish had managed to take advantage of the building materials offered by the railroad, and while some still lived in tents, more houses dotted the hillsides and valleys than before the November riot of the previous year. James had said there were at least eighty houses either completed or nearing completion, and all of them were filled with families living contentedly off the prosperity of the growing community.

But even with this, Carolina found herself discontent. Every day she would watch her husband saddle up and ride to the tunnel site, and every day she would find herself longing to go with him. She knew it was impossible. She simply did not live in a culture that would accept or allow her to participate in the masculine world of railroads. Even her dearest friends, Thomas Swann for one, chided her for her attempts to involve herself in places where she would only gain the disdain of those around her. Still she studied whenever time allowed. As was often the case, she would incorporate some of her own interests in the studies of her children, and while the two oldest attended the new school, she still tried to work with them to expand their minds and embrace new interests. Her interests.

Victoria couldn't care less. The time she spent in study was sheer misery, and Carolina knew she despised having to go to school. This alarmed Carolina, who had always seen the university in Victoria's future. It was becoming far more widely accepted to allow women to study, even if it was still rejected that they should want to do anything with that knowledge. But Victoria found no pleasure in learning. She seemed to enjoy reading and had even confided in her mother and father that she was attempting to teach Kiernan O'Connor to read, but outside of that, she wanted no part in formal education.

Kiernan was, of course, another matter entirely—one which Carolina refused to allow herself to dwell on for long. With her rambunctious Jordana and studious Brenton, she had little time to consider any matter at length. Jordana and Brenton both seemed to outgrow their clothes on a regular basis, and already she'd had to order shoes twice for the growing boy, refusing to let him go barefoot, as many of his friends were wont to do. Jordana, at four, was too young to go to school, and made it very clear that she thought this a terrible injustice. She spent her days pining for her siblings, running races around Carolina and Miriam, and generally getting herself into one mess after another.

Carolina no longer found it shocking to see Jordana walk into the house carrying frogs or insects, although she had obeyed her father's order to leave snakes alone. It was business as usual when she had to pull a curious Jordana back up after dangling over and nearly falling into the opening to their new well. It even ceased to be that startling when Jordana disappeared following an afternoon nap, only to be found atop the porch roof. It seemed she had come to her parents' bedroom in search of Carolina, but found instead an open window and the lure of what waited beyond.

For all of Jordana's busyness, Brenton was calmer and more easily occupied, but his interruptions came in the form of deep, introspective questions. "How high is the sky?" "How many days would it take to walk all around the earth?" "Why do we eat deer and cattle but not dogs and cats?" Nearing seven years old, Brenton felt that no bit of knowledge should be kept from him, including the operative workings of his father's musket. But where Jordana would have simply pulled the weapon off the wall for inspection, Brenton very calmly approached his father and asked for a demonstration and information concerning the matter.

Carolina was very grateful for Brenton's obedient, easygoing nature. She was also blessed by it. Her son's thoughtfulness came out in many ways. He generally did his chores without being asked, having learned early on that the sooner the necessary tasks were accomplished, the more time there would be to do what he wanted to do. He often found berry patches and surprised Carolina with a pail of fruit. On one occasion had told his father of a particular trinket that he wished to purchase for his mother, and worked extra chores in order to earn the money for the item. The gift turned out to be a broach locket, which Carolina cherished because it had come from Brenton's efforts, and was given for no particular occasion except that the giver wanted to bestow it upon her.

Even now, as she settled herself in her bedroom to read the latest letter from Oakbridge, Carolina knew that her blessings were many. Knew, in fact, that they outweighed any of her tribulations. So why should she feel so discontent?

She positioned her chair beside the open window and breathed deeply of the fading summer warmth. Soon autumn would be upon them, and after that she knew full well what to expect. The previous winter had brought heavy snows and moderate cold, but it was the isolation that Carolina didn't look forward to. Days and weeks when folks could scarcely come or go. Dark, depressing skies that threatened bad weather and kept the freighters and mail held up in Cumberland, leaving the residents of the small town to wonder if the rest of the world had fallen off the map and left them behind.

She tried to shake off these oppressive thoughts and opened the letter from home. Instantly she experienced a flood of joy over the feathery script of her mother's handwriting. How she longed to see her—to talk with her.

1850, August 20
Dearest Daughter,

I pray this letter finds you and your family in good health. Oakbridge is alive with activities as we prepare ourselves for the upcoming winter. We anticipate a good harvest and your father is pleased. The livestock, as well, have produced an abundance of young, and November will find us able to butcher and smoke some fifty hogs without at all compromising the stock remaining.

Virginia has been confined to bed by the doctor. Her condition grows more fragile as her time to deliver approaches. She seems to have lost her joy of living, and I cannot help but fear for her state of mind. As one who knows the delicacy of such matters, I see ever-growing telltale signs that Virginia is in peril. Please remember her in your prayers. She is much changed by the years and the bitterness in which she has surrounded herself. I wish I might have been here to help her in the early years of her marriage and motherhood, but alas, I cannot turn back the hands of time.

Otherwise, the state of affairs remains much unchanged. Your father is still working too hard and concerns himself overmuch with the issue of slavery. He says it tears at the very binding threads of this nation, and I fear he may be right.

Carolina, I cannot say how very much I long to see you and the children. Knowing that those dear babies live not so very far away, but much too far for me to journey to, is a great sadness. It is my dearest wish that you might come and bring your family home to Oakbridge.

Carolina felt hot tears slide down her cheeks. "I miss you so much, Mama," she whispered. Her tears fell upon the pages of the letter, and unable to go on, she set the letter aside and gave in to her longing and despair.

She wanted to go home. Wanted to see her family and to hold them. She wanted to show her children off and to know the comforts of the house she'd grown up in. She had no idea of the time that had passed until James' voice sounded from the doorway.

"Carolina? What is it?"

She looked up, startled to find him home. She hurriedly wiped her tears. "I'm sorry," she managed to say.

He came to where she sat and questioned her again. "What has happened? Did you have bad news from home?"

She tried to laugh but it came out sounding more like a stifled sob. "No, only good news. Well, Virginia is unwell, but other than that . . ." she trailed into silence, knowing her attempt at normalcy was impossible.

She folded the letter and looked up at her worried husband. "I am truly all right."

"That is why I find you sitting alone, sobbing?"

His voice was tender, and this was her undoing. "Oh, James," she said, and tears began to flow again.

He drew her into his arms and held her tightly against him. Carolina knew she had unduly worried him, but she couldn't keep the tears from coming. She clung to him, desperate to find strength in his embrace, but the longing inside would not be denied.

"Please," he whispered against her hair, "please tell me what is wrong."

She tried to shake her head. "Nothing is truly wrong," she answered. "At least if it is, I don't know what it is." She struggled to control her misery. "I know I miss my mother, and her letter only opened the longing to see her."

James lifted her chin, forcing her to meet his sympathetic expression. "I know you miss her. Carolina, why don't you go home for a time? I can't leave just now, but you could go with the children and Miriam. I'd get you to Cumberland somehow, and from there you could take the train into Baltimore. You could see Mrs. Graves and Cook and the house, and then go on to Washington and Oakbridge. Would you like that?"

Carolina felt her spirits soar. "Are you sure you wouldn't mind?"

"Not at all. In fact, it will free me up to give a more concentrated effort to the tunnel work. We're coming upon some particularly rough elements and my full attention will be needed. You could stay with your folks for as long as you like, although I would like you home before the first snows. Christmas wouldn't be the same without my family here."

She reached a hand up to touch his cheek. "You always seem to know exactly what I need."

"Maybe more so than you give me credit for."

She smiled ever so slightly. "You've always known, haven't you? Since I was fifteen and you played tutor to my curiosity. You've known me in ways that I'm only learning to know myself. How can this be?"

He returned her smile and reached a hand up to wipe a remaining tear from her cheek. "We are kindred souls, you and I. To know you better is to know myself. I've long felt your unhappiness and wanted to suggest you take this venture, but I didn't want you to perceive it as my trying to get rid of you. I'll be miserable while you're away, but I know it will do you a world of good."

"Who will escort us to Cumberland?" she asked hopefully.

James grew thoughtful for a moment. "I trust but one man at this point. Would you object to Kiernan being the one to take you?"

Carolina shook her head. "No, I have no objections to him, but I'd like to know what makes you so certain of his trust?"

James dropped his hold on her and walked to the window. Staring out, he spoke. "Kiernan has proven himself to be a reasonable man. He isn't hotheaded like his brother. He cares about the men, cares even more about Red, but he tempers it with logic and thoughtful consideration. He'd make an excellent supervisor one day, but he's still too young, even at seventeen. He's come to me many times with word of one dispute or another, and while his loyalties are torn between standing with his brother and maintaining the peace, he manages to betray neither one."

"If you think this highly of him, I should be honored for him to escort us. Will you be able to spare him soon?"

"Absolutely. This is a matter which cannot be put off," he said, turning back to face her. He leaned against the window frame and folded his arms across his chest. "This is the first week of September. We should have another month, maybe two, before any sign of snow. The sooner we get you headed for Oakbridge the better. Once you get to Cumberland, the railroad will make short order of your trip. But first we must deal with getting you there."

Carolina knew now that he was completely serious in this venture. "Thank you, James," she said, hoping that all the love she felt for him was conveyed in her words. The thought of being able to see her mother and father again overshadowed the nagging feeling that without him she would be only half of a whole.

The stage ride to Cumberland was less than desirable. Carolina constantly found herself battling with Jordana. If she wasn't fighting to keep the child from hanging out the window, she was trying to reason with her as to why it was inappropriate for four-year-old girls to ride topside with the driver and baggage. Miriam, sandwiched between Carolina and Brenton, tried her best to assist Carolina with the wayward child, but it often did little good. Brenton, ever the studious soul, concentrated first on his books, then on the passing scenery, and eventually he dozed off, using Miriam as a cushion against the rough, uneven ride.

Miriam was as excited as Carolina about visiting her childhood home and all her friends and family. But she had also been nervous about returning to Oakbridge until Carolina assured her that Hampton Cabot would have to walk over Carolina to get to Miriam.

Victoria was delighted to find herself with no other recourse but to sit opposite her mother. She sat next to the window, with Kiernan appropriately separating her from another man who'd chosen to make the journey with them. Carolina watched, and sometimes managed to listen in, as they conversed about the world around them and life in general. She suddenly realized, listening to Victoria speak on matters pertaining to the hardships of Irishwomen in America versus that of their homeland-bound counterparts, that her daughter had grown up a great deal in the past year. She was not only taking on the appearance of a young woman, but her thinking and concerns were more those of an adult than a child.

It shocked Carolina, although she tried to keep from revealing her thoughts. In a few short months Victoria would be fourteen, and Carolina knew it would be impossible to deny her interest in Kiernan O'Connor. Many of the Irish in Greigsville had taken wives of fifteen and sixteen. One girl was even rumored to be no more than thirteen, and already she was well along with child. Carolina shuddered. She wasn't ready for Victoria to be interested in marriage and a family of her own. There was still too much to teach her—still a great deal to tell her. Victoria didn't even know about the trust she'd set up for her, using a portion of Blake St. John's fortune. The trust was worth more money than either one of them could ever earn in a lifetime, yet here sat her daughter speaking of gold in California and the excitement of prospecting.

Carolina realized that the time would soon be upon them for her to have a very serious mother-daughter discussion with Victoria. Perhaps a time would present itself while in Baltimore, she reasoned. Perhaps she could have Mrs. Graves tend to Jordana and Brenton, while she and Victoria went to lunch or tea together. Already a plan was formulating in her mind, but her determination was further strengthened when she saw Victoria slip her gloved hand into Kiernan's when she thought her mother's attention was otherwise given to Jordana.

When she turned to give Victoria a reproving look, she found the child quite innocently sitting with hands folded in her lap. A calm, sweet expression met Carolina's, and suddenly Carolina felt very foolish and naïve. Her daughter was in love with this man. It was all too clear. What she had presumed to be an innocent flirtation, or at best, infatuation, was blossoming into Victoria's first real love.

"I'm not ready for this," she muttered under her breath. But it was clearly out of her hands.

Twenty-Nine

Reunion

Riding the rails of her own Potomac and Great Falls Railroad, Carolina couldn't resist straining her eyes to catch a glimpse of her childhood home. *Oakbridge.* The very word meant family and pleasant memories. It was odd, Carolina thought, how time away had caused her to set aside all of the bad memories and choose only the good ones.

"There it is!" Brenton declared. "I see the white pillars."

He was right. Through the trees in the distance, Carolina could just make out the glittering white marble. How happy she was for the late and lengthy summer weather. The trees had not even begun to lose their leaves, and the ground was still richly carpeted in green. The plantation looked gloriously clothed, like an aristocratic lady in all of her elegant finery. Carolina felt her breath catch in her throat. Soon. Very soon she would be back in the embrace of her childhood home. Soon she would know the contentment of her little-girl imagery and memories that had fueled her through the lengthy trip from Greigsville.

"It won't be long now," she told Miriam and the children. "Papa will have the carriage waiting for us just ahead."

And so he did. In fact, he had come himself to greet them. When Carolina saw her father, she couldn't contain an exclamation of girlish joy. She was instantly transported back in time. "Papa!" she shouted and jumped from the railcar without even awaiting assistance. She threw herself into his arms, trying not to notice how much older he looked, trying not to remember that she was no longer his little girl, but a grown woman, married, with children of her own. "Papa." This time the word was more a sigh of contentment. "How good of you to be here for us."

"I've scarcely thought of anything else this day," he admitted. "Now, stand back and let me look you over."

"Look at me, too!" demanded Jordana, who had somehow managed to exit the car closely behind her mother.

"Of course I will look at you," he replied, laughing. "Now, spin around for me and let me see how you've grown."

Jordana did this while the carriage driver assisted Victoria and Miriam from the railcar. "I'm big now, Grandpa. I'm four," she told him as she stopped twirling. "When you sawed me last time I was just three. Four is big. But they won't let me go to school."

Her jabbering made Joseph grin. He shared a quick glance with Carolina, then looked back to the dancing child. "Shame on them," he told Jordana, and for this he received a winning smile.

"Hello, Grandpa," Victoria said, coming to give him a kiss and a hug. "I've missed you so much. It seems forever since you visited us in Baltimore."

"Not much more than a year, but my, how you've grown into a handsome young woman."

"I'm almost fourteen, and—" She stopped midsentence as something else caught her eye. "Oh, look at the horse," Victoria murmured, and all eyes followed her gaze to the fine Arabian gelding that stood tied to the back of the carriage.

"I've had him since June," Joseph explained. "He is my birthday gift from Georgia."

"He's wonderful," Victoria said, stepping toward the beast. "May I pet him?"

"Be careful," Carolina called out. "He's no doubt a very spirited animal."

"That he is," admitted her father. "Stay away from his backside and approach him from side or front so that he's well aware of your presence."

"Grandpa?" Brenton spoke softly, and when he had Joseph's attention, he bowed low.

Joseph returned the bow and bent down to question his grandson. "Are we just to shake hands, or are you inclined to indulge me with a hug?" Brenton grinned and threw himself into his grandfather's arms. "I suppose that settles the matter," Joseph replied.

That only left Miriam, whom Joseph warmly welcomed back. "You will find your friends and family quite well," he told her. She nodded and thanked him before he turned to usher them all into the carriage. "The family is quite anxious for your arrival. Your mother hasn't stopped fussing all day."

"How is Mother?" Carolina asked, arranging herself and Jordana in the carriage.

"She is quite well," Joseph told her. "She is in many ways changed. She is quieter and more subdued, but she is also more attentive and loving. Her concern over social events and appearances is no longer a consideration, and this has freed her to focus on other things."

When they were all seated and the driver had finished loading their baggage, Joseph mounted his Arabian and motioned the driver to take them home. Keeping a steady pace beside the carriage, Joseph asked Carolina about James and the railroad.

"James is terribly sorry not to have been able to join us. The tunnel is at a critical point in its construction, and he simply could not get away."

"I completely understand," Joseph said, nodding. "I'm most joyous that he could spare all of you."

"He feared if we didn't come now, we might not come at all. The first snows will be upon us before long, and often the freighters—and even more so the stagecoaches—find it impossible to maneuver through the mountains in winter."

"We've been blessed with wonderful weather," Joseph said, glancing upward. "The rains have come just when we needed them most, and the sun has kept the weather otherwise warm and dry. We've had a good harvest of corn and wheat, and the orchards are overflowing. Naomi says we will hardly suffer for preserves and jellies and all manner of fruit desserts. I suppose you've had it just as good in Greigsville?"

Carolina smiled. "Yes. I planted a garden with Miriam's help, and the abundance was enough to give us a good hold on the winter months to come. Work at the tunnel has also benefited from the weather. They are ahead of schedule, and in spite of a few problems here and there with labor disputes and equipment failures, James is quite happy with the way things have gone."

"That's good news. Any idea what you will do once the tunnel is in place?"

Carolina shook her head. "None whatsoever. James says it will be at least two years before we can even think of completion."

"You'll be surprised just how quickly that time will pass."

Brenton and Jordana busily gawked at the scenery around them while Victoria and Miriam whispered comments conspiratorially. Carolina knew her father was indeed correct in saying that two years would pass quickly. Wasn't she only too well aware of how speedily her children had grown? Especially Victoria.

Their arrival at the house was heralded by Virginia's children. Nathaniel, or Nate as most everyone called him, was busy racing up and down the drive with a stick and hoop until he spied the carriage.

"They're here! They're here!" he shouted out, to which Levinia and Thora instantly left their quiet play to run out and greet the travelers.

All of the children eyed one another cautiously, with the exception of Jordana, who could not care less about the proprieties of deciding where one fit into a new situation. She was hanging over the side of the carriage, struggling to figure a way down, when the horses finally were drawn to a stop.

"Jordana, wait until the driver has put down the step," her mother chided.

Joseph reached over in his saddle and hoisted Jordana over the side. Sliding her to the ground, he laughed. "There, that should settle that." He quickly dismounted, just as a slave boy appeared and took the reins of his horse. Handing the beast over, Joseph made his way to the carriage to assist his daughter. "Welcome home, my dear," he told Carolina.

She smiled, gazing up at the fluted columns that lined the portico. She was just about to turn away and speak to Victoria when her eyes caught sight of someone stepping out of the massive front doors.

"Mama!" she called and, forgetting all decorum, ran up the steps, tears streaming down her face. Margaret Adams simply opened her arms and received Carolina like a long-lost child. Breaking into sobs, Carolina gripped her mother tightly. It was almost impossible to believe she was truly here. How long she had waited for this moment. How she had pleaded with God for the living proof of His goodness that now stood before her—embracing her—assuring her that all was well.

"Oh, my dear. My dear," Margaret whispered and soothed.

"I thought this day would never come," Carolina said, pulling away. She met her mother's dark eyes, now wet with her own tears of joy.

"I know."

"But here you are, and here we are," Carolina said, motioning to her children. "You have to meet your grandchildren." Victoria came up the steps first, with Jordana and Brenton bringing up the rear. "This is Victoria. She'll be fourteen in February."

Victoria curtsied and smiled. "I'm pleased to meet you, Grandmother."

Margaret wiped at her eyes and laughed. "We stand on no formalities here, child. Come give your grandmother a kiss." Victoria did as she was bid, and the older woman nodded approvingly as Brenton was introduced next. "He's the spitting image of his father."

"Yes, he is," Carolina admitted as her son bowed low, then went into Margaret's open arms.

"Are you feeling well now, Grandmother?" he asked innocently. "Mama says you were very sick, but now God has healed you."

Margaret smiled over his head at Carolina. "That is true, and yes, I feel quite wonderful. Especially now that you have come to visit me."

"I'm four," Jordana interrupted and smiled up with such a precocious expression that everyone burst out laughing.

"Oh, how like Maryland she is!" Margaret exclaimed.

A hush fell over the group, with exception to Margaret. Seeming to realize their uneasiness, Margaret laughed. "You all look as though you've seen a ghost. I'm truly all right, and being reminded of my dearly loved little girl is not going to hurt me as you fear it might."

Carolina reached out and touched her mother's arm. "It's just that I'd not thought of it. Jordana is very much like Mary. I'd really not considered how it might affect you until this very moment."

"I assure you all," Margaret said, exchanging a glance with her husband, "that I am fine. I am stronger than you might imagine. God has helped me to see that my strength does not lie in myself, but in Him. I could not be more delighted to find Jordana a pleasant replica of Mary." She smiled down at the child, who seemed most captivated to have suddenly become the center of everyone's attention. "You are a beautiful little girl, Jordana, and I think we shall very much enjoy each other's company."

"Will you show me where the toys are?" Jordana asked and quickly added, "So we can play—just you and me?"

Margaret nodded. "I would be very happy to show you the toys and to play with you."

Carolina let out a breath she'd not even realized she was holding. Jordana took hold of her grandmother's hand and turned to throw Carolina a look of sheer determination. "I'm going to play with Grandmama." She looked with the same self-confidence that she displayed at home after having caught a much-desired frog.

"I think that would be wonderful, Jordana," Carolina assured the child.

"Then we shall make for the nursery," Margaret said with a nod to Carolina. "We shall have time to talk later."

As they departed, Brenton spoke up. "May I go exploring?" His gaze was already darting from side to side as if to capture a view of everything at once.

"It's quite all right with me," Carolina answered. "But be careful. You don't know your way around."

"I can show you," a voice sounded.

"Ah, Nate. Come and meet your cousin Brenton!" Joseph declared.

Up until that moment, Carolina had forgotten about the children who had been there upon their arrival. Turning around, she found the twins eyeing her with a look of near contempt. Were they jealous that Jordana had so quickly captured their grandmother's attention?

"Nate, surely you remember your aunt Carolina," Joseph said matter-of-factly. "I'm not sure Levinia and Thora do, however. It's been at least two years, or has it been three, since you were here at Oakbridge?"

"It's been at least three. The girls were just toddling," Carolina said, smiling in a way that she hoped put the twins at ease.

"Well, the girls turned six last summer. Levinia, Thora, this is Brenton and Victoria."

The girls dropped a slight curtsy while Victoria did the same and Brenton bowed.

"There, now," Joseph continued, "the introductions are made and I suggest we get in out of the sun. Nate, you show Brenton around the plantation, and, Carolina, if you will excuse me for a time, I have business in the stables."

"May I come?" Victoria questioned suddenly. "I want to see your horses."

"Of course," Joseph replied. "If your mother can spare you."

Carolina laughed at the hopeful expression on Victoria's face. "By all means."

"We want to see them, too," the twins declared in unison.

"Well, then, come along," Joseph told them. "Will you amuse yourself while we are gone?"

Carolina nodded. "I will explore on my own and reacquaint myself with everything."

At this, Joseph looped his arm with Victoria's, and Carolina saw the scowling look that Thora gave her grandfather. She tried to ignore the implications of this reaction. She knew how contrary the twins could be and just had to hope that their jealousy would not cause conflicts among the children.

"Miriam, you might as well go ahead and visit your friends. I'll be just fine on my own," Carolina said. Miriam smiled and hurried off in the direction of the slave quarters. Smiling to herself, Carolina made her way into the house, pausing a moment in the foyer to take in all the sights, sounds, and smells of home.

The gold-framed paintings of Adams ancestors still lined the walls and seemed to welcome her with stoic approval from their canvas perches. Things were much the same as when last she'd visited. Virginia had arranged for the foyer to be repapered, and the gold-and-cream print fit well with the paintings and walnut furnishings.

Pulling off her bonnet and gloves, Carolina noticed the stuffiness of the house. Back home in Greigsville, the windows were always open to allow in the breeze. She hadn't realized until then just how refreshing this made her house.

She looked into the front drawing room, then made her way to the music room and across the hall to her father's first-floor study. She thought to linger here a moment and was halfway across the room when the door closed behind her.

"Well, well," Hampton said, coming toward her. "If it isn't my dear little sister-in-law. I heard you were due home today."

Carolina stiffened. He was just as she remembered him. Tall and foreboding. He had discarded his waistcoat and instead was casually dressed in little more than boots, trousers, and a white ruffled shirt. It was almost as if he'd noticed her arrival and had come to greet her in the midst of dressing for the evening. Carolina bolstered her courage, knowing there was no escaping the confrontation.

"Hello, Mr. Cabot."

"Tut, tut. We shall have none of that. After all, we are family, and we were once nearly engaged to be married."

"As I recall, you asked, and I refused," Carolina said, trying desperately to sound strong. In her years away from Oakbridge, she hadn't missed Hampton and Virginia's altercations, and she certainly hadn't missed the leering look that Hampton was throwing her way now.

"My, my, my," he said, looking her up and down, his gaze lingering in most inappropriate places. "You are all grown-up, and what a lovely seductress you've become. How long has it been since last we met? Let me think." He counted silently on his fingers, all the while moving closer to where she stood. "You visited some three years back, but, of course, I wasn't here then. Pity. As I recall, your father had me off on business."

He moved closer and Carolina started to feel trapped. The room had only one exit and he clearly blocked that path. "I believe it has been nearly five years. Yes, that's it." He took another step and let his gaze travel the length of her once again.

Carolina shuddered, hating the fact that he knew he'd unnerved her.

He grinned at her reaction. "I see childbearing has done nothing but improve your figure. Unlike my dear wife, who even now is confined to bed in order to give me another brat. Virginia has allowed herself to become so unappealing. But you, on the other hand, have fairly bloomed."

"Mr. Cabot, I find this conversation highly offensive." She moved back a pace, hoping to better position herself for a run at the door. Her quick glance in that direction betrayed her thoughts, and Hampton's laughter filled the air.

"Already planning your escape, eh?"

"I simply see no point in continuing this conversation. I've only just returned and am making a tour of the house. I do not desire to be further detained by you." Carolina fought with every ounce of strength to remain calm and collected. She might have succeeded but for Hampton's next statement.

"I saw Miriam from my bedroom window. She's looking fat and sassy. Time with you has done a great deal to improve her looks."

"You leave Miriam alone."

Hampton considered her for a moment. "Or you'll what?"

Carolina's rising anger in the face of protecting Miriam quickly quelled her fear. "Or I'll personally see to it that you never harm another person, black or white, again."

"Threaten all you like, dear sister, but the truth is, I am hardly concerned with your words. You will find yourself far too busy with visiting to worry about that darky."

Carolina stepped forward, feeling it might well be impossible to refrain from striking the man. "Miriam is my responsibility. Leave her alone. It's just that simple."

Hampton reached out to touch Carolina but drew his hand back as if he'd thought better of it. "Don't threaten me, Carolina. I don't take it well." His voice was low and menacing. "You are a slave owner's daughter, and you should well understand that Miriam is nothing more than property."

"She is not property. I freed her after you nearly killed her," Carolina declared, her hands clenched in fists.

"Well, if she's free, then you have no say over what she does."

"She's under my protection. Just as my children are under my protection," Carolina replied. "You would do well to understand, Mr. Cabot, that I will do whatever it takes to protect my own family."

"She's a Negro slave. Whether you call her free or not, she's still a slave at heart," Hampton said, and appearing completely bored with the conversation, he walked casually to his desk. "You would do well to rethink this situation. Slaves are property, nothing more."

"They are human beings, and whether they have papers to show their freedom or not, whether they are black, brown, white, or any other color you would choose, all mankind deserves respect and compassion."

"You scarcely practice what you preach," Hampton replied. "I've not had a decent word out of you in years, much less any respect or compassion."

Carolina considered him a moment before moving toward the door. "Miriam represents the very best of her people, while you are without a doubt the worst example of any white man I have ever known. I cannot offer even a shred of respect for any man who treats other human beings as worthless chattel."

She slammed the door behind her, hearing him mutter some incoherent response. Shaking from head to toe, she moved hesitantly down the hall. The peace of her visit had been shattered by Hampton's crudity and suggestive remarks. She could only pray that she might somehow manage to keep out of his way during their remaining time at Oakbridge.

Thirty

Sisters

Carolina stood outside of Virginia's room for a full five minutes before gathering the courage to knock. She hesitated in part because she feared her sister's reaction. She also feared her own, and it troubled her to the very core of her heart. Surely she didn't hold any malice toward Virginia. Not after all these years and everything that had passed. James belonged to Carolina and they shared a very happy marriage, while Virginia, having deceived everyone, had a miserable life with Hampton Cabot.

Knocking lightly, Carolina opened the door and called out, "Virginia, it's me, Carolina."

"Come in," a pathetically weak voice answered.

Carolina stepped into the darkened room. The windows were shrouded against the light, and the room felt stifling. Carolina approached the bed and found herself shocked at the sight of her elder sister. Desperately thin, with exception to the mounded proof of her pregnancy, Virginia was a mere shell of the woman she had once been.

"Hello, Carolina," she said, shifting uncomfortably.

"Hello, Virginia." Carolina wondered for a moment if she would resent an embrace. Deciding to throw caution aside, Carolina leaned down and gently hugged Virginia's bony shoulders. A quick peck on the cheek completed the greeting. "How are you feeling?"

"Terrible," Virginia said and gave a haughty laugh. "But how else would you expect me to feel under the circumstance?" Her eyes were glassy and lifeless and her face stark and pale against the lavender bed sheets.

"This is a difficult time," Carolina admitted, pulling a chair closer to the bed.

"Especially when you don't want the baby you're carrying."

This statement undid Carolina's composure. "What?"

Virginia shook her head. "Don't look so surprised. Everyone knows it's true."

"But how could you not want your own child?" Carolina asked, taking a seat.

"You wouldn't want it, either, not if it belonged to Hampton. He's brutal and vicious to all of us, but especially to me. He hates me."

Carolina thought of Hampton's earlier cruel words and reached out to take hold of her sister's hand. "I'm sure that isn't true."

"Just as I'm sure it is," Virginia replied and pulled her hand back. "It's no secret, so please don't think you need to defend him. We haven't been happy in years. Maybe we never were." She looked away toward the shaded window. "For at least ten years we've barely been civil to each other."

"But what of the children?" Carolina wanted to believe that their existence must be proof of some mutual love between husband and wife.

Virginia laughed. "They are merely the products of procreation. I was drunk or Hampton was when they were conceived. It was no more a matter of love than the coupling of animals in the fields."

"Virginia!" Carolina exclaimed. "How can you speak so?"

Shrugging, Virginia rolled her head back to fix her gaze on Carolina. "The truth is the truth, no matter how much we wish it to be otherwise. Hampton never loved me. He never loved you, either, but he especially never loved me. I lied to him, cheated him out of having you, and this is my punishment."

"I never loved or wanted him," Carolina said softly. "I only thought to marry him because you were so angry at me. You suggested I leave and go away, and I honestly thought it might make a difference."

"Always the good sister," Virginia said sarcastically.

"Not good—maybe practical, at least at that point. I thought I was being very practical. I truly wanted you to be happy."

"Well, I'm not and there is nothing you can do about it. I must endure yet another painful reminder of Hampton's virility while it takes a further toll on me."

"You'll feel differently after the baby comes. Once he or she is in your arms, you'll feel differently."

Virginia sneered. "Oh please, spare me your motherly platitudes. I have no such feelings for Hampton Cabot's children. I might have once, but those feelings are dead."

"But, if nothing else, your children need you, Virginia. Especially if what you've said about Hampton is true."

"Oh, it's true all right," Virginia admitted. "And perhaps that is the best reason for distancing myself from them." Just then their mother entered the room, but it didn't stop Virginia from continuing. "In the beginning I loved them, or at least I wanted to. But Hampton killed all my love."

"Virginia, you shouldn't take on so," Margaret said soothingly. "Why don't you rest for now? We can come back later."

"No! Hear me out," Virginia said, struggling to sit up. "No one will listen to me, and soon it will be too late."

"All right," Carolina replied before her mother could speak. "Tell us what it is you wish us to know so that we might help you."

"I'm beyond help. Hampton made sure of that. And he used our children to do so. Because every time he sought to hurt me, he did so through them. He would beat them for no good reason, deprive them of something they longed for or loved, and always, always, in order to get back at me."

"What are you saying, Virginia?" Margaret asked. Carolina glanced at her mother, afraid that Virginia's words might be too much for her. But Margaret appeared quite stoic.

Virginia shook her head with futility. "It's too late. My only hope is to die in childbirth."

"Virginia!" Margaret's face turned pale at her daughter's suggestion. "You simply mustn't say such things."

"But it is the truth. Doesn't anyone want the truth? For years you chided me not to exaggerate and lie, but now you rebuff me for the truth? Please make up your mind."

"Of course I want the truth from you, but I don't want you to feel this way," Margaret said, taking a seat on the bed opposite Carolina. She turned an expression of heartfelt despair on her younger daughter before continuing. "I only wish you would have spoken sooner. Your father did not know of these things, did he?"

"Of course not. Can you imagine my shame should anyone know? Now . . . I don't care anymore."

"Virginia, it's not too late. Your father will speak to Hampton—"

"No, Mother! He mustn't do that. Hampton will just take it out on the children or me. He wouldn't care. Besides, he would just as soon see us all destroyed."

"What are you saying?" Carolina feared her sister might be delirious.

"Hampton would see us all destroyed," Virginia repeated. "He wants Oakbridge, and he will do whatever he must in order to have it. He grows livid when Father speaks of selling or dividing it among us.

He rants and rages, until I think I might go mad, when Father speaks of freeing the slaves." She reached out to touch her mother's sleeve. "He is most determined to have this place for himself. It's the only reason he wanted Carolina to marry him. He thought I was off limits, and so he merely moved on to another of the Adams daughters. He would have gone after Georgia, no doubt, had Carolina and I both rebuffed him."

"But I hardly understand," Margaret said with a shake of her head. "He has wealth and money, and certainly he lacks for no good thing."

"But he doesn't want good things," Virginia said hatefully. "He wants things dark and evil. Things one would never speak of in good company. He does all manner of corrupt deeds and then leaves others to pay the debt. Ask the slave girls if you don't believe me. Mine are not the only Cabot children at Oakbridge." Virginia grimaced and threw herself back against the pillows. "You just don't know what he's capable of, but I do. He beats me, threatens to kill me, and then turns around to taunt me if I dare beg for mercy. Don't you see? I can't love my children or he'll do worse to them. At least now that he thinks I have no interest in them, he leaves them alone."

"Virginia, you mustn't allow Hampton to put a wedge between you and your own children. I'll find a way to deal with him," Margaret promised.

Virginia laughed bitterly. "I'm telling you, Mother, nothing can be done about it."

"We shall see," Margaret said, an undercurrent of anger in her tone.

"Of course something can be done," Carolina said with more faith than she felt. "You'll see. If we work together, we can come up with something."

"I'd like to believe that," Virginia said, her face drained of emotion, yet Carolina thought she detected just a hint of hopefulness in her sister's voice.

"Then count on it," Carolina said. "I for one will not rest until the matter is resolved."

"But please, Virginia," implored Margaret, "promise me one thing."

"What?" Virginia asked, shaking her head. "What could I possibly promise that would make any difference?"

"Promise that you won't give up on God. Promise me that you will at least try to believe He is in control." Margaret leaned forward to stroke her daughter's hair. "You have been sorely abused, but the time for that has come to an end."

Carolina heard the determination in her mother's tone and opened her mouth to add her agreement when Virginia lurched forward, crying out in pain.

"The baby," she said, gasping for air. "Oh, help me, Mother. Help me!"

If anyone would have noticed the gathering of the children at play, they might have commented on how amicably they worked together. The quiet huddle of figures brought no sounds of reproof from their parents as they quietly shared their stories and games. Only Victoria was absent from the group, as she had been drawn away to assist her mother and grandmother with her aunt's lengthy labor. Joseph and Hampton paid little heed to the children. Since no one was crying out about the injustice of some loss or seeking comfort because of some wound, the men were perfectly content to leave the children to themselves.

And this was just as Thora and Levinia Cabot preferred it.

"You'd better not tell anybody about this," Thora said menacingly to Jordana. "You may be just a baby, but I'll whup you good."

"I'm not a baby," Jordana protested.

"Hush," Brenton told her quickly. He had put a protective arm around her shoulder, but Jordana would have no part of it.

"I'll make something bad happen to you," Thora threatened, "if you don't do what I say."

"But I don't know how to get into the cupboard and find the cookies," Brenton said softly. "You know I don't live here."

"It doesn't matter," Levinia countered. "Everybody knows how to look for things."

"But it isn't right to steal," Brenton said solemnly.

"You get those cookies or I'll make you pay," Thora commanded. "Nate can help you."

"I don't want to," Nate replied.

Thora kicked him soundly, but in a way that was unobservable by the adults at the far side of the room. "Don't you cry, either, Nate. You're just a big baby."

"If we get caught, we'll be spanked."

"Too bad," Levinia said and pinched her brother's neck, just to add emphasis.

"Ow!" Nate exclaimed, causing the adults to glance over their way.

"I'm sorry, brother," Levinia said, leaning over to display a kiss on Nate's forehead.

"They are so good together these days," Joseph commented to Hampton.

"Well, they ought to be. The fear of the rod should bring about more than an occasional act of good behavior."

With that much said, the men moved on to other topics, and Levinia threw Nate and Brenton a menacing look. "See? Nobody will think we're bad." She smiled and Thora mimicked the action and nodded.

Thirty-One

The Phoenix

After several hours of anguish and suffering, Virginia was delivered of a stillborn daughter. As the doctor examined Virginia, who was extremely weak and sick with fever, he feared for her recovery.

"I am afraid these things are never easy to predict," the doctor later told the gathering of family, "but there is a good possibility she will not survive this ordeal."

Joseph watched carefully for Margaret's expression. Everyone in the household seemed as much concerned with Margaret's ability to cope as with the possibility that Virginia might die.

"Is there nothing more to be done?" Margaret asked.

"I wish I knew of something," the doctor answered. "Try to keep the fever down, see to it that she gets some sort of nourishment, and pray. That's all I can suggest."

"Thank you, doctor," Hampton said before anyone else could question the man further. "I'm sure we'll manage just fine." He took hold of the doctor's arm and led him to the front door, much to Joseph's astonishment. Upon returning, Hampton simply shrugged. "She didn't want the baby anyway."

"Hampton, your wife lies desperately ill upstairs, and that is all you have to say?" A fire burned in the depths of Joseph's soul. How could this man act so callous and indifferent when another human being, his own wife, lay perishing?

Hampton looked hard at both Joseph and Margaret, then shook his head. "I honestly don't know what to say."

"Of course you don't," Margaret responded, obviously trying to be conciliatory. "These are difficult times, but arrangements must still be made. I have already spoken to Virginia, and she seems not to have any idea what to call the child. I thought perhaps you would suggest a name for your daughter."

"The baby is dead. There is no need to assign her a name," Hampton said.

"Everyone deserves a name," Joseph interjected. "There will be a funeral, and there will be a name for my granddaughter." He did not bother to mask his hostility toward his son-in-law. Since Margaret had spoken to him of Virginia's confession regarding Hampton, Joseph had barely been able to control his wrath toward the man, only restraining himself because of the sudden rush of tragic events. He thought to respect Hampton's grief before confronting him. Now, however, Joseph decided to speak to him immediately after he'd had a chance to visit his daughter.

"Do as you like, then," Hampton replied. "I have work to do." He slammed the door hard behind him as he exited the parlor.

"I am so sorry, my dear." Joseph embraced Margaret tenderly, almost as much for himself as for her. The pain of recent events was only now beginning to settle on his heart.

"We mustn't give ourselves over to despair," Margaret replied. She clung to him for a moment, then pulled away. "I must see to Virginia."

"Of course, but may I see her, as well?"

Margaret's compassionate gaze fell upon him. "Come." She extended her hand, and together they climbed the stairs to the second-floor bedrooms.

Virginia lay perfectly still, almost deathly still. There was little evidence, except for her very shallow breathing and the flush of fever, to suggest that she was still among the living. Joseph sat in the chair beside her bed and reached out to take hold of her hand. Even then, Virginia did not stir. It was as if she had already made a choice between living and dying.

Joseph watched as Margaret ministered to her stillborn granddaughter. He wondered if this was how it had been the night Penny and Maryland had fallen ill with yellow fever. He had been away in Washington, and heavy rains had prevented his immediate return. When the messenger rode in to share the sad tidings that Maryland had died, and that Penny lay close to following her sister, Joseph had known an irreparable tear in his heart. He had always considered himself quite blessed. Of the nine children his wife had given him, only two had died in infancy. This, when all around him, friends and neighbors were constantly mourning the loss of their young. With the deaths of his two young daughters, Joseph knew more misery than he could put into words.

Even if he could have found words for his sorrow, there was Margaret and her inability to cope with the pain. Her temporary insanity had cost him much. And now, as he sat beside the bed of another ill child and thought of the possibility of her death, tears rose in his eyes. He couldn't abide that Virginia should die. Not now, not when her children were so young and in need of her. Not now, when Margaret had just regained her senses and could finally return to life with him.

A pang of guilt gave him cause for consideration. Did he fear more for Virginia's passing or for the idea that such a thing might well cause Margaret to slip back into her insanity? He looked at the child he'd so long ago welcomed into the world. Virginia had come after the deaths of their infant sons Hampshire and Tennessee. The birth of Virginia had given Margaret a strength to endure and a focus that pulled her out of the depression following the loss of her babies. Joseph had prayed they might never have to know such pain again. But, of course, that was an irrational prayer. Pain might well come again, but he must keep his strength fixed in God.

Then Margaret began a task that made Joseph's chest tighten and his breath catch in his throat. With the utmost tenderness and care, she was washing the dead infant. He fought within himself to keep from jumping up from the chair to take the task away from his wife and lead her from the room. He couldn't bear to lose her again. Not now. Not when she'd shared so little time with him.

As if sensing his concern, Margaret turned to meet his gaze. "I shall call her Martha," she told him. "Martha Cabot."

Joseph nodded, unable to speak. He watched her gently dry the baby and wrap her securely in a blanket. It was as if nothing at all was amiss. Had she already gone over the edge? Did she think the baby still lived?

"Ah, my dear," Joseph said, getting up rather uncomfortably. How could he approach the matter without risking further injury to his wife's delicate senses? "You needn't care for the child."

"Nonsense, Mr. Adams. This baby may have never drawn breath, but she deserves a loving hand to prepare her for burial."

He heaved a sigh of relief and sat back down. She knew. She knew the child was dead. Her mind had not slipped away. And then, as though watching that mystical phoenix rise from its own ashes, Joseph suddenly knew that she would never again slip away from him. She had once been defeated, dissolved, and destroyed, but she had arisen to find herself stronger than ever.

Now even as he watched her dress the tiny infant girl, Joseph felt a growing admiration for his wife. She would be his mainstay. She would give him comfort and support, and should Virginia die, it would be Margaret who would pull the family together and find a way to bring them solace. His heart soared and his spirits were renewed. It was as if God had given him a living proof of His goodness. He had seen the doubts and worries of Joseph's heart and mind and had offered assurance—when assurance was most needed.

"She's such a little one," Margaret said, fussing over the infant. "Martha seems a good name for her. Don't you agree?"

"Martha is perfect." Joseph was unable to keep the emotion from his voice.

Moans sounded from the bed and instantly their attention was directed to Virginia. Margaret motioned to a waiting servant girl and handed her the newly dressed baby. "Help me finish preparing her while I tend to Virginia." The house slave bobbed a curtsy and took the baby.

"No . . . no . . ." Virginia muttered the word over and over.

"There, there, child," Joseph said, patting her hand. "It will be all right."

"I've killed my baby," Virginia said with a mournful wail. "I want to die."

"No!" Margaret said emphatically. "Virginia, you cannot die. Your children need you."

"I would only hurt them," Virginia replied in a voice barely audible.

Throughout this exchange, Virginia had refused to open her eyes, but now she did so, and Joseph could see the suffering and misery in her soul.

"Virginia," he said, and she rolled her head to meet the sound of his voice. "Virginia, you must get well. We would suffer a great loss without you."

"No one would suffer," she managed to say.

"I would suffer," Joseph replied. "Your mother would suffer, as would your brothers and sisters and children." He hadn't realized he'd left out Hampton's name until Virginia herself brought it up.

"But not my husband. He would celebrate."

Margaret washed Virginia's face with a cool rag. "Virginia, you are needed here. Whether you like it or not, you have responsibilities and tasks that have gone undone."

Virginia shook her head from side to side. "I don't care."

"Virginia, it would break our hearts should you die. Your father and I love you so much. Please don't leave us now." Margaret's voice was full of tender emotion. Joseph could see that tears had come to her eyes.

"I'm so tired. . . ." Virginia closed her eyes. Her ragged breathing was their only clue that she'd not given up on life.

When she remained silent in unconscious oblivion, Margaret left the bedside, dried her own tears, and resumed her work with the infant. Joseph could see that the slave had already completed wrapping the child in a white crocheted blanket, but Margaret, obviously unsatisfied, reworked the arrangement until she deemed it just right.

"Has the coffin been completed?" she asked the girl. "And the front drawing room prepared to receive guests?"

"Yessum."

"Then go place the baby inside the coffin. Lay her out prettily so that she might be properly viewed."

"Yessum." The girl, scarcely more than fifteen, took the infant and left the room.

Joseph watched as Margaret finished putting away the items she had used. "Someone needs to remove this cradle," she told him.

"I'll see to it myself," he answered. He got to his feet and found Margaret studying their sleeping daughter. "We must have hope that she'll recover."

Margaret nodded. "She must find a reason to recover. If she has no will to live, I certainly can give her none. She has to do this for herself."

"There is one thing to be done," Joseph said as they left the room. "I will speak to that husband of hers and pray he has enough humanity in him to mend his ways. I am still shocked about the things you've told me, though they should not have come as a complete surprise. Hampton has long had a streak of greed and selfish ambition. I was a fool to have deceived myself into thinking his cruelty extended only to the slaves. And as far as his designs upon Oakbridge—well, he has a lot of nerve."

"Yes, and it extends much deeper than either of us realizes. Virginia confided in me once that Hampton has a great deal of money stored in a New York bank. Where he came by it, we can only guess, but Virginia is confident that the money once belonged to you, and I have little doubt that she is correct. It would be very easy for a man in Hampton's position to steal money from our pockets. Especially during his years as commission merchant."

Joseph tried not to appear shocked by his wife's astute assumption. For so many years his mind had been fixed solely on Margaret and her illness that he had been blind to so much around him. It was easy to see now how he had played into Hampton's hand.

"I only pray to be strong enough to deal with this," Joseph finally said, an undisguised heaviness in his voice.

"I will stand beside you, Joseph. Better still, remember the Lord is with you."

He pulled her close and held her tightly for a moment. Her sweet scent of lavender and jasmine made him think of their younger days. For a moment he did nothing but hold her and breathe deeply, as though the action could take him away from this misery, back to a more pleasant time.

Bolstered by his wife's encouragement, Joseph sought out Hampton, whom he located in the study. He was slouched in the leather chair, his collar open and a glass of whiskey in his hand. It appeared as if he'd already had a few glasses before this one.

"Well, Father Adams," he slurred, "how goes it in the sickroom? Does my wife still live?"

"Do you care, Hampton?" Joseph replied sharply.

"Would you prefer it if I gushed and wept all over you? I behave in the only way I know a man should."

"Are you saying that you really do care, but that you restrain your grief so as not to reveal weakness?" Joseph hated the hopefulness in his own tone. Even now he wanted to believe the best about his son-in-law.

Hampton drained the glass and reached for the crystal decanter for more. Joseph thrust out his hand to stop him. "Perhaps you've had enough."

"It's all I have to ease my grief."

"Then you do grieve?"

"Of course I do. Neither do I want Virginia to die."

Joseph could not be certain about the sincerity of the words, but he put that aside for the moment. "I've heard some things, Hampton—from Virginia. I must question you about them. She says that you have taken your hand to her and your children more than once. Is this true?"

A full gamut of emotions flickered across Hampton's visage—from outrage to fear, finally settling on something like regret. "I'm not proud of it," he said, or rather mumbled. "It's the only way I know to maintain discipline."

"Then it is time you learn a new way. Virginia is miserable. She doesn't care if she lives or dies. She needs a gentle hand, Hampton. You must learn."

The two men locked eyes. It was as if Hampton were sizing up Joseph as an adversary. In truth Joseph did not know if he could indeed force Hampton to change his ways. The law very consistently upheld the husband in such matters. A neighbor had experienced a similar problem with their daughter's husband and had attempted to take the man to court. But the judge had ruled for the husband, stating that it was not legally acceptable for anyone, even parents, to come between a man and his wife.

Thus Joseph felt great relief when Hampton said, "I will try to do better."

Joseph could do nothing but accept the man's word, despite the fact that Hampton had made many similar statements regarding the slaves. At least Hampton now knew his secret was in the open and he would be watched more closely. Perhaps that alone would be enough to protect Virginia.

Thirty-Two

Pardon and Mercy

"These done come for ya, Mizzus Baldwin," a tall, lean Negro boy announced.

Carolina took the letters he offered her and smiled. "Thank you, Zed." She glanced down and recognized her husband's handwriting on one letter, and that of Lucy Adams, her elder brother's wife, on the other.

Slipping to her room, which had been kept for her, she closed the door and took up a position at her old window seat. Enjoying her favorite spot at the window, Carolina could look down upon the grounds. She longed for the old feelings of peace and contentment to wash over her, but they were harder to come by with the passing years. Now with November upon them and the first snows imminent, Carolina longed for home and for her husband.

She took up his letter and broke the seal.

1850, October 20
Dearest Wife,

I do understand your desire to remain and see to Virginia's recovery. However, I was terribly disappointed to learn that you would not return until the middle of next month. There is always a threat that snow will keep you from me, and I long to see you and the children more than anything else in life. I cannot tell you the times I've nearly quit the tunnel and made my way to Oakbridge. Only my commitment to see this thing through has prevented my doing so.

She read on, learning the news of the small town. Saturday-night socials had been planned by a newly formed ladies committee, and the weekly event seemed to go over quite well with the tunnel workers. Of course, there remained conflicts between the Irish, but James was hopeful for amicable settlements as each new skirmish arose.

Carolina felt herself tense when James spoke of Kiernan's pining for Victoria. If his feelings were so evident that even James noticed, there must be much with which to concern themselves. Carolina was more determined than ever to speak to her daughter on the matter. She chided herself for having let so much time slip past without giving her a single word on the subject, but life at Oakbridge had consumed her most thoroughly—no, in truth, she had simply been reluctant to face these issues with her daughter.

> *And so it is with a lonely and heavy heart that I close this missive. Please know how much you are loved and how dearly I desire your return. These past weeks have been void of any joy. Hurry home.*
>
> *Ever your loving husband,*
> *James*

It had indeed been a terribly long time to be parted from her husband. Carolina smiled to herself when she thought of returning to him and telling him all her news. How she longed to lie in his arms and share secrets and dreams, as they were wont to do when the house grew quiet and all of the children were sleeping.

Lucy's letter was wordy and informative about the family. She spoke of life in Philadelphia and made a poor attempt at glossing over York's discontent by saying how he was holding fast to his duty toward her father's business affairs. He hoped to get into politics again, but she feared it could never be in Pennsylvania, where the issue of slavery distanced him from any possible constituency. The children were well. Amy was a real beauty at thirteen and already had several beaus. This made Carolina think of Victoria and Kiernan, but she forced herself to read on about the children's activities.

The letter concluded by stating that it was their desire to visit Oakbridge soon, but that they had no real plans to do so. York was extremely busy, and despite the fact that he had lost interest in his work, he proceeded without complaint.

Carolina folded the letter and thought of how good it would be to see Lucy. They had become such good friends that Carolina truly found the distance between them a curse. Would that they could live beside her in Greigsville, where she might see her best friend and favorite brother on a daily basis.

Thinking of visits, Carolina thought to take the letter and share it with Virginia. She was somewhat improved, but the doctor still held a grim view of her recovery. He had told her that should she regain her strength, there were definitely to be no more children. He then repeated the message to Hampton, who merely stated that God's will would be done.

"Virginia?" Carolina said, pushing open the door to her sister's room. Someone had pulled open the drapes, and light flooded the room to reveal a most distraught Virginia.

With tears streaming down her face, Virginia quickly turned away with a loud, sorrowful moan. Carolina put the letter in her pocket and rushed to her sister's side.

"What is it, Virginia? Are you in pain?"

Virginia only wailed louder. Carolina was uncertain what to do. No one appeared at the open door to assist her, and to leave Virginia unattended seemed risky.

"Please tell me how I can help you," Carolina said, reaching out to take hold of her sister's bony shoulders.

"Go . . . away. No one can . . . help me. I don't . . . deserve . . . help," Virginia managed to reply between sobs.

Taking a seat on the bed, Carolina pulled Virginia into her embrace. She fully expected her sister to refuse the gesture, but much to her surprise, Virginia clung to her like a drowning child.

"It's all my fault. I've killed my baby!" she declared and continued to wail and sob, her entire body trembling so hard that Carolina feared for her.

"You mustn't take on so," Carolina told her sympathetically. "You couldn't have avoided what happened. You did not kill your baby."

Virginia pushed away. "Oh yes, I did. I didn't want her. I didn't want my own child."

Carolina cast a quick glance at the open door. She was grateful that the children were all occupied downstairs with the Cabots' governess, Miss Mayfield. Even her own children were engaged in Miss Mayfield's scholastic instruction and would be thus contained for some time. Still, Carolina had no desire for anyone to overhear what Virginia was saying. It would only prove painful for her sister later in life, and so she quickly went to shut the door.

Coming back to the bed, Carolina shook her head. "You might not have thought you wanted her," she began, "but I know you did not wish her dead."

"Yes, I did," Virginia countered.

Her face contorted and the pain in her expression was so clear that Carolina realized she was speaking the truth. Stunned by this revelation, Carolina found it impossible to reply. Her sister had truly wished her child to die? Had Virginia somehow brought this about herself?

Was this why she was suffering such intense guilt and grief?

"I don't understand," said Carolina, who had cherished each and every one of her own children.

"I couldn't bear to have another of Hampton's children. I told you that before, but what I didn't tell you was that I purposely got myself drunk and threw myself down the grand staircase not long before you came to visit."

Carolina worked hard to hide her shock. "But that didn't necessarily kill the baby. We don't know why she died."

"I know why," Virginia said and turned to look away toward the windows. "She died because she knew I hated her. She knew I could never love her."

"If that is true, then why are you grieved? I think the real reason you suffer is that you tried hard not to love her, but in truth you loved her quite dearly."

Virginia snapped back around to meet her sister eye to eye. She opened her mouth to speak, then dissolved in tears. Burying her face in her hands, Virginia could not contain her misery.

Carolina knew she'd hit upon the truth. Coming closer, she sat on the bed again in order to hold Virginia while she spent her tears. Carolina prayed quietly and longed with all of her heart to give her sister peace of mind. Childhood memories haunted Carolina. It was as if she could visually turn the pages of their past experiences and see clearly the times when they had fought and bickered over petty differences. Then, too, were those times when Virginia had caused serious grief and harm, times when Carolina had felt a complete betrayal of their sisterly bonds.

But holding this broken woman now, Carolina let go of all the past hurts. She let go of her disappointment that they'd never been close. She let go of her bitterness and anger over the trials Virginia had put her through. And she let go of her fear of allowing herself to love her sister.

"It will be all right, Virginia. You will see. Little Martha knows that you truly loved her."

"But she couldn't," Virginia said, shaking her head from side to side. "I never told her."

"Tell her now," Carolina whispered. "Ask God to tell her if you doubt she can hear you."

Virginia grew still in Carolina's embrace. "I did love her. I do love you, Martha."

Tears stung Carolina's eyes as she heard the hope, the longing in her sister's voice. But it wasn't until Virginia spoke again that Carolina completely understood the weight of her sister's anguish.

"I love you, too, Carolina," she said, pulling away. Her face was mottled from crying and ravaged from sickness, but Virginia no longer was concerned about such things. "You might not believe me, but I do." Carolina opened her mouth to speak, but Virginia shook her head. "Let me say what I must." Carolina nodded, blinking back tears.

"I've envied you for so long. You had York's attention and Father's. You were intelligent and self-assured, and you cared not for what people thought of you." She paused for a moment to dry her eyes, then continued. "I hated that you were so capable, even though you were younger. You learned so easily, you loved so completely. And people loved you in return. Even James. Especially James.

"I knew James did not love me," Virginia continued. "I saw the way he looked at you when you studied together. I heard the patience in his voice, the admiration that he reserved only for you. I hated you for that. I hated you for being able to take him so completely under your spell, while I searched for ways to impress him. I took my first drink of liquor the night of your coming-out party and then I went in search of James in order to seduce him. I knew it was wrong, but I also knew that he was so besot with you, if I stirred his passions, he just might give in to me."

Carolina could scarcely believe her sister's confession. It was difficult to imagine anyone would do such a thing—that Virginia would have married James, even knowing that he loved another. How could she have been so desperate? As if the question had been spoken aloud, Virginia continued.

"I despaired of anyone ever marrying me. I was a laughingstock to my friends. They were married, or soon to be, and I had been so particular about men, I had chased off any potential suitors. When James came along, I felt certain it was my final chance. I had to make him agree to marry me, whether he loved me or not. But, of course, he didn't love me. He loved you." She paused and shook her head. "I don't deserve your forgiveness, Carolina, but I do need it, and I long for it."

Carolina wiped at her own tears and offered Virginia a weak smile. "But you've always had it. I never stopped loving you."

Virginia sighed. "If I truly have it, then I can die in peace."

"I forgive you, Virginia, but not in order to send you on your way to the grave," Carolina protested. "I give it freely as a healing balm. I want you to grow well and strong. I need you. Your children need you, even if Hampton doesn't."

"Hampton. Now, there's another mess I got into because of my treatment of you. No need to forgive me for that one, Carolina. I saved your life in that situation. You would have married the man in an attempt to please me, or at least to be rid of me. I have paid the price of my actions ever since that night."

"But in spite of that," Carolina began again, "you have three children who need a mother. The twins are deeply wounded by your distance, and Nate has grown quiet and withdrawn. You must find a way to love them again. Forget about Hampton if you must." Carolina let go of Virginia and got to her feet. "Father will find a way to control him."

"It's no use," Virginia replied. "He would rather see us all dead." She fell back against the pillows. "I don't feel so well."

Carolina felt a panic rise inside her. "I'll send for the doctor."

"There's nothing . . . nothing he can do," Virginia replied, her voice growing weak. "I'll just rest. It's enough to know you forgive me."

"Then rest easy, because I do forgive you, and I love you more dearly than you know." Carolina stroked her sister's cheek. "Nevertheless, I will send for the doctor."

Virginia looked up and the fear in her eyes was quite evident. "I'm going mad, just like Mother. My mind can't deal with these matters."

Carolina shook her head. "You are stronger than you realize. Childbed fever would have killed a weaker woman, but you have strength you've not even explored. God will strengthen you, Virginia. You must turn to Him. He can knit your body and mind back together and help you not be afraid."

"If only I could believe that," Virginia said and closed her eyes. "I want to believe that. I truly want to believe."

"Then do so," Carolina encouraged. "I'll send Zed for the doctor and then I promise to come back and sit with you until he arrives. In the meantime, you think about what I've said."

Virginia nodded, but Carolina worried that her efforts would be too late. Virginia seemed resigned to give up her life, and the sickness had already taken its toll. Could she recover with the love and help of her family? Carolina wished the answer might be evident, and soon. She longed to return to her husband, but she also felt bound to remain at her sister's side. It was not an easy choice to make. Especially now.

Thirty-Three

Troubled Times

James listened intently as Ben Latrobe outlined the various tasks being accomplished to connect the Baltimore and Ohio Railroad to the Ohio River. In the two days since his arrival at Cumberland, James had found Ben much preoccupied and greatly burdened. Contractors had failed to produce, some had even canceled, and supplies were slow to get to their destinations. Reletting contracts had taken time and additional monies, both of which Ben assured James the railroad could not afford.

"The Erie Railroad is nearly complete," Ben protested. "It will connect New York City with Lake Erie and produce the means by which to move vast quantities of goods from east to west and pull away business from the National Road and the B&O."

"Yes, but I heard they'd settled on a six-foot-wide gage for their rails," James offered. "There will be no interaction between railroads at that rate, so they will lose business from other lines. Our own four-foot, eight-and-a-half-inch gage is rapidly becoming the standard for all lines, and the Erie will simply find themselves having to rebuild in time."

"But for now their line will beat ours to completion, and much of our coveted business will go north. Baltimore simply must have this railroad to the Ohio!" Ben declared, his tone quite anxious.

"We will, Ben. We will. These setbacks you've described are only minor." James hoped to reassure his friend. "I understand the Erie has had its share of trouble, as well. I read about their iron bridge collapsing last July. Turned them completely off of iron truss bridges, as I understand."

"They were fools," Latrobe replied. "The iron truss bridge is the way of the future. The contractor allowed to build the Erie bridge obviously understood little about working with iron. They cut costs, used substandard equipment, and for what? To line their pockets with a bit more gold. Now the contractor is charged with gross negligence and will no doubt lose everything."

"But what of your designs?" questioned James. "I understood from Swann's letter that you have actually set the Mt. Clare shops to building iron frames for use on the bridges to be built west of this fair city. You obviously don't intend to follow the Erie's example and rid yourself of the notion of iron bridges."

Ben settled a bit and grew thoughtful. "I see nothing but good in the use of iron truss bridges. We have engineered the first for our line on the Washington Branch. So far it has proven to be ideal."

They spoke for some time of engineering feats and bridge building, subjects that fascinated James second only to engine designs.

Then Ben switched to a less enjoyable topic. "What of your Irish? Any more threats to strike?"

James shrugged. "They always threaten. I suppose it makes them feel as though they have some control. The real dilemma lies in the fact that they continue to despise each other and stir up a series of little problems, all in order to get back at each other. It costs me time and money whenever one side gets oppressive with the other."

"Well, I hope to allay that problem soon," Latrobe replied. "I have already contacted the Irish Immigrants League and requested the exact numbers necessary to even out all sides. I figure that the Connaughtmen are by far and away too demanding, and I mean to see that they meet their match in equal numbers. I'm certain this will settle matters nicely."

James shook his head. "Just as I'm certain it will only cause the problem to escalate."

"You're too close to the problem to see it accurately," Latrobe said simply. He put his glasses back on and met James' doubtful expression. "From where I stand, and from the standpoint of the board, it seems a very reasonable solution."

At that, a knock sounded at the door, and because it was James' hotel room, it was clearly his place to see to the disturbance. He opened the door to find Kiernan O'Connor reaching out to knock once again.

"Ah, Mr. Baldwin," Kiernan said, his voice emitting a tone of relief. "I feared ya might be gone."

"What is it, Kiernan? You look as though you've seen a ghost," James told him. The younger man was clearly shaken up. His eyes were wild with agitated fear, and his face was pinched and void of color.

"It's me brother," he said, lowering his voice to a whisper. "Can I come in and tell ya of the matter?" His Irish brogue was thick, further leading James to realize the degree of Kiernan's concern. It seemed the young man's voice always took on a much more decided brogue when he was upset or excited.

"Certainly," James answered and stepped back. "You know Mr. Latrobe, don't you?"

"Aye, I'm sure I do." Kiernan afforded the man a tight nod that also encompassed his shoulders and passed as the briefest of bows. He twisted his cap in his hand until James closed the door behind him. "Ya see," Kiernan continued without being prodded, "Red is afire because of the likes of the Corkians and Fardowns. They're bringin' in more men, or so Red has heard in town."

James had brought several men with him from the tunnel site, including Kiernan and Red, all in order to help transport equipment and machinery back to Greigsville. He should have known it was a mistake to bring the cantankerous Irishman. Red would find trouble wherever he went—or maybe it was just that trouble found him.

"What does your brother plan?" James asked, throwing Latrobe a look that suggested he knew full-out war was impending.

"Red rounded up the Connaughtmen here in town. He's riled 'em up, as if they needed the help, and he's convinced 'em they need to fight."

"But fight whom?" James questioned.

"Anyone who isn't one of us. He plans to send them all back to the city—or to their Maker," Kiernan answered. "Ya got to send them back, elsewise ya'll have a fight on yar hands."

"This makes little sense," Latrobe interjected. "Your brother merely fears having his authority usurped, but in truth, the authority has always belonged elsewhere. Mr. O'Connor would do well to remember he is employed to do a job, and if he is unhappy with the conditions, he can always leave."

Kiernan looked at James with a grief-stricken expression. "I didn't come here to get me brother fired. I shouldn't even be here, but I thought ya'd want to know. I hoped ya'd see the right in what I'm sayin'."

"I understand exactly what you're saying," James replied. "I'd like you to take me to Red so that we can talk."

"Now, I can't be doin' that," Kiernan protested. "He'd know I'd come to talk to ya. He'd call me a traitor. He's me brother, after all."

"You don't want him dead, do you?" James reasoned. "I simply mean to discuss the matter with him. He is here under my direction. It wouldn't seem all that strange if I should seek him out and speak to him on this matter. After all, I could approach it from the point of making it an announcement. I could tell him of the impending arrival of additional men, and let him respond to the matter from there."

"I suppose that would be all right," Kiernan admitted. "I just don't want him hurt. Ya understand?"

"No one intends to hurt your brother, Mr. O'Connor," Latrobe interjected, "but neither do we desire that your brother would stir up trouble and cause hurt to someone else. If he would only listen to reason—"

Kiernan cut Latrobe off with a short, painful laugh. "Red, listen to reason? And wouldn't our mum say the same thing if she could be a-speakin' from the grave? Red won't listen to ya. Yar not a Connaughtman."

"But you are," James interjected. "He'd listen to you."

"Nay. I'm his little brother. He'll tell me to shut me mouth and leave matters to him. He'll not listen to me."

"Then perhaps he'll listen to the sheriff," Latrobe suggested.

"Ben, that's not the answer," James replied. "At least not at this point. I know this man. I'll talk to him myself. Whether he listens or not, I have to give it a shot. You can speak to the sheriff, maybe suggest that a force of patrolmen would be wise, given the upcoming arrival of the new laborers. Even suggest that there could be trouble, but leave Red to me." He pulled on his outer coat and turned to Kiernan. "Will you take me to him?"

"Nay," he replied softly and bowed his head. He seemed to consider the matter for a moment before he added, "But I'll tell ya where I last saw him."

Thirty-Four

Facing the Dragon

Kiernan followed James into the street outside the hotel. His conscience bothered him something fierce, and there was no denying the conflict he felt within his soul. He cared about this man—cared about his family, too—and he didn't want to see any of them harmed. Neither did he want to see his brother hurt.

"Which way do I go?" James asked him.

Kiernan drew a deep breath. To send James to Red now would mean certain doom. Red was in a blood haze, and when he was like that, there was no dealing with him. He had set himself upon the mission of protecting his people from outsiders, and James' appearance would only fuel the fire.

"I still don't know that this is a good idea," Kiernan said, stalling for time.

"We haven't much choice," James replied. He looked Kiernan square in the face. "I agree with you, and in a way I agree with Red. This idea of evening out the various factions is only going to see us in a full-blown war. I can't convince Latrobe any more than I've had success in convincing your brother. But I have to try."

"Then I'll go with you," Kiernan said, heaving a sigh. There really was no other way. How could he ever explain to Victoria that he'd allowed her father to go into a fight without the slightest hope of winning? How could he look into her beautiful brown eyes and admit that he could have gone with James, could have stood beside him, but didn't?

James was watching him oddly. "Are you sure? Your brother will no doubt see this as a betrayal."

Kiernan nodded. "Aye. But if I don't go with ya, I'll be betrayin' meself." He motioned to James. "It's this way."

They walked through the town, weaving in and out of the mingling crowd. The good weather had held, making people eager to see to their shopping needs. Hammers rang out a rhythmic cadence as they passed by the smithy's shop. No one seemed aware that war was about to be waged in their city.

Kiernan took a right and motioned to James. They quickened their pace and moved past the depot to a clearing where railroad equipment had been stored. Several shacks blocked the view of any activity taking place behind. Kiernan knew that Red had chosen the place for this very reason. This, along with the fact that most of the laboring men were in the vicinity and could easily slip away to join the commotion.

As they rounded a corner, Kiernan jabbed James in the ribs. "Ya be keepin' yar mouth shut and I'll do the talkin'," he said gruffly.

James looked as though he might question Kiernan's demand when they caught sight of a man approaching.

"A man stands tall when he's respected," the man said rather stiffly.

"Aye, and when he's a Connaughtman, he's feared, as well," Kiernan countered with the expected passwords.

The man gave a quick jerk of his head in the direction of several cotton bales, and Kiernan touched the brim of his hat in respectful acknowledgment. He'd lived with passwords and countersigns most of his life, and even in America they were vital for staying alive, or at least staying out of trouble. Yet here he was going into trouble and dragging James Baldwin with him. It was senseless and he knew it. Red wouldn't listen to James. He would only seek to exact revenge upon him. With that thought, Kiernan paused, causing James to look at him questioningly.

"It's not too late if ya want to turn back," Kiernan told him.

"Red won't turn back," James replied. "Someone has to stand up to the man and make him see matters for what they are."

"Aye, I suppose yar right."

But in his heart, Kiernan didn't believe it. James was considered a landlord, a nobleman of American class, whom Red would just as soon run through as talk with. Already he could hear his brother's menacing tone. They rounded the corner, and Kiernan instantly caught sight of Red. He was speaking to a gathering of men who were clearly divided into opposing sides.

The two groups faced each other with about six feet of dirt between them. It was just enough space for James and Kiernan to approach through the crowd without having to ask or demand that they be allowed to pass. Red, instantly taking note of his brother, scowled down at Kiernan and narrowed his eyes. Kiernan lowered his head, feeling a mixture of shame and frustration.

"Ya fool. Why'd ya bring him into this?" Red demanded.

Before Kiernan could answer, however, James stepped forward. "I threatened to fire the both of you if he didn't." Kiernan's head shot up at this lie.

"Oh, ya did, did ya?" Red replied. "Well, I don't fear your threats, boss man."

"Well, perhaps you should," James answered him.

Red's face contorted and darkened in hue. "I'll deal with this jackeen first, and then I'll tend to yar senseless prattle."

It was only then that Kiernan realized his brother had two hefty Connaughtmen holding a member of the opposition. The victim had obviously been beaten; his eyes were even now turning black-and-blue, and his face was cut and bleeding. Kiernan felt sweat trickle down his neck, even though the November air was cold. He bit at his lip to keep from protesting Red's actions, but it was James who voiced his objection.

"Let him go, Red."

"Nay. He has to be taught a proper lesson."

"I'm asking you respectfully to let him go. All I want is for us to sit down and discuss this as reasonable men." James took yet another step away from Kiernan.

Kiernan feared that if James moved too far away, either side might well jump him. The Irish might be divided on issues surrounding their Irish heritage, but they'd no doubt unite to see to the demise of their taskmaster.

Red threw a punch into the injured man's midsection, then turned to James as though he'd just served the man tea. "Ya want to be next, boss man?"

"Not particularly," James answered him.

"Then leave off with yar clamorin' about discussions. Talk is for women. We men see settlin' our disagreements in a more physical way."

Kiernan didn't know if his brother's men had loosened their hold on the man because Red had so thoroughly beaten him, or if it was because they were enthralled at the oddity that any man should stand up to Red O'Connor. But for whatever reason, they were no longer paying much attention to their captive, and with one fell swoop, the man rammed his elbows backward into both men and sent them sprawling into the dirt. Next he threw out a punch in Red's direction, but he easily sidestepped it and raised his fist to defend himself. Kiernan was totally focused on the action when his concentration was broken by the firing of a gun.

James Baldwin had produced a revolver and, after firing the shot off, stood looking around to see if he had everyone's attention. "For those of you not yet familiar with a Dragoon, let me introduce you. I've just fired one shot. That leaves me five, and each one will walk a hole through a man big enough to drive a wagon."

Everyone kept their gazes fixed on James while stepping back a pace or two. Only Red and the man he had beaten remained frozen in place. "Ya can't shoot us all," Red said defiantly.

"No, I suppose you are right in that," James said, then turned to level the gun at Red. "But the next shot is reserved for you."

Red laughed. "Ya wouldn't dare be shootin' me. Ya haven't the guts."

"I'll do what I have to do," James countered.

Kiernan felt his mouth go dry. He could scarcely believe what was happening. James Baldwin looked as calm and collected as though he'd come for a church picnic. The man had to be ten kinds of fool to pull a gun on Red O'Connor. Red would never stand for this humiliation. He'd rather be dead than lose face with his men.

"Go ahead and shoot him," the injured man called out. "Here, better yet, let me."

James shook his head. "I've had it with both sides. I'd just as soon shoot you both as to see any more of your Irish brand of justice. You men give no thought to the consequences of your actions. You drive at each other like a man trying to rid his house of rats, but in truth, you've become the vermin. I have a railroad to build. I also have a wife and children to protect, as do many of the folks in this town. It may be no concern of yours, but it is uppermost in my mind."

"Yar stickin' yar nose in where it don't belong. I'm a-warnin' ya one last time," Red said, his words low and threatening.

"Don't bother," James replied. "I'm not interested in your warnings. I'm here to negotiate this matter, and if you won't listen to reason standing there on your own two good feet, maybe you'll listen to reason on a stretcher." He lowered the gun toward Red's thick, beefy leg and pulled back the hammer.

"No!" Kiernan said, putting himself between Red and James. "I didn't bring ya here to kill me brother. Nor will I be standin' by idle while ya put holes in him."

Red reached down, picked up a sledgehammer, and with lightning-quick speed lunged in the direction of James Baldwin. "Get out of me way," he told Kiernan, but Kiernan reacted quickly from years of brotherly wrestling matches. He pushed James out of harm's way, then gave Red a shove that threw him off balance.

The other men moved in as if to make it a free-for-all, but James fired off his second shot and once again the crowd moved back a pace. "Enough!"

"Ya traitor," Red said, spitting dirt from his mouth. He got to his feet and moved menacingly toward Kiernan. His eyes were ablaze with anger, and Kiernan saw instantly that he'd gone too far. Nothing he could say would be of the slightest interest to Red when he was in this state of mind.

"Don't touch him," James commanded. "I truly don't want to shoot you, Red, but if you give me no other choice—"

"Shoot me, then," Red interrupted, throwing James a hard look. "Ya might as well. It's ashamed I am to be the brother of this miserable cur." He turned back to stare long and hard at Kiernan. "Ya picked yar side of this fight, and now ya have to live with it."

"All I want is for ya to listen for once," Kiernan defended. "Our mum, God rest her soul, always told ya to stop fightin' long enough to see if anyone was still a-standin'. I swear, ya'd fight on whether we were all dead or not."

"It's me or him," Red whispered, his voice heavy with rage. "Yar choosin' yar side here and now."

Kiernan's stomach churned and his chest tightened. One look into his brother's fiery green eyes told him it was true. Their da had once told them a story about lookin' into the eyes of a dragon. He said that every man had to come to a point where he took a stand and met life's dragons face-to-face. If fear drove him back and caused him to set his standards aside, then he wasn't a man at all. But if he stood his ground, even feeling the heat of the dragon's breath upon him, and looked the dragon in the eye, then and only then could he call himself a man. Kiernan was looking the dragon in the eye and his time had come. He never thought his dragon would be his own brother, but to cower now would mean to lose all hope of self-respect—but to stand unmoved would mean to lose his brother. Maybe forever.

"I have no desire to fight ya on this," Kiernan told Red. Red stepped back a pace as though confident that Kiernan had made a choice to remain at his side. Kiernan quickly ended any hope of that, however, with his next words. "But James Baldwin is worth hearin' out. Yar way of doin' things is only leadin' to heartache and destruction."

Red was obviously stunned as Kiernan snugged his cap down on his head and turned to walk away.

"Yar no brother of mine," Red called after him.

Kiernan felt as though a knife were plunged deep in his heart. All of his life he had looked up to Red, admired him for his ability to get things done. He was a true leader, but his prejudices tainted his thinking and made his judgments unwise.

For the next few hours, Kiernan merely walked. He crossed the rails and headed down toward the river, hoping, even praying, for some form of solace. It seemed as if the world had been silenced around him, and the only thing he could hear was the pounding question in his head: *What have I done?*

He had sided with a stranger against his kin. Not only that, but he had done so publicly. Everyone—Connaughtmen, Corkmen—all of them had heard the declaration. But James wasn't a stranger. He was the father of the girl he loved and one day hoped to marry. Victoria knew of his difficulties with Red. He'd told her on more than one occasion of his fear that one day Red's temper would lead to his death. Victoria understood and was sympathetic. She was still terribly young, but she had the heart of a woman. She thought long and hard about her answers to his questions of what she wanted out of life. She was never one who was given to flippantly flirting and passing the time in idle chatter. Victoria cared about his brothers and sisters. Including Red.

"Yar no brother of mine."

The words echoed over and over in his heart. Red would sever their relationship with no more than those few words. And he meant them. No doubt when they returned to Greigsville, Red would demand he clear his things out of the new one-room cabin they had built together. It hadn't been much, but it was a whole sight better than living in a tent.

When night fell, Kiernan made his way back into town. He barely noticed the laughter coming from the saloons, or the conversations of those around him. He walked first up one side of the main street and then started down the other, only to realize that he really had no place to go. Sitting down on a bench in front of one of the hotels, he contemplated his situation for a while.

"Kiernan?"

He looked up to find James Baldwin standing not three feet away. "Evenin'," he said, trying to force a smile.

"I've been looking for you," James said and came to join him on the bench.

"I've been walkin'."

"Well, I've talked to your brother and the leader of the Corkians, Aidan Monahan. I don't think I've ever come across two more pigheaded individuals. They both refuse to back down. I'm afraid, however, when the new laborers arrive, there's going to be trouble anew."

"No doubt."

"Sadly enough," James said, appearing to have aged a score of years in a single day, "I can't very well allow Carolina to return to this. Not when the laborers are due anytime. God alone knows whether there will be another riot or merely a mild skirmish, but either way she'll be traveling with no one but Miriam and the children."

"What are ya goin' to do?" Kiernan asked, suddenly realizing the truth of James' concerns. He had little desire to see Victoria plunged into the middle of the Irish tug-of-war, either.

"I've sent a wire to Oakbridge. I can only pray it reaches Carolina before she departs. For now, I suppose all I can do is sleep on it."

"Aye. Sleep," Kiernan said, wondering what he should do regarding the same idea.

James looked at him sympathetically for a moment, then his expression changed to one of sudden revelation. "You have nowhere to go, do you?"

Kiernan chuckled. "It seems not. I was just chewin' on that bit of news when ya joined me."

"Well, I never got to thank you properly for what you did for me today," James said. "I think it only fair that since I was responsible for getting you alienated from your brother, it should also be my responsibility for seeing to your care. Come to my hotel with me. You'll sleep tonight in my room, then tomorrow we'll see about getting you a room of your own."

"I wouldn't want to impose."

"You won't be. Come on. Let Red sit in his misery, while you get a good night's sleep."

Kiernan nodded, knowing that James couldn't possibly understand the depths of the consequences from his earlier actions. He hadn't only alienated Red; he'd put off all of his own kind. There wouldn't be a Connaughtman high or low who would speak to him now. Even if they agreed with him, they were too afraid of Red to interfere. Getting to his feet in order to follow James, Kiernan felt as though the dragon had won.

Thirty-Five

Victoria's Declaration

Carolina finished looking over a report sent by Thomas Swann to her father. The accomplishment of a railroad to the city of Wheeling on the Ohio River was starting to take definite shape, and Carolina was terribly excited about it. Just poring over the facts and figures, she could see that it wouldn't be much longer, two years at the most, before the Baltimore and Ohio could boast completion. Contractors were building in sections all along the two hundred-some miles between Cumberland and Wheeling—some with varying degrees of success and others with overwhelming failure. Those failing contractors were being replaced or assisted as the circumstance merited it, but all in all the news was very positive. In addition to information regarding the new line, Swann had also included information regarding the line already in place. Passenger receipts were expected to greatly increase for the 1850 accounting year. Freight receipts had doubled.

"Mama?" Victoria called from outside the bedroom door.

Carolina folded the report and answered, "Come in, Victoria."

Victoria's dark curls swung and her eyes glinted with determination as she entered the room. "Mama, this dress is simply too tight in the bodice. I can't wear it anymore, and that hardly leaves me anything but this old thing and my Sunday best."

Carolina looked at the pale pink muslin gown her daughter held and then to the butterscotch calico gown she wore. Both looked ridiculously childish for the blossoming young woman who stood before her. Seeing Victoria as she did just now made Carolina all the more aware of her need to talk to her daughter.

"Come sit here." Carolina patted the window seat and moved over. "I've wanted to talk to you for some time, and now appears to be as good a time as any."

Victoria shrugged and tossed the pink muslin to the bed. "Can we have some more dresses made? I want some grown-up gowns."

"Victoria, you're not even fourteen. You've not come out, so there will be no floor-length gowns until that time. It's the same thing I've told you about pinning up your hair."

"But I don't want to wait until I'm sixteen."

Carolina smiled and reached a hand up to give her own stylish coif a pat. "You'll be grateful to have this freedom of wearing your hair down after you've had to pin it up for a time. Believe me, Victoria, being all grown-up isn't everything you believe it to be."

Victoria crossed her arms and shook her head. "You just want me to be a child forever. I hate it, and I hate having to be away from home for so long. When are we going back?"

Carolina was amazed at how quickly the girl had shifted the focus of their discussion. "I had planned to leave at the end of this week. I told you that at the first of the month."

"Yes, but you told me last month that we would leave by the twentieth and then the thirtieth and now this. I'm tired of being away from home. I miss everyone."

"Everyone?" Carolina questioned with a raised brow of suspicion. "You mean Kiernan O'Connor, don't you?"

Victoria squared her shoulders and jutted out her chin. "And what if I do?"

"You needn't take that tone with me," Carolina reprimanded. "I asked a simple question."

Victoria sighed and fell back against the wall. "I miss Papa, too."

Carolina smiled at her veiled response. "Papa misses you, as well. But I'd really rather we speak of this matter between you and Kiernan."

Victoria looked at her for a moment, and Carolina saw a range of emotions in her expression. It appeared that she wanted to confide and talk to her mother about the situation, but on the other hand she also seemed fearful of Carolina's reaction. It gave Carolina cause to retrace her steps. She didn't want to offend Victoria so that she refused to speak at all. Trying to put herself in Victoria's place, Carolina continued, this time in a less demanding voice.

"I'd really like to talk about what you're feeling for him, but only if you want to."

Victoria relaxed and smiled. "I love him. That's what I'm feeling for him."

She said the words so matter-of-factly that Carolina had to bite back a snide retort about Victoria being too young to understand what love was all about. Instead, Carolina focused on her own hands for a moment, studying the lines, the nails, anything to settle her nerves before replying.

"Love is a very confusing thing," Carolina began, "and we often find our perceptions clouded."

"Well, I'm not confused about what I feel for Kiernan," Victoria replied adamantly. "I think he's positively wonderful. We talk about such fascinating things and he tells me about Ireland and his family who still live there. Someday I hope to go to Ireland and see it all for myself."

"Perhaps someday we can all go abroad and see it together," Carolina countered.

Victoria seemed not even to hear her. "Kiernan has told me of his hard life there and how they all slept together in one room. Imagine it, Mama, nine kids all living in the same room." She didn't wait for comment before continuing. "Their life was so bad there. Their mother and father died, and the famine nearly took the lives of their youngest sister and brother. Kiernan's two older sisters, Bridget and Mary, are keeping the children and they nursed them back to health, but Kiernan wants to bring the entire family here to America and I want to help him. I can't imagine living in such poverty. All of my life I've had a room to myself and servants to help with the necessary duties. I've had dresses and toys—why, do you know Kiernan said his little sisters had rag babies with sewn-on faces? Not even a real doll. We've been very lucky to enjoy the wealth we have."

"I doubt luck had anything to do with it."

"You sound like Kiernan. He told me Red is always talking about the luck of the Irish, but that given all that has happened, he doesn't think it rings true."

"Yes, well, it's all very fascinating," Carolina said, trying to figure a way to bring up the subject of her daughter's youth. "As a *man*," she said, stressing the word man, "Kiernan has a tremendous responsibility to his family. He should focus on them before he does anything else. Especially if he feels that strongly about bringing them to America."

"I told him I would find work and help him save the money," Victoria told her mother matter-of-factly. The shocked expression that Carolina knew must be on her face was not lost on Victoria. "I will still manage my chores at home, so don't fret about that. I figure I can work after school and on the weekends and—"

Carolina held up her hand. "Wait just a minute. You aren't going to get a job."

"But there's bound to be something I could do to help. Maybe I could work at the store with the Kaberlines."

Carolina thought of the vast wealth that lay in a trust fund for Victoria. It would be more than enough to bring half of Ireland to America. "Victoria, I know you care about Kiernan's affairs—"

"I love him," she interrupted. "It's more than just caring about his affairs. I want them to be my affairs, too."

Carolina studied her for a moment. Her dark eyes were wide with excitement and her expression betrayed her passion for the topic. This was no child she was dealing with, and yet chronologically, she was no real woman, either. Still, her emotions and feelings for the man in Greigsville sounded very much like the feelings Carolina held for her own husband.

"You need to focus on your education," Carolina finally said, not certain how else to bring the conversation back in line. "I thought perhaps—that is, given the growing acceptability of women seeking to educate themselves—perhaps we would send you to a university."

Victoria jumped to her feet. "I don't want to go to a university! That is your dream, not mine. I have no interest in such matters. I want nothing more than to learn to keep a household in order and provide for the needs of my family. I want nothing more or less than that which will make me a good wife to Kiernan."

"Wife?"

Victoria smiled and bit at her lower lip. "Yes, well, that is what we hope for."

"We?" Carolina felt a sinking in the pit of her stomach.

"Kiernan and me. We hope to be married. In fact, as soon as the tunnel is complete, Kiernan plans to talk to Papa about it."

"But that's ridiculous, Victoria. The tunnel is scheduled to finish in less than two years. You'll barely be sixteen."

"Many girls younger than me get married, Mama."

"Not if they're my daughter, they don't!" Carolina retorted. "You can't be serious about marriage so soon. What will he do for a job? What about his relatives in Ireland? How can he save up money for them when he has a wife to support?"

"We plan to go west to California and look for gold. When we have enough, we'll send for his family."

"What?" Carolina couldn't believe what she was hearing. California? Gold? "Victoria, I cannot approve of this in any way. You are but a child and you need to think of your future. An education, even one from a lady's school, would do you better than running off at fifteen or sixteen to marry a man you scarcely know."

Victoria frowned. "I don't want to go to school. I hate it."

"But it's good for your mind," Carolina countered.

"People told you it was better for your mind to stay at home and knit scarves," Victoria protested. "You told me that yourself. You wanted to go to school, but everyone, including your mother, told you it was insanity. They told you it was sheer madness for a woman to educate herself—after all, what could she do with an education in this world?"

"But that was different," Carolina said, forcing herself to remain seated. She really wanted to go to the child and shake some sense into her.

"It's not any different at all," Victoria replied. "Not really. You wanted something for yourself that everyone else thought was crazy. I want something for myself that everyone thinks is crazy. You fell in love with Papa when you were fifteen. I'm barely a year younger. Why can't I know my heart as well as you knew yours?"

Carolina found it impossible to answer. How could it be that things looked so different now—now that she was the mother and it was her daughter whose lunatic ideas rang of insanity and waste?

For a moment, all Carolina could think about was the way her own mother had chided her for her desires. Margaret had recently confessed her regret at having stood in Carolina's way. If she'd had her mother's support on the matter, there was no telling where she might be today. Probably not here, and probably not with Victoria. Carolina loved her husband and children and knew her life had turned out well, yet she could not deny the bouts of discontent that still threatened her at times.

Calming her nerves, Carolina made herself realize that Victoria would mature and grow and soon be able to make her own decisions. She needed Carolina to help guide her choices, but if Carolina alienated her from speaking her heart, Victoria would simply choose someone else to assist her.

"How long . . ." Carolina began, then paused to take a deep breath. "How long have you and Kiernan been planning this?"

"Not long," Victoria admitted and plopped down on the end of the canopied bed. "At least not on Kiernan's part. I set my sights on him when the riots broke out last November. Remember how you and Papa had to go and help?"

Carolina nodded, not entirely certain that she wanted to know what her daughter would say next.

"Well, Kiernan came to the house. He was wounded and I hid him out in the cave behind the barn. I went there every day while he was getting well and he would tell me about Ireland, and we would just talk about all manner of subjects. I started teaching him to read when he was still there. He said he knew it would be a help to his getting a better job, and I saw it as a way of making myself useful to him."

Carolina could well imagine a great many uses Kiernan might have for her pretty young daughter, most of them unacceptable. "And when did Kiernan return your feelings?"

"Oh, I think he loved me from the first moment we met," Victoria said with a romantic sigh. "I think I did, too. But Kiernan, being older and wiser, said we should give it time to make sure we weren't just riding on the wind and hitching ourselves to stars. Isn't that a wonderful way of putting it?" Her eyes were alight with love.

Carolina nodded. "I suppose it is. But, Victoria, I think you should give it more time than just two years. I think both you and Kiernan need to think about the consequences of marriage. Especially in light of the fact that you want to journey to California. Many people have tried to find their fortune in gold. It isn't anything new. But it is a hard life and there isn't always a pot of gold to be found waiting for the searcher."

"You're just being negative," Victoria said, getting up and taking the pink muslin gown with her. "You just want to keep me a little girl, wearing clothes made for a baby. You don't care if I'm happy or not."

"That is not fair, nor is it true," Carolina said, getting to her feet. "My concern is born out of my love for you. Kiernan is a great deal older than you, and as a full-grown man he should know that such things are not to be considered lightly. If you are quite serious about this matter, then we need to sit down and discuss it with your father."

"Maybe Papa will understand better than you," Victoria replied. "After all, he's older than you, just like Kiernan is older than me. In fact, Papa is seven years older than you and Kiernan is only four years older than me. And my real father was a great deal older than you were and still you married him." She turned and walked to the door. "I think Papa will understand," she added and left the room, leaving Carolina to stare at the empty space where her daughter had stood only moments before.

Shaking her head, she wished most sincerely that James were with her at this very moment. What a thing to have to bear all alone. But a voice down deep inside reminded her that she was never alone. God was her constant companion, and she had but to turn the matter over to Him.

"It's so hard for me, Father," she whispered. "She's so very young, and I fear that the life she's planned out for herself is hardly the wisest choice. Help me in this." Just then voices could be heard in the hall, and with a sigh, Carolina moved to close the door against any further intrusion to her thoughts. This matter would not be easily resolved, and she had little desire to answer anyone's questions at this point.

Moving back to her window-seat perch, Carolina grew only too aware that she longed for her own home and for the comfort of her husband. Oakbridge had ceased to be her home, and while it held fond memories of carefree days, Greigsville was her home now. Wherever James was—that place was home.

Feeling that way, it wasn't hard to imagine her daughter's desire to share her life with Kiernan. Even if it meant dragging herself clear across the continent to do so, Victoria was in the process of transferring her little-girl attachments and affections to more grown-up propositions. There was still time, Carolina knew, and even comforted herself with the knowledge. But time wouldn't change Victoria's heart if Kiernan O'Connor was indeed the man God had chosen for her to love and marry.

"How difficult it is to let children grow up," Carolina said wearily. "And how very hard it will be to let her go."

Thirty-Six

Beyond the Wall

As the date for their departure grew near, Carolina felt an urgency to seek her mother out for a final moment of private consultation. Of course, they'd had many talks already, but with so much happening, they never seemed to get all the time they desired. She wanted to talk more with her mother about Virginia's mental state and illness, and Martha's death. Carolina had seen her sister's health improve, but her spirits were still dangerously depressed. Carolina had hoped to stay on until she knew for sure that Virginia was out of danger, but that appeared to be something that might well be slow in coming. Virginia had to want to get better, and she had to forgive herself and seek God. And while she was more open to do the latter, Carolina knew that forgiving herself came hard.

Then there were Carolina's own trials, small by comparison to Virginia's, but they nevertheless weighed on her. Nothing seemed right. Brenton and Nate had managed to get themselves into one conflict after another—not against each other, but always in trouble together. Several times they had been caught sneaking cookies, and what really perplexed Carolina was that she knew her son had no great love of sweets. Another time, the boys had broken a music box that had sat atop the mantel in the music room. When questioned about why he had tried to take the box down, Brenton had turned sullen and silent, not at all the open, reasonable child she had known in Greigsville. Nate, too, seemed unwilling to speak about each incident, and Carolina found herself perplexed as to how to treat the matter. Then there was Jordana, who seemed always to get in one fight or another with the twins, and finally, Victoria, who pined for home and Kiernan.

So now with her departure scheduled for the next day, Carolina was desperate to have her mother to herself.

It was her mother's routine of late to depart the company of everyone and seek a time of private rest in the afternoon. This always came after the noon meal and fell in a time that found the children well occupied with Miss Mayfield. And so it was that as they departed the dining room for their various corners of the house, Carolina followed her mother up the stairs.

"I wondered if I might intrude on your private time?" Carolina asked.

Margaret stopped midstep and looked at her daughter thoughtfully. "I've sensed that you had a great deal on your mind. I didn't want to pry."

"Nor did I want to trespass on your respite."

"Well, do not concern yourself with that," Margaret said, taking to the stairs once again. "Come and sit with me and we will speak of what's troubling you."

Carolina followed her mother upstairs, certain that she would seek out the family sitting room. It was a pleasant surprise, however, when she held to her routine and opened the door to her bedroom.

"No one will disturb us here."

Everything in the room was just as Carolina remembered it from childhood. Her mother's ornately carved wooden dressing screen, the wardrobe, and canopied bed were all designed in the same Gothic pattern. Everything held an air of familiarity. Of course, there had been changes. New blue damask drapes had been put in place shortly after Margaret's return home, and the canopy and quilts had been changed to match. But the furniture arrangement and scent of her mother's lavender and jasmine were the same.

"Come sit over here," her mother motioned, taking a seat on a blue velvet lounging couch.

Carolina drew up the dressing table chair and placed it beside the couch. It instantly struck her as ironic that only recently she'd shared a similar moment with Victoria. Only then she had been the mother and Victoria the daughter. Now Carolina took her position as daughter, and instead of feeling reduced in position or threatened in credibility, Carolina suddenly felt very comforted that she could seek this older woman out for counsel.

"I will miss you when you are gone," Margaret said, smiling sadly.

"You have no idea how I will miss you, Mother," Carolina replied, struggling to think of how she might share her heart in so short a time.

"But that's not the reason for your melancholy, is it?"

Carolina smiled. "You know me so well."

"Not half as well as I should," Margaret replied. "I remember clearly a time when I did not understand you or your desires. I regret that I did not even seek to learn."

"But you had more than enough with which to occupy yourself." Now that Carolina was a mother herself, she knew this was no mere lame excuse. "I hold you no ill feelings for that. I came up against all that was traditional and laid out for womankind, and that you should have found yourself unable to understand me was certainly no reflection on you."

"That's where you're wrong, Carolina. I believe it a mother's place to know her children better than anyone else. Her interest should be with them, or she should not have them. Look at Virginia's children if you doubt my word on this."

Carolina gave a heavy sigh. "I try to know my children, but I find that I constantly seek to interject my own philosophies and desires in place of their own. That's part of the reason for this discussion."

"Victoria?" Margaret asked, seeming already to understand Carolina's plight.

"Yes. I suppose I am confused by her desire to do nothing more than marry young and begin housekeeping. She has fallen in love with one of the Irish laborers, and from her own acknowledgment and what I've seen with my own eyes, I know that he also loves her."

Margaret smiled. "But you find this unacceptable, eh?"

"She's only thirteen. How can she possibly know her own heart?"

"How did you know your own at that age?" Margaret asked gently.

"But I didn't seek men's affections at thirteen."

"No, but you sought their minds." Margaret studied her carefully for a moment before continuing. "You knew, even then, that the education of masculine studies was something you had to obtain. You were striving to take in all that you could from your father and brother. I used to fret something fierce about it."

"I remember," Carolina said with a slight smile. And indeed she did remember. Listening to her mother speak of the matter helped her easily to see that her dilemma with Victoria was nothing new.

As if reading her mind, Margaret reached out to take hold of her hands. "You see, don't you? You understand that this thing with Victoria is much the same as it was with you and me?"

"Yes, I do see that. But now that it's more acceptable for a woman to continue her education, albeit only moderately so, I presumed that Victoria would desire such a thing for herself. After all, money is hardly the problem."

"I presumed you would want to run a plantation and be a planter's wife," Margaret replied. "You were raised to understand that this was to be your place in life, but you refused the confines of such a thing."

"But I am content being a wife and mother," Carolina said, then shook her head. "Well, maybe not in full. I still long to be allowed an active part in the railroad. Women's roles are still greatly limited and there is no need for my presence on the B&O."

"And you desire that there might be?"

Carolina nodded. "With all my heart." The conversation that she thought would center around Victoria had suddenly taken a new turn. "Maybe that's why Victoria is such an enigma to me. It seems only natural that a young woman, with the entire world at her feet, should choose something other than early marriage and motherhood."

"But why? I married young and immediately had children," Margaret replied. "I didn't regret it, even when my children died. I would not have traded roles with any other person in the world."

"I suppose I do understand that. I would not wish my marriage or children to be gone," Carolina admitted. "I suppose I just feel that there should be more. I long for more, and when Victoria implies that she can be content with this and nothing else, I grow frustrated."

"Because of her feelings," Margaret posed, "or yours?"

Carolina realized with an awareness that almost hurt that her mother had somehow uncovered a vital piece of information. "I fail to understand how a thirteen-year-old child can be content when I cannot."

Margaret chuckled. "Victoria doesn't have the knowledge and experience you have, for one thing. For another, her interests and ideals are different from yours. You know what's out there. You have seen beyond the wall, so to speak. You once played perfectly content in your own garden, but one day you climbed up the wall and saw with your own eyes what lay beyond. Victoria is content in her own garden."

"But what happens when she's no longer content? What if she marries and then learns the truth of there being many other opportunities out there?"

"But she has seen, hasn't she? Have you not already told her of the possibilities that await her?" Margaret questioned. "You have told her of college and the benefits of education. You've no doubt shared with her the possibilities and benefits of being an independent woman with means of her own. She has seen over the garden wall, but the world beyond doesn't appeal to her as much as the one within. Would you fault her for that, as I faulted you?"

"But she's only—"

"A child? Or an uninformed young woman?" asked Margaret. "Yes, she's young, but because she is young, she has a great long path ahead of her and will most likely change her mind several times in an attempt to fine-tune her desires. Carolina"—her mother squeezed her hands gently—"now that I've gone through all that I have, I can honestly say to you, this, too, will pass. It isn't that the situation is not important. Nor even that Victoria is very young and very vulnerable. No matter what you do, whether you forbid her to marry or accept the situation and help design her wedding gown, the only thing that really matters is that you stay true to God and true to her."

"I don't see how I can do one without stepping on the toes of the other," Carolina said with an exhausted sigh.

Margaret dropped her hold and leaned back against the couch. "It might appear contradictory at first, but what I've found with time and honest effort is that it fits perfectly together. First, you align yourself with God. You seek Him first and foremost and allow your thoughts, decisions, actions, to be based solely on the Word. In doing so, you allow Him to guide you into a peace and contentment that I cannot even begin to explain.

"When I was younger," Margaret continued, "and you children were small, I was convinced that my position in society revealed my true character and nature. I focused on the works I could do and how those works would be perceived. I fretted and stewed that someone might think ill of me, and when you children grew old enough to begin appearing publicly, I worried that your actions would become a reflection of me. So when York was expelled from college, and Virginia shunned suitor after suitor, I took it very personally. I felt that somehow I had failed, and that the general public would perceive this failure and find me to fall short of the mark.

"In turn, when you rode the locomotive and sought masculine studies, I feared that someone would see this as an error in your upbringing. I told you then how concerned I was that no respectable young man would seek you in marriage, but in truth, I felt a vast anxiety over whether or not my friends were speaking badly of me behind my back."

Carolina watched her mother absentmindedly smooth the material of her woolen skirt. It seemed odd to hear this confession after so many years had been lost to them.

"Perhaps I recognized it then for what it was, but I never allowed it to change me," Margaret admitted. "Remember the talk we had not long before your sixteenth birthday? I told you not to let fear keep you from living your life."

"I do," Carolina said, nodding. She remembered the talk as though it had only been yesterday. "You also told me that going my own way was more than having my own way."

Margaret smiled. "Yes, and that the truth God put inside you—the one that made you who you were, who you would become—was one that only you could know. It's no different now. Turning to God and reflecting on the Bible's teachings will help you see that truth for yourself, but you must remember, Victoria has God's truth inside of her, as well. Yes, she is very young. But that is fleeting. If she sees in you the ability to turn to God, even when things seem displaced and out of control, it will affect her more profoundly than any lecture. By being true to God, you can in turn be true to her. You can express your concerns for her, but turn your fears over to God and allow Victoria to begin finding the truth inside herself."

"You make it sound so simple."

"Oh, but it isn't," Margaret laughed. "And I would never tell anyone that it is. After all, this is a child you love. A child you have fought to keep from death's grip and life's hardships. This is a child for whom you would gladly give your life and fight to the death anyone who threatened to harm her. That kind of love is never simple. But let me share something else with you." Margaret leaned forward once again and this time reached out to touch Carolina's cheek. "Fear only kills love, and fear is not from God. The Bible says, 'For God hath not given us the spirit of fear; but of power, and of love, and of a sound mind.' "

She paused for several moments, her expression changing as she considered her next words. Carolina cherished the moment, knowing that her mother was reaching down into the depths of her own heart and soul to bear her weaknesses before her child. Somehow it humbled Carolina in a way that she could not explain, and her heart swelled with love so deep for this woman—her mother—that all else seemed dwarfed in importance.

"When I went to the hospital," Margaret began, "I was lost in my fear and suffering. I felt a bitterness toward your father for not having been at my side when our children fell ill. I felt a hatred toward the weakness and frailty of our human bodies, and I knew a deep abiding anger at God." Her eyes grew damp with tears. "I wanted no more of life because it seemed only to offer me death and suffering. I said to myself, 'If this is what living a godly life produces, then I want no more of it or of God.' But down deep inside, I knew it wasn't true. I knew it wasn't my heart's desire to turn my back on God, but my pain was so fierce and my fears were so overpowering.

"As time went on, I only wanted to push away those people who loved me. I didn't want to feel love or to love because that would only serve to make me vulnerable. I lay in my hospital bed, praying to die but believing that as some great joke of God's, I would live. My dear nurse, Esther, refused to allow me to bury myself in selfishness and sorrow. She read to me daily from the Bible, and she prayed for me when I could not and would not pray for myself. And always she left me with this verse I just quoted to you.

"Then one day she explained to me that if God had not given me this spirit of fear, I should examine the situation and recognize who was responsible. God was offering me power, love, and a sound mind, but only Satan stood to benefit from my fears—fears that rendered me helpless and useless, fears that drove me from my family and loved ones." Margaret gently stroked Carolina's cheek, then cupped her chin as though Carolina were a small child unable to focus. "I tell you again, my dearest daughter, do not let fear keep you from living your life. And I add, do not let it keep you from allowing your children to live their lives, as well. We can lock them away and secure them from all that might render them harm, but in the process we have hurt them even more. Protection is one thing, but isolation is another. They are human beings entrusted to us by God. We raise them for a time, teach them the truths we hold, and then, often uncomfortably, we must stand aside and allow them to think and plan for themselves. It isn't easy, and I certainly do not imply that you ever stop praying for them, but letting go is necessary for both their coming of age and yours."

It was indeed fear within her that made Carolina fret over Victoria. Perhaps it was even fear that kept her miserably discontent with her homelife. If she remained unhappily behind the garden wall because she was afraid to climb over and test what lay beyond, it was hardly anyone's fault but her own.

"Oh, Mama," she said and embraced her mother eagerly, "I want so much to grow up to be like you."

"Hopefully, you will be spared the years of a not-so-sound mind," Margaret said. Tears coursed down her cheeks, and Carolina's vision blurred with tears of her own. "I'd like to think that I went through my difficulties in order that my children might learn and be spared the same misery."

Carolina felt hope surge anew. She wiped at her tears and smiled. "Mama, I'm so happy to have had this time with you. I shall miss you so much when I go away again."

"But your home is in Greigsville," her mother said matter-of-factly.

"Yes," Carolina agreed. "And I miss it more than I had ever thought possible. Shortly before I left, I was fairly miserable and unhappy. I felt confused and homesick, and yet my home was there all along. Maybe I've just been too afraid to live the life God has given me."

Margaret nodded. "Perhaps so. Sometimes we let things creep in upon us without noticing them. But if you had never stepped out in faith, you wouldn't even have Victoria. Much less James and Brenton and Jordana."

Carolina smiled conspiratorially and leaned closer to her mother. "Or the baby I'm carrying now," she whispered.

"What? But why have you said nothing until now?" her mother replied with a look of sheer joy.

"Well, I suppose because I'm only now really certain of my condition, and then, too, with Virginia's pregnancy ending so tragically, I didn't want to make my joy any more painful for her."

"Well, this is delightful news," Margaret said, embracing Carolina. "Have you told your father?"

"No," she answered. "I wanted you to be the first to know. Somehow it just seemed right."

"I'm so glad," Margaret said, mirth edging her voice. "We should celebrate this evening."

"No," Carolina said, shaking her head. "I don't plan to tell the children until after I've told James. Perhaps we could just have a lovely farewell dinner, and you and Papa will know the heart of the matter for yourselves."

"I understand." They rose together and held hands for a moment before Margaret broke the silence to add, "God bless you, my dearest. You will never be far from Him, for my prayers will be uttered constantly on your behalf. There is power in the prayer of a friend for another, perhaps even more so in the prayer of a mother for her child. Never forget that power."

"I won't," Carolina said, knowing the truth of what her mother had said. "I promise you, I won't."

Thirty-Seven

Return to Cumberland

I'm so grateful the weather has remained fair," Carolina told Miriam as the locomotive slowed. They were approaching Cumberland, and Carolina strained to look out the window, anxious to catch a glimpse of her husband.

"Will Papa and Kiernan be at the station waiting for us?" Victoria asked in animated fashion. She smoothed her mulberry wool gown and added, "I want to show them my new dress."

Carolina smiled. She had hit upon a brilliant scheme in her final days at Oakbridge. Taking Victoria to the attic, they had managed to locate a trunk of Carolina's old gowns, and in turn had taken these to the sewing house to be remade for Victoria. The entire affair had proven to be a success. Victoria was pleased with the new array of gowns, as was Carolina. It seemed a perfect solution given their limited time.

"I 'magin' yo' papa will be there, Miz Victoria," Miriam told her, smiling broadly.

"I can't see him missing it," Carolina admitted. Then seeing the concerned perplexity of Victoria's expression, she added, "Nor Kiernan."

Victoria beamed a smile and resumed her vigilance at the window. Carolina tried to still her own excitement. The holidays were nearly upon them, and spending them together in their own home would be such a joy. She tried to imagine how they would decorate things and what they might dream up in the way of special treats and goodies. Carolina had managed to do some early Christmas shopping on the trip. And Naomi had overseen the packing and crating of several hundred jars of apple, plum, peach, and berry preserves and jellies, as well as fruit for pies and cobblers. Carolina had thought of the store in

Greigsville and what a treat it would be for the locals to experience this wealth of treasures from Oakbridge.

"We're here," Brenton said excitedly as the train finally came to a stop.

"Where's Papa?" Jordana asked, squirming down from Miriam's lap to join her sister at the window.

"I'm sure he's there somewhere," Carolina commented. Only one more leg of the journey and she would be home, she thought contentedly. They would spend the night in Cumberland; then in the morning they would make their way by stage to Greigsville. And through it all, she would have James.

A commotion outside their window caused Victoria to sit back with a start. "Kiernan's brother Red is out there arguing with someone."

Carolina glanced out and saw a gathering of about fifty men. Sure enough, Red O'Connor was in the middle of the entourage. He was speaking in loud, angry tones, but Carolina found it impossible to make out the words over the sounds of the train.

"I suppose the Irish trouble is still with us," she murmured and gathered up her children. "Let's stay very close together."

"If Red is here," Victoria stated, "then Kiernan probably is, too."

"And no doubt your father is, as well, Victoria. We will seek him out first. The others are probably here on his behalf."

Victoria nodded and followed her mother.

Carolina was assisted from the railcar by a porter and waited in turn for her children and Miriam to be helped down. Jordana, cantankerous from the long journey, put her hands over her ears and protested the noise of the arguing men and of the locomotive whistle and bells.

"Too loud!" she said over and over.

Miriam picked her up and patted her sympathetically while Victoria and Brenton joined hands and huddled near their mother. Carolina looked around for James but saw nothing of her husband. She moved away from the train, glancing first up one side of the platform and then down the other.

He wasn't there. Disappointment washed over her, and when the protests of the nearby Irish immigrants increased in volume, Carolina suddenly feared for her little family.

"Everyone stay close," she commanded.

"Where's Papa?" asked Victoria, drawing Brenton even closer.

Carolina positioned herself so as to put Brenton between them. "I don't know." She continued to look for James even as she began to doubt the wisdom of lingering too long near the rowdy group of men. Soon the other passengers had hurried off in their various directions.

A tingling sensation was edging up her spine as she suddenly realized that, with exception to the collection of arguing men, everyone else had deserted the area.

The sound of breaking glass caused Carolina and her family to press even closer to one another.

"Ya should ought to just go back to Ireland where ya belong," someone shouted. This was followed by several thudding sounds, and Carolina realized that rocks were being hurtled and some were hitting up against the railroad car.

Curses flew and accusations abounded as the argument reached a new height of intensity. "I say we hang 'em from the nearest tree," another voice cried out.

"We have to get out of here," Carolina told Miriam. She looked away from the growing crowd of men to see if the opposite direction might afford them an escape. But it looked no better. Even now another gang of laborers was making its way en masse toward the depot.

Red O'Connor caught sight of this at nearly the same moment Carolina did, and his shouts of displeasure rang out loud and clear. "And so here comes another pack of rats to chew at our bones."

The protests of those Carolina presumed were Red's Connaughtmen filled the air as vile cursing and threats rang out and tempers raged. Glancing back at the approaching gang, and then to Red and the crowd fixed in place to her right, Carolina suddenly realized her retreat was being cut off, with her and her family caught between the two warring groups.

"Dear God," she breathed, "help us."

"Mama, I'm scared," Brenton said in a trembling voice.

"I am, too," she told her son, then hugged him close. "Come on. Let's move this way." She pulled them along toward the depot, hoping and praying that somehow she could make her way through before the two sides rushed each other.

"Ya'll be lettin' our people go," one of the approaching men called out. "Men of Cork, are ya with me?"

A rousing cheer rose up from the men, while an equally disturbing counter cheer filled the air when Red proclaimed that the only good Corkman was a dead one. As if to add credence to their declaration, several rocks were thrown at the rival group, narrowly missing Carolina and Victoria.

"These are bad men," Jordana declared and hugged her arms around Miriam's neck.

Carolina pushed Miriam ahead of her, pulling Victoria and Brenton behind her as she turned to shield her children from the approaching men. Behind Red, Carolina's eyes caught sight of several mounted riders. The men carried muskets and were trying to make their way through the Connaughtmen. This only caused the crowd to surge forward, cutting off any chance of Carolina reaching the stationhouse.

As men attacked each other, oblivious to the women and children in their midst, Carolina began to pray as never before. She feared for her life, but more so, she feared for the lives of her children, including the unborn child she carried. Biting at her lower lip, she frantically searched the crowd for someone she knew. Of course, she recognized Red, but he would hardly do her any good.

Several feet away from her a fistfight broke out, and this quickly ignited the surrounding men into a full-blown battle. Boards, branches, mauls, whatever could be reached, instantly became a weapon for war.

Victoria screamed, and just as Carolina turned to see what caused this sudden outburst, a stunning blow hit her at the temple. For a moment, Carolina was too surprised to understand what had happened, but as her vision blurred and the images around her began to dance and spin, she completely comprehended the gravity of the situation.

"Mama!" Victoria screamed again, and this time Brenton, too, joined in.

Carolina tried to shake her head, but the pain was too intense. She reached her gloved hand up to the place where the rock had grazed her and brought it away bloody. Seeing her own blood was too much. Her knees gave out and blackness crowded her thoughts.

"James . . ." she whispered.

Suddenly strong arms grasped her. "This way," the voice instructed.

"My babies," she moaned, unable to see through the swirling darkness.

"I'll be seein' to them all."

Somewhere in her thoughts, Carolina recognized the voice of Kiernan O'Connor. "Don't let them get hurt," she pleaded, slipping further and further into the arms of unconscious oblivion.

"Hush," he told her. "I'll guard 'em with me life."

It was the last thing she would remember.

Thirty-Eight

Seeds of Prejudice

Carolina next opened her eyes to the worried frown of her husband. Hovering at her bedside, James' expression immediately reminded her of another episode of struggle and worry.

"I've not seen you look like that since I gave birth to Jordana," she said groggily.

"Carolina! Oh, thank God!" James declared, taking hold of her hand. "You can't imagine my shock when Kiernan brought you here."

"What happened?" she asked, fighting through the clouded images of her memory. Her head ached fiercely, and for the life of her, Carolina couldn't remember why.

"The Irish are rioting. It started at the station just as you arrived. Red is furious because Ben Latrobe has brought in additional Corkians. They were on the same train as you were. Now there's fighting going on all over Cumberland, and Red O'Connor is leading the Connaughtmen."

She nodded. Yes, somewhere in her memory she remembered Red O'Connor shouting and Irish voices being raised in anger.

"Where am I now?"

"My hotel room," James replied.

She nodded, supposing that somehow it all made sense. She lay quietly for several moments as bits and pieces came back to her. Suddenly she thought of Victoria screaming. "The children!" she cried, her eyes flying open in fright.

"They are fine. Kiernan has them all in his room. Miriam, as well."

"They are unhurt?"

"Yes," he replied. "You were the only one wounded." He leaned down to kiss her gently. "Why didn't you listen to me? Why didn't you stay at Oakbridge?"

"What are you talking about?" Carolina reached a trembling hand to her temple.

"I sent you a telegram. Didn't you receive it?" James asked gravely.

"No . . . I received nothing," admitted Carolina. "I had a letter dated from the first part of November, and that was the last I had from you." Things were coming clearer to her now, and the dull ache in her head didn't seem so troubling. A bandage had been placed over the wound, and bringing her hand back down, she once again saw the blood that was now drying on her glove. "It seems I can't keep a clean pair of gloves. It's either locomotive soot or blood or some such thing."

"Oh, Carolina," James said, and the heaviness in his voice immediately made her feel guilty.

"I am sorry," she said, slipping the soiled glove from her hand. She reached up to touch his face.

"You can't know what I went through when I saw you in Kiernan's arms. You were unconscious and bleeding, the children were crying, and even Miriam was so shaken that all she could do was weep. I thought you might even be dead."

"Not me," Carolina said, grinning gamely, trying hard to soothe his fears. "I've too much to live for. You need me to keep you out of trouble."

"Yes, but who will keep you out of trouble?" he asked softly. Pulling her gently into his arms, James held her close and stroked her hair.

Carolina relished the way he made her feel secure and loved. She didn't even mind that his actions had caused her head to throb painfully. She loved him so and had despaired of ever seeing him again.

"I want you to take the children and Miriam and return to Baltimore," James said suddenly. He pulled away to look her full in the face. "There are only going to be more problems. The labor situation isn't going to calm anytime soon. I can't even fire Red without concerning myself with a full-scale war. My only hope is to help him see reason. If we work together we can surely come to some kind of amicable settlement. But I won't risk your life, nor that of the children or Miriam."

"I'm not leaving you," Carolina said adamantly. "My place is with you. I probably never realized that so much as when I was at Oakbridge."

James shook his head. "It's going to be too dangerous."

"Life anywhere is dangerous, my love," Carolina said softly. "We're a family and we need to work together and remain together as one. I need to be with you. I need you. Especially now." She smiled and leaned forward to kiss him lightly upon the lips. "We're going to have another baby."

"What!" James exclaimed and held her at arm's length. The stunned expression on his face made her laugh.

"Poor man." She giggled. "First Ben overruns you with Irish, and now I do the same with children."

"Are you certain?"

"Of course I'm certain. I found out while I was at Oakbridge. Come June I will give you another daughter or son."

"Now I know that I want you to return to Baltimore."

"The doctor in Greigsville is good, and I want you near when I have our baby," Carolina countered. "James, see reason. Greigsville is just as safe as any place else. I wouldn't have been hurt today if I hadn't been in the wrong place. If I'd received your telegram, it might have made a difference, but who knows? I believe we are in God's hands and that all things happen for a purpose. Don't send me away," she pleaded.

"Don't look at me that way," James said in complete exasperation. "You know exactly how to get your way with me, and that look always seems to worm its way into my heart."

Carolina laughed. "I never knew that, but now that I do—"

"Don't you be getting any ideas, Mrs. Baldwin." He laughed and let go of her. Crossing his arms against his chest, he shook his head. "You know exactly how to get what you want out of me. I'm much too soft when it comes to you and your feminine wiles."

His expression was serious, but Carolina knew how to break through this facade. "It has nothing to do with feminine wiles," she said, her fingers lightly touching his cleanly shaven face. "It has more to do with my deep abiding love for you. You cannot know how very much I love you, how I live for you." She traced along his jaw, then placed the palm of her hand against his cheek. "I want to stay with you." She heard him sigh and knew that she'd won. She grinned.

"Stop looking like the cat who caught the mouse," he told her. "I know I'll probably regret this, but very well. We will all return to Greigsville together. Maybe the fact that you and the children are in tow will cause the men to behave themselves."

"What men?"

"I'm to escort the new laborers back to the tunnel site, along with the men who accompanied me here to Cumberland for my meetings with Ben Latrobe."

"Will there be very many?"

"Nearly fifty. If they choose not to behave themselves, then we'll all pay the price. I only hope Red will keep his mouth shut."

"Can't Red see the way he's dividing the people against each other?"

"He does and he doesn't care. He wants them divided. He's even put Kiernan away from him."

"What do you mean?" Carolina instantly remembered that it was Kiernan who had rescued her.

"Kiernan defended me against Red, and so Red has denounced him as a brother. He kicked him out of their room, and not only that, but the other Connaughtmen will have nothing to do with him. Either they are too afraid of Red or they totally agree with his politics and believe Kiernan to be a traitor."

"How sad."

"It is," James said. "But Red cares naught for anyone but himself. I would wager a bet that it isn't even the benefit of the Connaughtmen that drives him. He's filled with anger and hatred, and it pours out into everything he does. If I fire him, he'll only become more powerful as a martyr and sneak around behind my back without even the benefit of a job to keep him in line. And if I do nothing, then I'm seen as weak and an easy mark for further demands."

"It does seem an impossible situation."

Just then a knock sounded at the adjoining room door, and Kiernan O'Connor looked in when James answered. "How is she?" he asked.

Carolina lay back against the pillow as James moved aside. "I'm just fine, Kiernan, thanks to you and God."

Kiernan grinned. "Now, that's what I call keepin' high company."

"Mama! Mama!" Brenton pushed past Kiernan and rushed to his mother's bedside.

"Whoa there, son," James said, taking hold of him. "Your mother is going to be just fine, but you can't go jumping on her like she's a sack of flour."

There were tears in the boy's eyes as he nodded and turned toward Carolina. "I was a-scared that you were dead," he told her honestly.

Carolina opened her arms and James released the boy. Brenton snuggled down into her embrace and held on to her tightly. "I hate those Irish," he said angrily. "If I had a gun like Papa's, I'd kill them all."

Carolina knew without a mirror that her expression was one of absolute shock. The words coming from her young son's mouth were frightening and overwhelmingly filled with bitterness. James, too, appeared surprised by this sudden outburst.

"Son, that's no way to speak," he admonished.

"I don't care. They tried to kill my mama," Brenton said, rising up enough to see his mother's face. "They hurt you bad."

"No, not truly," Carolina told him, stroking his soft brown hair lovingly. "They weren't trying to hurt me, Brenton. They were fighting each other. I was simply in the way. They didn't mean to cause me harm."

"I don't care. I hate them. They're just a bunch of dumb old Micks."

"Brenton Baldwin!" Carolina exclaimed. "I don't know where you ever heard that term, but I'd better never hear you use it again. You may well think the Irish set out to hurt me, but I'm telling you otherwise, and as your mother I expect you to believe me. You should also remember that it was an Irishman who saved my life."

Brenton shook his head furiously and sat up. "Kiernan saved you."

"Son, Kiernan is also an Irishman," James said softly.

Brenton looked to his mother for affirmation, and Carolina nodded. "Kiernan is Mr. O'Connor's brother, and Mr. O'Connor is the one who started today's fight. At least from what I could see."

"I'm certain that's right," Kiernan offered from the door.

By this time, Victoria and Miriam had come into the room, with Jordana quietly watching the scene from Miriam's arms. The gravity of the situation was not lost on her, and it had subdued the active child for the moment.

Brenton looked up at the man he'd come to think of as a friend. Carolina knew it was difficult for him to understand. The seeds of bitter prejudice had been planted in her son's heart, and it was her utmost desire that they might be stomped out before being given a chance to grow.

"Brenton, there are all kinds of people in this world," Carolina explained. "Some look different from us. Some act different. Some live in other countries far across the ocean, and some have different colors of skin. But all are important to God. Do you understand?"

"Even when they're bad?" Brenton asked, his little-boy face contorting in confusion.

"Maybe even especially then," Carolina countered. "There are bad people everywhere, just as there are good people everywhere. The color of your skin or the country you were born in doesn't make you better or worse than anyone else. Remember what I told you about slavery?"

"You said it needed to stop," Brenton answered confidently.

"That's right. Grandfather Adams has slaves, but he intends to set them free. The slaves at Oakbridge are generally treated very well, but other slaves living elsewhere are often treated very badly. But no matter how good or bad they are treated, slavery is still wrong because no one has the right to own another person. Neither do they have the right to force people to work at one place or another. Mr. O'Connor is trying to force the railroad to not hire certain people just because he doesn't like them. A lot of the Irishmen feel the same way he does, but a lot of them don't."

"Me for one," Kiernan said.

Brenton seemed to consider all this for a moment, then got up from the bed and ran to Kiernan. "I didn't know you were Irish," he said. "I just thought you talked funny."

Kiernan laughed. "Now, 'tisn't me who talks funny," he said, purposefully thickening his brogue. "Folks in me homeland talk like this all the time. 'Tis yar own self who'd be talkin' funny."

Carolina smiled at James, then turned her attention back to her son. "Remember, Brenton, Kiernan saved my life. He's a good man, and we should all give him our thanks." She met his warm expression and knew that her opinion of him had been forever altered.

"Thank you for saving my mama," Brenton told him, extending his small hand.

Kiernan shook it and nodded. "I thank the good Lord that I could be there to help."

"So do we," James replied. "I can't thank you enough for protecting them. I had no idea Carolina wouldn't receive my telegram and not remain at Oakbridge. The shock of finding my family here, much less in the middle of a riot, is still taking a toll on me."

"Even if it isn't the first time James has found me in the middle of a brawl," Carolina said, trying to lighten the mood. "I'll have to tell you sometime about the fight that broke out at my coming-out party."

"Comin' out of what?" Kiernan questioned and everyone laughed.

"I can see," Carolina said, "that there is a great deal I shall have to explain. Suffice it to say, I tend to find myself in situations that would better be avoided."

"But she's stubborn and insistent," James added, "and when she bats those darks lashes at you and gets that pouting little-girl expression on her face, you'd might as well give up."

Kiernan threw a quick glance at Victoria, who Carolina noted was blushing. "I've had some experience with pouts," Kiernan said, returning his attention to James and Carolina.

"No doubt," Carolina replied, seeing clearly that the future was already mapping itself out before her.

Kiernan seemed instantly aware of Carolina's understanding, and instead of dealing further with the matter, he squatted down to meet Brenton face-to-face. "So are we still friends?"

"Sure," Brenton answered. "I'm sorry for saying those bad things."

"Apology accepted," Kiernan replied and hugged Brenton once again.

Carolina watched the scene, all the while her mind dealing with the idea that this man might one day be her son-in-law. It was hard to imagine Victoria growing up and one day getting married, but at least with her increasing awareness of the character of Kiernan O'Connor, Carolina no longer felt quite so fretful toward that day.

"Well, now I hope you will answer a question for me," Carolina said, turning to her husband. "When do we leave for home?"

James shook his head as if still uncertain that he should allow his wife to travel back to the isolated town. "Tomorrow, if you're up to it."

"I assure you, Mr. Baldwin, I will be up and ready. I long to be in my own home, and with the holidays nearly upon us, I want to celebrate in grand style."

James laughed. "Ever looking toward the future, eh, Mrs. Baldwin?"

Carolina glanced at Kiernan and then to Victoria. She gave a slow nod and met her husband's warm gaze. "I suppose it's best that way."

PART IV

September 1851–January 1853

I have been commended for the success of the grades,
for the tunnels and the bridges of this road;
but there is a source of pride more grateful to me just now,
in that I have been enabled to complete the line at the
precise time I had promised.

—Benjamin H. Latrobe, Jr.

Thirty-Nine

Cholera

The winter of 1850 passed with ease into the new year. It had been a mild winter with little in the way of snow and storms to slow the progress on the Kingwood Tunnel. This made the work and living conditions much improved over the previous winter, and the laborers and citizens of Greigsville found much to celebrate and feel joyous about.

Spring had been equally mild, and the workers reveled in the fact that with the light rainfall, landslides and cave-ins had been minimal. But by summer it was clear that the lack of snow in the winter and rain in the spring had led them straight into a drought. Without water by which to supply the steam-powered engines on the winches and locomotives, there was no steam. And without steam, the engines could not work. Progress slowed, much to everyone's dismay, and tempers flared, creating the first real tensions of the year. As water levels continued to drop and the creeks dried up even more, people became genuinely afraid and began seeking ways to hoard the precious commodity.

Meanwhile, the Baldwins welcomed a new member to their family on the twelfth day of June. Nicholas Baldwin was a plump, ruddy infant, with a wailing cry and a voracious appetite. Carolina found it nearly impossible to satisfy him by nursing alone and took up Miriam's suggestion that the child be supplemented with sugar water. This seemed to agree with the child, and since the Baldwin well seemed sufficiently supplied, there wasn't the same fear in their household of running out of water that haunted many others in the town.

The Baltimore and Ohio Railroad celebrated its July arrival at Piedmont, Maryland, some twenty-eight miles southwest of Cumberland. Then by fall, even this great accomplishment had been surpassed as the line reached Oakland, Maryland, not far from the Virginia border. Tunnels and bridges were being constructed at record paces, and everything seemed to be going well, with exception to the drought-plagued areas. Thomas Swann and his board of directors were very pleased with the anticipated completion of the line. This came in spite of the fact that the previous May had seen the celebrated achievement of the Erie Railroad in New York. The 467-mile, six-foot-gage railroad ran from the Hudson River, at a point just twenty-five miles north of New York City, and concluded in Dunkirk on Lake Erie.

Swann scoffed at the twenty-seven-million-dollar price tag on the Erie, and boasted that the Baltimore and Ohio would be completed for no more than sixteen million dollars. But even this boast required solid reserves and the cooperation of the investors. Swann felt that an injection of new money into the line was exactly what was needed to press the project forward to completion. What was not needed was the fierce cholera epidemic that hit the unsuspecting railroad workers.

Nothing rang fear in the heart of a mother more than to hear the announcement of yet another epidemic. Measles, mumps, and chicken pox were always to be endured, but epidemics of yellow fever and cholera were sporadic and unexpected. No one knew for sure how or why cholera struck. Medical reports suggested everything from poison airs secreted from the earth to the generally accepted idea that tainted water was somehow to blame. But even if doctors could agree on a cause, they seldom agreed on a cure.

Carolina watched the disease gradually take hold of the creek-side shantytown. Hundreds had fallen victim to the epidemic, and the mounting daily death tolls made it necessary to increase the size of the cemetery and eventually create another one altogether. Children were more susceptible than adults, and the Irish seemed destined to acquire the disease more often than anyone else.

Considering what little she knew of cholera, and wishing desperately that she could have access to some of the studies regarding the disease, Carolina had noted that the illness preyed especially upon those with poor standards of cleanliness. The shanties were hard to keep clean, and garbage and debris cluttered the streets and grounds surrounding the slapped-together houses. Because of this, Carolina and Miriam spent most of their waking hours cleaning their own home. This, coupled with the fact that during the outbreak Carolina refused to let the children attend the public school, seemed to work well for keeping the family healthy.

Brenton hated being cooped up in the house, but he busied himself as best he could. His activities often included tremendous battles fought with lead soldiers, which his father had purchased for him during a trip to Baltimore. Jordana, now five, also managed to keep her brother occupied. She demanded he read to her on a daily basis, and although she'd heard each of the books in Brenton's repertoire at least a dozen times, Jordana seemed not to care.

Victoria helped with the baby, and when little Nicholas demanded his mother's attention, Victoria assisted Miriam with the cleaning. Because the weather was fair, Carolina insisted that the windows be kept open to allow the breezes to blow through. She had read somewhere that fresh air was helpful in keeping down the growth of disease, and she meant to give it a chance.

"Mmm," Carolina said, dusting off the flour that clung to her apron. "Those pies smell wonderful, Miriam."

The black woman beamed a smile. "They be Mr. James' favorites."

"Mr. James would eat any kind of pie and call it his favorite," Carolina said, laughing. She turned her attention back to the bread she'd just kneaded down. "I think it would be impossible for you to displease him when it comes to your cooking."

"Yo' cookin' is plenty good, too," Miriam answered. "Don't know that I ever 'spected you to learn to cook, but yo' mama would be right proud."

"Yes, I think she would," Carolina admitted. "Papa said that when the railroad runs all the way to Greigsville, he and Mama will come and stay with us for a time."

"That will shorely be a grand day," agreed Miriam.

"Mama," Victoria called, coming into the kitchen, "couldn't I just go and tidy Kiernan's cabin a tiny bit?"

Carolina shook her head. "You know very well that I find that totally inappropriate. Miriam will see to it."

"But, Mama," Victoria began.

"No, Victoria. Your father may have arranged for Kiernan to live on our property, but he did not arrange for you to take over the housekeeping of that cabin."

"But I'm going to marry him someday. I might as well take care of his things now."

Carolina shook her head. "Victoria, nothing is settled in this matter. Your father and I have not given Kiernan permission to even court you, much less marry you."

"I think you're being mean," she said, plopping down on one of the straight-backed chairs. "You just don't care about my happiness."

"I'd say we've greatly considered your happiness. Your father hired Kiernan on as an assistant so that he wouldn't have to remain as a laborer with men who obviously hold great malice toward him. He could have sent Kiernan to Ben Latrobe, and who knows where he would have ended up on the line."

"Papa understands," Victoria pouted.

"No young missy has any reason to be tendin' a man's house. It ain't proper," Miriam offered in Carolina's defense.

"But Mama did it. Mama moved in with my father and took care of me. You weren't much older than I am now."

Carolina covered the bread dough and wiped her hands on a towel. "Victoria Baldwin, you know perfectly well that I had no love interest in your father. I fell in love with you. Besides, there were two other women there to oversee me. Cook and Mrs. Graves kept an eye out to make certain that everything remained on the up and up."

Victoria frowned, seeming to realize that bringing up the past wasn't going to help her case at all. "I just want to make sure he doesn't get sick. I care about him, even if you don't."

"Victoria, you are being unreasonable. Miriam and I have tended to Kiernan's needs. We clean his place the same as ours. He eats every meal with us, with exception to lunch, and that he eats with your father. I don't know how you can even pretend that we don't care about his well-being."

Carolina moved to where her daughter sat. "Don't be in such a hurry to grow up. You'll have plenty of time to clean cabins and see to the needs of a husband. Try being a child first. You may regret having thrown away these carefree days."

"I hate being this age," Victoria said, getting up in a huff. "I hate being young and I hate that nobody listens to me or takes me seriously." She stomped off in the direction of the front room, and in the meantime Nicholas awoke from his nap and began to cry.

"Well, I suppose one unhappy child is much the same as the next," Carolina said, untying her apron.

She could hear Miriam chuckling behind her, but Carolina didn't feel much like laughing. She was truly worried about Victoria. It seemed the child was ever in search of a way to grow up faster. She was so very discontent with her lot in life that at times Carolina wondered if she would simply wake up one morning to find that Victoria and Kiernan had run off together. Her comfort came in that Kiernan seemed, at least up to this point, to be a very reliable and responsible young man. She and James had already discussed Victoria's love interest, and James found it a satisfactory match. But, like Carolina, he agreed that time was needed to give them a better understanding of each other. He had also decided that when Christmas rolled around, he would give Kiernan permission to court Victoria.

"I'm not ready for that," Carolina murmured as she entered the nursery.

Nicholas had worked up to a full-blown rage by the time Carolina seated herself in the rocking chair and arranged him at her breast. He was so mad, in fact, that he hardly noticed that he was finally getting his own way. He continued to scream and cry, all without benefit of tears, until Carolina finally drew his attention to the offered meal.

Having silenced his cries, Carolina couldn't help but jump when Nicholas clamped down and began to suck. She laughed at his eagerness and cooed to him softly while he fed. "You are such a funny boy, my little Nicholas," she whispered and touched the downy softness of his sandy brown hair. She thought he favored James' mother, Edith. He seemed more fair than her other children, and his hair was lighter. Edith's hair had been a sandy brown, and where hers had been streaked with gray, Nicholas's appeared highlighted with honey tones. His plump baby fingers grasped at her offered index finger and his grip proved to be strong. Carolina knew without a doubt that should she pull upward, he would continue holding on.

As he fed, Nicholas watched her with his dark eyes. Carolina couldn't quite decide what color they were. At times they appeared navy blue, and other times they seemed black. This was in keeping with the way Brenton's and Jordana's had appeared, but both of them now sported dark brown eyes. What was different about Nicholas was the intensity with which he seemed to observe everything around him.

"You are a wonder, my little son," Carolina told the feeding baby. "I can't help but wonder what you will do with your life. Will you follow your father's steps and grow a desire for engineering and locomotives? Maybe you'll be like your grandfather and become a planter." At this, Nicholas seemed to choke a bit, and milk oozed down his chin before he resumed his meal.

Carolina laughed. "I suppose not," she said, wiping his face as best she could.

She loved times like these best of all. Here in the nursery, she could forget about the labor unrest and cholera epidemic. Here, alone with Nicholas, she could be at complete peace.

Gently easing the baby to her shoulder, Carolina thought of the infant her sister had lost the previous year. Virginia had been terrified of having another child and swore to have no interest whatsoever in her own flesh and blood. Carolina couldn't understand her sister's feelings. But then, there was nothing new in this. She and Virginia had never seen eye to eye. Thinking of Virginia brought to mind a letter she'd received only yesterday. Her mother was very faithful to write and tell

Carolina the news of Oakbridge. It seemed Virginia had spent the last year in various stages of recuperation. At one point, Margaret had written, she had even visited her infant daughter's grave. Carolina wished there might be something she could say or do to help Virginia, but she knew that short of praying and maintaining a correspondence, there was little else to be done. Virginia would have to find her own way.

Nicholas let out a hearty burp, and as she lowered him from her shoulder, Carolina could see that he'd already fallen back to sleep. He was a good baby and she couldn't imagine how life could have ever been complete without him. Funny how these things work, she thought.

"Just a few short months ago you were only an anticipated gift. A few short years ago, you weren't even considered. And now that you're here," she whispered, "I don't know what I would do without you."

Carefully she placed him back in the cradle, and for several moments all she did was watch him sleep. "Oh, Father," she prayed aloud, "I am so blessed to have my family. Watch over us. This is a grievous time. So many others have lost their children and friends. Please see fit to put an end to this sickness, and watch over my family so that they might not suffer the disease as others have."

Leaving the sleeping baby, Carolina made her way back downstairs. Her mind was already overworked with thoughts of what she would do that day when she heard the front door open. For a moment, she paused at the bottom of the stairs listening, but when she saw the face of her husband, Carolina smiled broadly and moved to embrace him.

"James, whatever are you doing here at this hour of the day?"

He looked up at her for a moment, and Carolina could see that his eyes were glassy and his face flushed. A sickening dread settled over her in such a way that Carolina nearly felt faint.

"James!" she exclaimed and hurried toward him. "What is it?" she asked, but in her heart she knew the signs. Cholera!

"I'm sick, Carolina," he whispered. "I thought it would pass, but I just keep getting worse. The pains in my stomach—the diarrhea—"

"It will be all right," she interjected and worked her arm under his and around his back. "Just lean on me and I'll get you into bed." Her heart pounded fiercely and her breath caught in her throat as his head rolled awkwardly to one side. She felt him go limp and slip from her grasp. "James!" she screamed.

Struggling to keep him from falling to the floor, she managed to slide him down against her until he lay in complete unconsciousness upon her new Persian rug. "Miriam!"

The woman didn't answer, and it was only then that Carolina remembered she was going to the cave to carve a piece of ham for their noon meal. Kneeling beside her husband, Carolina felt a frantic urgency. She needed help to get him to bed, but she couldn't bring herself to leave his side. Just then voices could be heard, and Carolina instantly recognized that the children and Miriam were coming into the house.

The children! She couldn't let them get near James.

"Miriam! Keep the children back!" she yelled, and fighting her desperation to stay at James' side, she got to her feet and ran to the archway. Miriam's confused expression was mirrored in the faces of Victoria and Brenton. Jordana, however, was too busy being occupied by a bug she had caught outside.

"James has the fever!" she exclaimed. "Oh, Miriam, he's lying on the floor in the front room. You have to take the children upstairs and keep them away."

"Dear Lord," Miriam said in a barely audible voice, "protect us."

"Papa is sick?" Victoria questioned, her voice filled with terror. "Is he going to . . . to—"

"Victoria, stop. You'll scare your brother and sister," Carolina replied in a much harsher tone than she'd intended.

Victoria's eyes filled with tears, and without another word she turned and ran out the back door. Carolina couldn't even call after her. She was too distraught with her own fears to deal with those of her daughter. Glancing back to where her husband lay, Carolina couldn't think of anything but the dreaded realization that James could well die.

"Oh, Miriam," she whispered, leaning against the archway. "It's finally come to us."

Forty

Victoria's Heart

Mindless of her mother's warnings to remain on their own property, Victoria went to the barn and saddled the one remaining riding horse. Her thoughts raced and her heart pounded so hard that she thought it truly might jump right out of her body. Her father lay sick, maybe even dying! The desperation of her mother's voice had made clear the gravity of the situation, and Victoria could think of only one way to deal with it.

"I've got to find Kiernan," she whispered, as if the horse had questioned their destination. "Kiernan will come and help us and everything will be all right."

Hiking her skirts, Victoria mounted the horse, throwing her leg over in a most unladylike manner. Sidesaddle might have been her mother's preference for the teenager, but Victoria knew that sitting astride would allow her the speed and maneuverability she needed.

With little other thought than reaching Kiernan quickly, Victoria dug her heels into the horse's side and made a mad dash across the yard and onto the dirt thoroughfare. The shortest distance to the tunnel was through the Irish shantytown. She knew this area was thought to be notoriously dangerous and unfitting for a lady, but aware that most of the men would either be at their shift or sleeping in preparation for the next shift, Victoria decided to ignore the warnings.

The street narrowed as it left the reputable part of town and headed into the poverty-ridden Irish settlement. Weathered gray unpainted wood was the standard decor for the slapped-together houses she passed. Most were without glass for their windows. In winter the residents would board up the openings, and the rest of the year they left them open come rain or shine. Victoria knew that most of the houses didn't have even a fireplace or stove, but rather the women would cook and wash from open caldrons and outdoor fire pits. This activity was performed in all manner of weather, almost as though the women enjoyed the ritual.

Kiernan had told Victoria otherwise, and it was through his education that Victoria knew the heartache and plight of many of these women. Still, traveling past their homes, Victoria found herself pensive, unable to imagine the strength of these families to continue in the face of such adversity. It was bad enough to have left their homeland and families only to find themselves destitute in their new home—the so-called land of opportunity. And now not only poverty but illness was taking its toll on their meager existence.

Every day Kiernan reported to her mother and father and told of the vast numbers of sick. Worse still, he reported the deaths of men and women he'd once called friends. Victoria didn't like the effect that the epidemic was having on Kiernan. She saw his worried expressions and knew his heavy heart as if it were her own. And in truth, it was her own heart. She felt so completely a part of his dreams and ambitions that it seemed only natural to take on his sorrows and miseries, as well.

They had talked on many occasions of Kiernan's regrets in leaving his siblings in Ireland. They had talked, too, of the railroad and the labor problems with the Irish. The one thing Victoria found Kiernan rather silent on, however, was Red. Kiernan never wanted to speak about his older brother and the painful, exacting way Red had dismissed Kiernan from his life. Victoria tried to be patient, but it troubled her greatly that Kiernan bore this burden and would not let her share it.

Putting the shanties behind her, Victoria pressed the horse on. Her mind went back to the problem at hand. Why should her father have to be one of those to fall ill? Was it not enough that he gave so unselfishly to everyone around him? Why would God let him get sick, especially now when they all needed him so much? After all, Victoria reasoned, there was the new baby and all the problems with the epidemic. Somehow she had just assumed they would go on being untouched by the disease. How very wrong she was.

Thinking of James made her also reflect back on her real father. Blake St. John was a mystery to Victoria. A mystery that she seldom spent time trying to understand. She couldn't remember him. Not really. There were fuzzy images in her head, and from some inner reasoning she had decided that they were images of her father. But otherwise there was nothing. Not even a painting to show her his likeness. In Baltimore, back in the house where she'd grown up, Victoria had a large oil painting of her mother and brother. Carolina had given it to her as a keepsake, reminding Victoria that while she counted herself Victoria's mother in every way that mattered, this was the woman who had given her life, and this was the brother she had never known.

Victoria didn't know the full story of their deaths. At least, she didn't believe that Carolina had given her the full story. Whenever her mother had been spoken of, the conversation had always been surrounded with mystery and conspiratorial glances between Carolina and Mrs. Graves. She knew that her brother had drowned in the Baltimore harbor, and that her mother had been the one to let him get too close to the water's edge. Carolina had said her mother's heart had been completely broken by this tragedy, and the only thing that had kept her alive was the fact that she was already expecting Victoria when her young son died.

But Victoria knew that shortly after giving birth, her mother had died. Carolina had told her quite honestly that Suzanna St. John had drowned in the same harbor as her young son, and that no one knew for sure what had happened. It was implied that the grief-stricken Suzanna had slipped off the walkway and, being unable to swim, had drowned without anyone realizing that she had fallen into the water. But Victoria felt this was probably a half-truth. As she'd grown up and found it possible to reason out the probable causes of her mother's death, Victoria had concluded that her mother had purposefully fallen into the water and killed herself. She had approached Carolina on the matter and had been told quite honestly that many people suspected this very thing. But still there were the veiled looks and glances that suggested even this was not the full truth.

And because of this mystery, Victoria found an unfillable void in her soul.

Why hadn't she been reason enough for her mother to live? Or worse yet, what if she was the cause for her mother's suicide? Maybe Suzanna had wanted another son, and the birth of a daughter was too despairing to deal with.

And interwoven throughout all of these questions were thoughts of her father. Why had he not kept her mother safe? Why had he allowed her to slip from the house so soon after the birth of her child? Victoria knew from her experience with Carolina's childbearing that women simply did not get up out of their bed for days, sometimes even weeks, after the birth of their children. Why, then, was her mother allowed to disappear in such a manner?

Such thinking inevitably depressed Victoria. Her real parents had not wanted her, or so it would seem. Even if her mother's death had been an accident, her father certainly had every opportunity to be a father to her and instead had chosen to distance himself.

Victoria shook her head and wiped at the tears that came unbidden to her eyes. She might not remember her father's face, but she remembered hearing his voice on many occasions—and his words as though he'd uttered them only yesterday. He often spoke to Carolina about Victoria's care, and while everyone assumed Victoria to be securely confined to the nursery, Victoria had often taken other courses of action.

More than once she would sneak into a room and hide under a cloth-covered table in order to listen to adult conversations. Other times she would stand outside the door, with her ear pressed against it, in order to hear what was being said. Unfortunately, she always heard more than she should have, and always it left her feeling totally displaced. Her father didn't want her. He made this abundantly clear. He had no desire to be reminded of the family he'd lost, and he had no desire to spend time with Victoria.

She couldn't count the number of times she'd heard Carolina pleading with Blake on her behalf. But instead of feeling grateful for Carolina's efforts, Victoria felt violated and worthless. Blake St. John's own daughter meant nothing to him. Nothing but trouble and expense. And while Victoria knew Carolina and James loved her as dearly as they loved their other children, it forever haunted her that the one man who should have loved her—didn't.

"Why was I not enough? What sin did I commit to make him show me such a lack of concern?" Victoria murmured aloud, as she had on many reflective occasions.

Pushing these thoughts aside she reminded herself that James, the only one to ever truly father her, lay desperately ill. If he died, she would lose yet another man in her life, and that was unacceptable to the insecure child.

Nearing the tunnel site, Victoria slowed the horse and glanced up and down the line, desperately seeking Kiernan. She had forgotten about her manner of dress and riding form until one of the laborers drew attention to the fact by whistling and calling down to her.

"Come on up here, lassy, and show me them pretty legs."

Victoria felt her face go hot and knew that she must be crimson with embarrassment. She pushed her skirts down as much as riding astride would allow her to do and urged the horse forward. She had no idea of where Kiernan would be. Usually he worked with her father, but since James had returned to the house, there was no way of knowing where to begin her search.

"What's the likes of you doin' here?" one man questioned as she drew near the mouth of the east tunnel entrance.

"I'm . . . I mean to say . . ." she stammered nervously. "I'm looking for Kiernan O'Connor."

"Bah! That useless piece of—"

"Please," Victoria pleaded, "my father, James Baldwin, is ill."

"So's half the town," the man replied and spit into the dust. "I don't know where yar Mr. O'Connor is." He turned his back on her and disappeared into the tunnel.

Nearly overwhelming panic began to settle upon Victoria. "Kiernan!" she called out, realizing too late the unwanted attention it would draw to her.

"Now, there's a pretty filly," a burly man with a thick red beard called.

"Wouldn't mind me a try at that one," another said, wiping sweat from his forehead.

Victoria studied the faces around her, then seeing that Kiernan wasn't among them, she urged the horse to where the small office shack stood.

"Kiernan! Kiernan, where are you?" she called, suddenly fearing that perhaps he wasn't on this side of the tunnel at all. Perhaps he was working at the west portal.

She looked upward to where temporary tracks crossed over the tunnel. Men were working with the winches and shafts to remove additional debris from the interior. Perhaps Kiernan was up there. Just as she made the decision to head the horse up the side of the mountain, Kiernan appeared at the door of the shack.

"Victoria?"

Unable to contain her sobs, Victoria leaped from the horse, catching her skirt on the horn and tearing it from the knee to the hem. She didn't care. Running blindly from her tears, she threw herself into Kiernan's arms.

"Oh, Kiernan, Papa has cholera!"

Kiernan's arms held her close for only a moment before he set her away from him. "Are ya certain?"

She nodded emphatically. "Yes. He just came home and collapsed on the floor. Poor Mama can't take care of him alone. You have to come and help her."

Kiernan nodded. "We'll have to be takin' yar horse."

She nodded, grateful for his ability to take charge of the matter. It seemed that for all she had done to occupy her mind with other thoughts on her journey to the tunnel, just seeing Kiernan caused her emotions to vent uncontrollably.

He helped her back up on the horse, this time sidesaddle, and then he mounted behind her and pulled her back snug against him. It was like being drawn into a private, protective haven, and in spite of the catcalls and lewd innuendoes being thrown at them from the observing workers, Victoria could not keep back tears of anguish.

Oh, God, please don't take my father away from me, she prayed. *Please let him be all right. Let Kiernan know what to do.*

Secure in Kiernan's strong embrace, Victoria realized how very much she counted on him to fill the aching void in her heart. Surely if Kiernan's love remained fixed and true, it would cease to matter that her real father had never loved or wanted her. After all, Kiernan had promised her that he very much wanted her. Needed her. Loved her.

Surely that would be enough. It had to be enough.

Forty-One

The Long Wait

Carolina sat dozing in the rocking chair. James lay not a foot away in a small bed fashioned by Kiernan. It had been decided to keep James downstairs, where they had easy access to needed supplies. It also allowed Miriam to keep the children upstairs and away from their father's sickness. Truth be told, Carolina had wanted the children to go elsewhere, but there was no place else to send them. The stage and freighters wouldn't come into town due to the quarantine, and even if they had, they wouldn't have been allowed to leave again. In fact, with the epidemic raging as it was, supplies were stored some miles from town, and payment was settled in like fashion.

Carolina found the entire ordeal so disheartening she could scarcely function under the weight of it. She longed to see James open his eyes and give her a reassuring smile, but after three days of constant diarrhea and vomiting, James was not likely to do either one.

Carolina could only watch and wait—doing what little she knew to do. The doctor had come and offered his remedies, but nothing helped. Miriam had insisted on brewing a concoction of turnip water and red pepper, and this they spooned into James every few minutes, but whether it helped or hurt, Carolina couldn't be sure.

The lamp had been turned down to a muted yellow glow, but even by this meager light, Carolina could see that James was slipping away from her. She lifted his hand and held it to her cheek.

"You must get well," she said softly. "I need you."

She kissed his hand, then looked at it as though seeing it for the first time. The skin seemed shrunken and wrinkled, giving his hand a bony appearance. The doctor had told her this was due to the drastic loss of fluids, which was the logical reasoning for adhering to Miriam's idea of turnip water. Miriam swore that Carolina's old mammy had used the very same thing whenever folks had been suffering from such violent purging.

"Am I interruptin'?" Kiernan asked from the kitchen archway.

Carolina shook her head. She'd given Kiernan free run of the house and had come to depend upon him heavily. "I'm afraid there's no news."

"I suppose 'tis the way of this thing," he told her and stepped toward the makeshift bed. "Two more little ones died earlier this evenin'. One of 'em belonged to the Kaberlines."

"Oh no," Carolina said, shaking her head. As much as she fretted over James' condition, she still felt an undeniable fear for her own children. So far they had managed to avoid the disease. But for how long?

Kiernan took up a stool and sat down. "I can sit with him while ya get some rest. It's nearly midnight. That fine boy of yars will be needin' to have a meal soon."

Carolina looked at him in surprise. "You are very observant of my family if you know things such as that."

Kiernan chuckled. "I have brothers and sisters of me own. Enough to know they plum wore me mum to a shred. Victoria says that Nicky eats like there's no tomorrow."

"Or if there is a tomorrow, he's convinced food will not be offered," Carolina agreed and stretched wearily. "I suppose some rest would be nice, but I hate to leave James."

"Aye. I know."

She looked at Kiernan and saw the understanding and compassion in his eyes. He had truly been a godsend during their ordeal. At a time when they needed to focus on the upcoming winter, Carolina found herself without their most beneficial source of help—James. But Kiernan had worked hard to fill the void, and when contractors temporarily shut down work at the tunnel due to too much sickness and death, he had devoted himself entirely to the Baldwin family.

"I can't thank you enough for all you've already done," Carolina said softly.

Kiernan ran a hand through his auburn hair and appeared uncomfortable with her praise. "Ya'd do the same for me."

Carolina nodded. "Yes, but you've given above and beyond what anyone could expect. Chopping all that wood. Keeping the livestock. Helping Miriam harvest the garden. We'd be in a sorry state if you'd not come along."

"Likewise for me."

Carolina knew of his troubles with Red. The man refused to even speak with Kiernan, and not only that, he had apparently forbidden any other Connaughtman to speak to him, either. Victoria had confided that it grieved Kiernan more than he could say, and for the most part he was silent on the matter.

"I'm sorry your brother has treated you so harshly."

Kiernan shrugged. "'Tis his way."

"But that doesn't make it right," Carolina said. She eased James' hand back under the cover and reached for the turnip water. Kiernan saw her action and immediately leaned forward to lift James' head. James didn't even moan as she spooned in the liquid. Much of it dribbled back out of his mouth, but Carolina worked patiently until she'd managed to get the better part of five spoonfuls into her husband's weakened body.

"People often do things without thinking," Carolina said as Kiernan lowered James back to the pillow. "Your brother is hardheaded, but I'm sure his heart is not as hard. He may feel that you chose against him, but James told me he'd also heard it said Red issued an order that no one was to touch you."

Kiernan smiled. "It'd be like him to do that."

"I doubt he would have if he didn't have some kind of love for you. Perhaps in time—"

Kiernan shook his head. "Ya don't know me brother. When he sets his mind to somethin', he stays with it."

"But God could change all of that," Carolina replied.

"Oh, He could, now, that's for certain," Kiernan agreed. "Me mum always said there weren't a problem too big for the good Lord. But Red thinks he's right, and he won't be likely to change his mind anytime soon."

"Then I feel sorry for him," Carolina said, contemplating the sorrow in Kiernan's voice. "I hope you know that you will always be welcome here."

"Thank ya," Kiernan answered, and again he looked away as if embarrassed by the intimacy of the moment.

Carolina had little desire to leave James' side, but she knew she also had an obligation to her children. Especially Nicholas, who would demand her attention for his insatiable appetite. Slowly she got to her feet and reluctantly put James' care into Kiernan's hands. "He needs the broth every few minutes."

"Aye. I'll see to it. Ya can count on it," Kiernan promised.

"I know I can or I'd not even think of leaving him." With one backward glance, Carolina left the room.

Wearily she took up a candle, lit it, and climbed the stairs to her bedroom. Stripping off her dress, Carolina found Miriam had left a pitcher of water and a soft washcloth. She relished the feeling of the cold water against her skin. It momentarily revived her, but even this brief respite couldn't give her ease from the heaviness in her soul.

Pulling on a nightgown, Carolina took up the task of unpinning her hair. She stared at her reflection in the mirror and found a stranger staring back. Who was this haggard-looking woman with sunken eyes and washed-out cheeks? She felt old and knew that her reflection confirmed the worst of it. James' illness had taken its toll on her. A vise of fear gripped her. What if this is just the beginning? she wondered. What if the children fall ill next, and then Miriam or Kiernan?

She heaved a sigh and took up the brush. With long, defined strokes, Carolina prayed for peace and strength to endure. She prayed for James' recovery and for the protection of her children.

"Oh, Father," she murmured, "please help us. Please."

Setting aside the brush, she slipped into bed and decided to rest until Nicholas sent up his cries of hunger. Surely after a little rest, things would seem better.

When morning came, Carolina stretched and yawned and for a moment felt very happy and very rested. She rolled over and found the empty space where James would normally have been, then startled to remember the circumstance that had taken him from her side. Worse still, she remembered that Nicholas had not awakened her in the night for his usual feeding.

Trepidation consumed her as she hurried into her robe. If anything had happened to Nicholas . . . oh, but she couldn't even finish the thought. She hurried from her room and burst into the nursery.

Glancing around the room, Carolina could see nothing amiss, and coming to her baby's cradle, she felt her heart skip a beat. Nicholas smiled up at her, cooing and gurgling as if quite pleased with himself.

"Oh, you darling boy," Carolina said, barely daring to breathe. She lifted the plump baby into her arms and felt tears form in her eyes. "Thank you, God. Thank you."

As if remembering his need for Carolina, Nicholas began to fuss. "Oh, you are soaked through!" Carolina exclaimed, realizing that the front of her robe was now wet, as well. She hurried to diaper him and put him to her breast, all the while anxious to see to her husband. How could she have slept the entire night away while James lay desperately ill downstairs? But even as she wondered, Carolina knew the truth. She had spent days and nights at his side, and last night had been the first night she'd slept in a bed for more than a few hours since James had fallen ill.

Nicholas fed, making slurping and smacking noises. His obvious pleasure with her attention gave Carolina yet another form of renewal. She'd not remembered much through these past days except James' condition, and now that she had a moment to reflect, Carolina knew she'd not done justice to her children. They were no doubt frantic with worry of their own, and she could not give them answers even if they voiced their questions.

Finishing with Nicholas, Carolina put him back in the cradle and went in search of Victoria. With the baby spending more and more time awake, she hated to leave him alone. Soon he would be crawling and sitting up and, before she knew it, walking and talking. It was the way these things went, and just as she felt Victoria's youth slipping by too quickly, Carolina knew she would find the same thing true of her infant son.

Peering in on Jordana and Brenton, Carolina found them still sound asleep. She was blessed by this. They were safe and well, and with God's help they would stay that way, and James would recover and they would all know a better day.

And it was with this thought that she descended the stairs. The house seemed deathly still, but around the corner came the voice of Victoria. She thought to reprimand the child for disobeying orders, but when her words registered in Carolina's ears, she could not be harsh with the girl.

"Papa, I love you so much," Victoria was saying.

Carolina peered around the corner and found her daughter on her knees beside James' bed. She held his hand against her cheek and stroked his arm lovingly.

"There are so many people who are sick, Papa. So many people who have died. But you can't be one of them. I lost my other father and I mustn't lose you. Don't you see? I can't lose another father." She kissed his hand, and Carolina could see that there were tears in her daughter's eyes.

"Mama is trying to be so strong," Victoria continued, her words deeply touching the aching in Carolina's heart. Sometimes she wondered if Victoria even recognized her struggles and griefs. Too often it seemed that Victoria considered Carolina the barrier to her own happiness in life. Now hearing these words of affirmation, Carolina felt a wonderful assurance that her daughter understood.

"Mama has always been strong. She takes it on herself, and even when things appear that they cannot work out, Mama makes them work. That's why I always want her on my side. She cannot help but see a thing accomplished. It's her gift. And so if for no other reason than Mama's will, you shall get better."

Carolina's tears fell in a steady stream down her cheeks. Victoria's faith in her was overwhelming. Just then James moaned and Carolina started toward him. Victoria glanced up and frowned. "Please don't be mad at me," she said defensively. "I came to pray with him when Kiernan left to bring in more wood."

"I'm not mad," Carolina assured her daughter. She watched her husband for any sign that he might open his eyes, but much to her disappointment they remained closed. "I'm afraid . . . but I'm not mad."

"Don't be afraid, Mama," Victoria said, getting to her feet. "Papa is strong."

"Yes, he is," Carolina agreed. "He's also headstrong, which is probably why he's sick right now. I love the railroad as much as he does. In fact, as much as it shames me to admit it, I've coveted his position. He can go and come at leisure and mingle among the men and the work, and no one finds it odd that he should do so. With me, on the other hand, I raise a fuss among the men just showing up at the work site. Women are bad luck, or so they say, and the miners are such a superstitious lot that they shut down work if I dare to appear."

She smiled sadly at her sleeping husband and took a seat beside him. "But James . . . well . . . James can do it all."

"But you can, too, Mama." Victoria knelt at her mother's side. "You've shown them all. You've studied and learned, and you came here with us just to be with Papa."

"But at what risk?" Carolina said sadly. "I've endangered all of your lives. The town is under quarantine and hundreds are dying. My envy and bitterness may well cost me my family."

"No," Victoria said firmly. "I won't believe that. Papa needed you. You may not believe that, but he told me it was so."

Carolina's curiosity was stirred. "He said that?"

"That and much more. He told me how lucky I was to have you for my mother. I told him I knew that, and while I might not always act like it, I thank God for giving me a mother like you."

Carolina's tears started anew, and Victoria smiled. "Don't do that or I'll cry again, too."

Carolina laughed. "It's just that you're such a blessing to me. I suppose I needed to hear something good. I feel like everything is so upside down, and my place is uncertain." She reached out and smoothed back a lock of hair from James' pale forehead. "I want to be faithful and trust

God for the outcome, but my heart is breaking. I'm so afraid, and that makes me feel guilty because surely if I trusted God, I would not be afraid."

"God understands, Mama," Victoria said, patting her mother's arm. "You've told me that over and over. He understands everything about us, even our fears."

"Especially those, I suppose. But, oh, Victoria, it is so risky to give your heart," Carolina whispered. She hoped Victoria didn't take her words in a wrong manner. She wasn't speaking of Victoria and Kiernan at all, but rather of herself.

"Remember when I was little and my cat got killed by the neighbor's dog?"

Carolina thought back to that tragic moment and nodded. "You were heartbroken."

"Yes, and I told you I was never going to love anything or anyone ever again," Victoria responded. "You told me that loving was a risk, but that the alternative was to never know the pleasure in giving love or in receiving love. You told me I would be cheating myself if I hardened my heart and hid myself away."

Carolina nodded and smiled. How blessed she was by her daughter's memories. "I suppose I should heed my own advice."

"I suppose we both should. I've been afraid, too."

"Maybe we can help each other," Carolina suggested, reaching out to stroke her daughter's hair. "Maybe we can help each other to remember that God is watching over us, and He has a very real plan for our lives. It may not always be the thing we think we need, but if we are obedient, He is sure to show us what He has in mind."

Victoria leaned forward and embraced Carolina tightly. "I love you so much, Mama. I will help you any way I can."

"And I love you, and you can count on me to be there for you," Carolina assured her daughter.

Forty-Two

Intentions

Carolina waited in the early morning silence for some sound that would betray the stirring of her family. As she sat by her husband's side, she prayed fervently for his recovery. Already James had survived the worst of the illness, and now it was just a matter of time. Time that Carolina prayed would pass swiftly. She agonized long hours over her circumstance, wondering exactly what she would do if James died. There was always the thought of returning to Oakbridge with her children, but that seemed hardly wise given the unrest of that place. Returning to Baltimore no longer held much appeal. The city could be delightful, but she'd actually come to love the stillness of this little mountain town. But could she remain here without a husband? Money, of course, would be no problem, but the idea of living in such an obscure little town without the protection of a man gave Carolina much to think about.

Now that there was definite hope of James' recovery, she shelved such thoughts, unwilling to further consider them. I mustn't borrow trouble, she thought and rubbed her eyes.

"Good morning," James whispered weakly.

Carolina smiled and opened her eyes. "Good morning, yourself. How do you feel?"

James attempted to chuckle, but the sound came out more like a cough. "I'm not sure. Not exactly. I know it's not really a good feeling, but then again, it isn't all that bad, either."

"Could you eat something?"

"Possibly. I would certainly try for you."

Carolina smiled. "You can't know how happy I am to hear you say that. I've been so worried about you. So many have died from cholera, and even the doctor didn't hold out much hope for you. But I told him you were a stubborn man and that if anyone could beat this disease, it would be you."

"I'm no more stubborn than you, dear wife. You bid me live, and I live."

"My pleadings to God have done the trick. Not my bidding, but His mercy."

James nodded and closed his eyes. "So what's for breakfast?"

"I think oatmeal might give you a bit of substance without being too heavy. I'll go put some on while you rest."

James nodded again but said nothing more. Carolina took this silence as her cue to get to work. She turned up the lamp to brighten the front room, then lit an additional lamp and took it with her to the kitchen. Bustling around the room she heard Miriam stir in the back bedroom and knew that before long the entire household would be up and running.

Several minutes later, Miriam appeared and headed to the barn to milk the cow and retrieve the eggs. This had been their routine for so long that neither woman felt the need to converse past their initial greeting of good morning. Carolina found comfort in routine. It was only when things broke from this organized pattern that she felt despair. Things like James falling ill to cholera and half the town dying.

Humming to herself, Carolina began stoking up the stove only to find the woodbox low. It didn't matter. Kiernan had chopped enough wood in his free time to see them through the winter. Grabbing up her woolen cloak, Carolina stepped into the brisk chill of the morning. The stars were still visible in the smudgy blue-black sky overhead. Carolina thought of how different they seemed here in Greigsville, compared to Baltimore or even Oakbridge. Everything was different here. There was none of the constant noise associated with city life, nor was the bustle of plantation life evident. Greigsville was a sleepy hollow, and even when it was active it came at a slower pace.

Leaning over the woodbox, Carolina started when she heard movement behind her. Fearful that some wild animal had come to make a meal of her, Carolina turned abruptly. Holding a log defensively, she squinted against the minimal light and breathed a sigh of relief when she found it was Kiernan.

"Mornin' to ya, Mrs. Baldwin," Kiernan said, with a tip of his cap. "I'll be getting the wood for ya, if ya'll allow me to."

"Why, thank you, Kiernan. That would be wonderful. I wanted to get the stove stoked up and start breakfast."

"Ah, well, now, we can't be delayin' that." He reached into the box and pulled out an armload of wood. "If ya'll just open the door for me,

I'll have ya taken care of in a minute's time."

Carolina nodded and complied with his instruction. She found herself watching him with unveiled interest. For some time now she'd longed to talk to him about his intentions toward Victoria, but she had remained silent. She didn't want to appear nosy or interfering, but Victoria was still so very young.

"This ought to do ya for a time," Kiernan said, breaking her thoughts. He stood before her with one final load of wood.

"Thank you," Carolina murmured. She remained fixed at the back door, drinking in the crisp morning air. Drawing a deep breath, Carolina waited for Kiernan to reappear.

"Was there somethin' more ya'd be needin' out here?" Kiernan asked as he peered round the door.

"As a matter of fact," Carolina began, "there is. I wondered if I might have a word with you for a moment."

"For certain," Kiernan said, stepping back outside. "I threw in a couple of logs so the stove should be a-warmin' up nicely by the time we're done here."

Carolina nodded acknowledgment, then looked back to the skies as though seeking strength from the One who made it all. "Kiernan, I have a very serious question to ask you, and because it is so serious, I pray you will give it the attention it deserves."

"All right."

She glanced back down. By now the beginning glow of dawn was lighting the skies enough that she could actually see his expression. He appeared very serious and reserved, and he looked at her with such intensity that Carolina nearly forgot what she wanted to ask.

"I . . . ah . . . well, you see," she stammered for a moment, then drew another deep breath and composed herself. "I would like to know your intentions toward Victoria."

Kiernan didn't laugh or act in the leastwise embarrassed. He merely looked thoughtful, then replied, "I have strong feelings for your daughter."

"Feelings? Exactly what do you mean by feelings?" Carolina pursued.

Kiernan looked down at his feet, and Carolina wondered if he was trying to decide how much to tell her. At eighteen, he struck Carolina as a full-grown man with the interests and ambitions of an adult. But when he looked back up to meet her gaze, Carolina also saw the youthful innocence of a boy.

"I'd be lying if I said I didn't love her," he answered. "I'd like to be plannin' a future with her as me wife."

Carolina nodded. "I have heard as much said by Victoria. James and I have strong feelings about such things."

"What things?" Victoria questioned, coming through the back door.

Victoria had probably come out on some errand for Miriam, but finding her mother and beau having a conversation, she lost all interest in any other purpose.

"Yar ma asked about me feelings for ya," Kiernan responded before Carolina could open her mouth to speak.

"Mother!" Victoria declared, obviously mortified with her mother's lack of decorum.

"Nay," Kiernan said. "She has a right to be askin' questions."

Victoria looked at him and instantly silenced her protests. Carolina could see things for herself now. Victoria might not have quieted for Carolina, but because the words came from Kiernan, she took it as absolute truth.

"I simply see things moving much too fast," Carolina resumed. "Victoria isn't even yet fifteen. She has very little interest in schooling, and she hasn't experienced very much in her young life."

"I've experienced plenty," Victoria countered. "And I told you I don't like books."

"Yes, you've made that very clear. You've also made clear the intention for you two to marry and move to California. How do you propose to earn enough money for such a trip? How will you tend to yourselves once you're there? Searching for gold with the man you love sounds very romantic, but it won't put food on the table when you're hungry." Carolina decided then and there that she would refrain from telling Victoria anything about her trust fund. It would be better for them to believe themselves destitute than have them make plans with money Victoria had not yet come to possess.

"Oh, Mama," Victoria said with a hint of amusement in her voice, "you worry about the strangest things."

"Do I?" Carolina's gaze fixed on Kiernan.

"Nay, yar mother's got a good head on her shoulders," Kiernan told Victoria. "And she's absolutely right. We'll have to be considerin' all these things."

"I only bring this up," Carolina continued, seeing Victoria's obvious distress, "because I want you to be realistic about marriage. In the first place, Kiernan has not spoken to your father on the matter, and there hasn't even been a courtship yet."

"But you won't allow—"

Carolina held up her hand. "Please let me speak my piece." Victoria nodded and stepped closer to Kiernan. "The order of things should first include James. He is the head of this household and you are his daughter. Kiernan, you are a fine young man, but there is a great deal that concerns me, given your state of affairs."

"Because I'm Irish?" he questioned.

"I suppose it plays a part, but not for the reasons you might imagine." Carolina refused to break her gaze, even though Kiernan's intense green eyes were boring holes through her heart. "I would never refuse you as a possible mate for my daughter simply because of your blood. I have made mention to James that I see the cultural differences as something to be dealt with, but otherwise, I don't care one whit that you are Irish."

"Then yar in the minority," Kiernan said with a grin.

"I suppose I might well be," Carolina admitted. "But it wouldn't be the first time. No, actually my problem with the aspect of your lineage comes in another form. Victoria tells me that you desire to see your brothers and sisters brought from Ireland to America. I commend you for that, especially given the fact that horrible struggles are still going on in your country. However, I must say that you will find it a great deal more difficult to save for their passage while experiencing the costs and duties of matrimony."

"Aye, I've thought of this. I wouldn't be forgettin' them, if that's what worries ya."

"It isn't necessarily a worry to me," Carolina admitted. "But I do wonder what bitter things might grow between the two of you if you find that a constant need to feed and clothe Victoria takes precedence over saving to bring your family to America." She caught sight of a change in his expression and drove the point home. "I can't help but believe it would be better for both of you to see to this family matter first, and then concern yourselves with marriage."

"You just don't want to let go of me," Victoria protested. "You want me to go to the university or some fancy women's finishing school, and I don't want to go. I want to spend my life with Kiernan. If we marry, then both of us can work to bring the family to America."

"And what will you work at?" Carolina questioned. "You have not had any training for a job, and you've not taken your studies seriously enough to consider teaching or bookkeeping. There may not even be such opportunities for a woman out west, even if you began in earnest to improve your writing and math skills. Your only options might be to take in extra sewing or laundry, and I doubt that you have any idea just what hard work that would entail."

"We're going to mine for gold," Victoria declared. "There's no reason I can't work with Kiernan. We heard tell that the stuff just lies about on the ground. You just pick it up, and when you have enough, you go to town and sell it."

"I hardly think that's very realistic," Carolina replied. "Consider the coal mines in this area. They hardly just pick up the coal off the ground. They have to dig and blast and haul, and it's all very difficult work that takes its toll on body and mind. Have either one of you bothered to look into the actual workings of a gold mine?"

"I've talked to a few blokes who've tried their hand at panning," Kiernan admitted. "Ya take a pan and stand in a stream and dig down in the muck. This gets swirled around, and as the water rinses the dirt away, the gold is left behind. The fellows told me that a man can get mighty rich this way."

"Then why aren't they still at it?" Carolina questioned. "It seems that if it is such a good way of life, they'd still be in California."

"I cannot say why they came back. Mebbe they aren't the greedy type," Kiernan offered.

"I suppose anything is possible," Carolina replied. "My point, however, is that neither one of you knows much about this endeavor. I'm only asking that you give yourselves time to grow up. I'm not even asking you to forget your interest in each other. Perhaps if Kiernan is really concerned about taking proper care of you, Victoria, he could go first and prepare a home for you."

"But I don't want him to go without me," Victoria protested rather loudly.

By this time, dawn was full upon them, and Carolina could see the fire in her daughter's eyes. She had dared to suggest something that would fail to coincide with Victoria's plans. Plans that Carolina knew would fall apart at worst, and be extremely difficult at best.

"I need to get your father some breakfast. I didn't want to start an argument," Carolina said quite seriously. "I merely want you both to think of the complications to this plan of yours. I want you to think of the cost."

Kiernan remained fixed in place for several moments after Carolina's departure. He knew the sense of her words, and she had awakened his mind to several issues he'd not allowed himself to consider before this time.

"I'm sorry Mother was so difficult," Victoria said, throwing her arms around Kiernan's neck. "She's too old to understand how we feel."

Kiernan looked down into the dark warm eyes and wrapped his arms around her. Her beauty astounded him. Her youth and vitality gave her added merit in his eyes. Youth generally meant strength, and strength was what would be needed if they were to forge a place in a new land. But her mother bore him sound counsel. Perhaps he should reconsider the situation. It would be unfair to ask Victoria to leave the conveniences and wealth she had grown up with. Maybe it would be best to establish a home for them in California and then come back for Victoria.

Seeming to sense his discomfort, Victoria pulled back and asked, "You aren't going to let her spoil our plans, are you?"

Kiernan set her away from him. "I think we need to heed all the advice we can get. A wise man considers his path before movin' ahead."

"I don't believe it. You *are* upset by this. Kiernan, we've been planning for this for a long, long time. I can't believe you've changed your mind."

Her distress was evident and Kiernan felt instantly sorry for the grief he'd caused her.

"Now, I'd not be sayin' that I've changed me mind. I still love ya very much, and I want to be yar husband. But I'd not be at ease if I left things to chance. Me brother might believe in the luck of the Irish, but I'm not so easily sold. Seems to me the family suffered much at the hands of that same luck."

"Papa says there is no such thing as luck. He believes in Divine Providence. He says that God has everything figured out and that luck has nothing to do with it."

"He does, now, does he?" Kiernan half questioned, half replied. "Well, then, I'd suppose a good, long talk with yar da would do us both some good."

When Victoria made no further comment, Kiernan tipped his cap and headed back in the direction of his small cabin. He had a great deal to contemplate, not the least of which was Carolina's sound advice. He loved Victoria. There could be no doubting that. He found her a lively companion and an amiable friend. He also admired her loyalty. She might not agree with her mother and father, but she was fiercely loyal to them both. She had a strong sense of family and of what that family meant. And why not? Kiernan reasoned. She'd lost both her mother and father when she was a young child. To accept Carolina and James Baldwin as her parents, Kiernan sensed that she had looked her grief in the eye and dealt with the fact that bitterness and anger wouldn't change a thing. But love could. Love could bring her peace and contentment. Kiernan knew it certainly had brought him something to hold on to.

In Ireland, he had known the love of a close-knit family. A family so loyal and true to one another that no outsider could ever come in and spoil it. Even now Kiernan felt the ties of those bonds tugging at him, urging him to hurry, to bring his family to America. An ocean might separate them, but nothing else stood between them. Nothing of consequence.

He wanted to share that kind of life with Victoria. But he knew, without anyone showing him the future, that to take her in a manner that would alienate her from James and Carolina would be to forever curse their union. It might not happen at first, but in the years to come, Kiernan had little doubt that it would be a constant wall to climb. Carolina had given him much to consider, and he would not take it lightly.

Forty-Three

Kingwood Tunnel

As Christmas neared, James regained his strength and made his way back to work on the Kingwood Tunnel. Bitter cold had set in, and where the previous winter had been mild—allowing for high performance from the workers—the winter of 1851–52 would be remembered for its record cold.

Tunneling was never easy, even under the best of circumstances. The simplest tasks became lessons in objectivity. Just when the crew had one plan figured out and in motion, some problem would arise to set the entire thing back and cause everyone to revert to drawing out new plans.

At four thousand one hundred feet, the tunnel was to be the longest in the nation. It would arch at a height of twenty-two feet and be twenty-four feet in width to accommodate a double-track line. In order to organize the beastly project into a workable feat, engineers had taken up the routine process of aligning the tunnel. This required that a survey be made over the top of the hill to be tunneled through. A surveying team, of which James had been a part, laid out a line for the tunnel and then plotted the positions of three shafts. The shaft sites were agreed upon by taking the lowest point on the ridge, equidistant from the ends of the tunnel and the other shafts. The shafts would be excavated by tunnelers to provide a number of things. First, they helped to keep the alignment of the tunnel. The shafts themselves were kept from deviating vertically by use of a plumb line and rule. In other places, nails were set in the roof of the tunnel, and string was stretched between them. These nails were kept centered with the transit, a surveying instrument used for measuring angles, and all of this worked together to keep the tunnel perfectly aligned.

The shafts also kept fresh air circulating, and tunneling at the three separate positions allowed the men to secure the tunnel against cave-ins. It was the preferred method of tunneling, and these men were well versed in their trade.

And so from the first ring of the hammer in the fall of '49, to the sound of blasting and the smell of black powder that currently filled the air, James had watched this tunnel take shape before his very eyes. He was proud of the work. As proud as if he'd accomplished it single-handedly, and yet he knew that without the hardworking Irish laborers, the tunnel wouldn't exist.

"Mr. Baldwin." Red O'Connor lumbered toward James as though he had all the time in the world. His unruly red hair was further accented by an equally unruly red beard, and his green eyes blazed as they ever did, in a mix of hatred and hostility. "If I didn't know better, I'd be sayin' that I was seein' a ghost."

"Well, I suppose I've been called worse," James countered.

"I suppose we both have," Red replied, coming to stand directly in front of James. They stood in silence for several moments, white puffs of steam billowing out around them with each breath they took.

"It's definitely cold enough," James replied.

"Aye. Makes tunneling hard."

"What is our status?"

Red shifted from one foot to the other as though trying to keep warm. James noted that he was dressed in a threadbare coat and that his boots had holes in them. He might have offered to help the man, but James knew better. Red was too proud to accept his help. He was the type of man who would rather die of exposure than accept the charity of another.

"There's ice in the shafts and on the cables. Makes workin' the winches impossible, and without them we can't take out the rock or have proper air down below."

James nodded. Not long ago, Ben Latrobe had replaced the slower horse-operated winches with steam-powered machines. This allowed for rapid excavation of the sandstone, shale, and limestone, and also doubled as a power source for ventilation fans in the tunnels.

"And there's precious little water," Red continued. "Ya got to have water to have steam, and without it ya cannot run a steam-powered winch."

"No, I suppose you can't," James answered. "Why don't we go inside and discuss what needs to be done."

Red followed him into the shack, where two of the supervisors were hugging a wood stove. James nodded to the men and greeted them.

"Glad to have you back, Baldwin," the older of the two men said.

"We've got a world of trouble with this cold."

"So I was just discussing with Mr. O'Connor," James admitted. "I suggest we sit down and combine our knowledge and see what is to be done."

"Water is a problem. There's very little of it, and what little there is happens to be frozen," the supervisor told James.

"Can we haul some in?" James questioned. "I know several families, my own included, whose wells are still holding at a good level."

"I hardly think it would do us much good," the younger supervisor replied. "After all, it's gonna freeze before you could get it from town to the tunnel."

"Yes, but we could set up caldrons and keep good fires going. It might take laborers off the tunnel, but it would be worth it if you could keep at least a portion of the work continuing."

"It might be worth a try, lads," Red said, surprising James with his congeniality.

"The birds can't take the cold," the older man announced. Birds were used with the mining efforts to alert the tunnelers to poison gases. Because the birds were smaller and much more sensitive to the gas, they would die from the slightest exposure. This in turn gave the tunnelers advanced warning of the gas leaks and saved many lives on more than one occasion.

"We can't tunnel without being sure that we aren't exposing the workers to certain death," James said.

Red laughed at this. "Mining has always carried a brand of certain death. Ya'd not understand the deathtraps of such a job, havin' never found yarself in such a position."

James eyed him sternly. "Neither have I ever performed as a surgeon, Mr. O'Connor, but I can appreciate the complications of such duties, just as I can appreciate the dangers associated with mining." He turned to the other two men. "Is there nothing else that would work instead of the birds?"

"Might be we could just work the men in two-hour shifts," the older man replied. "It's cold enough, so I doubt any of 'em could stand up to much more anyway."

"I'd hate to risk their lives," James said, thoughtfully considering the problem. "Perhaps we could have an early holiday and delay work on the tunnel for a few days and see if the weather improves. After all, given that Christmas is next week, it might do a great deal for the morale and health of these men."

"Morale and health is all well and fine," Red countered, "but a man can enjoy neither one without the funds to do so. If ya lay off work on this tunnel, the men won't have two pennies to rub together."

"Then we'll have to continue paying them," James answered evenly. "I don't propose to starve people at Christmastime; neither do I propose to see men die from exposure to cold or gas. The way I see it, we have no choice. The weather is against us, leastwise the temperature is, and we can't very well work the tunnel if we don't have the proper machinery to work it with. Let's give it a day or two and meet here again to see what our choices are."

"If this is on your authority," the older man replied, "then I'll adhere to it. I just want assurance that I'll not be made to suffer the consequences for the tunnel progress slowing."

"It's under my authority," James replied. "Now, I suggest we all head for home. Red, you tell your men to close up shop for a spell. If they need anything, they can come see me."

Red nodded. "And if the cold stays with us?"

"We'll cross that bridge when we get to it," James answered honestly.

But the cold held on, and days passed on top of each other, as record temperatures were recorded. Greigsville reported ten below zero, while to the north, Morgantown noted a temperature of eight degrees lower still. It wasn't a contest anyone wanted to win.

James felt a growing despair at seeing the tunnel stand idle. They were too close to completion to fall back now. Daily he faced the cold and rode the distance to the tunnel in order to contemplate what might next be accomplished. Kiernan generally accompanied him, as he had on this day, but usually very little was said between the two men. The cold made it impossible to converse for long. The icy air had a way of penetrating their bodies and stinging their throats and lungs. It was easily concluded that conversation could wait until they were in a warmer, more sheltered place.

Soon Christmas passed and James wanted only to see the weather warm up and the tunnel progress. He had spoken to several of the supervisors, and all agreed that they needed to resume the work. Whether they shared James' anxiety to see the project completed or worried about retaining control over the men, James couldn't say. And at this point he wasn't sure it mattered to him.

He couldn't explain it, not even to Carolina, but there was a driving force within him that made it necessary to see the Kingwood Tunnel completed. It was almost too personal to put into words, but somehow James saw it as his own private hurdle. For reasons that were beyond him, James felt desperately in need of completing the work.

"We can't put it off any longer," he told Kiernan, his eyes never leaving the eastern portal.

"Nay, I suppose not."

"It has to be completed. Ben is counting on me. The B&O is counting on me."

Kiernan nodded. "We could set up fires at either end and haul water like ya suggested."

James had shared many thoughts with Kiernan, including those ideas conveyed at his meeting with Red and the supervisors. Since that meeting, Red had stirred up a great deal of strife among the Connaughtmen. He was restless, as were they, to get back to the work at hand, and idleness only lent itself to arguments and fights. James also blamed Red's irritation on a desperately low supply of whiskey, but said nothing on this matter to Kiernan. The boy was troubled enough about his brother. There was no sense in adding fuel to that fire. Kiernan held a desperate fear that Red would get himself dismissed from the job, but James assured the boy that he'd rather not see that happen. Of course, James' reasons were entirely removed from Kiernan's. James desired to keep Red where he could maintain an account of his actions. Then, too, he knew that if Red were fired, he'd most likely convince the other Connaughtmen to walk off the job with him. That would set the tunnel construction back, and time was critical. Red knew it, as did his men, and this left James in a very precarious position.

Riding slowly back to town, James had more on his mind than he wanted to consider. He'd not been much good to Carolina, nor had he been a very good father to his children. First it was his bout with cholera, but now his mind was consumed with the tunnel and the urgency to see it completed. There wasn't that much left to do. The biggest task was to actually blast through to the other side. Workers had come from the western and eastern portals, and now there was estimated to be less than six feet of rock between them. One or two well-orchestrated blasts and they would be through. It was stimulating to imagine this happening. To complete the tunnel was everything!

As if reading his mind, Kiernan commented, "I'm supposin' there'll still be a great deal to do once we've blasted through."

"Yes," James said, nodding his head. His feet ached and his toes felt numb, but still he insisted on these daily rides. "We have to clear the tunnel out, support it with timbers, and eventually arch the weaker sections in brick. We can't very well have rocks flying down on passing trains."

Kiernan nodded. He appeared greatly consumed with his thoughts, and James wondered if something about the tunnel gave the younger man concern. When they were finally back in James' barn, he decided to press the issue.

"You've seemed mighty quiet," James began. "Not only on our rides, which we both know negates much in the way of conversation, but also here. You scarcely said two words at breakfast."

Kiernan busied himself by taking the saddle from the back of his horse. "It's nothin' to worry over."

James eyed him over the back of his own mount. "You're a poor liar, Kiernan O'Connor. What is it that has you so concerned? Is it something about the tunnel? Something with your brother? If there's something I should know, man, speak up."

Kiernan shook his head. "No, there's nothing. I mean, not in the sense that ya might suppose." He pulled the bridle off and hung it on a nearby peg. Turning, he shrugged. "I've just been thinkin' about what I'll do once the tunnel is finished."

Suddenly James realized the implication of such a matter. Once the Kingwood Tunnel was completed, the bulk of the men would either be let go or reassigned to other places on the line. Kiernan knew this would mean his own job, and the life he'd known in Greigsville would also come to an end.

"I can always use a good assistant," James told him, hoping the words would somehow comfort the young man. "I don't know what my own responsibilities will be after the tunnel is finished, but there is plenty left to be done. Why, they are still struggling to complete Section 77 just five miles to the east of us. That's some of the most glorious country you would ever want to see, but it has proven an infuriating nightmare to complete. Before the cholera put me down, Latrobe had me ride over to the site and give him a firsthand account of what seemed to be the problem."

"And what did ya find?"

"Steep ravines, razor-sharp cliffs, and, of course, the Cheat River," James answered. "Add to this that the five-mile stretch between there and this place climbs some four hundred and fifty feet with numerous ravines to be crossed, which, of course, will require bridges. The work is coming right along, but there will be work on this section for years to come. Even after the line is in place, I know Latrobe plans to change out any masonry and timber bridges for iron. I may well stay on to do whatever I can. I suppose it will depend on where they can best use me."

"Aye."

"Latrobe has talked of having me go west to Fairmont. They are working hard to negotiate the Monongahela River, and the bridge Latrobe proposes there will be the largest iron bridge in America. It might be interesting to find myself involved," James said absentmindedly. He knew that such an endeavor would send him away from his family. It would be unlikely that he would move them the forty miles just to be with them every night. Such a move would slow things down, and the Baltimore and Ohio was only now starting to speed up its production. Once the weather warmed, and the rains replenished the water levels, James knew it would be just a year or so before the line was completed.

No, Carolina might not like him taking on a project that sent him away from her, but once he pointed out that it was only for a short time, surely she'd share his enthusiasm. Surely she'd sense the importance and stand beside him in his decision.

Forty-Four

A Clannish Breed

January 16, 1852, showed no signs of warming, and James Baldwin found the entire matter infuriating. He had put the men back to work at the first of the year, but still they struggled to accomplish their main objective—that of blasting through to open the tunnel.

"It's me own thought that we be done with it already," Red told James. "Me men are half frozen. Better to keep them busy workin' than send them back to their cold, drafty houses. Haulin' rock and pickin' through limestone will get their blood up."

"We still can't be sure about the gas," James countered.

"And for sure we'd be worryin' about that," Red replied, "but not so much that the work wouldn't get done."

Kiernan stood not a foot away from James, but Red refused to even acknowledge his presence. When James turned to Kiernan, he saw the pained expression in the younger man's eyes. Having been an only child, James could barely imagine the anguish in having a brother reject you. Seeing the misery caused his young friend, he found himself almost grateful to have never known brothers or sisters.

"What do you think, Kiernan?" James asked. He knew it would infuriate Red, but he didn't care. He wanted to reassure Kiernan that his position was important. The entire island of Ireland might snub him, but James wanted him convinced that here in America he had a place to belong.

"I suppose me brother knows his own mind on the matter," Kiernan replied. "We've been haulin' rock by hand ever since the winches went down. I'm doubting it would hurt anythin'."

Red waited impatiently, and James could hear a low, almost inaudible growl coming from the man. He turned back to face Red. "Kiernan thinks it would be worth a try. I suppose if the men are willing to take the risk," James said thoughtfully, "we could move ahead."

"The men will do what they're told to do," Red replied, appearing even more hostile. James could only presume it was from his further loss of power. With James suggesting the men be given a choice, Red would find himself very nearly out of the picture altogether. Not an acceptable means for a bully whose self-appointed power fed on the fears of others.

"I don't want any man to feel forced," James answered. "While you speak to your men, I'll travel over to the other side to see what's going on there. When I get back, we'll know better what to do."

Red, obviously annoyed, said nothing as he stormed off in the direction of the Connaughtmen. Kiernan watched him, and James could see only too well the misery the younger man felt.

"I'm sorry, Kiernan," James said sympathetically. "Why don't you come with me?"

Kiernan nodded, his eyes ever on the back of his burly brother. "I suppose it might keep me out of trouble."

James spoke quickly with two of the eastern portal supervisors. He told them of his thoughts to get the tunnel blasted through, and each man agreed it would be better to push forward than to wait, frustrated and idle.

"Better bundle up," James told Kiernan and handed him an extra wool scarf. "The winds will bite right through us up there."

Kiernan gazed upward to the mountaintop. "Too bad the train can't run."

James agreed. Tracks had been placed over the top for hauling supplies and transporting crew, but with the bitter cold and lack of water, the supply train was temporarily disabled. No doubt about it, the cold slowed their productivity even more than the drought of the previous summer or the cholera epidemic of the fall.

As they started up the inclined path, James heard the sound of arguments coming from the men below. Halting only momentarily to see what was happening, James worried about the men and what Red might do to them. Either he would work them into a fighting frenzy, or he would forcibly demand their allegiance and actions. Neither was acceptable to James. He was tired of Red O'Connor running the show. Every argument or delay usually found its conception in that man, and it was beginning to be more than James wanted to deal with. Over and over, Red had forced situations that James either had to accept or find a compromise for.

"He hasn't always been like this," Kiernan confided as if reading James' mind.

James nodded and resumed their hike to the western portal. "No, I suppose not."

"He once was a good and lovin' man. He had a wife and child, but they both died before their first anniversary. Red came home to the family a broken man."

"I can well imagine."

"He was good to me family. Worked harder than any man ya'll ever know. He even used to be a prayin' man, but that ended with the death of his Kathleen."

"How did she die?" James questioned.

"Childbirth. She struggled a long time and our mum tried hard to save her. She gave Red a son. He called him Brian. But the next day they both died. Her from bleedin' to death and the boy from bein' too small."

"How awful for him," James said, no longer feeling such frustration with Red. The man obviously carried a heavier load than even James had imagined.

"Aye," Kiernan replied sadly.

James thought of how he would feel should Carolina die in such a manner. He would rather die himself than lose her. And yet, for all his occupation with the railroad, it might be hard just now to convince her of his loyalty to her. James instantly felt guilty for the long periods of time he'd spent away from his family. It wasn't like he couldn't have remained at home during the past few weeks, but the need to finish the tunnel had become almost an obsession. Maybe that was why he was eager to accept Red's ideas on blasting through. It might not be safe, but then again, it might prove absolutely successful and James would be able to send word to Ben Latrobe that the tunnel had finally been completed. Of course, it wouldn't be a true completion, but just opening it from end to end would offer James the success he was looking for.

Suddenly realizing that Kiernan had fallen in step behind him, James stopped and turned. "Why such a slow pace?" he asked with a grin. "Have you a hankering to freeze?"

Kiernan shook his head. "Nay. I'm just lost in me thoughts."

"Care to talk?"

Kiernan shrugged. "I love your daughter."

James laughed at this. "Yes, I know. But that hardly seems a reason for such a long face. After all, I've given you permission to court her, and even if it has been too cold to have socials and church services, the time will come when you two can walk about together."

"Aye. I've no doubt of that. I suppose thinkin' about Kathleen gave me reason to worry. I'm not sure I'd be able to live with meself if I caused Victoria to die."

James sobered. "Life comes with no guarantees. We have no way of knowing who will live and who will die. My own sister-in-law lost a baby, and it gave Carolina a fearful time when she was carrying Nicholas. She kept wondering if she would fare any better than her sister. She prayed continuously and found it difficult to look forward to his birth with anything other than trepidation. But I told her there was simply nothing to be gained in worry. It wouldn't stop whatever the good Lord had planned, and it certainly wouldn't ease her fears. I suppose it would be much the same for you and Victoria. Perhaps that's another reason you should give her time to grow up. She's precious to me. As precious as if she were my own flesh and blood. I can't deny that it tears at my heart when she looks at you the way she once looked at me."

Kiernan lowered his gaze to the ground. "I'd not thought of it that way."

"It's the way of these things. The passing of daughters from fathers to husbands. Just remember, you may have her heart—but she has mine," James said quite seriously. "I would be just as sorely grieved as you should anything ever happen to her."

"I suppose it makes marriage a great risk," Kiernan replied and looked up with tears in his eyes.

"A risk? Oh, decidedly that," James countered. "But one well worth the taking. I know you love her, and that gives me great pride and joy. You love her for herself. For the woman she will become. For the heart that beats within her. I only ask that you consider the future and the tasks at hand. I ask that you pray for wisdom and knowledge, that you might go forward with clear thought for tomorrow."

"She brooks no idea of waiting," Kiernan said softly.

"Women are often that way in matters of the heart," James answered. "Especially Victoria. She has little patience. It greatly vexes her to find her plans interrupted."

"But ya think those plans should be interrupted, don't you?"

James was rather taken aback. "Why do you ask that?"

Kiernan shrugged. "I suppose from havin' heard Mrs. Baldwin speak on the matter, and listenin', too, to the things ya say. It's given me reason to think."

"There's nothing wrong with that, Kiernan. Thinking a thing through is sound and wise. I doubt when you've come to the conclusion of your contemplation that you'll love my daughter any less."

"Aye, it's certain I am on that point," Kiernan replied. "I think if anythin' I'll be lovin' her more. Maybe even enough to leave her here in yar care while I make a way for us in California."

"She won't like that," James replied, "but perhaps it would be the clearest act of unselfish love I've ever witnessed. Even to hear you say that such a thing would be a possibility proves more than ever the truth of your love for my daughter."

"Never doubt that, sir," Kiernan said, meeting James eye to eye. "I cannot say I've ever loved another more."

James smiled. "And that is how it should be." He clapped Kiernan on the back. "Come along, lad. My feet are fairly frozen, and there's still work to be done."

They'd barely stepped out to continue their journey, however, when the air was rent with the unmistakable sound of an explosion. The earth shook fiercely under their feet, nearly knocking Kiernan and James to the ground. From up ahead, shaft number two gave off billowing clouds of dust. Someone had blasted in the tunnel, and James would bet money on who that someone might be.

Kiernan, too, looked at him with a panicked expression that suggested his own understanding of the situation. Without words they ran for the tunnel, hoping, praying, that the worst would not be realized.

"What happened?" James called out to the first supervisor he found.

"It was O'Connor," the man said, his face stricken with a look of disbelief. "He grabbed up a keg of powder and headed in there before anyone could stop him. Said he'd blow the hole through or die trying."

James turned toward Kiernan but found that the boy had already left his side. Glancing up, James watched him disappear into the dusty haze that still poured out from the mouth of the tunnel.

"Kiernan, wait!"

James rushed after him, calling his name over and over. He coughed fitfully when he drew in a lungful of dust and reached inside his coat to find a handkerchief. Putting this over his nose and mouth, he drew up a nearby lantern with the other hand and pressed into the tunnel.

At this point, the tunnel was fine; there were no cave-ins or other signs of damage from the blast. Pushing deeper, James felt a strange foreboding as the silence engulfed him. He passed the first shaft, peering upward at the dusty light overhead. Sunlight did its best to filter through, but it was as though someone had pulled a veil across the opening.

As the dust settled, James called out again to Kiernan, but again his call went unanswered. The boy had no doubt set out at a full run in hopes of finding his brother. But James knew that the situation did not suggest Red's survival. No one had seen him come out, and he certainly hadn't passed James along the way. The closer James drew to the last of the tunnel's obstacles, the more certain he was that Red was either severely injured or dead.

The first thing to break the silence was the periodic rumble of rock as it fell from the roof of the tunnel. James knew he'd walked into a very dangerous situation, but he couldn't leave Kiernan to face this alone. Neither could he ignore the fact that other men might well be involved. After all, no one had given the blasting signal that always saw the tunnel emptied of men. No doubt the laborers on the western side would have been hard at work on preparations to break through. James could only wonder how many lives this grandstanding of Red's might have cost them.

And then James saw it. A pinpoint of light that grew with every step he took. Light that suggested something other than a torch or lantern. Soon enough it became clear that the blast had breached the hard, rocky wall. They were through! The tunnel was open!

But even as this thought came to him, James was aware of the moans and groans of injured men. Running now, he came to the point where the worst of the debris lay in haphazard piles. To the right he finally found Kiernan—cradling the lifeless body of his brother and sobbing as though he had lost his best friend.

"Let me help you get him out," James suggested, placing the lamp on a large piece of limestone.

"Nay," Kiernan said, shaking his head over and over. "Leave me be."

James eyed him for a moment, then backed away. There were others who needed his help, and clearly Kiernan wanted to be alone with Red. Turning to the job at hand, James had managed to throw aside several good-sized rocks before hearing Kiernan move.

He glanced over his shoulder and found the young man struggling to lift his brother. His heart went out to Kiernan, and he thought to go to him and at least help him secure Red's weight, but something inside held back. Little by little, Kiernan wrestled with the body, until he bore the full weight across his shoulders. As James watched him walk away, others had come to join the cleanup and rescue. Without thinking, James followed after Kiernan, compelled to stay near his friend—hopeful that he might offer some manner of comfort.

As they passed through the oncoming men, caps were doffed and heads bowed as Kiernan bore Red's body. James thought it strange that even though the group was now mingled with Corkians, Fardowns, and Connaughtmen, all of these fierce Irish seemed of one mind. They were united through the death of one man in a way that they had never been joined in life. They all seemed to understand the finality of the moment—seemed to know that there was no hope of life in Redley O'Connor's body. They simply stood back, caps in hand, heads bowed as the dead passed by.

There would be no celebration for the tunnel now opened. The price paid had been too high. This clannish breed understood that price—had paid it elsewhere in other forms and had lived to tell their tales of danger and adventure. Red would become one of those tales now. They would speak of him around campfires and in taverns where the drink ran free.

"Aye, I knew Red O'Connor," the men would say. "He was as fine a Connaughtman as ever there was, and he died drillin', as many a good tarrier has. Oh, the stories I could tell ya . . ."

James smiled sadly, thinking of how it would be, knowing it was no less than Red would have wanted.

Forty-Five

Troubled Days

Two years and eight months after breaking ground at the Kingwood Tunnel, James sent word of completion to Ben Latrobe. Carolina shared her husband's excitement and enthusiasm for the finished tunnel but knew she shared little else. As her children grew and Nicholas's first birthday was less than a month away, Carolina found herself in the middle of some strange sort of balancing act. She didn't want James to know how much she resented his opportunities as a man. It wasn't a proper attitude for a lady, nor was it Christian. Yet Carolina struggled against herself daily. James had the world open to him. He could come and go at will, and she was expected to keep his home and children in order and busy herself with her hands.

She couldn't recall how many times her mother had spoken to her of a married woman's place being at home. So she really tried to be happy doing the things she knew were proper. Yet inside there was a turmoil that kept the fires of envy constantly stirred. She would study her husband's papers, read the reports sent by Thomas Swann and the ever-educational *American Railroad Journal,* but she knew she was only peering through a closed window into a place where she could not go. It was just as her mother had suggested. She had seen the world beyond the garden wall and found it more to her liking.

Staring out on Greigsville from her bedroom window, Carolina gave a heavy sigh.

"I'm thirty-two years old," she murmured. "I have a loving husband and four beautiful children. I have good friends and a fine house, and more money than I'll ever have need of. So why am I so unhappy?"

For the longest time, Carolina thought she had dealt with her frustration. After all, when James had been so desperately ill with cholera, Carolina had felt perfectly content to remain at his side. She had no interest in books or railroads when his life was ebbing away. It was then that she realized how her life centered around James. She wanted to share his life. His dreams. His job. She longed to know what his day consisted of and where he went that took him away from her for so many hours.

Whenever Ben Latrobe came to visit, she listened to their discussions, envious of James' abilities and position. The men spoke of iron truss bridges and problems with the line at Fairmont; negotiating the Monongahela River had proven more difficult than they'd planned. It was fascinating to hear the details of each crisis and resolution.

All through the rainy spring, Carolina had felt James' anticipation. With every problem, with every conflict, she urged James to explain the situation and detail his thoughts on solutions. She tried to offer her own suggestions, as well. But this only furthered her frustration, as James would point out to her where her thinking was flawed.

And another source of frustration now made itself visible to her. In the yard below, Kiernan and Victoria were walking hand in hand. She paused momentarily to glance up at him with such love and adoration that Carolina found herself unable to look away.

"My child can be content, but I cannot?" she questioned aloud.

Of course, she had convinced herself that the source of Victoria's satisfaction came in the fact that she had set her sights very low. She wanted nothing more out of life than to be a wife and mother.

"You seem very deep in thought," James announced as he came through the door to their room.

"I didn't expect you to be home this soon," Carolina said, turning from the window but remaining fixed in place. She offered him a smile, feeling love for him that she knew must surely outweigh all of her discontentment. I am simply taking my eyes off of what is real and important, she thought. I get all worked up over issues that have no validity in my life.

" . . . or so it would seem."

Carolina shook her head. "What? I'm afraid I was thinking of something else. I didn't hear what you had to say."

"I said the fair weather has given over to stimulating young love, or so it would seem," he said, throwing his frock coat on the bed. "I saw Kiernan and Victoria walking about town."

"I know. I was just watching them."

"Oh, spying, are we?" James teased and went to the small rolltop desk where he kept his business papers.

"I was just thinking," Carolina said, sitting down on the edge of the bed, "how Victoria is happy with what she has because she's set her sights so low."

James stopped what he was doing and looked at her hard. "That's not a very gallant thing to say. Do you mean to suggest that her desires to marry and keep house for the man she loves is less than admirable? That is the normal expectation of most women, you know."

Carolina felt slapped by his words. "It's just that there's a whole world out there."

"A world she doesn't want if it means having it without Kiernan O'Connor." James came to stand in front of her. "Carolina, I'm rather surprised by your attitude. Are you that unhappy here?"

"No!" she declared defensively. "It's not that." She paused and looked down at the floor. "Not truly. I don't know why I feel this way. Just when I think I have an understanding of my feelings, it flees me and I find myself as confused as ever. I pray, seek the Scriptures, and ask God for direction, and while I know I'm doing the job set out for me, I can't help but feel—" She fell silent.

"Feel what?" asked James.

Just then Miriam knocked on the door. "Miz Carolina, I gots the mail and this here done come for you." She extended a letter and smiled. "It's from Oakbridge."

Carolina took the missive and smiled. "Thank you, Miriam." She waited until the woman left before breaking the seal to read the contents. With the very first line, she felt the blood drain from her face. "Oh no." She glanced up at her husband.

"What is it?" James asked, reaching for the letter.

"Papa has been hurt. The doctor says it's serious enough to call for the family."

James read the remainder of the letter aloud.

> " 'The slaves revolted two nights ago. Your father was a week in Washington, and during his absence, Hampton acted most unreasonably. He made impossible demands on the slaves and took to beating several of them on a daily basis. His nocturnal abuse of the young women became evident, and when I confronted him about it, he accused me of lunacy. I sent word to your father, and, of course, he returned home. But by then it was too late. Hampton had already stirred the fires of hatred to a raging inferno. His behavior alone can be blamed for the revolt. Your father tried to ease the tensions, but even as he tried to speak, one of the slaves lashed out—I'm certain Hampton had been his target, but your father was struck instead and rendered unconscious.

'Oh, my dear daughter, you are needed here at my side. I cannot bear this thing alone. I have sent for York and Georgia, but, of course, Maine is too far away to reach. I pray you will come see your father. The doctor does not hold much hope for him at this point.' "

James handed her back the letter. "Of course you must go. I'll make immediate arrangements. Thank God the railroad is in place. You can be to Oakbridge in sight of three days."

"You'll come with me, won't you?" Carolina asked, her voice mingled with fear and dread.

"I can't—" he said, stopping in midsentence as he donned his coat. His expression was stricken. "I have too much to take care of in regard to the celebration Ben has planned. They're opening the line to Fairmont on the twenty-second of June, and there's much to be done. I still have timber supports falling down in the tunnel. I can't very well have a cave-in during the celebration, so I must see that section tended to."

Anger welled up in Carolina at his response. The concern in his expression was genuine, but his refusal to accompany her was more than she expected. "I can't believe you would deny me this." She got to her feet. "My father may well die. Would you have me bear that alone?"

"Of course not," James said. He came to take her in his arms, but Carolina remained stiff and unyielding. "I would accompany you if—"

"Don't!" she exclaimed. "Don't give me any more excuses. I don't know why I should expect you to stand by me in this. You're seldom ever here for any other reason." She knew the bitterness in her voice but found it impossible to dam up the flow of words. "You see the railroad as your own personal legacy—a legacy of iron and rails—but your real legacy is here. We have a legacy in our children, but you hardly know them. I thought moving here would resolve that problem, but I was wrong. You spend long hours absorbed in the building of your precious tunnel and leave us to make our way. We've scarcely seen you since you recovered from the cholera last year."

"The cholera made me feel a sense of urgency," James offered. "I saw my own mortality, and I knew that I had to complete this tunnel. I thought you understood that dream."

Again he approached as if to embrace her, but Carolina backed away. "I understand a great deal that I'm not given credit for. I understand my place is in this house, nurturing the children I've been given. I understand the ledgers and reports that deal with the building of this railroad. I even understand the properties and mechanics involved in some of the newest engine designs. What I fail to understand, however, is how you can leave me out of our dream." At this she broke down, hating herself for her tears. Burying her face in her hands, she despised her behavior. How could she treat so cruelly the man she loved so dearly?

He came to her, as she knew he would, wrapping her in his arms—hushing her tears.

"I can't abide myself," she told him, breaking into yet another series of sobs. And that was what hurt her most. She couldn't stand the way she had acted. Did education do this? Had she allowed herself to become some sort of freak? Was that why there was such discontentment inside of her?

"I find that I can abide you very well," James said softly.

"Don't!" She tried to jerk away from him, but he held her tight. "Don't be kind to me. I don't deserve it. I've been cruel and hopelessly critical."

"You've just received bad news from home," James countered gently. "You have a right to be upset."

"But I think I'm more upset with myself than over this news about my father," she said tearfully. "And that makes me an even worse person. I'm so selfish and bitter. I try to do what's right, but I keep looking over the wall and wishing for what I can't have."

"And what is it you want that you don't already have?" questioned James, his expression serious but loving.

"You," she whispered, her heart aching from the way she'd behaved.

"But you've always had me," he answered, tracing her jaw with his fingers.

"I know," she said, and exasperation filled her voice. "I know." And she did know it as well as she knew her own name. But there was more to it, and that was what confused her. Especially now, with her father's injuries and the impending trip to Oakbridge. Where she once had longed to return to her childhood home, she now dreaded the thought of it.

"Look, I've got to go take care of a couple of things. I'll send Miriam up here to help you pack and be back to take you to the station. All right?" He kissed her lightly without waiting for her to answer.

Carolina watched him go and felt like crying anew. He couldn't possibly understand her feelings. How could he, she thought, when she herself didn't understand them?

An hour later she stood ready, purse in hand and bags loaded in the carriage. She kissed each of the children good-bye, and only Nicholas seemed particularly out of sorts at her leaving. He was newly weaned, and Carolina knew he still considered her his private source of nourishment.

"I'll take care of everything," Victoria told her confidently. Carolina knew her fifteen-year-old daughter was quite competent in helping with her siblings and tending the house.

Miriam sniffled into a handkerchief and promised prayers for Master Joseph. Carolina knew that Miriam's heart was breaking at the thought that Joseph might pass away. She supposed they both fretted over what his death might mean to the other slaves at Oakbridge.

She glanced around impatiently for James. Five minutes ago he had returned to the house. He had handed her some money, as well as a slip of paper, and then was just as quickly off and out the back door. She had no idea what he was doing. The carriage was already standing ready in the front yard. Perhaps he hadn't seen it, but no doubt one look into the barn would assure him that he needn't ready her transportation.

Nicholas began to wail for all he was worth, and Victoria, seeming to sense Carolina's uneasiness, motioned to Brenton and Jordana. "Come on. We'll take Nicky to play inside."

"You children remember to obey Miriam and say your prayers," Carolina called out. She hated to see them go, but perhaps it was for the best. Good-byes were never easy.

"I can't imagine what's keeping James," she told Miriam in complete exasperation. "He said we had to be at the station in ten minutes, and that was five minutes ago." She shook her head and rechecked the contents of her purse. Her traveling money was securely contained in a small drawstring bag Victoria had embroidered and given her as a birthday gift, and the slip of paper James had given her assured her safe and free passage all along the Baltimore and Ohio Railroad. Now the only thing missing was James.

But just then he appeared. Coming at a mad dash through the front door, James threw another bag into the carriage and reached out to help Carolina. "Come on, we've only got a few minutes to spare."

"What's that?" Carolina asked, nodding toward the extra bag.

"It's my carpetbag. I mean to travel to Oakbridge with you," he told her, then grinned devilishly. "That is, if you still want me to."

Stunned, Carolina found it hard to speak. "Of . . . course."

"Miriam, we'll be back soon. I've already instructed Kiernan to make himself available to you. If you need anything, go to him."

Miriam nodded.

"But the children," Carolina said, realizing they'd not know of their father's departure.

"I've already bid them good-bye," James told her, smacking the reins against the horse's rump. "I saw them in the house and told them to mind and I'd bring them all a present."

Carolina smiled, remembering all the times her own father had done the same thing.

"And the railroad?" she asked.

"I put Kiernan in charge. He'll do just fine," James assured her.

"You certainly changed your mind in a hurry," she commented.

"Let's just say I saw the wisdom in it," he replied.

They hurried through the town and made their way to the depot just as the train whistle gave its first blast. James jumped from the carriage, motioned one of the baggagemen to take charge of their luggage, then helped Carolina down.

They were seated, with the train already in motion before either one said another word. With James at her side, Carolina felt both joy and guilt, and with her gloved hands folded demurely on her lap, she searched for words to tell him she was sorry.

"I want to say something," James spoke before she could compose her thoughts.

Carolina turned and looked into his blue eyes—eyes she had so long searched for love, hope, and strength. She knew she deserved his anger and consternation, but instead she found only compassion.

"I've been wrong to stay away from home so much. After all, the real reason you came to Greigsville was in order to keep us together as a family. I'm sorry. I can't explain it, but this whole matter seems to have grown into an overwhelming mess. When Red was killed, I thought I'd never take joy in the tunnel again. It seemed our drive to see the thing completed had taken the life of a good man. But then I rationalized that Red's impatience and inability to heed authority had killed him, not the job itself.

"I don't want my actions to kill what we have between us, Carolina. We have a good marriage and a fine family, and I know those things better than you would imagine. I don't want you to be unhappy, but I don't know how to help you."

"How could you?" Carolina responded. "I'm uncertain as to how to help myself. I'm uncertain about a great deal."

"But surely not about us? Surely you aren't uncertain about your love for me, and mine for you."

She smiled. "No. But I do become jealous," she admitted sheepishly.

"Of what?" he asked, his expression confused.

"You," Carolina replied. "You can't know the battle I wage inside of myself. On one hand I want only to make you happy and be a good wife and mother. Then I see or hear something to do with the railroad, and you are a part of it and I am not. I envy your respected position among the men of the B&O, and I wish I could somehow hold that same respect. I—or should I say we?—own thousands, hundreds of thousands of dollars worth of stock, yet I'm not allowed to vote my own shares. You vote them, and yes, I know you always ask me what I desire you to do. We always discuss the matters as they come." She laughed nervously and twisted her hands together. "I know how silly this sounds. Believe me. My mother used to chide me for it. My father sympathized and everyone else fell somewhere in between."

"Except me," James said quite seriously. "I understood. I promoted your learning."

"Yes, for what good it has done. I see only that it has made me discontent. Perhaps Mother was right. It is a danger to educate a woman. After all, she cannot do a thing with her knowledge."

"Bah!" James said, shaking his head. "We neither one believe that rhetoric. No, what I think you need is simple. You need a task that involves you with the railroad. Something you can legitimately do without facing the disapproval of the general public."

"And why should I care what the public thinks?"

"I've often asked that same question. So why don't you answer it for me?"

Carolina shrugged. "I'm not sure I have an answer."

"I think you do. I think you've convinced yourself that you can't have any other role in life, and I'm telling you differently. If you desire to sit at home and keep track of the railroad's progress, then so be it. You know very well that most of my reports are done from the desk in our bedroom. There's no reason you can't sit there and tend to the matter instead of me. That way I'll have more time to share with our children, and you will have a purpose and occupation that includes your participation with the railroad."

"Do you really suppose it would work?" Carolina asked, suddenly excited at the prospect.

"I do. I have business in Baltimore to tend to. I'll talk to Thomas Swann myself and inform him that the task shall now fall to you."

Carolina grew quiet, remembering her reason for being on the train in the first place. "You will still accompany me to Oakbridge, won't you?"

"Absolutely," he said, squeezing her hand. "I was wrong to suggest you should ever make this trip alone. It was heartless of me, and nothing made me see things as clearly as that one thoughtless action. Will you forgive me?"

Carolina felt instant contrition. "So long as you forgive me."

"And for what should I forgive you? The desire to share in the dream we built together?"

"No," she said, seriously considering her heart. "For the bitterness and envy I have harbored against you. I know now they alone are the sources of my unhappiness."

"Then harbor them no longer," he said, leaning close to whisper in her ear. "Harbor only love, as I feel for you."

She turned, and when she did so, their lips brushed together. Regardless of the public display, James kissed her long and lovingly. Carolina sighed. She knew there was much yet to be done in her heart. Knew that it was entirely up to her to make her way and be glad. She offered up a prayer for her father's safety and recovery, and followed it with her sincerest request for forgiveness. The road ahead held promise. A promise for their love. A promise for tomorrow.

Forty-Six

The Issue of Slavery

Delighted to find her sister-in-law Lucy and brother York already in residence at Oakbridge, Carolina embraced them both with enthusiasm.

"I am so glad we could all be together," she told her brother.

"Even if it does have to be for such a dismal reason," York replied. "However, there is good news. Father is recovering, in spite of the doctor's lack of hope."

"Thanks be to God for that," James replied, shaking hands with York.

Lucy and Carolina were still holding hands and chattering on about their children when Georgia and her brood were admitted to the house. Lydia appeared and whisked all of the children up to the nursery while the women greeted one another warmly.

"Have they told you that Father is better?" Georgia asked Carolina as she entered with her husband, the Major.

"York was just mentioning that. I'm so anxious to see him. May we go up now?" Carolina asked, looking to York.

"Of course. In fact, Father said we were to gather in his room for some sort of family meeting," York replied.

"Family meeting?" questioned Carolina. "Whatever could that be all about?"

"He's been quite agitated ever since the slave revolt," Lucy said.

Georgia acknowledged the truth of this, as well. "He's not been at all happy. He's totally convinced that something must be done and done quickly."

"About the slaves?" Carolina asked.

"He really won't say until we are all assembled. I tried to get him to talk to me about it, but he refused," York answered before Georgia or Lucy could speak a word.

Just then Virginia appeared in the foyer. Carolina had to restrain herself from gasping. Her sister was hideously thin. The image of a walking skeleton would serve perfectly to describe the once beautiful woman.

"Virginia!" Carolina finally managed to say without sounding too stunned. She hurried to embrace her sister, lest she see her shocked expression.

Virginia barely returned the gesture, then quickly stepped back. "I'm glad you could come." She looked beyond Carolina to where James stood. "I'm glad you could come, too, James."

James stepped forward and gave her a bow. "I only wish it might have been under better circumstances."

Carolina watched them for a moment. She couldn't help but wonder what might be passing through her sister's mind. Would she be further depressed by James' appearance at Oakbridge? Would it only serve to deepen her obvious melancholy? Virginia looked like some macabre apparition, a pitiful figure sent to haunt the house in which she'd once been so happy. Carolina was deeply concerned.

"We were just going up to see Father," York told Virginia. "Is Mother still up there?"

"I'm sure she is," Virginia replied. "She is scarcely far from him."

"Then I suggest we make our appearances. He was quite adamant about discussing this matter before Hampton returns from his hunt."

"Hunt?" Carolina questioned.

"Slave hunt," Virginia said flatly. "He's out trying to retrieve the runaways. He's already been gone three days, and we expect him back anytime."

Carolina nodded and shuddered. She hated to think of what Hampton might do if and when he caught up with the slaves. James seemed to sense her worry and very gently took hold of her arm. She glanced up at him, seeing the concern in his expression. How thankful she was for his presence. She could hardly imagine having to face this ordeal on her own.

They mounted the stairs as one assembled mass. Silently, they paired off, with exception to Virginia, who brought up the rear, very much on her own. Carolina pitied her sister. Yet even as she thought of such a thing, Carolina knew it would be the last thing Virginia would want. Virginia had always despised pity. Carolina silently vowed to figure out some way to help her. She would speak to Lucy later, and perhaps together they could figure out a way to bring Virginia back to health.

They entered their parents' bedroom, and Carolina tightened her grip on James' arm. Her father's head was swathed in bandages, and his face was still bruised and discolored from where he'd been struck. The swelling seemed to bloat his features, and Carolina wanted to cry out in despair. That anyone should have hurt him this way was unthinkable.

"Papa!" she breathed and, leaving James, went to his side. "Mama," she added, taking hold of her mother's extended hand.

"Ah, so you came," her father said in a weak voice that sounded nothing like his normal, strong baritone.

"It's good to have you here," Margaret told her daughter.

Margaret squeezed her hand, and Carolina leaned down to kiss her cheek. Her mother looked tired but surprisingly strong. Carolina found herself breathing a sigh of relief. She hadn't even realized how this issue had weighed on her mind. Her mother had suffered so much through her life, and her previous inability to deal with tragedy gave Carolina cause for worry. Should anything happen to Joseph, Carolina feared it would be her mother's final undoing.

"How are you feeling, Papa?" Carolina asked, reaching out to take hold of his hand. She longed to throw herself into his arms and kiss his whiskered cheeks, but she refrained, fearing that she might cause him further injury.

"I've been better," Joseph admitted. He smiled as best he could. "I see you have brought your brother and sisters."

"We're all here, just as you requested," York replied, escorting Lucy to a chair. He took his place behind her, then looked to the others. "We might as well be seated. Unless I miss my guess, this could take some time."

"What is this about?" Georgia questioned.

York shrugged. "Ask Father. I only know that he said it was important."

"Don't speak as though I'm not here," Joseph interjected. "I may have one foot in the grave—"

"Joseph!" Margaret said, her voice stern, "don't scare your children that way."

He smiled at his wife. "My apologies. Please do make yourselves comfortable."

Carolina returned to James and allowed him to pull up a chair for her to sit on. Why was her father so hard pressed to speak to them all? Did he believe he was dying? Was he simply awaiting their arrival en masse so that he could explain his last wishes? She shuddered again, and James, seeming to sense her discomfort, put his hand gently on her shoulders as if to steady her.

"I've asked you here so that we could talk about what happened," Joseph began slowly. "As you know, I've long struggled to keep a balance here at Oakbridge. Even as children you were taught not to judge a man by his skin color, but by his deeds. However, that hasn't been the belief of many in this country. It seems most people would relegate the slaves to a status somewhere beneath us, and treat them accordingly."

He shifted uncomfortably, and Margaret leaned forward to help him prop up with an extra pillow.

"The revolt," her father continued, "was the clear result of improper treatment. As you may or may not know, Hampton has been unduly harsh with the slaves."

"That's putting it mildly," Virginia said sarcastically. All eyes turned momentarily to her, and she shrugged. "Unduly harsh is the only thing Hampton really understands."

Then without warning, the man himself appeared in the doorway. He was sweat soaked and covered in grime and dirt, but he strode into the room as though going to church.

"I'm back," Hampton announced. "I got three of them. They're chained to the post in the back. Tomorrow I'll see to it that they never run away again."

Carolina looked at Hampton with what she knew was undisguised horror. Margaret and Joseph, too, looked at Hampton as though sickened by his words. Then, as if seeing the gathering for the first time, Hampton's expression changed from elation to puzzlement.

"What have we here?" he asked. "The whole family is gathered."

"Yes," Margaret replied, settling back in her chair. "With exception of Maine."

"May I ask what this is all about?" Hampton scowled at Virginia, as if she might have been responsible.

"I called them here," Joseph answered, suddenly sounding surprisingly strong. "I have need to talk to my children about the future of Oakbridge."

"I see. And did you not think this might affect me, as well?"

Joseph nodded. "I did and I still do. You were represented here by your wife."

"Bah!" Hampton declared. "She's hardly a worthy representation."

"I'll ask you not to speak of my daughter that way," Joseph said, his blackened eyes narrowing. "What I have to do here today is as much because of your actions as anything else."

"I see. You continue to blame this revolt on me, is that it?"

All eyes turned to Joseph, and Carolina feared what would happen next. Would her father suggest Hampton pack up his family and leave?

"There are revolts all over the South," Joseph replied. "We are most generally considered to be southerners, but we share a unique situation in that our nation's capital is only hours away. While in Washington, I was privileged to be included in conversations with many congressmen and cabinet members, all who spoke of the growing unrest surrounding slavery. States are affected, no matter where they are positioned, because each state is either titled 'free' or 'slave.' The issue is tearing this nation apart, and mark my words, if the issue is not resolved, there will be war."

"You preach doom and gloom," Hampton said, shaking his head. "You don't understand the truth of the matter. Keep these slaves in their place and the issue will go away."

"I don't believe that," Carolina replied.

"Neither do I," Georgia said supportively. "I have long shared the opinion that owning slaves will one day be a thing of the past. I even heard tell that there were plans to ship the slaves back to where they were taken from. I think that would be an admirable solution, as many of them have been in this country for less than fifty years and still have families on another continent."

"The same could be said of many white men," Hampton retorted.

"Yes, but white men may come and go at will. No one ties them to whipping posts and plots to keep them from running away again," Carolina returned sarcastically.

"Discipline is necessary to keep people in line, be they black or white," Hampton countered. "The Major knows full well about such things. Tell them if I lie."

The Major nodded. "Discipline is necessary, but so, too, is respectable leadership."

"It is indeed," Joseph replied. "Now, hear me out, because I haven't the strength to make this a lengthy debate. I've spoken with your mother, and it is our conclusion that the slaves of Oakbridge should be set free. We have already educated many of them and taught them additional skills in order to be able to work in the community. We have prepared papers to free several within the month. More will follow soon. After they are all released, your mother and I have plans to draw up papers dividing this property among you children. If you choose to sell it to one or the other, that will be up to you. As for the house, well, I'm uncertain at this point."

"You can't be serious!" Hampton exploded. "It's illegal to educate the slaves, and if you set them free, they'll only be snatched up by someone else."

"I think Father has a good plan," Carolina interjected. "I've already set Miriam free. I've taught her to read and write, and I pay her a good wage to act as my housekeeper. We have a good working relationship, and I'm sure other people would find such a situation to work just as well for them."

"We personally prefer free Irish whites," Georgia responded. "We keep no Negroes on our property and find that men who fear the loss of job and wage are better kept than those who fear the whip."

"There are always ways to motivate people," Carolina said, staring hard at Hampton, "and it might surprise you to know that many of them do not require physical abuse."

"I would expect such talk from women," Hampton replied, seemingly unconcerned with their comments. "But the truth is, you could not afford to hire laborers to keep Oakbridge in place of using slave labor. It simply wouldn't be prudent; nor would it be profitable."

"I agree," York said, surprising everyone. "I can't believe, Father, that you'd break up this plantation all because of a revolt brought on by mismanagement. We've known good years here, and now the property is more prosperous than ever before.

"In the North," he continued, "there are those who believe that slave owners are the next thing to the devil himself. We are looked down upon, as sons of the South, because they say the blood of the slave is on our hands. They make their lewd suggestions and comments about our 'peculiar little institution,' as they call it, and believe us to be some form of deranged deviants. But I challenge that this is a time-honored tradition. I challenge that while there are those"—he stared hard at Hampton—"who would defile and harm women and children, and mercilessly beat and maim the men, there are even more who would never consider such a matter. How can we let the actions of one fool determine the future for the rest of us?"

"So you see nothing wrong in things continuing as they are?" Carolina questioned.

"Of course I would not see things continue as they are. That madness only led to Father being injured. No, I would make changes and see to it that things went back to the way they used to be."

"There's no profit in that. The laziest of men will grow only more lazy unless you stand over them with the whip," Hampton proclaimed. "I helped to see this place double its profit."

"Money isn't everything, Hampton," Joseph said from his bed.

"Unfortunately, I think you believe it is."

"It is what gives a man power and brings him respect. It keeps a roof over the heads of his family and puts food on the table. You cannot live in this luxury and suggest to me that money means nothing to you," Hampton countered.

"Perhaps that is why I suggest leaving this luxury," Joseph replied. "Margaret and I have talked of traveling."

"That, too, comes at a price," Hampton replied.

"Yes, but I have more than enough money to see me through life. There must come a point where a man puts down his duties and allows himself to rest."

"Not if you rid yourself of your labor force." Hampton began to pace the room. His eyes blazed in anger, and his expression was frightening to Carolina. "You are a fool, Joseph, if you allow this to happen. I've told you before, go and travel, live elsewhere if you like, but allow me to stay on and make your land profitable. I can't believe you'd drive your grandchildren out into the street—" he paused to glance at Virginia—"all in order to free those ignorant darkies."

"I've never suggested putting my grandchildren out into the street," Joseph replied. "You have managed to put a good amount of my money into your own pocket with which you can support them should they choose to leave with you." At this, all faces turned to Hampton as if to question how this happened. Joseph continued by adding, "I know exactly what your stake is in all of this, Hampton—and it has nothing to do with your concern for your family."

The words were very nearly a challenge for Hampton to deny the unspoken accusation, and Carolina remembered Virginia's confession regarding Hampton's desire to take over Oakbridge. No doubt he'd already robbed her father of a great deal of wealth.

"But what will the slaves do once they are set free?" York questioned, bringing the subject back around to slavery. "You can't believe that they will be eagerly hired to work jobs that were intended for whites."

"If they are skilled to do those tasks, why not?" Joseph questioned.

"Because they are not white," York said emphatically. "I live in Philadelphia, and while those good folks would have you believe their disdain for slavery, I can tell you honestly that the institution is still kept—even in and around that city. Of course, there are also free blacks, and they are often without job or home. I've seen many a black man hanged for thievery and murder, all because he was hungry or desperate to provide for his family. Would you do that to our people? People you've known since their childhood?"

York left Lucy's side and went closer to the bed where Joseph lay. "I cannot believe this to be a good thing, and quite frankly, I can't see standing by idly and allowing it to happen. It has always been my place to take over Oakbridge, and now I intend to do so. Lucy and I will leave Philadelphia and return immediately to Oakbridge so that I may take up my rightful place as heir." Without waiting for his father's acknowledgment, he turned to Hampton. "I will not be needing your assistance. I don't approve of your heavy-handedness. I hold you completely responsible for what has happened here and for Father's injuries. I don't care if you remain here or leave, but you will have no say in the running of this plantation." Then without even looking to Lucy for approval, York strode out of the room, slamming the door behind him.

Carolina was stunned by her brother's explosive declaration. She looked at Lucy, who sat openmouthed, staring at the door. In one brief moment, her husband had changed their entire future. Carolina reached out to take hold of Lucy's hand and squeezed it supportively. This in turn caused Lucy to look at Carolina with such an expression of grief that Carolina thought she might break into tears.

"I won't tolerate such treatment!" Hampton roared. "I stayed when everyone else left to seek his own way. Will you stand by and allow this to happen?" he asked Joseph angrily.

Joseph seemed just as stunned as everyone else. "I . . . don't . . . know. I suppose I must consider it," he replied. "York is my son and the rightful heir. If it is his desire to take over Oakbridge, then I should not deny him that opportunity."

"Madness!" Hampton stormed to the closed door, then threw it open with such force that it boomed against the wall behind it. "You'll see! You'll all see!"

He left them without bothering to close the door, and each of the remaining members of the room could only sit in stunned silence.

It was difficult to take in all that had just happened. To Carolina, her beloved Oakbridge had been forever altered. The issue of slavery held the potential for dividing a nation, Carolina thought. Why not a household?

"I suppose there's no hope for a peaceful conclusion to this matter," Joseph said sadly.

Carolina met his gaze with sympathy. He had suffered so much, and all because of this plantation—this obligation. The issue of slavery was merely a catalyst, a spark of fire to ignite the already tumultuous battlefield. But now, instead of strangers, her father and brother were at odds, as well as her brother-in-law. And who could possibly win a battle such as this? Surely someone would have to suffer loss.

Forty-Seven

Adams Women

"Of course, I believe the winters to be much milder here," Lucy Adams told her sister-in-law.

Carolina smiled. "You should have seen what we endured last year in Greigsville. The temperatures were so cold that every normal operation was suspended. We all doubled up in our sleeping arrangements. Victoria and Jordana slept with Miriam, while Brenton and Nicholas slept with James and me. Otherwise the children would have frozen to death. In fact, that very thing happened to several of the families in our community."

"How awful," Lucy replied, picking up her cup of tea. "I can scarcely imagine."

"I know," Carolina agreed. "We grew up so blessed. Here at Oakbridge such things were never a consideration. But in Greigsville—oh, Lucy," Carolina said, shaking her head, "there are so many poor families. James and I started a store, just in order to help out. We barely break even, but there is so much need in that town, and by our keeping prices low, the other stores have to follow suit. I'm sure we are despised for such dealings, but how could we do otherwise?"

"Indeed," Lucy said, nodding. "I have long performed acts of charity in Philadelphia, but I suppose it never has come to rest upon my doorstep as it has upon yours."

"I know the railroad will improve the plight of Greigsville in general. But there is no way of knowing if it will help the families there or not. Most are Irish and have a half dozen or more children. Their fathers are common laborers and most have already lost their jobs. Some will move on with the railroad, moving west as the various lines develop, but many will find themselves trapped and without hope for their future."

"It's so sad. I suppose—" She fell silent as the drawing room door opened to admit Virginia.

"Oh, I'm sorry," Virginia said and immediately started to back out of the room.

"Virginia, you needn't go," Carolina declared with a welcoming smile. "We're just having tea and cakes. There's plenty here and we would love to have you join us, wouldn't we, Lucy?"

"Oh, indeed. I've scarce had an opportunity to visit with you since our arrival."

"I can't say that I am good company," Virginia remarked, sounding rather embarrassed.

"Nonsense," Carolina said, getting to her feet in order to move over. "Come sit here beside me on the sofa."

Virginia did as she was bid, but it was clear she was uncomfortable. Carolina, too, found herself uncertain as to how she should act. While she had long since forgiven her sister's bitterness toward her, she and Virginia had never been close and probably never would be.

"We were just discussing last winter's cold," Lucy offered.

"Yes, but that topic is long exhausted," Carolina countered. "What I haven't heard much about is you and the children," she told Virginia.

"There isn't much to tell. All are well."

Carolina poured her sister a cup of tea and offered it to her. "I understand from Mother that you have been sick these past months."

Virginia took a sip of tea and shrugged. "Another miscarriage. It seems to be my lot in life."

"I'm so sorry," Carolina and Lucy murmured in unison.

"I had no idea," Carolina added. "Mother only mentioned that you were ill."

"I'm not certain that she knew," Virginia said casually. "It matters little if she did."

An uncomfortable silence fell around them, and for several awkward moments they did nothing but drink tea and stare at the floor.

"I knew this was a bad idea," Virginia finally said, putting her cup down. "I heard the two of you talking quite eagerly before I came into the room. I will leave now so that you might reacquaint yourselves to that conversation."

"No, please don't go," Carolina said, reaching out to take hold of Virginia's arm. "It's just that . . . well . . . I'm uncertain as to what to say. I don't wish to make you uncomfortable, but in truth I had intended to speak to Lucy on this matter of York taking over Oakbridge."

"I assure you, nothing that you can say will make me uncomfortable. I would welcome York's command here. I would love nothing more than to see Hampton deposed."

"Very well," Carolina said, realizing she was only making matters worse by maintaining her silence. "Lucy, in these past days since York declared his intention to return here permanently, I've been reluctant to ask you about his decision. Is he intent on carrying through?"

Lucy put down her tea, and the look she wore was one of pure misery. Her delicate face, accented by dark eyes and finely arched black brows, contorted into an expression of anguish. "He is intent, and I am most heartbroken." She fell silent for a moment, then continued. "I cannot say that this is what I want. I personally abhor slavery. I've even attended several abolitionist lectures and found the entire matter to be one which I can in nowise support."

Carolina suddenly realized the depth of Lucy's distress. "Whatever will you do?"

Just then Margaret entered the room, her soft brown cotton day dress billowing out around her. "I'm not sure but what this skirt is too full," she said, her voice almost youthful. She looked up with a radiant smile, then seemed to note the seriousness of the moment. "Am I interrupting?"

"Not at all, Mother," Carolina replied, now uncertain she could ever get Lucy to continue speaking. "Come join us. We are having tea and discussing our futures."

Lucy looked away, appearing to concentrate on her cup.

"I have interrupted, haven't I?" Margaret inquired, taking the chair beside Lucy. "My dear, if I have done something to make you unhappy—"

Lucy looked up. "Absolutely not, Mother Adams. It's just that . . . well . . ." She looked to Carolina as if seeking the words to explain.

"We were just confiding in each other about Oakbridge and our concern about the slavery issue."

"Ah," Margaret replied, taking the cup of tea Carolina had just poured for her. "York's declaration must have been difficult for you to take, Lucy. After all, I presume it came as a complete surprise."

"Indeed it did," Lucy replied, tears in her eyes. "I don't wish for you to think that I find such an idea abominable. I love Oakbridge, truly I do. But there are matters which I cannot abide, and it will be impossible to separate myself from them when we are living here."

"What matters?" Margaret asked. She saw Lucy's hesitant glance at Carolina and reached out to pat her daughter-in-law's hand. "Come now, Lucy. We have much past between us. I love you as I do my own daughters, so let there be no secrets between us."

"I cannot abide slavery, ma'am," Lucy finally admitted.

"Is that all?" There was a hint of amusement in Margaret's voice. "You must surely know that I could never condemn you for such thoughts. I am in complete agreement with Mr. Adams. I want them to be set free. I never honestly considered their circumstance to be a wrong one until Hampton's mistreatment became so evident. Of course, you always heard about the various problems in the surrounding counties. But most of our friends and neighbors were good to their people. So we were very isolated here. When the rest of the country spoke out against the atrocities done to the Negro, we could honestly look to one another and have little idea of what was being said."

"I, too, know that to be true," Carolina offered. "Until I went to Baltimore, which is in general very supportive of slavery, I heard very little of the debates and arguments surrounding the institution. Then when I moved to Greigsville, I learned only too quickly about antislavery sentiment. When I came to town with Miriam at my side, people were offended that I would impose slavery in their town. I quickly gave Miriam her freedom, which I had intended to do anyway, and I taught her to read and write. Now she stays on as a paid worker and a friend."

"But there will be none of that here," Virginia said sadly. "Plantations do not run themselves, and my brother will find much to repair. Hampton has done this place grievous harm, and it will take more than a change of masters to bring harmony back to Oakbridge."

"Your father feels quite badly about this," Margaret interjected. "He simply couldn't keep Hampton under control with so many other matters pressing upon him. He talked to him, pleaded with him, and even threatened him on more than one occasion, but Hampton knew only too well that he had Joseph in a bad position."

"York will see this as more than a challenge," Lucy finally said. "He has come more and more to regard Oakbridge as his birthright and as the future he can hand down to his children. His difficulties with antislave sentiments in Philadelphia probably had the effect of crystallizing his views on the subject. But I don't want my children to be slave owners," she said and burst into tears.

"There, there, my dear," Margaret said, putting down her tea and reaching an arm around Lucy's shoulders. "You mustn't fret so about that which has not yet come to pass. Joseph still desires to free the slaves. Perhaps he will even convince York of the wisdom in this. After all, I believe it is Oakbridge York is most intent upon preserving, not slavery. York has more love of this land than he ever realized. It seems his time up north has proven that to him."

"I want to stand by his side on this," Lucy said, trying hard to compose herself. "But I don't even know how to speak to him on this matter. He'll see me as a traitor if I tell him my heart."

Margaret sighed sadly. "Listen to me, all of you. This issue will not be easily dismissed, and your father is right to worry about it. The way I see it, no one man will resolve this problem. It will take everyone agreeing to abolish slavery or it will simply continue wherever it is allowed. However, there are other matters at hand that cause me as great a concern as the issue of slavery. We face a tremendous challenge here, and of that we cannot be mistaken. Virginia, your husband will not accept defeat easily and so we must be ever watchful of his actions. You once spoke to me of your fear for this place and for your father. Do you still feel that way?"

"More now than ever," Virginia replied with a slow nod of her head.

"Then you must help me to make sure that Hampton harms no one else. It would be wise to keep him under a watchful eye. If you see that he is about to cause us grief, then I want you to come get me."

"But what if I am uncertain?" Virginia questioned. "Hampton is often argumentative and temperamental, but whether he carries through and actually becomes violent is another issue. I have seen the time when he has been provoked to absolute rage and yet he holds back. Other times, he flies off at a mere word."

"If there is anything at all that suggests to you the possibility of violence and tragedy, then come to me. Don't allow him an upper hand by worrying that you will appear foolish or out of line. Understand me?"

Virginia nodded and Carolina thought that she actually took on a better color. Suddenly she had support and confidantes. She would no longer face Hampton alone.

"And, Lucy, I want you to help me teach more of the slaves to read. Virginia, you will no doubt have your hands full in trying to keep tabs on that husband of yours, so Lucy can pick up where you have left off. That is, if you are willing to help."

"Of course," Lucy replied, her eyes still glinting tears. "If it means moving toward the release of those people, I will happily do whatever I can."

"I have another request to ask of you, as well, Lucy."

"What is it?"

Margaret glanced to Virginia and then back to her daughter-in-law. "No matter what happens, whether Joseph and I remain here or go abroad, whether the slaves are freed or kept on, I would ask that you allow Virginia and her children to make their home here for as long as they desire."

"I would never consider it any other way," Lucy assured Margaret, then turned to Virginia. "I mean that most sincerely. I know life has not treated you well, but I would not see you sent from your home, and neither would York. He's already told me as much."

Virginia's expression reflected obvious gratitude. "I don't know what to say." She bowed her head and looked at the teacup in her hand. "I don't deserve such goodness."

"You deserve much better than you've had," Margaret countered. "We have all sinned and fallen short of God's glory. Not one of us here hasn't been guilty of one thing or another, but no one deserves to live in fear for his or her very life."

Carolina took this all in, watching her family with great love and admiration. She wanted to break through her reserve with Virginia and extend some sort of symbolic gesture that might prove once and for all that the past was forgiven.

"I once told you that you were welcome to come to Baltimore," Carolina said, turning to her sister. "That offer still holds."

"I think in the future I would prefer to live somewhere other than Oakbridge," Virginia said, surprising them all. "Baltimore is so big, and, well, I'm not certain that I would be comfortable there. But perhaps some town not so very far away where I can raise my children in peace."

"Do you mean to divorce your husband?" Carolina questioned before thinking.

"I doubt that would be possible," Margaret said, eyeing Virginia seriously. "Unless Hampton agreed with such a move."

"He never would. I don't know what the future holds," Virginia answered honestly, "but I know I'm tired of being afraid. And I'm tired of letting my children slip away from me."

"Then stay here with us," Lucy said softly. "Stay here and be safe. York won't allow Hampton to hurt you anymore. He won't be away as much as Father Adams had to be, and thus he will be able to keep Hampton in line."

"Joseph longed only to do the decent thing," Margaret replied. "He has a good heart. His way has always been to recognize a problem and then hope and pray that it will resolve itself. Just like this issue of slavery. He'd much rather it take care of itself than force him to choose sides."

"There isn't a one of us who can't understand that sentiment," Carolina interjected. "I weary of these issues. Let us be speaking on matters less depressing. I for one have had enough."

Margaret chuckled. "Spoken like a true Adams woman. You may

carry different surnames, my daughters, but you are Adams women. You, too, Lucy. You now bear the name and you have shared the family ways for many years. It's in your blood and it will forever shape your life. Come, the day is beautiful. Let's plan a picnic or some outdoor activity that will add a bit of merriment to our lives."

Lucy and Margaret immediately linked arms and headed to the door. Margaret laughed at the fullness of her skirt. "With these new undergarments, I believe we shall find it difficult to walk arm in arm."

"Surely it's only the latest fashion. Next year will see us wearing something different," Lucy declared.

"I fear it may take longer than that," Margaret said as they disappeared through the door. "I heard it said . . ."

As their words faded, Carolina looked to Virginia. "Shall we join them?"

"I suppose so," Virginia replied, getting to her feet.

"Before we do," Carolina said, reaching out to halt her sister, "I want you to know that I was serious about offering you and the children a home. Divorce may not be possible, but no one would deny you a roof over your head should Hampton desert you and the children."

"Thank you." Virginia murmured the words and looked in the direction of the far wall.

"I would happily purchase a place, even in Greigsville. Or perhaps even give you our home if James finds that we must move yet again. I just don't want you to live without hope. As Mother said, we are Adams women, and God made us strong. We need to help one another, and while you and I have never been close, it is my desire that we somehow find a comfortable place with each other for the future."

Virginia turned. "I desire that, too. Perhaps more than you will ever know."

Carolina smiled. "Then we have already started our journey." She reached out to link her arm through Virginia's. "To the future," she added, as though proposing a toast.

"Yes," Virginia half said, half sighed. "To the future."

Forty-Eight

Carolina

When the time came for James to make a brief trip to Baltimore on business, Carolina accompanied him to the B&O station in Washington. Newly constructed, and still not completely finished, the station was now located at New Jersey Avenue and C Street. Carolina liked the brownstone and stucco building with its Italianate style. A seventy-foot clock tower stood in ample view of the Capitol, and inside gas-lighting and rich wood paneling completed the depot in grand style. Plush cushioned seats and comfortable armchairs were promised as finishing touches, and Carolina thought it all very grand and lovely. Who wouldn't want to find themselves awaiting a locomotive in such a beautiful setting?

"I shall miss you," Caroline said, her voice full of emotion. She had promised herself she wouldn't cry when James left, but the ordeal of the days now spent at Oakbridge were nearly more than she could bear. "Everyone is so tense and unhappy at Oakbridge. Poor Lucy seems on the verge of tears nearly every minute of the day, and while Father is doing better, he's still so weak."

"I know," James told her and patted the gloved hand that held him so tight. "But all will soon be set to right. You'll see. York is a fine man, and he will see the sense in adhering to his father's council."

"Then it will be the first time," Carolina said lightly. "York is headstrong."

"I can't imagine that trait in *your* family," James countered with a grin.

"Oh, go on and tease. Mark my words, however, this issue is far from settled. York seems to have some definite goals in mind for the future of Oakbridge."

James glanced around at the growing number of people, and Carolina did the same. It seemed James would have a full load of companions to accompany him to Baltimore.

"Come along," James said, suddenly maneuvering them through the crowd. He pulled Carolina along with him until they were well beyond the gathering travelers and nearer to the iron-roofed train shed behind the depot. Stopping here, James pulled Carolina into his arms and kissed her passionately.

Surprised by this display, but pleasantly so, Carolina wrapped her arms around her husband's neck and melted in a most unladylike fashion against him. She knew her mother would have once frowned on such public behavior, but given her change of attitude, Margaret Adams would now not only understand but completely approve of Carolina's actions.

"You make it hard to say good-bye, even for a short time," James whispered against her ear.

"I didn't start this," Carolina replied, barely able to contain a girlish giggle as her husband started to pull away. She held him fast and added, "But if you hadn't, I surely would have." This time she initiated the kiss.

The blast of the train whistle startled them both and caused them to jump as though they were naughty children caught in the act of some mischief. They laughed heartily at the expressions on each other's faces.

"Here we are at a respectable age in life, stealing kisses like youthful sweethearts," James chided mockingly.

"I feel like a youthful sweetheart," Carolina said, linking her arm with his. "I've very much enjoyed our time alone and I've determined that as much as I love our children, we should definitely have more moments to ourselves."

"Why, Mrs. Baldwin, are you proposing we slip away from our family on a regular basis?"

Carolina grinned. "Yes, I am. And I further suggest that it be to some far-removed location where we have neither kith nor kin."

James pulled her close and whispered in her ear, "I've always appreciated the way your mind works, Mrs. Baldwin."

"I had a good teacher, Mr. Baldwin. A handsome, studious man who taught me to expand my thinking and stretch my imagination." She glanced up at him, giving him what she knew to be her most inviting expression.

"Hmm," he sighed against her ear, "I should like to further explore that imagination. Perhaps I shall shorten my stay in Baltimore."

"I wouldn't argue with that."

They made their way back to the depot platform just as the final boarding whistle was sounded. James kissed her hand lightly in appropriate fashion, then threw her a roguish look that caused Carolina's face to flush. Glancing quickly around to see if anyone else had noticed her husband's wanton behavior, Carolina was rewarded with James' hearty laughter.

"See you soon, my love," he told her and then was gone.

Carolina waited and watched, mindless of the soot now collecting on her peach-colored walking-out suit. She already missed him, and yet the train hadn't even pulled out from the station. A part of her longed to motion the conductor to help her board—to just forget her family at Oakbridge and let them resolve their conflicts on their own. Her father would surely understand, as would her mother. Yet Carolina couldn't just leave them without a word.

The steam whistle blasted long and mournfully, but even so, Carolina thrilled to the sound. She loved the railroad. Loved the sights and sounds and smells of everything to do with the massive iron beasts and their ribbons of iron and steel.

She waited until the lumbering locomotive had disappeared from sight before returning to her hired hack. The driver assisted her into the carriage, then asked her for her desired destination.

"Just take me around the city for a time," she told him.

He seemed to sense her mood and nodded. The open carriage was exactly what she needed to promote her reflective feelings. They pulled away from the station, and Carolina found herself eager to memorize every sight they passed in this constantly changing city. The Capitol stood in its gleaming white radiance, an ever-present reminder of this city's prominent purpose. Stretching out in front of this symbolic building, in angles between Pennsylvania and Maryland Avenues, was the parklike area known as the Mall, where an impressive structure of a monument was being built to honor General George Washington. It was to be a white marble obelisk, which would rise hundreds of feet to tower over the city as a watchful sentinel, though now it was little more than a white stony stump barely one hundred feet high.

The driver picked up the pace as they joined in with numerous other carriages and made their way down Pennsylvania Avenue. Passing the presidential home, Carolina's mind wandered back to the days of Andrew Jackson. The wiry old man had treated her with great affection, even continuing their friendship after his departure from Washington and public life. He was dead now, having succumbed to his old age and a broken heart some seven years earlier. In one of his final missives to Carolina, he had mentioned that he had many accomplishments to be proud of but added wryly that he had two regrets: "I was unable to shoot Henry Clay or to hang John C. Calhoun."

Even now it made her smile to recall the battles he had fought in his younger days with both of these men. Politics could ruin the best of friends and incite the worst of enemies. Had she not seen this herself? Yet this city that she held in great affection was the very birthplace of such affairs.

She sighed, wishing fervently that the old president might have joined her on this excursion around the city. She thought of the letter, still preserved with her other Jackson correspondences, that told of her friend's passing. His final words still warmed her and left her with the satisfaction that he had made his peace with God.

"Do not cry. Be good children, and we shall all meet in heaven."

Tears came to her eyes, but they weren't tears of sorrow. No, Carolina felt joyous in the memory, for one day she would see her good friend again. They would meet in heaven, and knowing Andrew Jackson, he would already have God's ear regarding the affairs of that wicked little city called Washington.

"Take me to the Potomac and Great Falls Railroad stop," she instructed the driver.

"Yes, ma'am," he said with a nod, then applied the whip to the back of the horse.

Carolina eased back against the leather upholstery and closed her eyes to the sights and sounds of the city. She had taken in enough, and now her thoughts were better put to use on her family and the few remaining days she had with them.

She thought of her wounded father and of his desire to leave the responsibilities of plantation life behind. "The wanderlust," she whispered in a barely audible tone and smiled. More than anything in this world, Carolina wanted to see his dreams of travel come true. She wanted to see her father and mother happily together, with their greatest concerns and responsibilities centering around each other.

Whatever it takes, Lord, she prayed silently, *please show my father the way. Show him how to properly discharge his duties so that he might enjoy his remaining days with my mother. They've known such heartache and misery, but they've also had happiness and love. I only ask that you would deal with them according to your merciful love. Give them the desires of their hearts, even as you have given me mine.*

In that moment, Carolina had never known such peace. She truly was happy. She could see the future laid out before her. Her husband held her in highest regard and loved her enough to make her a part of his masculine world. Her children, although growing up much too quickly, were healthy, happy, and well adjusted to life. They knew the goodness of God and held a healthy respect and honor toward Him, as well. All that money could not buy, all that force and greed could not command, Carolina possessed because of the goodness of God.

Forty-Nine

Hampton's Plan

Carolina walked into the foreboding silence of Oakbridge and shuddered. Her pleasant mood of the morning was quickly absorbed by the ominous atmosphere of her childhood home. Reaching for the banister of the main stairway, Carolina felt a cold, almost nauseating sensation invade her. Something was wrong, but what was it? She listened, straining to hear something amiss—some voice calling for help. But there was nothing.

I'm being silly, she told herself and gathered up her soot-smudged skirt. She tried to laugh at her feelings, but the strangeness refused to leave her.

Deciding to seek out her mother, Carolina remembered that she had planned to teach Lucy about the workings of Oakbridge. Perhaps she would find them together in the family drawing room. Quickening her steps, Carolina made her way to the second-floor room and threw open the doors without so much as a knock.

A startled house servant looked up from her dusting, but otherwise there was no one else in the room. "Kitty, do you know where my mother is?"

"Yes'um, Mizzus Baldwin. She's done gone to show young Mizzus Adams de sewin' house."

Carolina nodded. "Thank you." She left the room, hardly remembering to close the doors behind her. Just as she turned to go back to the steps, her gaze fell on Virginia's open bedroom door. Perhaps her sister might enjoy a visit. After all, Carolina would be leaving in only a few short days, and there was still much that needed to be said between them.

"Virginia?" she called softly and knocked lightly on the open door. But to her disappointment no one was inside the room. With a shrug,

Carolina backed out of the room and looked down the opposite wing. At the end of the hall was her parents' bedroom. She knew without a doubt that her father would be one resident whom she would find exactly where she expected him to be.

She thought about sending Kitty for refreshments, then changed her mind. No, she'd simply pop in on her father and if he was up to a visit, then she would go after Kitty and have tea brought up.

"Papa?" she called as she opened the ornate oak door.

The scene that met her eyes was all of her worst nightmares come true. Hampton Cabot stood bent over her father's bed, holding a pillow tightly pressed over Joseph Adams' face.

"No!" she screamed, running toward the scene on legs that seemed made of lead.

She threw herself at Hampton, catching him off guard. "You beast! You vile monster! How dare you!" She struck at him with her fists, her blows falling against whatever part of him she could reach.

"Get off of me, you witch!" Hampton raged, throwing her backward by simply standing upright. He turned to face her, pure hatred in his expression. "Have you come to die, too? Well, so be it."

He stepped toward her, seeming to expect her to cower at his threatening presence. And in truth, it was exactly what Carolina knew she should have done. But instead, she hurled herself at him once again.

"You murderer!" She was blinded by her own rage. He had just killed her father, or at least that had been his plan, and it looked as though he had succeeded. "My father loved you like a son. How could you be so heartless—so cruel?" She pummeled him with her fists.

"Cease this!" he demanded before slapping her hard.

Carolina's vision blurred and dizziness instantly commanded her. Before she could react, Hampton charged at her with the full force of his weight, but not before both of them heard the unmistakable gasping of Joseph Adams.

"Leave her . . ." Joseph breathed out the words in a raspy, gurgled sound.

"See what you've done?" Hampton said as their bodies slammed against the hardwood floor.

Carolina felt the air forced from her lungs as Hampton let his full weight fall upon her. She struggled against him, pushing at his chest, gasping painfully for air, but to no avail.

Laughing at her feeble attempts, Hampton grabbed both of her wrists and pulled her arms up high above her head. "I should have done this a long time ago," he said, then pinning both of her arms to the floor with his left hand, he reached down and tore open the jacket of her gown with his right hand. " 'Miss High and Mighty, I'm too good for the likes of you.' Well, you aren't so good now, are you? Your education is hardly going to help you out of this situation, is it?"

"No! No!" Carolina tried to scream, but because her lungs were empty, no sound came out. The dizziness had cleared to give her a full picture of the situation. Hampton was breathing heavily upon her face, his hand doing its best to tear through the layers of her clothing.

"Leave her alone," she heard her father whisper once again. There was a sound as though he had tried to get up, but in weakness had fallen back against the bed.

"Shut up, old man. Your time is coming soon enough. There's no one to concern themselves with your circumstance this time, Carolina. No stupid sister to steal my victory of having what I want. And I do want you," he said, his expression leering and evil. "I always did. Even when I lied and promised you an education if you would marry me. But you were too high-and-mighty for the likes of me. Weren't you?" He touched his lips to her neck. "I guess this brings you down a few notches, eh?"

Carolina struggled against him, and for the tiniest moment his weight seemed to lift off of her, and she was able to breathe. Gulping a great lungful of air, Carolina nearly cried aloud from the crushing sensation that gripped her chest. She tried to kick at him, hoping against all odds to gain some kind of control in the situation, but it only served to amuse him.

"You are a fool if you think your attempt at fighting is going to serve any purpose but mine."

"No!" Joseph called from the bed once again.

"You won't get away with this," Carolina finally managed to say loud enough for Hampton to hear. The words seemed to catch him off guard, and for a moment, he stilled his attempt to destroy her bodice.

"I suppose you really believe that," he said in an almost thoughtful manner. "But the truth is, I will get away with not only this, but much, much more. There's so much about me you can't even begin to imagine. Power and ability beyond even your mind's capability." He reached up to touch her face, but Carolina turned away, then quickly rethinking, turned back and bit him hard in the fleshy space between his thumb and index finger.

"Ow!" he yelled, instinctively drawing his hand back. Recovering quickly, he growled and put his hand to her throat. "You should die for that."

He pressed against her throat hard enough that Carolina felt the blackness threaten her once again.

"Of course, you could save yourself by making it worth my while."

Carolina closed her eyes. She couldn't bear to have Hampton Cabot's face be the last thing she ever saw. Barely able to conjure any other image to mind, Carolina focused on remembering James' blue eyes. She saw them clearly, then his face and his smile.

"Let her go or I'll blow a hole clear through you." The voice sounded remarkably like her mother's, but Carolina was certain she had imagined it, along with James' sweet expression. Nevertheless, when Hampton's grip went limp, Carolina forced herself to open her eyes.

"Move this instant!" Margaret commanded again.

Hampton rolled off of Carolina, his hands up as though to ward off the threatening presence of Margaret Adams. Carolina struggled to sit up, gasping for air, desperate to put space between herself and Hampton Cabot. She managed to scoot about a foot away before a spell of coughing wracked her body.

"Lucy, Virginia, help Carolina, then see to your father," Margaret ordered.

Carolina glanced up to find her sister-in-law and Virginia coming toward her. Their expressions were matched in terror and shock. Reaching down, they gently helped Carolina to her feet. It was then that Carolina saw her mother standing in the doorway, shotgun leveled at Hampton Cabot.

Carolina gripped her bodice and tried to assess the damage. Only the outer jacket and gown showed signs of the savage attack. Her chemise shielded her from complete embarrassment, and as if sensing her need, Virginia took her own shawl and put it around Carolina's shoulders. Glancing up, Carolina offered her sister what she hoped was an expression of gratitude. Virginia's face was ashen and marred with pain, but she nodded in acknowledgment and turned to help Lucy tend to Joseph.

"You can't seriously mean to threaten me with that," Hampton said, trying to sound unimpressed. "You couldn't possibly know one end of that gun from the other."

"I know the end I have pointed at you is capable of taking off your head, and believe me, Mr. Cabot," she said in a low, even tone, "I'd have little trouble pulling the trigger and doing just that. You yourself are always reminding me of my insanity."

It was then that Carolina noticed the two field slaves who stood behind her mother. Carolina wasn't familiar with either man, but they were obviously there to lend aid to her mother. Their presence gave Carolina reason to calm down and see to her father's condition.

Joseph was extremely pale, but other than that, he seemed fine. In fact, much to Carolina's surprise, he was actually smiling. He seemed to be enjoying the scene before him. And then Carolina realized why. Margaret had been weak and fragile for so long, and during the past years Joseph had gone out of his way to protect her from further harm. Now she was the one offering him protection. She was suddenly the strong one.

Carolina couldn't keep from smiling herself. He was proud of her, and so was Carolina. Standing there at her father's side, Carolina had never known a moment when she'd been more surprised by her mother, nor when she'd admired her more.

"Get up," her mother commanded, then lowering the gun, she glanced at the men behind her. "You have finally gone too far, Mr. Cabot. Now you'll have to face the hand of the law for your actions. Your family will now be our responsibility."

Hampton laughed, seeming more confident now that the gun was no longer pointing at him. He got to his feet, dusted off his coat and pants, then shook his head. "You don't know what you're doing."

"I know well enough that you tried to rape my daughter. Virginia heard you in here arguing and knew it wouldn't amount to anything good."

"He tried to smother Father," Carolina added quickly. "I came in here to visit and found him standing there with a pillow over Father's face."

Margaret eyed her husband as if for confirmation. "It's true," Joseph said, his voice gradually regaining strength. "I'd nearly lost all hope of life when Carolina appeared."

Margaret's face reddened. "So not only rape of a defenseless woman, but murder of a wounded man."

"Oh, try to prove any of it," Hampton said in a lackadaisical manner that suggested he was not at all threatened.

"I don't have to prove anything," Margaret said wearily. Carolina saw her mother's shoulders droop slightly and knew instantly that the enormity of what had just happened was finally sinking in. "Malachi, Ezekiel, take Mr. Cabot to see the constable. One of us will be there directly to press charges."

The color drained from Hampton's face as Margaret passed the shotgun to the taller of the two men. "You can't be serious," Hampton objected, his voice now clearly registering concern. "You can't give a firearm to a darky. They'll kill everyone in sight."

There was a scuffling sound out in the hall, and Carolina wondered if the other slaves had gathered to watch in anticipation of Hampton finally receiving his comeuppance. She leaned forward to look into the corridor, but there was no one else to be seen.

"Leave us," Margaret said sternly. "You've caused this family enough grief and pain."

"I won't be pushed around this way," Hampton said, seeming to cower despite the bravado of his words. "You . . . can't . . . do this. I have a family . . . you need me. Your husband is daft . . . senseless when it comes to taking these Negroes in hand."

"Malachi, if Mr. Cabot so much as attempts to get the upper hand, you have my permission to shoot him," Margaret told the large black man.

The man nodded and grinned, his white teeth gleaming in contrast against his ebony skin. He took a step forward, which caused Hampton to nearly scream out in terror.

"No! You don't understand. I've whipped this boy before. He was one of the runaways. He's hungry for revenge." Hampton's voice dropped to a whimper. "You can't turn me over to him. I . . . I can see it in his eyes—he wants my blood."

"So do I, Mr. Cabot," Margaret said, coming to stand beside Lucy at Joseph's bed. "But being a Christian woman, I'll turn my desire for revenge over to the good Lord and the legal authorities. May God have mercy on your soul."

"We have a secret!" Levinia declared, bursting into the nursery to find Nate consumed with his toy soldiers.

"I don't care," Nate replied in obvious indifference. His sisters seldom told him anything of much interest to him. Usually they only managed to get him into trouble.

"You'll care about this," Thora announced, following Levinia's lead.

Nate gave up his struggle to remain focused. At nearly ten years of age, he still found it difficult to maintain his own ground against his twin sisters. "Then tell me."

"Grandmother is sending Papa away," Levinia said, nearly bursting to share this vital information.

"What are you talking about?" Nate questioned, getting to his feet. "You're just playing games with me."

"No, no," Thora assured, "it's all true. Father tried to hurt Grandfather Adams and Aunt Carolina. We saw. Aunt Carolina's dress was all torn and everybody was really scared. Grandmother had a gun."

"A shotgun," Levinia corrected. "The same one Grandpa used to take hunting."

Nate shook his head. This news was too much to take in at once. It exceeded even his sisters' wildest imaginations. "I don't believe you."

"Well, go look out the window. Grandmother gave the gun—" Thora paused, correcting herself—"shotgun, to one of the Negro slaves."

Levinia nodded, approving of the correction and reaffirming the event. "Yes, and she told him to shoot Father if he had to. He might even kill him!"

This was too much even for Nate. He went to the window and glanced down at the circular front drive. Sure enough, his father's white stallion had been saddled and brought round along with two other horses.

The three children waited in silence for several moments before Thora ran to the nursery door and opened it enough to peek out. The sound of a door slamming across the hall sent the wide-eyed child up against the nursery door, closing it with a thud.

"They're taking him downstairs!" she exclaimed.

Nate still found it hard to believe. Maybe his father was just going for an afternoon ride. His heart began to pound hard in his chest. Surely he wasn't really being sent away. Surely Nate wouldn't be so lucky as to have his most fervent prayer answered.

He hated his father, and the thought that someone big and strong could make him go away excited Nate in a way he couldn't explain. That the someone should be a slave almost made the experience too rich to be believed. His father hated the Negroes and said so on every possible occasion. He told Nate they were a necessary nuisance, far beneath the consideration of real human beings, except that they could do menial tasks and lighten the work load of the plantation owners. But Grandpa didn't feel that way, nor did Grandmother. They seemed to take almost the same trouble and concern with the house servants as they did any other family member.

"Look! There they are!" Thora declared, jumping up and down in anticipation of what might happen next.

"Do you think they will shoot him?" Levinia asked quite seriously.

"I hope so," Nate muttered inaudibly.

"What?" Thora exclaimed, eyeing her brother with avid curiosity.

Nate shrugged. "I said I don't know," he lied, guilt already eating at him as he watched the scene. The two slaves held their distance while his father, the man who had caused him so much misery and pain, mounted his horse. One of the slaves tied up his hands like he was a real captive. Then the slaves mounted their horses and they rode away. But Nate's father paused, turned the horse slightly, and glanced back at the house.

Nate gasped, fearing that his father could see him standing at the nursery window. With raised fists, Hampton shook a fierce farewell, then continued to ride.

"Well, there he goes," Levinia said, as though already bored with the whole matter.

"Did you see him shake his fists?" Thora asked, moving away from the window. "I think he wanted to hit us."

"Well, he can't now," Levinia said, then dismissed the idea. "Let's go get some cookies. I saw Naomi leave some in the window to cool."

"Yummy. Let's hurry," Thora agreed.

They left Nate to stand staring out the window, and for a long, long time, that was exactly what he did. Guilt consumed him for wishing his father dead, but the pain of his life spent cowering in fear, hiding from punishment for imagined wrongdoing, was enough to cause the boy to feel great relief in his father's dismissal from Oakbridge. He could only hope that it meant forever.

"Is everyone all right?" Joseph asked, and Carolina, having witnessed Hampton's departure from the window, turned and nodded.

"I'm fine, Papa, honestly."

"I'm better than fine," Virginia announced. "I feel as though I've been emancipated. Mother, you should have taken a gun to him long ago. Better yet, I should have."

"I'm not proud of my actions," Margaret said, sitting quite soberly by her husband's side.

"Well, I am," Joseph said, a smile of admiration clearly brightening his face. "You did a good job there, Mrs. Adams. Saved my life, and possibly Carolina's, as well."

"Well, for that I am grateful," Margaret admitted.

"I can't believe I was afraid of that sniveling coward. Did you see the way he reacted when Ezekiel took hold of him?" Virginia said almost gleefully. "I've never seen that expression on his face. Oh, Mother, thank you. I finally believe in the power of prayer. God must truly have forgiven me for the past, or He'd never have found a way to rid me of Hampton."

"Don't be so certain we've seen the last of him," Margaret said, sharing an anxious look with her husband.

"I don't think we have to worry," Joseph replied. "Our name carries a great weight in this community. I'm sure he will be prosecuted for his actions."

"I pray you are right," Margaret said, glancing upward to catch Carolina's eye.

Carolina saw the worry in her mother's expression and smiled. "Virginia is right, Mama," she said. "God has delivered us this day. I, for one, am grateful and will not give myself over to worrying about the future."

"Neither will I," Virginia countered. "I intend to pick up the pieces of my life. I also intend to have a long talk with God, and maybe I can sort out all the things in the past that I shouldn't have said or done."

Margaret smiled and nodded. "I suppose you are right. Lucy, you are terribly quiet. Are you all right?"

Lucy's dark eyes seemed to quietly take in the entire scene. "I'm still stunned by what has happened. Why did he come here?"

"To kill me," Joseph replied.

"But why?"

"I suppose because he thought he would stand a better chance of convincing York that he would change. That he would run Oakbridge for him and keep it for his sons, if only York would allow him to stay on as caretaker and overseer. I'm sure Hampton would have played on York's torn loyalties."

"Torn loyalties?" Lucy questioned.

"Between remaining in Philadelphia or returning here."

Lucy nodded and exchanged a quiet, knowing glance with the women in the room.

"I think you've had enough excitement for one day," Margaret told Joseph. "In fact, I think we all have."

"Yes," Carolina agreed. "Perhaps enough for an entire lifetime." She gripped Virginia's shawl tightly against her neck. Now that everything was said and done, she longed only for a hot bath and her husband's protective embrace. But with James in Baltimore, she would have to settle for the bath alone.

Fifty

Bittersweet Partings

"Papa?" Carolina called hesitantly from the bedroom door.

"Come in, child. Come in."

She peered around and smiled. "I've come to say my good-byes."

"Then come here and sit by me and do so properly," Joseph told her, easing himself up against the headboard. He still looked rather fragile, but he smiled most sincerely. "I know you must go, but I shall miss you greatly."

Carolina arranged herself beside him on the bed. She sat stiffly, almost warily, lest she jostle him too much and cause him pain. Joseph immediately sensed her discomfort and reached out to take hold of her.

"I will not break," he assured her and pulled her into his arms for a tender embrace.

Carolina relished his touch. Her father had been such a mainstay in her life. He always understood her needs. He alone saw her desires, very nearly before she could recognize them for herself. Sitting here now, she felt twenty years younger. In her father's arms the world seemed far away and unable to hurt her.

"James is lucky to have you, my dear," Joseph murmured and released her. "You are a ray of sunshine that brightens an otherwise gloomy existence."

"Oh, stop it, Papa," Carolina declared, straightening her ruffled lace collar. "Your existence is hardly gloomy."

Joseph's expression grew thoughtful. "I hadn't realized how dismal it had become, to tell you the truth. No, I think it was good to see the bad that came to light. It helped me to understand how my complacency allowed evil a foothold. Often we think we are doing nothing to aid the devil, when just by doing nothing we are giving him the upper hand."

"I hadn't thought of it that way," Carolina replied, realizing the wisdom in her father's words.

"Well, we see the sense of it now, don't we?"

She smiled. "Yes, we do." She reached out to touch his muttonchop whiskers. For as long as she could remember, he'd held to this same fashion. There was now a liberal sprinkling of gray, but overall his hair was still dark, as were his whiskers. He was nearly sixty, but his body remained strong, and in spite of the beating he'd taken only weeks earlier, she was confident he would recover to full health.

"So you are content to give Oakbridge over to York?" she asked, suddenly realizing the time was slipping away from her. A quick glance at the mantel clock proved her concerns were valid.

"Yes, but with certain provisions. We are even now working through those."

"Will he agree to free the slaves?"

"I believe in time he will come to understand my position. If not, I'm convinced the matter will be taken out of his hands and decided for him."

"What of you and Mother? Will you travel abroad?"

Joseph smiled. "My wanderlust should do us both justice. I intend to see the world and all its wonders. But you know, it wouldn't have meant anything at all if your mother hadn't been willing to accompany me. I couldn't bear to travel without her, and our years of separation proved that to me more so than anything else could."

"I know," Carolina replied. "It's the same with James and me. I hate being parted from him, and even knowing that he's not so very far away isn't enough. He isn't with me, and that's what truly matters."

"I pray it will always be good between you two," her father said with a bittersweet smile. "I want only the best for you, my dear."

"I have the best, Papa," Carolina replied, leaning down to kiss him. "I have extraordinary parents, a loving husband, and wonderful children. And soon I will be helping my husband with his work on the railroad, and I shall truly be a part of the dream."

Joseph shook his head. "But you were always that. Can't you see? Being a part of the railroad is more than swinging a pick or driving a locomotive. You saw the future—the potential. You envisioned the dream as a reality. It's people like that who make dreams come true. You. Me. James. And countless others. We're all necessary to breathe life into the scheme of things."

As Carolina realized the truth in his words, contentment bubbled up from inside and threatened to overflow. "Oh, Papa, you are right. I do see." She kissed him again and smiled. "I guess even dreamers sometimes lose sight of things."

"It's often easier to focus on what hasn't come about," he told her. "Just keep your trust fixed firmly in God and don't be afraid to dream big. You never know what might happen."

Carolina laughed. "Yes. You just might get everything you ever wanted."

Later, with bags packed, Carolina made her way downstairs. Everyone had chosen to assemble themselves in the first-floor family drawing room, all in order to bid her farewell. She embraced Virginia first, impressed that her sister actually looked happy.

"Don't forget what I told you," Carolina whispered. "Baltimore is always open to you. Or you could come to Greigsville—at least for a visit."

"I won't forget," Virginia told her and surprised her by kissing her cheek.

Carolina moved on to where York and Lucy awaited her. York's features seemed to have hardened in the days since her arrival. Even now he looked at her with an expression of mixed emotions.

"I'm so sorry I wasn't here for you the other day," he said.

Carolina put her hand on his arm. "It's over. Don't worry yourself any longer. What happened was unpleasant and very nearly tragic, but God watched over us and He interceded. Hampton is to be pitied, not hated."

York shook his head. "He needs to know that he cannot treat people in such a manner. And I will at least see to it that he is punished to the full extent of the law."

"He's not worth too much of our bitter anger," Carolina said. "Peace in our home is far more important than anything. And remember, we must guard the honor of his children and his wife."

York leaned down to kiss her on the cheek. "You may be an intelligent woman," he said with a hint of a smile, "but you know nothing of how men deal with matters of importance."

Carolina laughed. "Oh, you might be surprised, my dear brother." Lucy, too, laughed and Carolina was glad to see her sister-in-law smile. "I think you should give Lucy and me credit where credit is deserved. After all, we've put up with you all these years. Surely we must have learned something in that time."

"I shall miss you dearly," Lucy said, hugging Carolina close. "I pray you'll come back soon for a visit."

"I have no way of knowing," Carolina answered honestly. "I'm uncertain where the future is taking me, but of one thing I feel confident—James will be by my side, and it will most likely involve the railroad."

She finished saying her good-byes, then turned to find Margaret awaiting her at the door. "Come. I'll walk out with you," her mother said softly.

Carolina nodded, and taking up her bonnet and purse, she clasped hands with her mother. "I'm ready."

They came out onto the porch and gazed across the broad, intricately groomed lawn. "My heart is so full, I can scarcely speak the things I feel," Carolina said. Tears came to her eyes as she leaned over to kiss her mother's cheek. "I long to stay. But I long equally to go. Ours is a bittersweet parting."

"Those are often the best, for we are neither too sad nor too glad to take our leave," Margaret offered. "You belong elsewhere now, and while you will always have a special place here and in my heart, this is the proper order of things."

"I know you're right. I see the truth of it down deep within my soul." Carolina looked away to the awaiting carriage and then beyond to the open expanse of fields. "Granny once said God puts a special truth inside each of us that only we can know. I think I'm starting to understand what that truth is for me." She turned back to see her mother's tender smile. "There is a purpose and a plan for my life. A plan that only I can fulfill. It doesn't require the actions of anyone else, but it does rely heavily upon my willingness to go where I am called and to do what I am to do."

"A willing heart that seeks to do what God would have you do," Margaret said, reaching up to lovingly stroke her daughter's cheek, "will take you much farther than all the book knowledge and education that man can afford you."

"Yes," Carolina replied, embracing her mother tightly. "I haven't always been satisfied with who I was or the paths I had chosen, but I will endeavor to put such thinking aside and lose myself in God's vision of what I can become."

Margaret held her for several moments, then released her and nodded. "I have always . . . and will always . . . love you."

"I love you, too, Mama," Carolina whispered, barely able to speak. "Now and always."

Fifty-One

To Wheeling and Beyond

Having arrived in Wheeling on an earlier mail train, Carolina and James anticipated the arrival of the official celebration locomotives with as much excitement as the rest of the crowd. Carolina had found the new line to perch perilously in spots where high, narrow passageways made it necessary for the railroad to cling to the side of scenic cliffs. She had held her breath with the other forty-some passengers when they passed over the Monongahela River bridge, wondering if such a vast expanse would hold up to their imposing weight.

But they had arrived safe and sound, and now they awaited the governors and board of directors who would set the official celebration in order. Bands had been put in place to entertain with a variety of marches and reels, while military units, including the Steubenville Grays and the Bridgeport Artillery, were on hand to offer salutary cannon fire. The air was crisp and cold on that January tenth of 1853, but few people seemed to notice. And even as night came and dampness rolled in from the river, the people refused to give up their party. Wheeling was finally going to have its railroad, and even though the line came in south of the city proper, it was enough for now, and the people were stirred to a frenzy unequaled by anything they'd ever known.

Carolina found herself remembering the first time she'd ever wandered through a crowd like this. She had been a child of fifteen, yet it seemed like only yesterday. The blast of a steam whistle caused her to strain to see beyond the pressing crowds around her, and for a brief moment, she could nearly hear her mother's voice chiding her to act like a lady.

James leaned down and whispered something in her ear, but she couldn't hear it as cheers rose up from the men and women all around her. The bands struck up, each playing something different, adding to the confusion and revelry in their own disorganized ways, and Carolina stretched up on tiptoe in order to see better.

"I ain't never seen no train," a man wearing a straw hat told the plump woman beside him.

"I heard tell they set ever'thin' on fire with them thar sparks," another man behind Carolina spoke out.

She laughed to herself, remembering the comments of the Washington Branch crowd when she was fifteen and viewed her first locomotive. Women had fainted dead away, children had cried, and men had been notably impressed. Then, Virginia had supposed it to be indecent to expose women in a family way to such activities. But the memory hadn't stopped Carolina, who only that morning had advised her husband that she would give him yet another child in the summer. It only made her celebration of the railroad more complete. One promise fulfilled. Another yet to come.

The whistle blasted again as the steam locomotive came into view. Even against the night skies, moonlight illuminated the billowing smoke. Steam hissed and the whistle blew several more times before the great lumbering monster came to a stop.

But to everyone's surprise, this wasn't the celebration train they'd anticipated at all but was in fact yet another mail train. Everyone laughed and the festive spirit remained, even as it began to rain and it was realized that the expected locomotive had somehow been delayed. But hours later the trains were still delayed, and so the crowd dispersed and went back to their homes for a good night's sleep.

Disappointed, Carolina and James made their way back to their room at McClure House. "I pray they have not met with trouble," Carolina told her husband as they prepared for bed that night.

"As do I," James replied. "I especially pray that it wasn't my tunnel that slowed their progress."

Carolina laughed and blew out the lamp. "I suppose we shall all know what the problem was when they finally arrive." She settled down in her husband's arms, her mind racing with thoughts of the celebration and the people who waited so patiently for their step into the future of railroad travel.

Finally, three days after having begun their journey in Baltimore, the two trains of dignitaries arrived in Wheeling. Because it was the middle of the night, no one was on hand to greet them, but the passengers hardly concerned themselves with this matter. In pure exhaustion most everyone went happily to a peaceful night's sleep, not even noticing that they had arrived at their final destination.

But later in the day, the celebration spirit was revived and the people of Wheeling paraded and bands played and children squealed with delight at the wondrous sights and sounds. A procession was led to the courthouse, where a formal reception was headed up by Maryland's young governor, Enoch Louis Lowe. He made a dignified speech congratulating the Baltimore and Ohio Railroad for their fair and faithful dealings with the state, and predicted that this was only the beginning of many destinations yet to come. He easily saw the future as connecting the Chesapeake and San Francisco bays via the railroad.

"Who can measure her destiny?" he had cried out to the crowd, and a tingling sensation had run down Carolina's spine. Who indeed?

Later that night they sat down to a banquet dinner of mass proportions, and Carolina laughed to see grown men act like schoolboys.

"They are behaving as though they've just won a game," Carolina said, leaning over to tell James, only then to remember her husband had been positioned several chairs down.

"What was that?" the formally attired gentleman at her right questioned.

"Never mind," she said, smiling her apology.

The aroma of huge quantities of food mingled throughout the banquet hall, and Carolina welcomed the succulent flavors of roasted lamb and rice. The gentleman beside her had cutlets of veal smothered in a truffle sauce, while the woman across from him had boned turkey and lobster salad. There truly seemed no end to the variety and choices afforded them.

At eight o'clock the champagne was brought around, and attention turned to speeches and toasts. Thomas Swann lifted high the silver trowel that Charles Carroll had used at the B&O ground breaking on July 4, 1828. "If the people of Baltimore could have seen the country through which we were trying to build a railroad," he told the crowd, "it would have been abandoned." He continued by singing the praises of Ben Latrobe and others before giving up the floor to someone else.

One after another, men stood and toasted the Baltimore and Ohio, the men who had worked the rails, the engineers who had designed such feats, and the investors who had remained faithful backers of the dream. The thirteenth toast came to Benjamin Latrobe, who stood and thoughtfully greeted his fellow revelers with a smile. He admitted that he'd been too busy to complete a speech for the occasion. Last-minute conflicts and problems, including the excursion's lead train breaking an axle, had consumed his mind. But he thanked his friends, including

James Baldwin, and Carolina felt her heart swell with pride for the husband she had so long loved.

"I have not, however, a right to call it finished," Latrobe told them all very seriously. "No railroad, indeed, is finished while the trade for which it was constructed continues to grow; and progress is the genius of our people."

Cheers and toasts continued for some time, until to her surprise, James stood and held his own glass aloft. "I give my praise to all of you," he told his comrades. "To those who are with us now, and to those who could not make our celebration." Carolina knew he spoke of Philip Thomas and Louis McLane, both of whom had sent their regrets. "We accomplished this task," James continued, "only because we pledged ourselves to the dream. I salute you." Cheers went up yet again, and Carolina smiled when her gaze met James'. His expression turned from serious to loving. "And," he shouted out above the din, waiting only momentarily for the crowd to quiet, "to my dearest friend and confidante. To the woman who has made my life worth living and who shares in our dream. I could not have become half the man I am today without her. She has endured the building of this railroad and has poured every bit as much time, sweat, and tears into the completion of this line as has any man in this room. To you, my darling Carolina."

Hearty approval was rendered by the men around her, and even the women in attendance couldn't help admiring the praise given their dining companion. Carolina could barely see through her tears. She had never expected such praise, and yet she found herself so blessed by James' words. He had publicly drawn her in, given her credit and validity. He had shown them all that he found her worthy of a place outside of mere convention.

The celebration continued into the late hours, but when James appeared at her side and suggested they leave, Carolina willingly followed him into the starry night. Signaling a carriage driver, James helped his wife up, then joined her, spreading a blanket over their legs.

"Take us along the river," he told the driver. Then turning to Carolina, he whispered against her ear, "I thought perhaps a moonlit drive would be the perfect ending to our evening."

Carolina snuggled against him, grateful for his warmth, content in his love. The evening had been exhausting, but magical—so, too, the journey from that first moment in Washington City when she'd stained her kid gloves with locomotive grease and soot, to the completion of the railroad to the banks of the Ohio River.

After riding for a while in silence, James turned and said, "I hope you know I meant every word I said tonight." He put his arm around her shoulder and pulled her close. "I love you more than you will ever know." He lowered his mouth, pressing his lips tenderly against hers.

Carolina felt the old feelings of passion and desire ignite. He had only to touch her and she was completely and totally his. He pulled away and she sighed. "So where do we go from here?" she asked softly.

"There's a whole country out there begging to be settled."

She straightened and caught his contemplative expression in the moonlight. "Mr. Sullivan of the Central Ohio Railroad has promised to connect his railroad to ours within eighteen months."

"Then there's that whole transcontinental matter," James said, a twinkle in his eye. "I suppose," he added with a mock sound of exasperation, "that you will want to be a part of that, as well."

Carolina laughed and the sound echoed into the night air. "I suppose that shall depend on a great many things, Mr. Baldwin."

"Such as?" His brow arched in question.

"Such as whether you will be a part of it, for I could not consider such a thing without you by my side."

"I suppose I might be persuaded to consider it," James teased. "But, of course, there's a great deal of work remaining here. Just because the line is through does not mean it is in any way finished."

"I know. I heard Ben's speech," she said, grasping his gloved hand in hers. "But it honestly doesn't matter. So long as we are together."

Just then the melancholy sound of a steam whistle broke through their thoughts. Like Noah's rainbow and the promise God gave him, the whistle touched something deep within her soul. Carolina squeezed her husband's hand. "One dream fulfilled and another just beginning," she said, unable to hide her enthusiasm.

James nodded and removed his hand from hers, placing it against her rounding stomach. "A never-ending journey," he said, pure pride radiating from his eyes.

"One we'll make together," Carolina replied, putting her hand over his and looking out across the expanse of the river.

The land seemed to stretch out forever and disappeared into the blackness of the night, but Carolina knew there was more there than met the eye. The western horizon beckoned them with a promise for tomorrow. A promise Carolina intended to embrace.